Remembrance
DANIELLE STEEL

WARNER BOOKS

A *Warner* Book

First published in Great Britain by
Hodder & Stoughton Ltd 1982
Published by Sphere Books Ltd 1982
Reprinted 1982 (twice), 1983 (three times), 1984,
1985 (three times), 1986 (twice), 1988 (twice),
1989, 1990, 1991, 1992, 1993
Reprinted by Warner Books 1994
Reprinted 1995, 1996 (twice), 1999 (twice)

Printed in England by Clays Ltd, St Ives plc

ISBN 0 7515 0555 2

Warner Books
A Division of
Little, Brown and Company (UK)
Brettenham House
Lancaster Place
London WC2E 7EN

To Popeye;
A different dedication this time,
One that's never been done before:
Me,
For the rest of my life.
With all my love,
Olive

A tomb is only an empty box. The one I love exists
entirely in my memory, in a handkerchief that's
still scented when I unfold it, in an intonation that
I suddenly remember and listen to for a whole long
moment, my head bent . . .

. . . and what bitterness at first—but what calm
relief later!—to discover, one day when spring
trembles with cold, uneasiness and hope—that
nothing has changed: neither the smell of the
earth, nor the quiver of the brook, nor the shape,
like rosebuds, of the chestnut shoots . . . to lean
down in astonishment over the little filigree cups of
the wild anemones, toward the carpet of endless
violets—are they mauve, are they blue?—to let
one's gaze caress the unforgotten outline of the
mountains, to drink with a sigh of hesitation the
piquant wine of a new sun . . . to live again!

Colette
*A Retreat from
Love*

Book One

SERENA:
THE EARLY
YEARS

CHAPTER ONE

The train rolled relentlessly into the Italian darkness, its wheels chattering rhythmically against the rails. There were fat peasants crowded everywhere, and skinny children, and seedy-looking businessmen and hordes of American GI's. There was a sad, musty smell in the train, like a house that hasn't been cleaned in years and years, and added to that the ripe smell of tired bodies, long unwashed, unkempt, unloved. Yet no one had thought to open a window. No one would dare. The old women would scream as though they had been assaulted, faced with a rush of the warm night air. That would have offended them. Everything upset them. Heat, cold, fatigue, hunger. They had reason to be disturbed. They were tired. They were sick. They had been hungry and cold and afraid for a long time. It had been one hell of a long war. And now it was over. For three months now. It was August 1945. And the train rolled on relentlessly as it had for two endless days.

Serena had boarded the train in Paris, and ridden, without speaking to anyone, across France and Switzerland, and at last into Italy. This was the last of her journey now . . . the last of it . . . the last of it. . . . The wheels of the train chattered out her thoughts as she lay huddled in a corner, her eyes closed, her face pressed against the glass. God, she was tired. Every inch of her body ached now, even her arms, as she hugged them tightly around her, as though she were cold, which she was not. The heat on the train was stifling, her long blond hair felt matted against the back of her neck, as the train began to slow, and then a few moments later it stopped, and she sat there, without moving, wondering if she should get out and walk, even if only for a moment. She had been traveling now for almost nine days in all. It had been an endless journey, and she wasn't home yet.

She kept thinking of home, reminding herself of it over and over. She had forced herself not to let out a whoop of joy as they crossed the Alps and she knew that she was back in Italy at last. But this was only the beginning. In fact, she reminded herself again as she opened her eyes slowly in the glare of lights from the station, for her the journey hadn't even begun. It wouldn't begin until sometime the next morning, when she reached her destination, and then she would see, she would find out . . . at last. . . .

Serena unraveled herself sleepily, stretching her long graceful legs under the seat in front of her. Across were two old women, sleeping, a very thin one and a very fat one, with a scrawny child pressed between them, like a pathetic offering of pink meat between two loaves of old stale bread. Serena watched them expressionlessly. One could read nothing in her eyes, they looked like icy cold green pools of very fine emeralds, incredibly beautiful, but with very little warmth. But there was something about the depth of the young woman's eyes. One was drawn to them, as though one had to look into her, had to discover what she was thinking, as though one had to see inside her . . . and could not. The doors to Serena's soul were firmly shut, and there was nothing to see except the perfect precision of her finely carved aristocratic face. It had the translucence of white marble. Yet it was not a face one would have dared to touch. Despite her obvious youth and beauty, there was nothing inviting about her, nothing beckoning, nothing warm. She had surrounded herself with an aura of distance that carefully masked tenderness and vulnerability.

"*Scusi.*" She murmured the word softly as she tiptoed past the sleeping women and over an old man. She felt wretched sometimes for what she thought, but she was so tired of old people. She had seen nothing but old people since she had arrived. Was there no one else left, then? Only old women and old men, and a handful of children cavorting crazily everywhere, showing off for the GI's. They were the only young men one saw now. The Americans, in their drab uniforms, with their bright smiles and good teeth and shining eyes. Serena had seen enough of them to last a lifetime. She didn't give a damn whose side they were on. They were part of it. They wore uniforms, just like the others. What

12

difference did the color of the uniforms make? Black or brown or green or . . . purple for that matter, or scarlet . . . or turquoise. . . . She let her thoughts run wild in the warm night air . . . she watched the uniforms cascade out of the train behind her as she stood on the platform and turned to look the other way. Even with her back turned, she could hear them standing near her, talking to each other, laughing at some joke, or speaking softly in the late night silence, broken only by the scraping metal noises of the train.

"Smoke?" A hand reached out suddenly toward Serena, crossing her field of vision in spite of the way she had turned her back, and startled, she shook her head and hunched her shoulders, as though to protect herself further from what had happened, from what had been. One had a sense of something hurt about Serena; even in all her powerful young beauty, one sensed that there was something broken, something damaged, and perhaps forever spoiled, as though she were carrying some terrible burden, or existing in spite of an almost intolerable pain.

Yet there was nothing on her surface to show that. Her eyes were clear, her face unlined. In spite of the ugly, wrinkled clothes she wore, she was striking. And yet, if one looked beyond the first glance, one could not help but see pain. One of the GI's had noticed it as he watched her, and now as he took a last drag on his cigarette and dropped it on the platform, he found his eyes drawn toward her again. Christ, she was pretty. That white-blond hair peeking out from under the dark green cotton scarf she wore tied around her head, as though she were a peasant woman. But it was unconvincing. Serena could not pass for a peasant, no matter what she wore. Her carriage gave her away almost instantly, the way she moved, the way she turned her head, like a young gazelle, bounding with grace. There was something almost too beautiful about Serena. It almost hurt to look at her for too long a time. Just seeing her in the drab clothes she wore was troublesome. One wanted to tap her on the shoulder and ask why—why are you dressed that way and what are you doing pressed amongst the dregs of humanity on this over-crowded train? And more questions: Where had she come from? Where was she going? And why was there that faraway look in her eyes?

As she stood on the platform in the warm summer darkness, she offered no answers. She only stood there. Very straight, very tall, very slim, and so young, in the crumpled cotton dress. She looked down at the deep creases in the cheap fabric and smoothed the skirt with a long delicate hand as her mind seemed to snag on a memory, a gesture . . . her mother doing the same thing . . . her perfectly manicured hand smoothing the skirt of a dress . . . a white silk dress . . . at a party in the garden of the palazzo. . . . Serena squeezed her eyes closed for a moment, forcing the memory back. She had to do that often. But the memories still came.

One of the GI's was watching her as she opened her eyes again and walked quickly down the platform to reboard the train. She looked as though she were running away from something, and he wondered what it was, as she put a foot on the steps up to the train and swung herself gracefully aboard again, as though she had just mounted a Thoroughbred and was about to ride off into the night. He watched her closely for a long moment, the tall thin frame, the elegantly squared shoulders. She had an extraordinary grace about her. As though she were someone important. And she was.

"*Scusi*," she whispered again softly as she made her way down the aisle and back into her seat, where she let out a soft sigh and leaned her head back again, but this time she did not close her eyes. There was no point. She was bone tired, but she wasn't sleepy. How could she sleep now? With only a few more hours before they arrived. Only a few more hours . . . a few more hours . . . a few more. . . . The train began moving and picked up the refrain of her thoughts again, as she gazed out into the darkness, feeling in her heart, her soul, her very bones, that whatever happened, at least she had come home. Even the sound of Italian being spoken around her was a relief now.

The countryside outside the train window was so familiar, so comfortable, so much a part of her, even now, after four years of living with the nuns in the convent in Upstate New York. Getting there four years before had been another endless journey. First, making her way across the border into the Ticino with her grandmother and Flavio, one of the few servants they had left. Once into the Italian part of Switzerland they had been secretly met by two women carrying weapons, and two nuns. It was there that she had left her grandmother, with rivers of tears pouring down the young girl's cheeks, holding tightly to the old lady for a last time, wanting to clutch her, to beg her not to send her away. She had already lost so much in Rome two years before, when—She couldn't bear to think of it as she stood in the chill air of the Italian Alps, locked in her grandmother's firm embrace for a last time. . . .

"You'll go with them, Serena, and you'll be safe there." The plans had been carefully laid for almost a month now. There was America. So terribly far away. "And when it is over, you'll come home." When it is over . . . but when would it be over? As they had stood there, Serena felt that it had already gone on for a lifetime, ten lifetimes. At fourteen she had already lived through two years of war and loss and fear. Not so much her own fear as everyone else's. The adults had lived with constant terror of Mussolini. The children had tried at first to pretend that they didn't care. But one had to care. Sooner or later, events made you care. Sooner or later it all grabbed you by the throat and throttled you until you thought you would die.

She remembered the feeling, still . . . of watching her father dragged away by Mussolini's men . . . watching him try not to scream, to look brave as he tried, helplessly, with his eyes to protect his wife. And then the horrible sounds of what they had done to him in the courtyard of the palazzo, and the terrible noises he had made at last. They hadn't killed him then though. They had waited until the next day, and shot him along with half a dozen others in the courtyard of the Palazzo Venezia, where Mussolini was head-quartered. Serena's mother had been there when they shot him, begging, pleading, screaming, crying, while the sol-diers laughed. The Principessa di San Tibaldo crawling as she begged them, as the men in uniform taunted her, teased her. One had grabbed her by the hair, kissed her roughly, and then spat and threw her to the ground. And it was all over moments later. Serena's father had hung limply from the post where they had tied him. Her mother ran to him, sobbing, and held him for a last moment before, almost as a matter of amusement, they shot her too. And all for what? Because they were aristocrats. Because her father hated Mussolini. Italy had been sick with a special kind of poison then. A poison based on hatred and paranoia and greed and fear. A horror that had turned brother against brother, and sometimes husband against wife. It had turned Serena's uncle against her father, with a kind of passion Serena couldn't understand. Her father thought that Mussolini was a savage, a buffoon, a fool, and said so, but his brother had been unable to accept their differences. Sergio di San Tibaldo had become Mussolini's lapdog at the beginning of the war. It was Sergio who turned Umberto in, who insisted that Umberto was dangerous and half mad, that he was involved with the Allies when in fact he was not. The truth was, Sergio stood to gain a great deal if he could dispose of Umberto, and he had. As the younger son he had inherited almost nothing from their father, only the farm in Umbria, which he had hated even as a boy. And he couldn't even sell that. He had it for the use of his lifetime, and then he was obliged to leave it to his children, or Umberto's if he had none. As far as Sergio was concerned, his older brother had it all, the title, the money, the looks, the palazzo that had been in the family for seven generations, the artwork, the importance, the charm, and Graziella, of course, which had been the final spark to ignite his hatred for his older brother.

He hated her father most for possessing Graziella, the golden fairy queen with the incredible green eyes and spun-gold hair. She had been exquisite, and he had loved her since he had been a boy. He had loved her always . . . always . . . when they all spent their summers together in Umbria or San Remo or at Rapallo, when she was a little girl. But she had always loved Umberto. Everyone had loved Umberto . . . everyone . . . especially Graziella.

Sergio had knelt, sobbing, at her funeral at Santa Maria Maggiore, asking himself why it had all happened. Why had she married Umberto? Why had she run to him after he was dead? No one at the funeral had fully understood the part that Sergio had played in his brother's and sister-in-law's deaths. To their friends, he had always seemed ineffectual, a weakling. And now no one knew the truth, except Serena's grandmother. It was she who prodded and pried and inquired and pressured in all the right places, she who pressed everyone she knew until she learned the truth. Only she had been brave enough to confront him in a rage of horror and grief so overwhelming that when it was over Sergio understood as never before the nightmare of what he had done to his own flesh and blood. And for what? A white marble palazzo? A woman who had died at the feet of her husband, and had never loved anyone but him in any case?

For what had he done it? his mother had screamed. For the love of Mussolini? ''That pig, Sergio? That pig? You killed my firstborn for him?'' He had trembled in the wake of his mother's rage, and knew that he would spend the rest of his lifetime trying to live with the truth. He had denied everything to his mother, denied that he betrayed Umberto, denied that he had done anything at all. But she had known, as had Serena. Those brilliant green eyes of hers had bored into him at the funeral, and he had been grateful to escape at last. Unable to fight the tides of Mussolini, and unwilling to expose the horror of her son's fratricide to the whole world, the elderly Principessa di San Tibaldo had taken Serena and the oldest of the servants and removed them from Rome. The palazzo was his now, she told him as she stood for a last moment in the brilliantly lit black and white marble hallway. She wished never to see him, or the house, again. He was no longer her son, he was a stranger, and for a last moment she had gazed at him with tears filling the wise old eyes once more. She shook her head slowly then and walked silently out the door.

She and Serena had never seen her uncle, or the house, or Rome again. She had been twelve the last time she walked out the richly ornate bronze doors on the Via Giulia and yet even as she stood in the chill air of the Alps two years later she felt as though they had left Rome that afternoon. It had been a difficult two years, years of figthing off the memories of the sounds of her father being beaten by the soldiers in the courtyard, the frantic look of her mother as she had run out

17

of the house the next morning, her hair barely combed, her eyes wide with fear, a red wool coat clutched around her, and the sight of their bodies when the soldiers had left them at the gate, sprawled on the white marble steps, their blood trickling slowly down into the grass . . . and Serena's endless screams as she saw them . . . saw them lying there . . . even as she said good-bye to her grandmother. The memories were not yet dim, and now she was losing her too. Losing her by being sent away, to safety, her grandmother had insisted. But what was safe now? Nothing was safe, Serena knew that at fourteen. Nothing would ever be safe again. Nothing. Except for her grandmother, she had lost it all.

"I will write to you, Serena, I promise. Every day. And when Italy is a nice place again, you will come back here and live with me. I promise you that, my darling. I promise. . . ." In spite of her strength the principessa had choked on the last words as she held Serena close to her, this last bit of her own flesh, this last link she had to her firstborn. She would have no one now when Serena went away. But there was no choice. It was too dangerous for the child to stay. Three times in the last two months the soldiers in the Piazza San Marco had accosted Serena. Even in plain, ugly clothes, the child was too beautiful, too tall, too womanly, even at fourteen. The last one had followed her home from school and grabbed her roughly by the arms and kissed her, pressed against a wall, his body crushed against hers. One of the servants had seen them there, Serena panting and frightened, wide eyed with terror yet silent, afraid that this time they would take her, or her grandmother, away. She had been terrified of the soldiers' faces and their laughter and their eyes. And the older woman knew each day that there was danger for Serena, that letting her out of the house at all was dangerous for the child. There was no way to control the soldiers, no way to protect Serena from the madness that seemed to run wild. Any day a nightmare could befall them, and before it happened Alicia di San Tibaldo knew that she had to save the child. It had taken several weeks to find the solution, but when the bishop quietly suggested it to her, she knew that she had no choice. Quietly, that night, after dinner, she had told Serena about the plan. The child had cried at first, and begged her, pleaded not to send her away, and surely not so far away as that. She could go to the farm in Umbria, she could hide there, she could cut off her hair, wear ugly dresses, she could work in the fields . . . she could do anything, but please, *Nonna* . . . please. . . . Her heart-wrenching sobs were to no avail. To let her stay in Italy was to destroy her, was to risk her daily, to walk a constant tightrope, knowing that she could be killed, or hurt or raped. The only thing left for her grandmother to do for her was to send her away, until the end of the war. And they both knew, as they stood inside the Swiss border, that it could be for a very long time.

"You will be back soon, Serena. And I will be here, my darling. No matter what." She prayed that she wasn't lying as rivers of tears flowed from the young girl's eyes, and the slender shoulders shook in her hands.

"*Me lo prometti?*" Do you promise me? She could barely choke out the words.

The old woman nodded silently and kissed Serena one last time, and then, nodding to the two women and the nuns, she stepped gracefully backward and the nuns put their arms around Serena and began to lead her away. She would walk for several miles that night to their convent. The next day they would take her with a group of other children to their sister house by bus some hundred miles away. From there she would be passed on to another group and eventually taken out of Switzerland. Their goal was London, and from there, the States. It would be a long and difficult journey, and there was always the danger of a bombing in London, or at sea. The route that Alicia had chosen for her grandchild was one of possible danger and an even greater chance for safety and survival. To stay in Italy would have meant certain disaster, in one way or another, and she would have died before she would have let them touch Serena. She owed Graziella and Umberto that much, after what Sergio had done. She had no one now, except Serena . . . a tiny speck of dark brown, her pale gold hair shoved into a dark knitted hat . . . as they reached the last knoll and then turned, with a last wave from Serena, and then they disappeared.

* * *

For Serena it had been a long and terrifying journey, complete with five days and nights in air-raid shelters in London, and at last they had fled to the countryside, and left on a freighter out of Dover. The crossing to the States had been grim, and Serena had said not a word for days. She spoke no English. Several of the nuns accompanying them spoke French, as did Serena, but she had no wish to speak to anyone at all. She had lost everyone now. Everyone and everything. Her parents, her uncle, her grandmother, her home, and at last her country. There was nothing left. She had stood on deck, a solitary figure in brown and gray, with the wind whipping the long sheets of pale blond hair around her head. The nuns had watched her, saying nothing at all. At first they had been afraid that she might do something desperate, but in time they came to understand her. You could learn a lot about the child simply from watching her. She had an extraordinary sort of dignity about her. One sensed her strength and her pride and at the same time her sorrow and her loss. There were others in the group of children going to the States who had suffered losses similar to Serena's, two of the children had lost both parents and all their brothers and sisters in air raids, several had lost at least one parent, all had lost beloved friends. But Serena had lost something more. When she learned of her uncle's betrayal of her father, she had lost her faith and trust in people as well. The only person she had trusted in the past two years was her grandmother. She trusted no one else. Not the servants, not the soldiers, not the government. No one. And now the one person she could count on was nowhere near. When one looked into the deep green eyes, one saw a bottomless sorrow that tore at one's heart, a grief beyond measure, a despair visible in children's eyes only in times of war.

In time the look of sorrow was less apparent. Once at the convent in Upstate New York, she laughed, though rarely. She was usually serious, intense, quiet, and in every spare moment she wrote to her grandmother, asking a thousand questions, telling her each detail of every day.

It was in the spring of 1943 that the letters from the principessa stopped coming. First Serena had been mildly worried, and then it became obvious that she was deeply concerned. Finally she had lain awake every night in terror, wondering, imagining, fearing, and then hating . . . it was Sergio again . . . he had come to Venice to kill her grandmother too. He had done it, she imagined, because her grandmother knew the truth about what he had done to his brother and he couldn't bear to have anyone know, so he had killed her, and one day he would try to kill Serena too. But let him try, she thought, the extraordinary green eyes narrowing with a viciousness even she hadn't known she had. Let him, I will kill him first, I will watch him die slowly, I will. . . .

"Serena?" There had been a soft light in the corridor, and the Mother Superior had appeared at her door that night. "Is something wrong? Have you had bad news from home?"

"No." The walls had come up quickly, as Serena sat up in bed and shook her head, the green eyes instantly veiled.

"Are you sure?"

"No, thank you, Mother. It is kind of you to ask." She opened up to no one. Except her grandmother, in the daily letters, which had had no response now for almost two months. She stepped quickly to the cold floor and stood there in the simple cotton night-gown, a curtain of blond hair falling over her shoulders, her face a delicately chiseled marvel, worthy of a statue, and truly remarkable on a girl of just sixteen.

"May I sit down?" The Mother Superior had looked gently at Serena.

"Yes, Mother."

Mother Constance sat on the room's single wooden chair as Serena hovered for a moment and then sat back on the bed, feeling uncomfortable, and her own worries still showing in her eyes. "Is there nothing I can do for you, child?" The others had made a home here. The English, the Italians, the Dutch, the French. The convent had been filled for four years now with children brought over from Europe, most of whom would eventually go back, if their families survived the war. Serena was older than most of the others. Other than Serena the oldest child had been twelve when she had arrived, the others were mostly much younger children, five, six, seven, nine. But the others had acquired a kind of ease about them, as though they had come from nowhere more exotic than Poughkeepsie, as though they knew nothing of war and had no real fears. The fears were there, and at times, at night, there were nightmares, but on the whole they were an oddly happy-go-lucky group. No one would have believed the stories that had preceded their arrivals, and in most cases there were no visible signs of the stress of war. But Serena had been different from the beginning. Only the Mother Superior and two other nuns were fully aware of her story, apprised of it in a letter from her grandmother that came shortly after she arrived. The principessa had felt that they should know the full story but they had heard nothing of it from Serena herself. Over the years she had never opened up to them. Not yet.

"What's troubling you, my child? Do you not feel well?"

"I'm fine. . . ." There had been only the fraction of a second of hesitation, as though for an instant she had considered opening a sacred door. It was the first time, and this time Mother Constance felt that she had to be persistent. Even if it was painful for Serena to reveal her feelings, it was obvious that the girl was in greater distress than she ever had been before. "I'm . . . it's only that—" Mother Constance said nothing, but her eyes reached out gently to Serena until she could resist no more. Tears suddenly filled her eyes and spilled onto her cheeks. "I've had no letter from my grandmother in almost two months."

"I see." Mother Constance nodded slowly. "You don't think she could be away?"

Serena shook her head and brushed away the tears with one long graceful hand. "Where would she go?"

"To Rome perhaps? On family business?"

Serena's eyes grew instantly hard. "She has no business there anymore!"

"I see." She didn't wish to press the girl further. "It could just be that it's getting harder and harder to get the mail through. Even from London the mail is slow." During her entire stay in New York the letters from her grandmother had reached her via an intricate network of underground and overseas channels. Getting the letters from Italy to the States had been no easy feat. But they had always come. Always.

Serena gazed at her searchingly. "I don't think it's that."

"Is there anyone else you could write to?"

"Only one." There was only one old servant there now. Everyone else had had to leave. Mussolini wouldn't allow anyone of the old guard to keep as many servants as the principessa had been keeping. She was permitted one servant, and one only. Some of the others had wanted to stay on without pay, but it had not been approved. And the bishop had died the previous winter, so there was no one else she could write to. "I'll write to Marcella tomorrow." She smiled for the first time since the nun had entered her room. "I should have thought of it earlier."

"I'm sure your grandmother's all right, Serena."

Serena nodded slowly. With her grandmother having just turned eighty, she was not quite as sure. But she had said nothing of being ill or not feeling well. There was really no reason to think that something was wrong. Except for the silence . . . which continued, unexplained. The letter to Marcella was returned to Serena four weeks after she wrote it, unopened and undelivered, with a scrawled note from the postman that Marcella Fabiani did not live at that address anymore. Had they gone to stay at the farm? Things must be worse in Venice. With a growing sense of panic, Serena grew ever more silent and strained. She wrote to her grandmother at the farm in Umbria then, but that letter came back too. She wrote to the foreman, and the letter came back marked "Deceased." For the first weeks and then months, she had felt panic-stricken and desperate, but in time the terror ebbed into a dull pain. Something had, happened, of that there was no doubt, but there seemed to be no way to get an explanation. There was no one left. No family except Sergio of course. And now, in her desperation, there was nowhere for Serena to turn. All she could do was wait until she could return to Italy to find out for herself.

There was still enough money for her to do that. When Serena had left, her grandmother had pressed on her a fat roll of American bills. She had no idea how the old woman had got the American money, but it had amounted to a thousand dollars when Serena counted it out quietly, alone in the bathroom the next day. And the nuns had received another ten thousand through elaborate international channels, for her care and whatever she might need during her stay at the convent. Serena knew that there had to be a great deal of that left. And every night, as she lay in her bed, thinking, she planned to use the money to get back to Italy the moment the war was over. She would go straight to Venice and find out, and if something had happened to the old woman, because of Sergio, she would go directly to Rome immediately thereafter and kill him.

It was a thought she had cherished now for almost two years. The war had ended in Europe in May of 1945, and from the very moment it ended she began making plans to go back. Some of the others were still waiting to hear from their parents that things were ready for their return, but Serena had nothing to wait for, except her ticket, her papers. She didn't even need the permission of the nuns. She was over eighteen, and she turned nineteen on V-J Day on the train. It had seemed to take forever to get passage over, but at last she had.

Mother Constance had taken her to the ship in New York. She had held Serena close for a long time. "Remember, my child, that whatever happened, you cannot change it. Not now. And you couldn't have then. You were where she wanted you to be. And it was right for you to be here, with us."

Serena pulled away from her then, and the elderly nun saw that the tears were pouring down the delicate cheeks and flooding the huge green eyes that seemed brighter than any emerald, as the girl stood there, torn between affection and terror, grief and regret. "You've been so good to me all these years, Mother. Thank you." She hugged Mother Constance once more, the boat horn sounded again, this time more insistently, and the stately nun left the cabin. Her last words to Serena were "Go with God," and Serena had watched her wave from the dock as she waved frantically from the ship, this time with a smile on her face.

That had been only nine days before. The memories of

Mother Constance seemed to fill her mind as Serena glanced out the window and saw that the dawn had come as they sped along on the train. She stared at the pink and gray sky in amazement as they raced through fields that had not been harvested in years and that showed signs of the bombs, and her heart broke for her country, for her people, for those who had suffered while she was safe in the States. She felt as though she owed them all something, a piece of herself, of her heart, of her life. While she had eaten roast turkey and ice cream on the Hudson they had suffered and struggled and died. And now, here they were, together, the survivors, at the dawn of a new era, a new life. She felt her heart rise within her as the train continued on its journey, and she watched the sun ride up in the early morning sky. The day had come at last. She was home.

Half an hour later they rolled into Santa Lucia Station, and slowly, almost breathlessly, she stepped from the train, behind the old ladies, the children, the toothless old men, the soldiers, and she stood there, at the bleak back door of Venice, looking at the same scene she had seen twice a year as a child when she and her parents had come to visit from Rome. But they were gone now, and this was not an Easter vacation. This was a new world, and a new life, and as she walked slowly away from the station she stared at the bright sunlight shining on the ancient buildings and shimmering on the water of the Grand Canal. A few gondolas bobbed at the landing, and a fleet of random boats hovered near the quay, drivers shouted to prospective passengers, and suddenly everything was in frantic motion around her, and as she watched it Serena smiled for the first time in days. It was a smile she hadn't felt in her heart for years.

Nothing had changed and everything had. War had come and gone, a holocaust had happened, she had lost everyone, and so had countless others, and yet here it was as it had been for centuries, in all its golden splendor, Venice. Serena smiled to herself, and then as she hurried along with the others, she laughed softly. She had come of age, in that one final moment, and now she was home.

"*Signorina!*" A gondolier was shouting, staring admiringly at her long graceful legs. "*Signorina!*"

"*Sì . . . gondola, per piacere.*" They were words she had said a thousand times before. Her parents had always let her pick the one she wanted.

"*Ècco.*" He swept her a low bow, helped her to her seat, stowed her single, battered suitcase, and she gave him the address and sat back in her seat, as deftly the gondolier sped into the swirling traffic of boats on the Grand Canal.

CHAPTER TWO

As the gondolier made his way slowly down the Grand Canal, Serena sat back and watched with awe as the memories unfolded, memories she had barely dared to indulge herself in for four years, and suddenly here it all was. With the sunlight shining on his gilded body the Guardian Spirit of the Customs seemed to watch her as they passed majestically below, the gondola moving in the familiar rhythm that she had all but forgotten and that had enchanted her so extravagantly as a child. And just as they had remained unchanged in centuries of Italian history, the landmarks of Venice continued to roll into sight with a beauty that still took her breath away, the Ca' d'Oro in all its splendor, and the Ca' Pesaro, and tiny piazzas and small bridges and suddenly the Ponte di Rialto as they glided slowly beneath it, and on further into the Grand Canal, past endless palazzi: Grimani, Papadopoli, Pisani, Mocenigo, Contarini, Grassi, Rezzonico, all the most splendid and visible palaces of Venice, until suddenly they were swept gently under the Ponte dell'Accademia, past the Franchetti Palace Gardens and the Palazzo Dario, and the church of Santa Maria della Salute standing gracefully by on the right, as the gondola suddenly drifted in front of the Doges' Palace and the Campanile, and was almost instantly poised before the Piazza San Marco. He slowed there and Serena gazed at it in wonder, its devastating beauty leaving her speechless as they paused. She felt as the ancient Venetians must have, after their endless journeys to foreign ports, only to return to rediscover with wonder and enchantment what they had left behind.

"Beautiful, eh, *signorina?*" The gondolier glanced at San Marco with pride, and then back at her. But she only nodded. It was extraordinary to be back after so many years, yet nothing had changed here. The rest of the world had been turned upside down, but even the war had not touched Venice. Bombs had fallen nearby, but miraculously, Venice itself had remained untouched. He swept slowly under the Ponte di Paglia then, and rapidly under the illustrious Ponte dei Sospiri, the Bridge of Sighs, and then drifted into the maze of smaller canals, past other less important palazzi and ancient statues carved into the magnificent facades. There were balconies and tiny piazzas and everywhere the ornate splendor that had drawn people to Venice for a thousand years.

But now Serena was no longer fascinated by the architecture. Ever since they had turned into the maze of smaller canals, her face had been tense, and her brow furrowed as she watched familiar landmarks begin to slide by. They were coming closer now, and the answers to the questions that had tormented her for two years now were within reach.

The gondolier turned to confirm the address with her, and then, having seen her face, he said nothing more. He knew. Others had come home before her. Soldiers mostly. Some had been prisoners of war, and come home to find their mothers and their lovers and their wives. He wondered who this young beauty could be looking for and where she had been. Whatever she was looking for, he hoped she found it. They were only a few hundred feet from the house now, and Serena had already sighted it. She saw the shutters falling from their hinges, boards over a few of the windows, and the narrow canal lapping at the stone steps just beneath the iron grille on the landing. As the gondolier approached the building Serena stood up.

"You want me to ring the bell for you?" There was a big old-fashioned bell and a knocker, but Serena was quick to shake her head. He held her arm to steady her as she stepped

27

carefully onto the landing, and for an instant she looked up at the darkened windows, knowing only too well the tale they told.

She hesitated for an endless moment, and then quickly pulled the chain on the bell and closed her eyes as she waited, thinking back to all the other times her hand had touched that bell . . . waiting . . . counting the moments until one of the old familiar faces would appear, her grandmother just behind them, smiling, waiting to embrace Serena and run laughingly up the steps with her to the main salon . . . the tapestries, the rich brocades . . . the statues . . . the tiny miniatures of the exquisite golden copper horses of San Marco at the head of the stairs . . . and this time only silence and the sounds of the Canal behind her. As she stood there Serena knew that there would be no answer to the bell.

"*Non, c'è nessuno, signorina?*" the gondolier inquired. But it was a useless question. No, of course there was no one home, and hadn't been in years. For a moment Serena's eyes rested on the knocker, wanting to try that too, to urge someone from the familiar depths within, to *make* them open the door, to make them roll back the clock for her.

"Eh! . . . Eh!" It was an insistent sound behind her, almost an aggressive one, and she turned to see a vegetable merchant drifting past in his boat, watching her suspiciously. "Can't you see there's no one there?"

"Do you know where they are?" Serena called across the other boats, relishing the sound of her own language again. It was as though she had never left. The four years in the States did not exist.

The vegetable man shrugged. "Who knows?" And then, philosophically, "The war . . . a lot of people moved away."

"Do you know what happened to the woman who lived here?" An edge of franticness was moving back into Serena's voice and the gondolier watched her face, as a mailman on a barge came slowly by, looking at Serena with interest.

"The house was sold, *signorina*." The postman answered the question for her.

"To whom? When?" Serena looked suddenly shocked. Sold? The house had been sold? She had never contemplated that. But why would her grandmother have sold the house? Had she been short of money? It was a possibility that had never occurred to Serena before.

"It was sold last year, when the war was still on. Some people from Milano bought it. They said that when the war was over they would retire and move to Venice . . . fix up the house. . . ." He shrugged and Serena felt herself bridle. "Fix up the house." What the hell did he mean? What did they mean? Fix what up? The bronzes? The priceless antiques, the marble floors? The impeccable gardens behind the house? What was there to fix? As he watched her the mailman understood her pain. He pulled his boat close to the landing and looked up into her face. "Was she a friend of yours . . . the old lady?" Serena nodded slowly, not daring to say more. "Ècco. Capisco allora." He only thought he understood, but he didn't. "She died, you know. Two years ago. In the spring."

"Of what?" Serena felt her whole body grow limp, as though suddenly someone had pulled all of the bones out of her. She thought for a moment that she might faint. They were the words she had expected, the words she had feared, but now she had heard them and they cut through her like a knife. She wanted him to be wrong, but as she looked at the kind old face she knew that he wasn't. Her grandmother was gone.

"She was very old, you know, signorina. Almost ninety."

Serena shook her head almost absentmindedly and spoke softly. "No, she turned eighty that spring."

"Ah." He spoke gently, wanting to offer comfort but not sure how. "Her son came from Rome, but only for two days. He had everything sent to Rome, I heard later. Everything, all her things. But he put the house up for sale right away. Still, it took them a year to sell it."

So it was Sergio again, Serena thought to herself as she stood there. Sergio. *He* had everything sent to Rome. "And her letters?" She sounded angry now, as though within her there was something slowly beginning to burn. "Where did her mail go? Was it sent to him?"

The mailman nodded. "Except the letters for the servants. He told me to send those back."

Then, Sergio had got all her letters. Why hadn't he told her? Why hadn't someone written to her to tell her? For more than two years she had gone crazy, waiting, wondering, asking questions that no one could answer. But he could have answered, the bastard.

"*Signorina*?" The mailman and the gondolier waited. "*Va bene*?" She nodded slowly.

"*Sì . . . sì . . . grazie* . . . I was just . . ." She had been about to offer an explanation but her eyes filled with tears instead. She turned away and the two men exchanged a glance.

"I'm sorry, *signorina*." She nodded, her back still turned, and the mailman moved on. Only her gondolier waited.

In a moment, after a last look at the rusting hinges on the gate, she fingered the bellpull one last time, as though making contact with some piece of her, some tangible part of the past, as though by touching something that her grandmother had touched she could become part of her again, and then slowly she came back to the gondola, feeling as though some vital part of her had died. So Sergio finally had what he wanted now—the title. She hated him. She wanted him to choke on his title, to rot in his own blood, to die a far more horrible death than her father, to . . .

"*Signorina*?" The gondolier had watched her face contort with anger and anguish, and he wondered what agony had seized her soul to make someone so young look so tormented. "Where would you like to go now?"

She hesitated for a moment, not sure. Should she go back to the train station? She wasn't ready. Not yet. There was something she had to do first. She turned slowly to the gondolier, remembering the little church perfectly. It was exquisite, and perhaps someone there would know more. "Take me please to the Campo Santa Maria Nuova."

"Maria dei Miracoli?" he asked her, naming the church where she wanted to go. She nodded, and he helped her back into the gondola and pushed slowly away from the landing, as her eyes held interminably to the facade she would always remember and never come back to see again. This would be

30

her last journey to Venice. She knew that now. She had no reason to come back. Not anymore.

She found Santa Maria dei Miracoli as she remembered it, almost hidden by high walls, and as simple externally as she recalled. It was inside that Mary of the Miracles showed her wonders, inside that the marble inlays and delicate carvings startled the newcomer with its beauty and still entranced those who knew it well after seeing it for dozens of years. Serena stood there for a moment, feeling her grandmother beside her, as she had every Sunday when they had come to Mass. She stood silently for a few moments and then walked slowly toward the altar, kneeling there, and trying desperately not to think . . . of what to do now . . . of where to go. . . .

Dwelling on her loss wouldn't help her. But still, the reality of it was almost intolerable and two lone tears traveled slowly down her cheeks to the delicately carved chin. She stood up again a moment later and went into the office at the back of the church, to attempt to find the priest. There was an old man in a priest's robe sitting there when she entered. He sat at a simple desk, reading from a frayed leather book of prayer.

"Father?" He looked up slowly from what he was reading, gazing directly into Serena's green eyes. He was new to the parish, she suspected. She did not remember him from before she left. "I wonder if you could help me. I am looking for some information about my grandmother."

The old man in the cassock sighed and stood up slowly. There had been so many inquiries like this since the end of the war. People had died, moved away, got lost. It was unlikely that he would be able to help her. "I don't know. I will check the records for you. Her name?"

"La Principessa Alicia di San Tibaldo." She said it softly, not meaning to impress anyone, but nonetheless his manner changed. He became more alert, more interested, more helpful, and in spite of herself, Serena was annoyed. Did the title mean so much, then? Was that what would make the difference? Why? It all seemed so unimportant now. Titles, names, rank, money. All that mattered to Serena was that her grandmother was dead.

He was whispering softly to himself as he shuffled through drawers of papers, and then checked a large ledger for what seemed like an interminable time, until at last, he nodded his head and looked up at Serena again. "Yes." He turned the book toward her. "It is here. April ninth, 1943. The cause of death was natural. A priest from this church administered last rites. She is buried outside in the garden. Would you like to see?" Serena nodded and followed him solemnly out of the office, through the church, and out a narrow door, into a brightly sunlit little garden, filled with flowers and small ancient tombstones, and surrounded by small trees. He walked carefully toward a back corner where there were only a few tombstones, and all of them seemed to be new. He gestured gently toward the small white marble stone, watched Serena for a moment, and then turned and left as she stood there, looking stunned. The search was over, the answers had come. She was here, then, beneath the trees, hidden by the walls at Santa Maria dei Miracoli, she had been here all along as Serena wrote her letter after letter, praying that her grandmother was still alive. Serena wanted to be angry as she stood there, she wanted to hate someone, to fight back. But there was no one to hate, no fight left. It was all over, in this peaceful garden, and all that Serena felt was sad.

"*Ciao, Nonna.*" She whispered as she turned to leave at last, her eyes blurred with the tears that filled them. She did not return to say good-bye to the priest, but as she made her way out through the beautiful little church again, he was standing in the doorway and came to her, looking solicitous and interested, and he shook her hand twice as she left.

"Good-bye, Principessa . . . good-bye. . . ." Principessa? For an instant she stopped in her tracks, startled, and turned to look at him again. Princess, he had called her. . . . Princess? . . . And then slowly, she nodded. Her grandmother was gone now. Serena was the principessa, and as she ran hastily down the steps to the landing where she had left her gondolier, she knew that didn't matter at all.

As the gondolier made his way away from the church, her

thoughts were spinning. Sergio. What had he done with the money he got for the house? What had he done with her parents' treasures and her grandmother's beautiful things? Suddenly she wanted an explanation, a recount, she wanted the despicable man who had destroyed her family to make up to her what he had taken from her. Yet even as she thought of it she knew that he could not. Nothing Sergio would ever do would make up to Serena what she had lost. But still, for some reason, she felt an urge now to see him, to demand something of him, to make him account for what was, in a sense, hers as well. And now as she sat in the gondola, heading slowly back toward the Grand Canal and the Piazza San Marco, she knew where she was going. Venice had belonged to her grandmother. It was a part of her. It *was* her. But it wasn't home to Serena. It never had been. It had always been foreign and different and intriguing, exciting, a kind of adventure even during the two years she had lived there after her parent's death. But now, having come this far, Serena knew that she had to go further. She had to go all the way to her beginnings. She had to go home.

"Do you want to go to the piazza, *signorina*?"

"No." She shook her head slowly. Not to the piazza. She had finished what she had to do in Venice. Three hours after she'd got there, it was time to move on. "No, *grazie*. Not the piazza. Take me back to Santa Lucia."

They glided slowly under the Ponte dei Sospiri, the Bridge of Sighs, and she closed her eyes. Almost instinctively, the gondolier began to sing; it was a sad, plaintive song, and he sang it well. A moment later they were back in the bright sunshine and the song went on as they rounded the bend in the Grand Canal and passed in front of the splendor of the Piazza San Marco, the Campanile, the Doges' Palace, and back down the canal, past all the miracles of Venice. But this time Serena did not cry. She watched all of it, as though drinking it in this one last time so that she could remember, as though she knew that she would never come back again.

When they reached the station, she paid him, including a

handsome tip, for which he thanked her profusely, and his eyes sought hers.

"Where are you going now, *signorina*?"

"To Rome."

He nodded slowly. "You haven't been back since the war?" She shook her head. "You will find it very different." But it couldn't be any more different from what she had found here. For her everything was changed, everywhere. "You have relatives in Roma?"

"No . . . I . . . all I had was my grandmother. Here."

"That was her house this morning?" Serena nodded and he shook his head.

"I'm sorry."

"So am I." She smiled softly at him then and reached out to shake his hand. He took her delicate white hand in his rough brown one, and then patted her on the shoulder as he helped her out and handed her her bag.

"Come back to Venice, *signorina*." He smiled at her, and she promised that she would, and then solemnly picked up her little suitcase and began to walk back in the direction of the train.

CHAPTER THREE

As the train drew into Termini Station shortly after sunset at eight that evening, there was no smile on Serena's lips. Instead she sat in her seat as though at any moment she expected something ghastly to happen, her entire body tense, her face white. She watched landmarks she hadn't seen in almost seven years begin to drift past her, and it was as though for the first time in years a door deep inside her was being torn from its hinges, as though her very soul was exposed. If someone had spoken to Serena at that moment, she wouldn't have heard them.

She was lost in another world, as they rolled along on the edge of the city, and suddenly she felt a longing well up in her that she had not allowed herself to feel in years. It was a longing for familiar places, an ache for her parents, a hunger to come home. She could barely wait for the train to stop in the station. As it lurched the last few feet forward she stood up and pulled her suitcase out of the overhead rack, and then with rapid strides she threaded her way to the end of the car and waited, like a horse anxious to return to its stable. The moment the train stopped and the doors opened, she leaped down and began to run. It was like a wild, instinctive gesture, this mad pounding of the pavement, as she ran past women and children and soldiers, heedless of everything except this wild, mingled feeling. She wanted to shout "Here I am everybody! I'm home!" But beneath the excitement was still the tremor . . . of what she would find here in Rome . . . and of the terrible memories of her parents' last day alive. Her emotions were wild—was coming here a betrayal? Was there reason to be scared?—oh, God, she was glad to be home. She had had to see it. Just once more. Or had she come in search of her uncle? Of an explanation? Of apologies or solace . . .?

She flagged down a small black taxi and flung her suitcase into the backseat. The driver turned his head with interest to watch her, but made no move to assist her. Instead he looked long and hard into her eyes. It was a look that startled her in its frank appraisal, and she lowered her eyes suddenly, embarrased at the desire she saw in the man's eyes.

"*Dove?*" It was a question that startled her in its directness, but it was hardly unusual for him to ask. The only problem was that she wasn't sure how to answer. He had asked her simply "Where," and she didn't know. Where? To the house that had been her parents' and was now her uncle's? Was she ready? Could she face him? Did she want to see that house again? Suddenly all her assurance melted as quickly as it had sprung up in her and she felt her hands tremble as she smoothed her dress and averted her gaze again.

"The Borghese Gardens." The tremor in her voice was

audible only to Serena, and the driver shrugged and thrust the car into the traffic. And as she sat in the backseat staring out at the city that had drawn her like a magnet, Serena felt suddenly like a child again, her hair loose and flowing softly in the breeze coming in the windows, her eyes wide. She knew from familiar landmarks that they were approaching the Porta Pinciana. She could see the Via Vittorio Veneto stretched out ahead, and just before them suddenly the dark expanse of the gardens, lit here and there along the walkways, the flower beds visible even in the growing dark. She realized suddenly also how strange the driver must have thought her. The Borghese Gardens at nine o'clock at night? But where else was she to go now? She already knew the answer, but tried not to think of it as she counted out the fare to the driver, tossed her hair off her shoulders, and picked up her suitcase and got out. She stood there for a long moment, as though waiting for someone, and then, as if seeing everything around her for the first time, she took a deep breath and began to walk. Not hurriedly this time as though she had somewhere to go, and someone to meet her, but slowly, aimlessly, as if all she cared about was imbibing the essence of Rome.

She found herself walking along one of the grassy paths for strollers along the edge of the park, watching bicyclists hurrying along, or women walking dogs, and here and there children playing. It was late for them to be out, but it was summer and a balmy evening, the war was over, and there was no school the next day. Serena noticed for the first time that there was a kind of holiday atmosphere everywhere, people were smiling, young girls were laughing, and everywhere, as they were all over Europe, the young GI's were walking in groups, or with their girl friends, chatting, laughing, and trying to make friends with passing young women, waving candy bars and silk stockings and cigarettes, half laughing at themselves and half serious, and almost always getting a laughing response or an invitation. Even the refusals were kind ones, except Serena's. When two GI's approached her, her face turned to stone and her eyes were angry as she answered in Italian and told them to leave her alone.

"Leave her alone, Mike. You heard the lady."

"Yeah, but did you see her?" The shorter of the two whistled as Serena rapidly made her way toward the Via Veneto and got lost in the crowd. But the attempts to pick her up were all harmless. She was a pretty girl, and the soldiers were lonely, and this was Rome.

"Cigarettes, *signorina*?" Another cluster of uniforms waved a pack almost in her face. They were everywhere, and this time she only shook her head. She didn't want to see them all over the city. She didn't want to see any uniforms. She wanted it to be as it had been before the war. But it wasn't. That much she could see now. There were scars. There were differences. There were still remnants of signs in German, and now American ones posted over them. They were occupied once again.

It made her sad as she remembered back to when she had been a child . . . when she had come to the Borghese Gardens to play. It was a rare treat to do that with her mother. Usually they went everywhere by car. But now and then there had been wondrous adventures, just she and her mother—the beauty with the tinkling laughter, the big hats, the huge laughing eyes. Serena suddenly dropped her face into her hands in the darkness. She didn't want to remember anymore. She didn't want to remember what had happened, how it had happened, what was no more. But it was as though whatever she did now that she had come back here there was no way to run from the memories anymore. The ghosts that had haunted her for seven years now didn't have to go far to find her. She had come home to find them.

Without thinking, she wandered in the direction of the Fontana di Trevi, and stood there mesmerized by it, as she had been as a little girl. She sat quietly for a few minutes, hunched against a wall, watching, and feeling refreshed by the breeze that came off the water. Then slowly, approaching the fountain, she tossed a coin quietly into the water, and then smiled to herself as she wandered in the direction of the Palazzo del Quirinale and then into the Via del Tritone. She came rapidly to the Triton's Fountain, and then to the Piazza Barberini, where she stood for a long moment wondering where to go next. It was almost eleven o'clock now and she was suddenly exhausted as she realized that she had nowhere to spend the night. She had to find a hotel room, a pensione, a convent, some place, but as she enumerated the possibilities in her head, her feet seemed to follow their own direction, and then suddenly she realized where she was going and caught her breath, knowing what had happened, what she was doing, and not wanting to continue or turn back. It was for this that she had left the peaceful convent on the Hudson, crossed the Atlantic, and taken the train from France.

A tiny part of her told her to wait until morning, until she was rested and her head was clear. It had been a long trying day, first in Venice and now here, with hours on the train, but it suddenly didn't matter, and Serena stopped letting her feet wander and stopped pretending to herself, that she had nowhere to go. She did have somewhere to go, a place she wanted to go to desperately, no matter how tired she was . . . and her feet moved relentlessly toward the familiar address on the Via Giulia. She had to see it, just to stand there for a moment, before she turned her back on the past forever and began the rest of her life. As she turned the last corner she could feel her heart beat faster, and suddenly her pace quickened as she could feel the building before it even came into view. And then suddenly . . . suddenly . . . under the street lamps, just past the trees, was the gleaming expanse of white marble, with the long French windows, the balconies, the lower floors hidden by tall hedges, and the long marble steps just inside the front gate, the whole of it surrounded by a border of flower beds and lawn.

"My God. . . ." It was the merest whisper. In the darkness it was easy to delude oneself that there had been no changes, that everything was as it had once been. That at any moment a familiar face would appear at a window, or her father would step outside with a cigar, for some air. Serena's mother had hated it at night when he had smoked cigars in the bedroom, and once in a while he had gone for a walk in the garden. When Serena awoke at night, as a little girl, sometimes she saw him there. Unconsciously she found herself looking for him now. But she saw no one, and like the house in Venice, it was shuttered. Only now she imagined her uncle sleeping here and even though he might be inside, she had lost the urge to see him—to fight him. What difference now?

She stood in front of her home for what seemed an endless time, unable to take her eyes from it, unable to go closer, and unwilling to try. This was as far as the dream had brought her. She would go no closer. She had no need to. The dream was all over now.

And then, as she turned slowly, her eyes filling with tears, her head held high, her suitcase still in her hand, she saw the copious form of an old woman, standing, watching her, a shawl around her corpulent shoulders, her hair pulled into a bun, as she continued to stare at Serena, as though wondering what this girl was doing here, with a suitcase, gaping at the Palazzo Tibaldo in the middle of the night. As Serena continued down the street with a determined step, the old woman suddenly rushed toward her, with a piercing shriek and a wail, both arms extended, as the shawl fell from her shoulders into the street, and she suddenly stood before Serena, her whole body trembling, her eyes streaming as she held out her arms to the girl. Serena made as though to step backward, stunned by the old woman, and then suddenly she looked into the heavily lined face and she gave a gasp of astonishment and then she too was sobbing softly as she reached out and held the old woman to her. It was Marcella, her grandmother's last remaining servant in Venice . . . and now suddenly she was here . . . at their old house in Rome. The old woman and the young one stood there, holding tightly to each other for what seemed like forever, unable to let go of each other, or the memories they shared. They stood there together, for a very long time.

"*Bambina . . . ah, Dio . . . bambina mia . . . ma che fai?* What are you doing here?"

"How did she die?" It was all Serena could think of as she clung to the old woman.

"In her sleep." Marcella sniffed deeply and stood back to get a good look at Serena. "She was getting so old." She gazed into Serena's eyes and shook her head. It was remarkable how much the girl looked like her mother. For a moment, as she had stood there in the street, watching her,

Marcella had thought she was seeing a ghost.

"Why didn't anyone tell me?"

Marcella shrugged in embarrassment and then looked away. "I thought he . . . that your uncle . . . but he didn't have time before . . ." She realized something then. Serena knew nothing at all of what had happened since her grandmother's death. "No one wrote to you, *cara*?"

"*Nessuno*." No one. And then, gently, "Why didn't you?"

This time the old woman looked at her squarely. The girl had a right to know why she hadn't written to her. "I couldn't."

"Why?" Serena looked puzzled as they stood there in the lamp-light.

Marcella smiled shyly. "I can't write, Serena . . . your grandmother always told me that I should learn, *ma* . . ." She shrugged in a helpless gesture as Serena smiled in answer.

"*Va bene*." It's all right. But how easily said after two terror-filled years. How much anxiety she would have been spared if the old woman had at least been able to write and tell her of her grandmother's death. "And . . ." She hated to say his name, even now. "Sergio?"

There was a moment's pause and Marcella took a careful breath. "He's gone, Serena."

"Where?" Her eyes searched the old woman's. She had come four thousand miles and two and a half years for this news. "Where is he?"

"Dead."

"Sergio?" This time Serena looked shocked. "Why?" For an instant there was a flash of satisfaction. Perhaps in the end they had killed him too.

"I don't know all of it. He made terrible debts. He had to sell the house in Venice." And then, almost apologetically, she waved at the white marble palazzo behind them. "He sold this . . . only two months after your grandmother died and he brought me back to Rome." Her eyes sought Serena's then, looking for condemnation. She had come with Sergio, he who had betrayed her parents, whom even the principessa had come to hate. But she had come home to

40

Rome with him. She had had nowhere else to go, Serena understood. Except for the elderly principessa, Marcella had been alone in the world. "I don't understand what happened. But they got angry with him. He drank. He was drunk all the time." She looked knowingly at Serena. He had had good reason to be drunk all the time. He had had a lot to live with, the murder of his own brother, his brother's wife. . . . "He borrowed money from bad people, I think. They came here, to the palazzo, late at night. They shouted at him. He shouted back. And then . . . Il Duce's men came here too. They were angry at him too . . . perhaps because of the other men. I don't know. One night I heard them threatening to kill him. . . ."

"And they did?" Serena's eyes lit up with an ugly fire. Perhaps he had come by his just desserts after all.

"No." Marcella shook her head. Her voice was without pity in the summer night. "He killed himself, Serena. He shot himself in the garden, two months after the principessa died. He had no money left, he had nothing. Only debts. The lawyers told me that it took everything, the money from both houses and everything else, to pay his debts." Then there was nothing left. It didn't matter. She hadn't come home for that.

"And the house?" Serena looked at her strangely. "Who does it belong to now?"

"I don't know. People I have never seen. They rent it to the Americans now since the end of the war. Before that, it was empty. I was here by myself. Every month the lawyer brings me my money. They wanted me to stay, to see that everything is all right. Once, the Germans almost took it over, but they never did." She shrugged, looking embarrassed again. Serena had lost everything, and yet Marcella was still living here. How odd life was.

"And the Americans live here now?"

"Not yet. Until now they only worked here. Now . . . next week . . . they will move in. Before, they only used it for offices, but they came yesterday to tell me they will move in on Tuesday." She shrugged, looking like the Marcella that Serena had known as a child. "For me, it makes no difference, they have all of their own people. And they told me yesterday that they will hire two girls to help me. So for me it changes nothing. Serena?'' The old woman watched her closely. ''*E tu? Vai bene?* What happened in all those years? You stayed with the nuns?''

''I did.'' She nodded slowly. ''And I waited to come back.''

''And now? Where are you staying?'' Her eyes glanced down at the suitcase Serena had dropped at her feet. But Serena shrugged.

''It doesn't matter.'' She suddenly felt oddly, strangely, free, fettered to no place, no person, and no time. In the last twelve hours every tie that she had ever clung to had been severed. She was on her own now, and she knew that she would survive. ''I was going to find a hotel, but I wanted to come here first. Just to see it.''

Marcella searched her face, and then hung her head as tears filled her eyes again. ''Principessa . . .'' It was a word spoken so softly that Serena barely heard it, and when she did, it sent a gentle tremor up her spine. The very word conjured up the lost image of her grandmother . . . Principessa. . . . She felt a wave of loneliness wash over her again, as Marcella lifted her face and dried her eyes on the apron that she eternally wore, even now. She clung to Serena's hand then, and Serena gently touched it with her own. ''All these years I am here . . . with your grandmother, and then·here, in this house.'' She waved vaguely toward the imposing building behind Serena. ''I am here. In the palazzo. And you''—she waved disparagingly at the dismal little suitcase—''like a beggar child, in rags, looking for a hotel. No!'' She said it emphatically, almost with anger as the corpulent body shook. ''No! You do not go to a hotel!''

''What do you suggest, Marcella?'' Serena smiled gently. It was a voice and an expression on the old woman that she recognized from a dozen years before. ''Are you suggesting that I move in with the Americans?''

''*Pazza, va!*'' She grinned. Crazy! ''Not with the Americans. With me. *Ecco.*'' As she spoke the last word she snatched the suitcase from the ground, took Serena's hand more firmly in her own, and began to walk toward the palazzo, but Serena stood where she was and shook her head.

"I can't." They stood there for a moment, neither moving, and Marcella searched the young girl's eyes. She knew all that she was thinking. She had had her own nightmares to overcome when she had first returned to Rome after the old lady's death. At first all she could remember here were the others . . . Umberto and Graziella . . . Serena as she had been, as a child . . . the other servants she had worked with, the butler she had once so desperately loved . . . Sergio when he had been younger and not yet rotten from within . . . the principessa in her prime. . . .

"You can stay with me, Serena. You must. You cannot be alone in Rome." And then, more gently, "You belong here. In your father's house."

She shook her head slowly, her eyes filling with tears. "It's not my father's house anymore."

More gently still, "It is my home now. Will you not come home with me?" She saw in those deep green eyes the agony that had been there on the morning of the death of her father and knew that she was not speaking to the woman, but the child. "It's all right, Serena. Come, my love. . . . Marcella will take care of you . . . everything will be all right." She enfolded Serena in her arms then, and they stood as they had in the beginning, holding tightly across the empty years. "*Andiamo, cara.*" And for no reason she could understand, Serena allowed herself to follow the old woman. She had only come to see it, not to stay there. To stand and gaze and remember, not to try and step inside the memories again. That was too much for her, she couldn't bear it. But as the old woman led her gently toward the rear entrance, Serena felt exhaustion overwhelm her . . . it was as though her whole day was telescoping into one instant and she couldn't bear it any longer. All she wanted was to lie down somewhere and stop thinking, stop trying to sort it all out.

Soon she stood at the back door of what had once been her parents' palazzo. Marcella quickly inserted the heavy key and turned it, and the door creaked, just as Serena had remembered it, and as the door swung open she found herself standing downstairs, in the servants' hall. The paint was yellowing, she saw as Marcella turned a light on; the curtains were the same, only they were no longer a bright blue but a faded gray; the wood floor was the same only a little duller, but there were fewer hands around now to wax it and Marcella had grown old. But nothing had really changed. Even the clock on the wall in the pantry was the same. Serena's eyes opened wide in amazement, and for the first time in years there was no anger and no pain. At last she had come home.

She had come full circle, and there was no one left to share it with but Marcella, clucking like an old mother hen as she led her down a familiar hallway into a room that had once belonged to a woman named Teresa, who had been a young and pretty upstairs maid. Like the others, she was long gone now, and it was into her room that Marcella led Serena, grabbing old frayed sheets and a blanket from a cupboard as she went. Everything was old and growing shabby, but it was still clean, and every bit of it was familiar, Serena realized as she sat down in a chair and watched Marcella make the bed. She said nothing. She only sat and stared.

"*Vai bene*, Serena?" The old woman glanced at her often, afraid that the shock of all she'd heard and seen and learned would be too much. She could neither read nor write, but she knew people, and she knew from the look in Serena's eyes that the girl had been through too much. "Take your clothes off, *bambina mia*. I'll wash them for you in the morning. And before you go to sleep, a little hot milk." Milk was still hard to come by, but she had some, and on this precious child of hers she would have lavished all she had.

Serena looked content to be where she was. It was as though suddenly all of her defenses had given way at the same time and she couldn't bear to stand up a moment longer. Coming home to Marcella was like being nine years old again, or five, or two.

"I'll be back in two minutes with the hot milk. I promise!" She smiled gently at Serena, cozily tucked into the narrow bed in the simple room. The walls were white, the trim gray, there was a narrow faded curtain in the room, a small ancient rug that dated back to the days of Teresa and the others, and the walls were bare. But Serena didn't even see them. She lay back against the pillow, closed her eyes, and when Marcella returned a moment later with the precious warm milk and sugar, she found Serena fast asleep. The old woman stopped just inside the doorway, turned out the single bulb that lit the room, and stood in the darkness, watching the young woman in the light of the moonlight, remembering how she had looked as a child. Like this, she thought to herself, only so much smaller . . . and more peaceful. . . . How troubled Serena had looked to her that evening . . . how angry . . . and how hurt . . . and how afraid. It hurt her to think back on all that had happened to the child, and then suddenly she realized as she watched her that she was gazing at the last remaining principessa of the Tibaldos. Serena di San Tibaldo. Principessa Serena . . . asleep at last in the servants' quarters of her father's house.

CHAPTER FOUR

When the sun streamed in the narrow window the next morning, Serena lay sprawled across the bed like a young goddess, her hair fanned out behind her like a sheet of gold. Marcella stood once more in the doorway, watching her, awed by the sheer brilliance of her beauty, and even more amazed than she had been the previous evening that Serena had come back at all. It was a miracle, she had told herself.

"*Ciao*, Cella." Serena opened one eye sleepily and smiled. "Is it late?"

"For what? You have an appointment? One day in Rome and you're already busy?" Marcella bustled toward her and Serena sat up and grinned. Years seemed to have fallen from her in the hours that she had been sleeping. Even after all that had happened the day before, she was less worried than she'd been since leaving the States. At least now she knew. She knew everything that she had been dreading hearing. The worst had come. Now there was the rest of her life to consider.

"What would you like for breakfast, *signorina*?" And then she changed it quickly. "*Scusi*, Principessa."

"What? You're not going to call me that! That was *Nonna*!" Serena looked half amused, half outraged. That was another era, another time. But Marcella looked dragonlike as she drew herself up to her full five feet at Serena's bedside.

"Now it is you. And you owe it to her, and to the others before her, to respect who and what you are."

"I'm me. Serena di San Tibaldo. *Punto. Finito. Basta.*"

"Nonsense!" Marcella fussed as she smoothed the covers over Serena, and then looked at her gravely. "Don't ever forget who you are, Serena. She never did."

"She didn't have to. And she didn't live in the world we do now. That's all over, Marcella. All of it. It died with—" She had been about to say "my parents," but couldn't bring herself to say it still. "It died with a whole generation of people whom our charming Duce attempted to destroy. Successfully, in a lot of cases. And what's left? People like me, who don't have ten lire left to their name, and have to get jobs digging ditches. Is that what being a principessa is all about, Cella?"

"It's in here." She pointed heatedly to her vast breast, indicating where her big generous heart was, and then to her head, "and in here. Not in what you do and what you don't do and how much money you have. Being a principe or a principessa is not money. *She* had not so much money either at the end. But she was always the principessa. And one day you will be like that too."

Serena shook her head firmly. "The world has changed, Marcella. Trust me. I know that."

"And what have you seen since you've been back here? The train station and what else?"

"People. On the train, in the streets, soldiers, young people, old people. They're different, Cella. They don't give a damn about principesse, and they probably never did. Only we cared about that stuff, and if we're smart, we'll forget about it now." And then with a return of cynicism she looked at the old woman. "Do you really think the Americans are going to care about that? If you told them you were hiding a principessa in your basement, do you think they would give a damn?"

"I'm not hiding you, Serena." Marcella looked sad. She didn't want to hear about this new world. The old world had been important to her. All of it. She believed in the old order and how it had worked. "You are staying here with me."

"Why?" Serena looked at her cruelly for a moment. "Because I am a principessa?"

"Because I love you. I always did and I always will." The old woman looked at her proudly, and tears rapidly filled Serena's eyes and she held out her arms from where she sat on the bed.

"I'm sorry. I didn't mean to say that." Marcella went to her and sat down. "It just hurts me to think about the old days. Everything I loved about them is gone. To me all that mattered were the people I loved. I don't want the damn title. I'd rather have *Nonna* still here, and just be me."

"But she isn't, and this is what she has left you. It is all she has left you, and I know she would want you to be proud of it too. Don't you want to be a principessa, Serena?" She looked at the girl in surprise.

"No." Serena shook her head solemnly. "I want my breakfast." She had only eaten bread and cheese at the station the day before. And she had forgotten dinner completely. But now she laughed at Marcella's earnestness, and the old woman dried her eyes and growled.

"You haven't grown up at all! You're just as impossible as you always were! Fresh . . . rude. . . ." The old woman grumbled and Serena stretched and got lazily out of bed with a grin.

"I told you. Princesses are a bad lot, Cella. Bad blood."

"Stop making light of that!" This time the growling was for real.

"Only if you stop taking it so seriously." Serena looked at her gently, but there was something very determined in her eyes. "I have better things to think about now." The old woman made no further comment, but went back to the pantry to make a steaming pot of coffee, another precious commodity that was still difficult to get enough of, after the war. But from Serena she was hoarding nothing. She lavished it all upon the young princess with the modern ideas. Crazy, all this nonsense about not wanting the title, not using it, not . . . it was ridiculous, Marcella grumbled to herself as she made breakfast. She had been born to be a principessa. Imagine not using the title! Ridiculous! She had obviously been in America for too long. It was high time she came home and remembered the old ways. Ten minutes later she called Serena to breakfast and the striking young beauty appeared in a blue cotton bathrobe they had given her at the convent, and her hair was brushed until it shone like gold in the bright morning sun. "What's for breakfast, Cella?"

"Toast, ham, jelly, peaches, coffee." A wealth of treasures some of which, like the jelly and the sugar, she had been saving for months. Serena instantly understood, and kissed the wrinkled old cheek before she sat down. She promised herself that she would eat sparingly, no matter how ravenously hungry she was.

"All of this just for me, Marcella?" She felt guilty eating all of the old woman's treasures, but she knew also that not to eat them would be to hurt her feelings. So she ate, carefully, but with obvious pleasure, and they shared the coffee, right to the last drop. "You cook like an angel." She closed her eyes and smiled happily in the morning sunshine, and the old woman touched the smooth young cheek with a smile.

"Welcome home, Serena." There was a moment of happy silence and then Serena stretched her long legs out in front of her and smiled.

"You make me want to stay forever." But she knew that she couldn't, and she wanted to leave before the temptation became too great to venture into the rest of the house. She didn't really want to do that. Even if part of her did. The rest of her did not.

Marcella was eyeing her thoughtfully as she stood up. "Why couldn't you stay, Serena? You don't have to go back to the States."

"No. But I have no reason to stay here." Except that she

loved it and it was home.

"Don't you want to stay?" Marcella looked hurt and Serena smiled.

"Of course I do. But I can't just move in. I have to have a place to live, a job, all of that. I don't know that I could find work in Rome."

"Why do you have to work?" The old woman looked annoyed. She wanted to hold on to the past, Serena realized with a smile.

"Because I have to eat. If I don't work, I won't eat."

"You could live here."

"And eat your food? What about you?"

"We'll have plenty. The Americans throw away more than all of the Romans eat put together. There will be everything we need here once they move in upstairs."

"And how do we explain me, Marcella?" Serena continued to look amused. "Resident principessa? Good luck charm? Your good friend? We just tell them they're lucky to have me, and I stay?"

"It's none of their business who you are." Marcella looked instantly defensive.

"They might not agree with you, Cella."

"Then you can work for them. As a secretary. You speak English. Don't you?" She looked at Serena with curiosity. After four years, she should, she was a bright girl after all. And as she listened Serena grinned.

"Yes, I do, but they wouldn't hire me as a secretary. They have their own people for that. Why should they hire me?" And then suddenly, her eyes began to sparkle. She had an idea.

"You thought of something?" Marcella knew that look only too well. It always made her faintly nervous, but often Serena's most outrageous ideas had been good.

"Maybe. Who does one speak to about jobs here?"

"I don't know. . . ." She looked pensive for a moment. "They gave me an address, in case I knew of any girls to help me with the house." She looked instantly suspicious. "Why?"

"Because I want to apply for a job."

"To do what?"

"I'll see what they have." It was one thing to arrive, oblivious with exhaustion, and spend a night in Marcella's cozy servants' quarters. It was quite another to live eternally belowstairs in a house that had once been her own. And she knew that she wasn't ready yet to go upstairs. But if they gave her a job, she would have to. She would just have to tell herself that it was their house, that it had nothing to do with her, or anyone she knew, and that she had never seen it before, but she was still quaking a little inside as she rounded the end of the Via Nazionale and passed the Baths of Diocletian as she turned into the Piazza della Repubblica and found the address. What if they didn't give her a job? Then what would she do? Scrape up the last of her money and make her way back to the States. Or stay here, in Rome? But for what? For her heart, she told herself as she pushed open the heavy door into the American offices that had been established there. Rome was where she had to be. She smiled as she thought of it, and she was still smiling to herself as she stepped into the building and collided almost instantly with a tall man with a boyish grin and a headful of thick blond curls under his military hat. On him the hat looked jaunty and he had it perched at a rakish angle, and his gray eyes seemed to dance with amusement as he looked into Serena's green eyes. For an instant she was tempted to smile at him, but her face grew rapidly serious, and as always when confronted with a uniform, she averted her eyes. No matter how handsome the man was, or how friendly, the uniforms always reminded her of her old nightmares, and she couldn't bear to look the men in the eyes.

"I'm sorry." He gently touched her elbow as though to convey his apology in case she did not speak his language. "Do you speak English?" His eyes combed her face, and he was instantly struck by her perfect creamy satin beauty, the wheat-gold hair, the huge green eyes, but he noticed too the stiff way she pulled away from him after their brief collision, and then the chilly way she looked at him once she had regained her composure, caught her breath, and stepped back. She seemed not to understand what he was saying, and he smiled and said a few words to her in Italian. "*Scusi,*

50

signorina. Mi dispiace molto. . . .'' And then he faltered with a captivating smile. But Serena did not appear captivated, inclined her head, indicating that she understood and murmured, *"Grazie.''* Her attitude would have annoyed him except that in the brief moments he had watched her he had seen the pain lurking deep within the bright green eyes. He had seen others like her. Everyone had suffered in the war. The Ice Maiden, he dubbed her to himself as he went on his way.

He had noticed instantly her spectacular beauty, but chasing the locals had never been Major B. J. Fullerton's forte. He had managed not to do any of that since he had arrived. He had ample reason not to. The major was engaged to one of the most beautiful young socialites in New York. Pattie Atherton had been the most ravishing debutante of 1940, and now at twenty-three, she was engaged to be his wife. B.J. smiled to himself again, with a little whistle as he hurried down the steps to the waiting limousine. He had a lot to do that morning, and his encounter with Serena slipped quickly from his mind.

Inside, Serena had pondered the available desks for a quiet moment, headed toward one marked EMPLOYMENT, with a subheading in Italian *LAVORO*, and had then explained in halting English what it was she wanted in the way of work. She was anxious not to let them know how well she spoke English. It was none of their business, she had decided. And above all, she did not want a job as translator, or as Marcella had suggested, as a secretary. All she wanted was to scrub floors in her old home, beside Marcella, and for that she barely needed to speak English at all.

"You're familiar with the existing housekeeper, you say, miss?" She nodded. "Did she send you here?" The Americans spoke loudly and precisely to the Italians, assuming that they were both stupid and deaf. Serena nodded again. "How well do you speak English? A little? More than that? Can you understand me?"

"*Si. Un po'* . . . a leetle. Enough." Enough to clean floors and polish silver, she thought to herself, and apparently the woman in uniform at the desk thought so too.

"All right. The major moves in on Tuesday. His aide-de-camp will be there too, and the sergeant who attends

51

to his household. In addition, there will be three orderlies. I think they're going to be housed in some old
servants' rooms upstairs.'' Serena knew immediately which
ones. The rooms under the roof were hot but well aired, and
had been occupied by several of her parents' servants over
the years. The better quarters were belowstairs, and she was
pleased that she and Marcella were keeping those. ''We
haven't found another girl yet, but we're still looking. Do
you think that, in the meantime, you and this woman
Marcella can handle it alone?''

''Yes.'' Serena answered quickly. She was not anxious to
have an intruder belowstairs.

''The other woman seemed quite old when I saw her.
What about heavy work?''

''I'll do.'' Serena stood to her full height and made an effort to stand even straighter and taller than usual. ''I am
nineteen.''

''Good. Then maybe we won't need another girl.'' The
American woman mused, as suddenly Serena realized that if
she did the heavy work and discouraged them from hiring
another young woman to help her, then she would be spending most of her time upstairs with ''them,'' in the rooms she
had hoped to avoid. But one couldn't have everything. She
would just have to brace herself and do it. It was worth it,
not to have a stranger around, downstairs with her and
Marcella. She would have resented that more than she
resented the American officers living upstairs in what had
once been her house. It was crazy really, this business of her
living with Marcella in a house that had once belonged to
her family and now belonged to someone else and was being
rented to the American army. What in hell was she doing
there? She wasn't really sure, but for the moment it seemed
to feel right, so she'd stay. ''We'll send someone out to
inspect the place on Monday and give you any necessary
details. Please see to it that all the rooms are clean, especially
the master bedroom. The major''—she smiled coquettishly
and Serena thought she looked absurd—''is used to very
handsome quarters.'' The comment was wasted on Serena,
who didn't really care. The American woman stood up then,
handed Serena some papers to sign, and explained that

she'd be paid in lire on the first and fifteenth of every month. Fifty dollars a month plus room and board was what it amounted to. And it sounded good to Serena. Very good. She left the building on the Piazza della Repubblica with a happy grin, and by the time she got back to her own house and stepped into her little apartment with Marcella in the basement, she was singing old familiar songs.

"My, my, so happy. They must have hired you to work for the general."

"No." She grinned at Marcella. "Or should I say yes? They hired me to work for my very own general: you." For a blank moment Marcella didn't seem to understand her.

"What?"

"You heard me. I will be working for you. Starting on Monday. Or before, if you'd like."

"Here?" Marcella looked stunned. "In the palazzo?"

"That's right."

"No!" Marcella turned on her instantly, outraged. "You tricked me! I gave you that address so that you could get a good job! Not a job like this!"

"This is a good job." And then gently, "It's good enough for you, Cella. And I want to be here with you. I don't want to work in an office. I just want to be here. In the house."

"But not like that. Santa Maria . . . what an insanity. But you're crazy. You can't do that!"

"Why not?"

And then it began. "Because," Marcella railed at her, "you are forgetting who you are again, Principessa."

Serena's eyes began to flash green fire as she looked down at the little woman who had worked for her family for forty-seven years. "And you'd better forget it too, Marcella. Those days are over. And whatever my title, I don't have a dime to my name. Nothing. If it weren't for you taking me in, I'd be sleeping in some fleabag, and if it weren't for their giving me work scrubbing floors, I would starve to death damn soon. I'm no different than you are now, Marcella. That's all. It's that simple. And if I am satisfied with that, then you'd damn well better be too."

The older woman was silenced by Serena's speech, at least temporarily. And late that night, on tiptoe, Serena ventured upstairs at last. The visit was less painful than she had feared it would be. Almost all the furniture she had loved was gone now. All that remained were a few couches, an enormous grand piano, and in her mother's room the extraordinary canopied antique bed. It had been left here because it would fit nowhere else. It was only that that distressed Serena. That bed in which she could still see her mother, radiant and lovely in the morning when Serena had come in to see her for a few moments before school. Only in that room did she truly suffer. In the others she stood for a quiet moment, seeing things that were no more, remembering evenings and after-noons and dinners, Christmas parties with all of her parents' friends, and tea parties when her grandmother visited from Venice . . . visits with Sergio . . . and others. It was a quiet pilgrimage from room to room, and when she came back downstairs to Marcella, she looked strangely peaceful, as though she had laid the ghosts to rest at last. There was nothing left that she was afraid of. It was only a house now, and she would be able to work in it for the Americans, doing whatever she had to, to go on living there, in the palazzo, and to stay in Rome.

CHAPTER FIVE

Serena was up at the crack of dawn the next morning. She washed and pulled her golden hair into a knot at the nape of her neck, and then concealed it beneath another dark cotton scarf. She wound the piece of navy blue cloth around her head, bandanna fashion, and then slipped into an old blue cotton dress, which she had worn at the convent in Upstate New York to go berry picking with the younger girls. It had already been patched in a number of places, and it was faded to a color that suggested long years of use. Beneath the dress Serena put on thick, dark stockings, sturdy shoes, and over the front of the blue dress she tied a clean white apron, and then looked into the mirror with a serious face. It was certainly not an outfit for a principessa. But even with the dark blue bandanna there was no concealing the beautiful face. If anything, it seemed to provide a contrast for the pale peach hue of her cheeks and the brilliant green of her eyes.

"You look ridiculous in that outfit." Marcella looked at her with instant disapproval as she poured their coffee and the first hint of daylight crept over the hills. "Why don't you wear something decent, for God's sake?" But Serena said nothing to the old woman. She only smiled as she sipped the hot coffee and closed her eyes in the hot steam as she held the cup in her hands. "What do you think the Americans will think of you wearing that old dress, Serena?"

"They will think that I'm a hard worker, Marcella." The green eyes met hers quietly over the cup of coffee, and she looked older and wiser than her years.

"Ah . . . nonsense!" She looked more annoyed than she had the night before. She thought the whole thing was ridiculous. Worse than that, she felt guilty for suggesting to Serena that she get a job at all. She was still hoping that Serena would forget herself and speak to her new employers in good English and that by the next morning she would be working for the commanding officer as his secretary, in one of the large handsome rooms upstairs.

But half an hour later even Marcella had forgotten those hopes. They were both busy running up and down stairs, helping the orderlies to carry boxes, and figuring out what to put in what rooms. It was mostly Serena who helped them. Marcella was too old to run up and down the stairs. But Serena ran rapidly alongside them and seemed to be in a thousand places, saying little, overseeing everything, and seeming to assist with a dozen pairs of hands.

"Thank you." The head orderly smiled at her at the end of the afternoon as she brought him and his men six cups of steaming coffee. "We couldn't have managed without you." He wasn't sure if she understood him, but he knew that she spoke a little English and she would easily understand the tone of his voice and his broad smile. He was a heavyset man in his late forties, he had a broad chest, a bald

head, and warm brown eyes. "What's your name, miss?"
Serena hesitated for only a moment, and then knowing that
it would have to come sooner or later, she spoke softly.

"Serena."

"Sereena." He repeated immediately with the American
pronunciation, but she didn't mind it. And after a day of
watching him work as hard as his men, she didn't mind him.
He was a good man and a hard worker, and he had helped
her often, taking heavy boxes from her, in spite of her
protests. But he simply took them in his huge hands and
continued up the stairs.

He was the first man in the uniform of any country who
had actually won one of her rare smiles. "My name is
Charlie, Serena. Charlie Crockman." He put out one of
his thick hands and she extended hers. Their eyes met for
a moment and he smiled again. "You worked very hard
today."

"And you too." She smiled shyly, not looking at the
other men.

But Charlie laughed. "Not nearly as hard as we're going
to work tomorrow."

"More?" Serena looked shocked. They had already filled
every room with boxes and files and cabinets and luggage,
desks and lamps and chairs and a hundred other things.
Where on earth would they put anything more? she wondered, but Charlie Crockman shook his head.

"No, nothing like that. Tomorrow we get down to the
real work here. The major will be here tomorrow morning."
He rolled his eyes with another grin. "And we'd damn well
better have everything unpacked and moving by noon."
The men groaned and broke into conversation.

"I thought he went to Spoleto for the weekend?", one of
the men complained loudly, but Charlie Crockman shook
his head again.

"Not him. If I know the major, he'll be here tonight until
midnight, setting up his files and his desk." Now that he and
his men had moved in, the army had also assigned the major
a fresh load of tasks. B. J. Fullerton had been something of a
hero during the war, and now he was getting his first shot at
something important behind a desk. Hence the palazzo.

56

"Shit." Serena heard one of the men say it and appeared not to hear them, and a few minutes later as they continued the conversation she slipped away. In the cozy kitchen she found Marcella, soaking her feet and sitting back in a chair with her eyes closed. Serena slipped her hands onto the old woman's shoulders and began to massage gently, as Marcella smiled.

"*Sei tu?*"

"Who do you think it is?"

"My little angel." They both smiled. It had been a long day.

"Why don't you let me cook dinner tonight, Cella?" But the old woman wouldn't hear of it. She already had a tiny chicken in the oven, and there was pasta bubbling softly on the stove. There would be fresh lettuce from the garden, and some carrots and some basil, and the little tomatoes Marcella had just started to grow. It was a delicious meal when it was all over, and Serena could hardly keep her eyes open as she helped clear the table and urged Marcella to go to bed. She was too old to work as hard as she had. "And tonight I'm making you hot milk and sugar. And that's an order!" She smiled at the woman who had taken her in only days before, and the old woman inclined her head.

"Ah, Principessa . . . you are too good. . . ."

But Serena was quick to bridle. Her eyes flashed as she took a step back and straightened her head. "Stop that, Marcella."

"I'm sorry." Tonight the old woman didn't argue. She was too tired, and she ached all over. It had been years since she worked so hard. Even if Serena had done most of it with the Americans, just being there trying to help had exhausted Marcella. She felt guilty for having let Serena do so much. She had tried in the beginning to keep her from it with whispers of "Principessa!" But Serena had silenced her rapidly with a ferocious scowl, and gone on with her own work.

"Go on, go to bed, Cella. I'll bring you the milk in a minute." With a sleepy yawn the old woman complied and shuffled off, and then with a glance over her shoulder, she remembered something and paused in the doorway with a frown.

57

"I have to go back upstairs."

"Why?"

"To lock up. I don't know if they know how to do it. I want to check the front door before I go to bed. I told them I would. And they told me to make sure that all of the indoor lights are out."

"I'll do it for you."

She hesitated for a moment and then nodded. She was too tired to argue, and Serena could do that. "All right. But just for tonight."

"Yes, ma'am." Serena smiled to herself as she poured the milk into a cup and went to get the sugar. A few minutes later she stood in the doorway to Marcella's tiny bedroom, but the gentle snores from the bed told her that it was already too late. She smiled and then took a sip of the warm liquid, and then slowly she walked to the kitchen, sat down, and drank the milk herself. When she finished, she washed the cup and saucer, dried them, and put away the last of the dishes, and then with a sigh, she opened the door to their basement quarters and walked slowly up the back stairs.

She found everything in order in the main hallway. The grand piano still stood there as it had for decades, and the chandelier in the entry burned as brightly as it had when her parents were there. Without thinking, she turned her face up toward it, smiling to herself as she remembered how much it had enchanted her when she was a child. It had been the best part of her parents' parties, standing on the circular marble staircase, watching men in dinner jackets or tails and women in brilliantly colored evening clothes drift beneath the many faceted crystal chandelier as they wandered through the hall and out into the garden, to stand near the fountain and drink champagne. She used to listen to them laughing, trying to hear what they were saying. She used to sit there in her night-gown, just around the bend, peeking at them, and now as she thought of it again she laughed to herself as she walked up the same stairs. It gave her an odd feeling now to be here in the dark of night, with all of the others gone. The memories at the same time delighted and chilled her. They filled her with longing and regret all at the same time, and as she began to walk down the second-floor landing, she suddenly felt a wave of homesickness overtake her, the likes of which she hadn't felt in years. Suddenly she wanted to be in her old room, to sit on her bed, to look out the window at the garden, just to see it, to sense it, to become part of it again. Without thinking, she put a hand up to the now dusty navy blue bandanna and pulled it slowly off her head and released the long shining blond hair. It was not unlike the gesture she used to make when she took off the hat to her school uniform as she came home every day and ran up the stairs to her room. Only now she checked in the doorway, and the room was almost empty. There was a desk there, a book shelf, several file cabinets, some chairs . . . none of the familiar furniture, none of the things that had been hers. It was all long gone.

With a determined step she walked to the window, and there she saw it . . . the fountain . . . the garden . . . the enormous willow tree. It was all exactly as she had left it, and she could remember standing at precisely the same spot in the same window, gently frosting the glass with her breath in winter as she looked out there, wishing that she didn't have to do her homework and that she could go outside to play. And if she closed her eyes very tightly, she would hear them, her mother and her friends, laughing outside, talking, wandering along, playing croquet in the springtime, or gossiping about their friends in Rome. . . . She would see her there in a blue linen suit . . . or a silk dress . . . or a big picture hat . . . perhaps holding some freshly cut roses, looking up to Serena's windows and waving and—

"Who are you?" The voice she heard behind her sounded ominous, and with a small scream Serena flung out her arms and jumped in terror, wheeling around quickly and clutching the wall behind her with both hands. All she could see was the frame of a man silhouetted in the darkness. The room was still dark, and the light in the hallway was too dim and distant to be of much assistance. She didn't know who he was or what he was doing there, or if he would hurt her, and then as he took a step toward her she saw the shine of the insignia on his lapels. He was in uniform and suddenly she remembered what the head orderly had said earlier that evening, about the major being there until midnight, setting up his desk.

"Are you"—it was barely a croak as her entire body trembled—"the major?"

"The question I asked was who are you?" His voice sounded terrifyingly firm, but neither of them moved and he did not turn on the light behind him. He just stood there, looking down at her, wondering why she seemed so familiar. He sensed something about her, even in the moonlight filtering in from the garden. He had the impression that he had seen her somewhere before. He had been watching her since she had entered the room that was to be his office. He had just turned off the light when he heard her footsteps on the stairs. At first his hand went automatically to the pistol lying on his desk, but he had decided quickly that he didn't need it, and now he only wondered who she was and where she had come from, and why she was here, at the Palazzo Tibaldo, in his office at ten o'clock at night.

"I—I'm sorry. . . . I came upstairs to turn off the lights." For an instant she had almost wanted to say "Sir," and then she was annoyed at her own reactions. It was something about the uniform that she could see more clearly now, the clustered insignia on his lapel, and the imperious tilt of his head. "I'm sorry."

"Are you? That still doesn't answer my question." His voice was cold and even. "I asked you who you were."

"Serena. I work here." Her English was better than she wanted it to be, but under the circumstances she decided not to play any games with him. It was better that he understood her, otherwise, God forbid, he could have had her arrested, or fired, and she didn't want that. "I am a maid here."

"What were you doing upstairs here, Serena?" His voice was gentler than it had been at first.

"I thought I heard sounds . . . noises. . . ." Her eyes darted from his in the darkness. Perhaps she would have to play games with him after all. "I came to see what was wrong."

"I see." He looked at her more closely and knew that she was lying. He had made no sound at all for several hours, not even when he turned off the light. "You're very

60

courageous, Serena." His eyes mocked her and she knew it. "And what would you have done if I had been an intruder?" He looked down at the slim shoulders, the long graceful arms, the delicate hands, and she understood the look he gave her.

"I don't know. I would have called for . . . someone . . . to help me . . . I suppose."

He continued to watch her and slowly walked toward the light he had turned off only moments before. Now he switched it on again and turned to look at her more closely. She was a strikingly beautiful girl, tall and graceful and lovely, with eyes of green fire and hair like Bernini's gold. "I suppose you know that no one would have come to help you. There is no one here."

But this time it was Serena who bridled as she watched him. Was that a threat he had just made her? Would he dare to assault her in this room? Did he think that they were alone? She looked at the tall, lean, young American, and she could sense that, even in the uniform, he was something more. This was not just another American major, this was a man who was accustomed to command, and to having his wishes granted, and if what he wanted now was her, she knew that he would see to it that that was what he got. "You are mistaken." This time she felt no urge to add "Sir." "We are not alone here." She spoke with precision and certainty and a look of fury building in the green eyes.

"Aren't we?" He seemed surprised. Had she brought someone with her? She was a cheeky little thing if she had, but nothing would surprise him, perhaps she and her boyfriend had come to the lovely palazzo to make love. He raised an eyebrow and Serena took a step back.

"No, we are not alone."

"You brought a friend?"

"I live here with my . . . *zia* . . . my aunt." She faltered again on purpose.

"Here? In the palazzo?"

"She is waiting for me at the foot of the stairs." It was a brazen lie, but he believed her.

"Does she work here too?"

"Yes. Her name is Marcella Fabiani." She just hoped

that the major had never met her. She had hoped to conjure an image of a dragon who would not allow him to hurt her. But a mental image of the ancient, heavyset, soundly snoring Marcella crossed her mind and she almost groaned aloud. If truly this man meant to hurt, or rape, her there would indeed be no one at hand to help her escape.

"And you are Serena Fabiani, then, I imagine?" He looked her over carefully once again and Serena paused for only a moment before nodding.

"Yes, I am."

"I'm Major Fullerton, as I imagine you've gathered. Not an intruder. This is my office. And I do not want to see you here again. Not unless it's during daytime hours and you're working or if I ask you to come up here. Is that clear?" She nodded, but despite the stern words she had the feeling that he was laughing at her. There were little lines beside the gray eyes that made one suspect that he wasn't nearly as serious as he seemed. "Is there a door between your quarters and the palazzo?" He gazed at her with interest, but this time she was looking him over too. He had a thick handsome mane of blond hair given to curls, broad shoulders, and what appeared to be powerful arms. He had well-formed hands and long graceful fingers . . . long legs . . . in fact he was very attractive, but also terribly cocky. She found herself wondering what kind of family he came from. He reminded her all of a sudden of some of the old playboys of Rome. And perhaps that was why he was asking her if there was a door between her quarters and the palazzo, and suddenly she stood a little taller and made no attempt to hide the fire in her green eyes.

"Yes, Major, there is. It goes directly into my aunt's bedroom."

Understanding what had happened, B. J. Fullerton had to fight not to burst into laughter. She was really an outrageous young girl and in a way she amused him, but he had no intentions of letting on. Here she was in the middle of the night, in his office, and she was staring him down and implying that *he* might try to intrude on *her*. "I see. Then we'll attempt not to disturb your aunt in the future. I was going to suggest that we have the door between your quarters and the rest of the palazzo permanently closed, so that . . . er . . . you are not tempted to go wandering. And of course, once I move in here tomorrow, there will be a sentry posted outside the palazzo, so that if you hear anything at night''—he looked at her pointedly but her eyes didn't waver and she didn't flinch—''you won't need to come to my rescue.''

''I did not come to your rescue, Major. I came to see if there was a robber. It is my responsibility''—this time she struggled with the word for real and once again he had to fight not to smile—''to protect the house.''

''I'm sure I'm deeply grateful for your efforts, Serena. But in future that won't be a necessary part of your job.''

''*Bene. Capisco.*''

''Very well then.'' He hesitated for only a moment. ''Good night.''

She made no move to leave him. ''And the door?''

''The door?'' He looked blank for a moment.

''The door to our quarters. You will have it closed tomorrow?'' It would mean that they would have to go outside and up the front steps each time someone rang for them or they had an errand to do in the main body of the palazzo. For Marcella it would be a real hardship, and a nuisance for Serena as well. But now the major began to smile slowly. He couldn't resist any longer. She was really very funny, and so stubborn and so brave and so determined, he wondered what her story was, and where she had learned to speak English. In her nervousness at being discovered in his office, she had allowed him to see that she spoke his language very well.

''I think we can let the door go for the moment. As long as you can resist the urge to wander up here at night. After all,'' he said, looking at her mischievously for an instant, ''you might accidentally wind up in my bedroom, and that would be awkward, wouldn't it? I don't recall your knocking tonight before you came in here.'' This time he saw her blush almost purple, and for the first time since he had spoken to her in the darkness, she lowered her eyes from his. He was almost sorry that he had just teased her. He suddenly realized that she was probably even younger than she looked. For all he knew she was a tall girl of fourteen and just looked a few years older. But you never knew with Italian women. He realized now that he was being unfair to Serena. She was still looking in the direction of her sturdy convent shoes and dark stockings and he cleared his throat and walked to the door, held it open, and this time said firmly, "Good night."

She walked out without looking at him again and with her head held high she answered, "*Buona notte.*" He heard her clatter down the stairs a few seconds later, and then walk across the endless marble hall. He saw all of the lights go out beneath him, and then as he listened he heard a door close gently in the distance. The door to her aunt's bedroom? He grinned to himself, remembering the outrageous story.

She was a strange girl—also quite a beauty. But she was also a headache he didn't need. He had Pattie Atherton waiting for him in New York and just thinking about her brought forth a vision of her in a white organdy evening dress with a blue velvet sash, over it she had worn a blue velvet cape trimmed with white ermine, in sharp contrast to the shiny black hair, creamy skin, and big baby-doll blue eyes. He smiled to himself as he walked toward the window and stared out into the garden, but it wasn't Pattie he thought of as he looked out there. It was Serena who wandered back into his head, with her huge, determined green eyes. What had she been thinking as she stood there, staring out at the garden? What had she been looking for? Or who? Not that it really mattered. She was just one of the maids assigned to cleaning the palazzo, even if she was very pretty and very young.

But still the thought of her gnawed at him as he looked around his office for a last time before going to his room.

CHAPTER SIX

"Serena! Stop that!" It was Marcella whispering fiercely over her shoulder as Serena stooped to scrub the bathroom floor in the room occupied by Charlie Crockman, and seeing her that way was something Marcella could still not bear.

"Marcella, *va bene*. . . ." She waved the old woman away like a big friendly dog, but the woman stooped down again and attempted to take the cloths from Serena's hand. "Will you stop that?"

"No, I won't." And this time Marcella's eyes filled with mischief as she sat down on the rim of the tub and whispered to Serena. "And if you don't listen to me, Serena, I'll tell them."

"Tell them what?" Serena brushed a long strand of blond hair from her eyes with a grin. "That I don't know what I'm doing? They probably already know that themselves." She sat back on her heels with a smile of her own. She had been working for the Americans for almost a month now and it suited her perfectly. She had food in her belly, a bed to sleep in at night, she was living with Marcella, who was the only family she had left, and she was living in what had once been her home. What more could she want? she asked herself daily. A great deal, she answered now and then, but that was neither here nor there. This was what she had. She had written to Mother Constance that everything had worked out well. She had told her of her grandmother's death. She went on to report that she was living once again in her parents' home in Rome, though she did not explain under what circumstances.

"Well, Serena?"

"What are you threatening me with now, you old witch?" The two were bantering in whispered Italian. But it was a pleasant break. Serena had been working ceaselessly since six o'clock that morning and it was almost noon.

"If you don't behave yourself, Serena, I'll expose you!"

Serena looked at her, amused. "You'll steal all my clothes!"

"Shame on you! No, I'll tell the major who you are!"

"Oh, that again. Marcella, my love, to tell you the truth, I don't even think he'd care. The bathrooms have to be scrubbed, by a principessa or whoever else is around, and as hard as he works at his desk every night, I don't even think he'd be shocked."

"That's what you think!" Marcella looked at her meaningfully and Serena tilted her head to one side.

"What does that mean?" The major had developed a fondness for Marcella since he had moved into the palazzo, and Serena saw them chatting often. A few nights before, she had even seen Marcella darning his socks. But she herself had steered clear of him since their first meeting. She had never quite been sure of his intentions, and he seemed a little too quick and too perceptive for Serena to want to hang around him very much. He had been curious about Serena during his first week in the palazzo—she had seen him watching her on several occasions, with too many questions in his eyes. Thank God her papers were in order, in case he checked. "Have you been hanging around with the major again?"

"He's a very nice man." Marcella said it with a reproachful glance at the young principessa still on her knees on Charlie Crockman's bathroom floor.

"So what? He's not our friend, Marcella. He's a soldier. He works here just like we do. And it's none of his damn business who I used to be."

"He thinks you speak very good English." Marcella said it with defiance.

"So what?"

"So maybe he could get you a better job."

"I don't want a better job. I like this one."

"Ah . . . *davvero*?" The old eyes glittered. "Really? I thought I remembered you crying last week over the cracks in your hands. And wasn't that you who couldn't sleep because your back hurt so much? And how are your knees from scrubbing the floors, and your feet and your—"

"All right . . . all right! Enough!" Serena sighed and

tossed the brush back into the bucket of soapy water. "But I'm used to it now, and I want to be here." She lowered her voice and her eyes pleaded. "Don't you understand that, Cella? This is my home . . . our home." She corrected quickly and the old woman's eyes filled with tears as she patted Serena's cheek.

"You deserve more than this, child." It broke her heart that life had been so unfair to the girl. But as she brushed the tears away with the back of one hand, Charlie Crockman found them that way and stared down at them in sudden embarrassment.

"Sorry." He muttered before backing out quickly.

"*Fa niente*," Serena called after him. She liked him, but she seldom spoke to him in English. She had nothing to say. She had nothing to say to any of them. She didn't have to. It didn't matter. Nothing did. Except that she could go on living here. It had become an obsession with her in the past month, being at home again and clinging to the memories. It was all she thought of now as she went from room to room, cleaning, waxing, dusting, and in the morning when she made the major's enormous bed, she pretended to herself that it was still her mother's. The only thing that disturbed the dream was that the room smelled of lime and tobacco and spice, like the major, not of roses and lily of the valley as it had almost ten years before.

When she had finished scrubbing Charlie Crockman's bathroom that morning, Serena took a hunk of bread and a piece of cheese and an orange and a knife and wandered slowly into the garden, where she sat down, looking at the hills beyond with her back against her favorite tree.

It was here that the major found her half an hour later, and he stood there for a long moment, watching her as she peeled the orange carefully and then lay in the grass and looked up at the tree. He wasn't sure whether or not to approach her, but there was still something about her that intrigued him. There was a special aura of mystery that surrounded Marcella's hardworking young niece. He still seriously doubted the story that they were related, but her papers were in order, and whoever she was, she worked damn hard for them. What difference did it make who she was? But the strange thing was that it seemed to make a difference to him. He thought of her often as he had seen her on that first evening, standing in his office in the dark, leaning against the window, looking out at that willow tree.

He wandered slowly closer to where she lay and then sat down quietly beside her, looking down into her face as she looked up at the tree and the sky and then him. She gave a little start as she saw him and then she sat up quickly, smoothing her apron over her skirt and covering her thickly stockinged legs, before she allowed her eyes to meet his.

"You always seem to surprise me, Major."

Again he noticed that her English was better than she usually let on and he suddenly found himself wanting to tell her that she always surprised him. But instead he only smiled, the thick blond hair brushed softly by the September breeze. "You're drawn to this tree, aren't you, Serena?"

She nodded with a childlike smile and offered him part of her orange. For her, it was an enormous step. After all, he was a soldier. And she had hated all soldiers for so long. But there was something about him that made her want to trust him. Maybe because he was Marcella's friend. His eyes were kind as he accepted half of the orange and began to peel off sections as he sat beside her. For a moment she looked very far away. "When I was a little girl, I lived in a house . . . where I could see a tree . . . just like this one . . . from my window. Sometimes I used to talk to it at night." She blushed then, and felt silly, but he only looked amused, as his eyes took in the smoothness of her skin and the long lines of her legs spread out ahead of her on the grass.

"Do you talk to this one?"

"Sometimes," she confessed.

"Is that what you were going to do in my office that night, when I surprised you?"

She shook her head slowly, looking suddenly sad. "No, I just wanted to see it. My window—" She seemed to pull herself back. "The window of my room looked out just as this one does."

"And that room?" He looked at her gently. "Where is it?"

"Here in Rome."

"Do you still visit it?" He didn't know why, but he wanted to know more about her.

She shrugged in answer. "Other people live in the house now."

"And your parents, Serena? Where are they?" It was a dangerous question to ask people after a war and he knew it. She turned slowly with a strange look in her eyes.

"My family are dead, Major. All of them." And then she remembered. "Except Marcella."

"I'm sorry." He hung his head and riffled the grass with his hand. He had lost no one in this war. And he knew that his family was grateful that they had not lost him. Friends of his had died, but no cousins, no brothers, no uncles, no distant relations. It was a war that had barely touched the world he had lived in. And one of these days he knew that he would be going home too. Not yet though. He was still enjoying his work in Rome.

An orderly had come then and interrupted them. There was a phone call from General Farnham and he had to come at once. He looked at Serena regretfully over his shoulder for a moment and then he hurried inside and she didn't see him again.

When she climbed between the cool sheets that night after bidding good night to Marcella, she found herself thinking of the interlude that afternoon in the garden, of the long slender hands playing with the grass, the broad shoulders, the grey eyes. There was something so startlingly handsome about him, as though one expected to see him in evening clothes or playing football. He looked like other Americans Serena had seen in her four and a half years on the Hudson, but he was far more beautiful than any she had seen.

Oddly her thoughts were not unlike what Bradford Fullerton was thinking at that precise moment about her. He was standing alone in his office with the lights off, his jacket cast over a chair and his tie on the desk, looking out at the willow tree. He could still see the sun reflected in her eyes as she handed him half of the orange, and suddenly for the first time in a long time he felt a physical yearning, an overwhelming hunger, his body craving hers, as it had craved no one else's for a long time. He had been home on

69

leave once for a week at the end of the war, and he had made passionate love to Pattie, but he had been faithful to her since coming back, and he really had no desire to stray. Until now. All he could think of as he stood there was Serena, the shape of her neck, the grace of her arms, the way her waist narrowed to almost nothing beneath the starched white apron strings. It was insane. Here he was, engaged to the most beautiful woman in New York, and he suddenly had the hots for an Italian maid. But did that matter? He knew that it didn't, that he wanted her, and he didn't just want her physically—he wanted something more from Serena. He wanted her secrets. He wanted to know what lay in the deep mysterious shadows of those huge green eyes.

He stood there for what seemed like hours, staring out the window, his eyes glued to the tree, and then suddenly he saw her, like a vision, a magnificent ghost darting past the tree and then sitting quietly in the darkness, the long hair flowing in the breeze behind her, almost silver in the moonlight, the delicate profile turned up as though to sniff the night air, her eyes closed, and her body shrouded in what looked like a blanket as she stretched out her legs on the grass. He could see that her legs and feet were bare, and as he watched her he suddenly felt his whole body grow tense, as everything within him surged toward the mysterious girl. Almost as though he had no control over his actions, he turned and left the room, closing the door softly behind him, and hastily he ran down the long flight of marble stairs. He walked down the long stately hallway to a side door that he knew led into the garden, and before he could stop himself, he had walked softly across the grass until suddenly he stood there behind her, shivering in the breeze, trembling with desire and not sure of why he had come. As though she sensed him standing there, she turned and looked up at him with wide startled eyes, but she said nothing, and for a long moment he stood there and their eyes met and she waited, and silently he sat down beside her on the grass.

"Were you talking to your tree?" His voice was gentle, as he felt the warmth of her body beside his. He wasn't sure what to say to her, and it seemed foolish, but as he looked down into her face he saw now that it was shimmering with tears. "Serena? What's wrong?" For a long time she didn't answer, and then she shrugged with a little palms-up gesture and a lopsided smile. It made him want to take her in his arms, but he still didn't dare to. He wasn't sure what she would think. And he still wasn't sure what he thought himself. "What's the matter?"

She sighed then, and almost without thinking, she rested her head on his shoulder and closed her eyes. "Sometimes . . ." She spoke softly in the cool darkness. "Sometimes it is very lonely . . . after a war." Her eyes burned into his then. "There is no one. Not anymore."

He nodded slowly, trying to understand her pain. "It must be very hard." And then, unable to resist the questions that always plagued his mind, "How old are you, Serena?"

"Nineteen." Her voice was like velvet in the darkness. And then, with a small smile, "And you?"

He smiled too. "Thirty-four." He wasn't sure why, but he suddenly felt that she accepted him as a friend now. It was as though something different had begun to happen between them that afternoon. She shook her head from his shoulder, and he found that he missed the gentle pressure, and more than ever he found himself desperately hungry for her, as his eyes lingered over her lips and her eyes and her face. "Serena . . ." He wasn't sure of how to say it, or of what he wanted to tell her, but he knew that he had to say something about what he felt.

"Yes, Major?"

He laughed then. "For God's sake, don't call me that." It reminded her of when she scolded Marcella for calling her Principessa and she laughed too.

"All right, then what do I call you? Sir?" She was teasing now, and suddenly more woman than girl.

He looked down at her for a long moment, his smile gentle, his eyes a deep sea-gray, and then he whispered, "Yeah . . . maybe you do call me Sir." But before she could answer, he had taken her in his arms and kissed her, with a longing and a hunger and a passion that he didn't know he had. He felt his whole body press toward her, his arms held her close, and he never wanted to take his mouth from hers, as her lips gave in to his and their tongues probed and

71

danced between his mouth and her own. He was almost breathless with desire when finally he peeled himself away slowly and she seemed to melt into his arms with a gentle sigh. "Oh, Serena . . ." Without saying more, he kissed her again, and this time it was Serena who came up for air. She shook her head slowly, as though to clear her head, and looked at him sadly in the moonlight, with fresh tears in her eyes.

"We shouldn't do this, Major . . . we can't."

"Why can't we?" He wasn't sure she was wrong, but he knew that he didn't want to stop. "Serena . . ." He wanted to tell her that he loved her, but that was crazy. How could he love her? He barely knew her. And yet he knew that there was some extraordinary bond between him and this girl.

"Don't." She put up a hand and he kissed the delicate fingers. "It's not right. You have your own life. This is only Rome," she said, smiling sadly, "working its magic." She had seen the photographs of Pattie Atherton in his bedroom and on his desk.

But the major was thinking only of Serena as he stared at the exquisite face in the moonlight and kissed her gently on the lips before pulling away to look at her again. She wasn't sure why she let him do it, but it was as though she had to, as though she had sensed from the first where it would end. But it was crazy . . . an American . . . a soldier? What would it lead to? She cringed at the thought.

"Why were you crying tonight, Serena?"

"I told you. I was lonely. I was sad." And then, "I had been thinking about—" She didn't know how to say it. Her world was no more. "About things that are gone."

"Like what? Tell me." He wanted to know everything about her. Why she laughed, why she cried, whom she loved, whom she hated, and why.

"Ah . . . " She sighed for a moment. "How can I tell you what it was like? A lost world . . . another time, filled with beautiful ladies and handsome men. . . ." She thought suddenly of her parents and their friends, so many of them dead now, or having fled. She stopped talking for a moment as she thought of the faces that haunted her lately more and more, and the major watched her and saw her eyes grow bright with tears.

"Don't, Serena." He pulled her into his arms and held her there as the tears rolled slowly down her face.

"I'm sorry."

"So am I. I'm sorry that it happened to you." And then he smiled to himself, remembering the story that she was Marcella's niece. That hardly matched up with her "lost world filled with beautiful ladies and handsome men." He looked at the delicately carved face for a long time then, wondering who she really was and knowing that, to him, it didn't matter, and perhaps never would. She was special and lovely and he desired her more than he had ever desired anyone, even the woman to whom he was engaged. He didn't understand why that was true, but it was, and a part of him wanted to tell her that he loved her, but he knew that that was mad too. How could he love a girl he barely knew? And yet, he knew, as they sat huddled in the moonlight, that he did, and as she felt his arms around her Serena knew it too. He kissed her again then, long and hard and with passion and hunger. And without saying anything further, he stood up and pulled her up beside him, kissed her again, and then walked her slowly to her back door. He left her there, with a last kiss, and he said nothing further. There was nothing that he dared to say. And Serena stood there watching him for a long moment before she disappeared into the servants' quarters that she shared with Marcella and softly closed the door.

CHAPTER SEVEN

For the next few days Major B. J. Fullerton was as a man tormented, as he drifted through his duties without thinking or seeing, and Serena moved as though in a dream. She did not understand what had happened between her and the major, and she was not at all sure that she wanted it to happen again. For years now she hated wars, soldiers, uniforms, any army, and yet suddenly there she had been in the arms of the major, wanting no one else but him. And what did he want with her? She knew the answer to that question, or she thought so, and it made her bristle with anger each time she remembered the photograph by his bed of the New York debutante. He wanted to sleep with his Italian maid was what he wanted, a casual wartime story, and yet even as she bridled she remembered his touch and kisses beneath the willow tree and knew that she wanted more of him. It would have been difficult to say which of them looked the most unhappy as each struggled through their duties, observed by all, yet understood by only two. The major's orderly, Charlie Crockman, had exchanged a speaking glance with Marcella two days later, and yet the two had said nothing. The major barked at everyone, accomplished nothing, lost two folders filled with moderately important orders, and then found them again as he fumed. Serena waxed the same patch of floor for almost four hours and then walked off leaving all her cloths and brushes abandoned in a central doorway, she stared right through Marcella, and went to bed without eating dinner.

They had not spoken to each other once since the night beneath the willow tree. By the next morning Serena had known that it was hopeless, and the major had been consumed with both guilt and fear. He was certain that Serena was innocent in every way, and surely a virgin, and the girl had suffered enough without adding a wartime affair with a soldier to her pains. In addition he had his fiancée to think of. But the problem was that it wasn't with Pattie that his thoughts were filled each morning and each evening and for a dozen hours in between. Every moment seemed to be filled with visions of Serena, and it wasn't until Sunday morning, as he looked down at her working in Marcella's vegetable patch in the garden that he decided he couldn't bear it any longer and he had to speak to her, at least to try to explain things before he went totally insane.

He hurried downstairs in khaki slacks and a light blue sweater, his hands in his pockets, and she stood up, surprised to see him, and pushed the hair out of her eyes.

"Yes, Major?" For an instant he thought there was accusation in her tone, but a moment later she was smiling, and he was beaming, and he knew that he was so damn glad to see her that he didn't care if she threw all her gardening tools at him. He had to talk to her. It had been agony, attempting to avoid her for the past four days.

"I wanted to talk to you, Serena." And then, almost shyly, "Are you busy?"

"A little." She looked very grown-up suddenly as she put the tools aside and stood up, her green eyes meeting his gray. "But not very. Do you want to sit down over there?" She pointed to a small wrought-iron bench, chipping but still pretty, left over from better days. She was relieved to speak to him now, and there was almost no one around to observe them. All of the orderlies were off on Sunday, Marcella had gone to church and to visit a friend. Only Serena had stayed home to tend the garden, she had gone to church early that morning, and Marcella didn't even try to drag her to visit the elderly friend. On the street side of the house were the usual two sentries, but other than that, they were alone.

The major followed her quietly to the little bench, and they sat down together. He lit a cigarette and stared into the distance, at the hills. "I'm sorry. I think I've behaved very badly this week, Serena. I think I've been a little crazy." The gray eyes looked into hers frankly, and she nodded slowly.

"So have I. I didn't understand what happened."

"Were you angry?" He had wondered for four days now.

Or was she frightened? He knew he was, but he was not entirely sure why.

"Sometimes I was angry." She smiled slowly and then sighed. "And sometimes I was not. I was frightened . . . and confused . . . and . . ." She looked at him, saying nothing further, and once again he felt an overwhelming desire to hold her and to touch her, and an even greater urge to make her his right there, under the trees in the autumn sunshine, on the grass. He closed his eyes as though in pain, and Serena reached out to touch his hand then. "What is it, Major?"

"Everything." He opened his eyes slowly. "I don't understand what I'm feeling . . . what's happened. . . ." And then suddenly, with his whole mind and soul and being, he knew that he couldn't fight it any longer. "I love you. Oh, God. . . . " He pulled her to him. "I love you." And as his lips found hers she felt desire surge up within her too, but it was more than that. It was a quiet longing to become his forever, to be a part of him, in order to become whole. It was as though here, in her parents' home, in their garden, she had found her future, as though she had belonged to this tall blond American major from the beginning, as though she had been born for him.

"I love you too." It was the merest whisper, but she was smiling as she said it, and at the same time there were tears in her eyes.

"Will you come inside with me?" She knew what he was saying, but he didn't want to take her, to sweep her off her feet and carry her inside. He wanted her to know what she was doing. He wanted her to want it too.

Slowly she nodded and stood up beside him, her face turned up to his, her eyes larger than any he had ever seen, and solemnly he took her hand in his and they walked across the garden together, and Serena felt in an odd way as though they had just been married. . . . Will you take this man . . .? Yes. . . . She felt her own voice ring out deep within her soul, as they mounted the stairs together and he closed the door behind her as they stepped inside. He put an arm around her waist then, and they walked slowly up the main staircase together to the bedroom that had been her mother's, and then as she stood on the threshold she began to tremble, her eyes riveted to the enormous four-poster, her eyes wide with memory and fear.

"I—I . . . can't. . . ." She spoke barely above a whisper, and he nodded. If she couldn't, then he wouldn't force her, but he wanted only to hold her, to caress her, to feel her and touch her and let his lips linger across her exquisite flesh.

"You don't have to, my darling . . . never . . . I won't force you . . . I love you. . . ." The words tumbled amid the extravagant satin of her hair, as his lips moved to her neck and her breasts and he gently pushed open the dark cotton dress with his lips, lusting after every inch of her, tasting her like nectar as his tongue traveled everywhere and she began to moan softly. "I love you, Serena . . . I love you. . . ." It was no lie, he both loved and wanted her as he had loved no woman before, and then, forgetting what she had said in the doorway, he picked her up gently and laid her on his bed, and slowly he peeled away her clothes, but she did not fight him, and her hands gently searched and held and nestled until he felt the powerful thrust of his own desire, and he could barely hold back anymore. "Serena," he whispered her name hoarsely, "I want you, my darling . . . I want you. . . ." But there was a question in his words as well, and he watched her face now as her eyes sought his and she nodded, and then he slipped off the last of her clothing and she lay before him naked. He shed his own, and almost instantly he lay beside her and held her close to him, as his flesh pressed against hers. And then, ever so gently at first, and then with ever greater hunger, he pressed inside her, pushing himself deeper and deeper into her center until she cried out in pain, and he lunged forward, knowing that it must be done at once, and then the pain was over and she clung to him and he began to writhe mysteriously as he carefully taught her love's wonders, and with great tenderness they made love until this time she arched her back suddenly and gave a shout, but not of pain. It was then that he let himself go unbridled until he felt hot gold shoot through him, until he seemed to float upon it in a jewel-filled sky. They clung together like that, drifting for what seemed like a lifetime, until he found her lying beside him, as beautiful as a butterfly having lighted in his arms.

"I love you, Serena." With each passing moment the words had ever deeper meaning, and this time with the smile of a woman she turned toward him, and kissed him, gently fondling him with her hands. It seemed hours before he could bring himself to pull away from her, and he lay in the huge handsome bed, propped up on one elbow and smiling at this incredible golden mixture of woman and child.

"Hello." He said it as though he had just met her, and she looked up at him and laughed. She laughed at his expression, at what he had just said, and at the ghosts they had pushed aside, not roughly, but certainly with determination, as she lay in her mother's bed and looked up at the blue satin panels that reminded her of a summer sky. "It's pretty, isn't it?" He looked up at the cerulean satin and then smiled down at her again, but she was grinning strangely, and her laughter was that of a mischievous child.

"Yes." She kissed the end of his nose. "It always was pretty."

"What?" He looked confused.

"This bed. This room."

He smiled at her gently. "Did you come here often with Marcella?" He asked the question in all innocence, and Serena could not restrain a gurgle of laughter. She had to tell him now. She had to. They had been secretly married in the garden by friendly spirits, and consummated their union in her mother's bed. It was time to tell him the truth.

"I didn't come here with Marcella." She hung her head for a moment, touching his hand and wondering how to say the words. And then she looked into his eyes again. "I used to live here, Major."

"Do you suppose you could call me Brad now? Or is that too much to ask?" He bent to kiss her, and she smiled afterward as she pulled away.

"All right. Brad."

"What do you mean, you used to live here? With Marcella and your folks? Did the whole family work here?"

She shook her head solemnly, with a serious expression in her eyes. She sat up in bed then and pulled the sheets around her, as she held tightly to her lover's hand. "This was my

78

mother's room, Brad. And your office was my room. That was—" Her voice was so soft he could barely hear her. "That was why I went there that night. The first time I saw you . . . that night in the dark. . . ." Her eyes bore into his then, and he stared at her in astonishment.

"Oh, my God. Then, who are you?" She said nothing for a long moment. "You're not Marcella's niece." He grinned. He had suspected that long before.

"No." There was another pause and then Serena drew a breath and hopped from the bed to drop him a deep and reverent curtsy. "I have the honor to be the Principessa Serena Alessandra Graziella di San Tibaldo, . . ." She rose from the curtsy then and stood before him in all her extraordinary elegance and beauty, naked in her mother's room, as Brad Fullerton stared at her in amazement.

"You're what?" But he had heard it all. As she began to repeat it he put up a hand quickly, and suddenly he began to laugh. So this was the Italian "maid" he had worried about seducing, Marcella's "niece." It was wonderful and perfectly insane and delightfully crazy, and he couldn't stop laughing as he looked at Serena, and she was laughing too, and then at last she lay in his arms in her mother's bed and he grew pensive. "What a strange life for you, my darling, living here, working for the army." He suddenly let his mind run over the work she had had to do in the past month and it no longer seemed so funny. In fact it seemed desperately cruel.

"How in hell did it all happen?" And then she told him, from the beginning, how it had been, from the days of dissent between her father and Sergio, her parents' death, the time in Venice, her flight to the States, and her return. And she told him the truth, that she had nothing, that she was no one now except a maid in the palazzo. She had no money, no belongings, nothing, except her history, her ancestry, and her name. "You have a great deal more than that, my love." He gazed at her gently as they lay on the bed, side by side. "You have a magical gift, a special grace that few people have. Wherever you are, Serena, it will serve you well. You will always stand out. You are special, Marcella is right. You are a principessa . . . a princess. . . .

I understand that now." For him, it explained the magic about her. She was a princess . . . his princess . . . his queen. He looked at her with such tenderness then that it almost brought tears to her eyes.

"Why do you love me, Major?" She looked strangely old and wise and sad as she asked.

"I'm after your money." He grinned at her, looking very handsome and younger than his years.

"I thought so. Do you think I have enough?" She smiled into his eyes.

"How much have you got?"

"About twenty-two dollars after last payday."

"That's perfect. I'll take you. That's what I want." But he was already kissing her, and they both wanted something else first. And after they had made love again, he held her and said nothing, thinking back to what she had gone through, how far she had come, just to come home, to return to the palazzo, where, thank God, he had found her. And now he would never let her go. But just as he thought that about Serena, his eyes drifted across to the photograph of the smiling dark-haired young woman in the silver frame on the marble-topped table beside his bed. It was as though Serena sensed where he was looking and she turned to see the photo of Pattie, smiling down at them both. She said nothing, but her eyes went to the major's and there was a question in them and he sighed softly and shook his head. "I don't know, Serena. I don't have the answer to that yet." She nodded, understanding, but suddenly worried. What if she lost him? And she knew that she had to. The other woman was part of his world in a way that Serena wasn't, and perhaps could never be.

"Do you love her?" Serena's voice was gentle and sad.

"I thought I did. Very much." Serena nodded and said nothing, and he gently took her chin in his hand and made her raise her eyes to his again. "I will always tell you the truth, Serena. I won't hide anything from you. That woman and I are engaged to be married, and I have no idea what in hell I'm going to do. But I love you. I honestly, truly, love you. I knew it the first minute I laid eyes on you, tiptoeing through my office in the dark." They both smiled at the

80

memory. "I have to think this thing out. I don't love her the way I love you. I loved her as part of a familiar, comfortable world."

"But I'm not part of that world, Brad."

"That does not matter to me. You are you."

"And your family? Will they be satisfied with that too?" Her eyes said that she doubted it.

"They're very fond of Pattie. But that doesn't mean a damn thing."

"Doesn't it?" Serena tried to look flip as she slid out of bed, but he pulled her back.

"No. I'm thirty-four years old. I have to lead my life, Serena, not theirs. If I wanted to lead their life, I'd already be out of the army, working for one of my father's friends in New York."

"Doing what?" She suddenly had an insatiable curiosity about him.

"Working in a bank most likely. Or running for office. My family is very involved in politics in the States."

She sighed tiredly and there was a cynical smile in her eyes. "My family was very involved in politics over here." She looked at him with sorrow and wisdom and a hint of laughter, and he was glad to see that she could see the irony in the situation. "It's a little different there."

"I hope so. Is that what you want to do? Go into politics?"

"Maybe. To tell you the truth I'd rather stay in the army. I've been thinking of making that my career."

"How do they feel about that?" It was as though she had instantly sensed how great a power they wielded over him, or attempted to. And there were times when it was a battle royal. "Do they like that idea?"

"No. But that's life. And this is my life. And I love you. So don't you forget that ever. I'll make my own decisions." He glanced at the photograph again. "About that as well. *Capisci?*"

She grinned at his American-accented Italian. "*Capito.*"

"Good." He kissed her then, and a moment later he made delicious love to her again.

CHAPTER EIGHT

"You what?" Marcella looked at her in total amazement. For a moment Serena was afraid that she might faint.

"Relax, for heaven's sake. I told him. That's all."

"You told the major?" Marcella looked as though she were going into shock. "*What* did you tell him?"

"Everything. About my parents. About this house." Serena tried to look nonchalant, but it didn't come off and she burst into a nervous grin.

"What made you do that?" The old woman studied her shrewdly. She had been right, then. Serena had been falling in love with the handsome young American. Now all she had to do was hope that he married her, and her prayers would have been answered for the beloved girl. It was the only hope she could see for Serena, and she could tell from details she was used to observing that he was well brought up, probably from money, and she had long since decided that he was a very nice young man.

"I just did it, that's all. We were talking, and I felt dishonest not telling him the truth." Marcella was too old and too wise to believe a word Serena was saying, but she nodded sagely and pretended to accept the tale.

"What did he say?"

"Nothing." She smiled to herself. . . . That he loves me. . . . "I don't think that he cares about the title. Hell," she said, grinning at Marcella, "I'm still just the upstairs maid to him."

"Are you?" Cella watched her reactions. "Is that all you are to him, Serena?"

"Of course. Oh, well . . . I suppose we're friends now. . . ." Her words drifted off and Marcella considered for a moment, and then decided to push for an answer to the question that was on her mind.

"Do you love him, Serena?"

"Do I . . . why that's . . ." She began to bluster, and then dropping the pretense, she nodded slowly. "Yes. I do." The old woman went to Serena to take her in her arms.

"Does he love you too?"

"I think so. But," she sighed deeply and pulled free of the old woman's arms to wander about the room, "it doesn't mean anything though, Cella. I have to face the truth. He's here, it's the romance of Rome—the war. One day he'll go back—to the world he knows."

"And he'll take you." The old woman said it with pride. This special girl was, after all, like a part of herself.

"I don't think so. And if he did, it would be out of pity. It would be because he would be sorry to leave me here."

"Good. Then go with him." As far as Marcella saw it, everything was set. But Serena saw a great deal more than that.

"It's not that simple."

"It is if you want it to be. Do you? Do you love him enough to go with him?"

"Of course I do. But that isn't the point. He has a life there, Cella. He isn't the kind of man to take a war bride home. . . ."

"War bride!" Marcella jumped to her feet. "War bride? Are you crazy? *Sei pazza?* You're a princess, or don't you remember? Did you remember to tell him that too?" She looked suddenly anxious and Serena laughed.

"Yes, I told him. But that's not everything. I have nothing, Cella. Not now. Nothing at all. No money, nothing. What will his family think if he comes home with me?" She had overnight become wise in the way of things, but Marcella didn't want to hear it.

"They'll think he's very lucky, that's what they'll think."

"Maybe." But Serena didn't believe it. She was remembering the face she had seen so often in the pictures. . . . "My family is very fond of Pattie," she could hear him say. But would they be fond of her? It seemed unlikely. She felt ashamed now. As though she had been disgraced along with her Uncle Sergio and Il Duce, her country had fallen apart around her and her life had too. She wandered out into the garden then and Marcella watched her go.

October was a dream month for Serena. She and Brad had worked out their affair with miraculous precision, and every night after dinner he went to his room, as Serena waited in hers. When Marcella went to bed, the orderlies had usually retired, and she tiptoed softly into the main house and made her way quietly up the marble staircase to his bedroom, where he waited for her with things to tell her, funny stories, sometimes a letter from his younger brother, white wine or champagne, or a plate of cookies, or photographs he had taken of her the previous weekend, which they sifted through. There was always something to share, to chuckle over, to enjoy, to discuss, and then inevitably a little while later there was the miracle of their lovemaking, the endless discoveries and pleasures she found in his arms. Eventually the photographs of Pattie had been relegated to his office, and now she never saw them at all. They spent the nights cozily tucked into his bed, and then they rose together, before the rest of the household, just before six in the morning. They sat for a moment, watching the sun come up, looking down at the familiar garden, and then with a last kiss, a last touch, an embrace, she went back to her quarters, and they each began the day. In a strange way it was like being newly married, because each lived to return to the other at the end of the day.

It was on a day at the very end of October that Serena came to him and found him upset and vague. He seemed jumpy when Serena put her arms around him, and when she said something to him about it, he appeared not to hear.

"What?" He looked up at her from the chair he'd been sitting in as he stared into the fire with a distant expression. "I'm sorry, Serena. What did you say?"

"I said that you looked worried about something, my darling." Her voice was a whisper on his neck, and he sighed deeply and laid his head against hers.

"Not really. Just distracted." As she looked at him closely she thought again what a proud head he had, what fine gray eyes, and now she knew also that he was both intelligent and kind. Sometimes too much so. He was a man whose greatest

84

virtue was compassion, and he always struggled to understand and assist his men. Sometimes it made him not quite firm enough as a leader. He was never heartless. He always cared.

"What are you distracted about, B.J.?" He smiled at the nickname his men used. Serena seldom used it. When she teased him, she called him Major. Otherwise she called him Brad.

He looked at her thoughtfully now, and then decided that he had to tell her. He had wanted to wait until the next morning, but what was the point—there was never going to be a right time. "Serena . . ." Her heart stopped as she heard the way he said it. She knew what was coming. He was leaving Rome. "I had a telegram this morning." She closed her eyes as she listened, fighting back her tears. She knew she had to be brave when she heard it, but her insides had just turned to jelly. Her eyes fluttered open again quickly and she saw the pain in her eyes mirrored in his own. "Now come on, sweetheart, it's not that bad." He took her in his arms and let his lips roam slowly over the soft spun-gold hair.

"You're leaving?" It was a hoarse whisper, and quickly he shook his head.

"Of course not. Is that what you thought?" He pulled away from her gently, his eyes loving yet at the same time sad. "No, darling. I'm not leaving. This is nothing official." And then he decided to plunge ahead and tell her. "It's Pattie. She's coming over. I'm not sure why. She says the trip is an engagement present from her father. Frankly I think that she's worried. I haven't been writing much lately and she called here the other morning, right after . . . I don't know. I couldn't talk to her." He stood up and wandered slowly across the room, his eyes troubled and vague. "I couldn't say the things she wanted." And then he turned to face Serena. "I couldn't play the game with her, Serena. I don't know. I'm not sure what to do. I probably should have written to her weeks ago, to break the engagement, but—" He looked desperately unhappy. "I just wasn't sure."

Serena nodded slowly, the knife of pain slicing swiftly

through to her very core. "You still love her, don't you?" It was more a statement than a question, and B.J. looked at her with fresh anguish in his eyes.

"I'm not sure. I haven't seen her in months now, and that was all so unreal. It was the first time I'd been home in three years. It was all so heady and so romantic, and our families were cheering us on. It was like something in a movie, I'm not sure it's something in real life."

"But you were going to marry her."

He nodded slowly. "It's what everyone wanted." And then he knew he had to be honest. "It was what I wanted too. It seemed so right at the time. But now . . ."

Serena closed her eyes for a moment as she stretched out in front of the fire, trying to bear the pain of what she knew would come. And then she looked at him again, not in anger, but in sorrow. She knew that she couldn't fight the pretty dark-haired woman. She had already won him. And Serena was no one. Just the upstairs maid, as she had said to Marcella. The ugliness of it all was that it was true.

"I know what you're thinking." He said it miserably as he dropped into a chair near the window and ran a hand through his already tousled curly hair. Before she had come to him that evening, he had been sitting there for hours, thinking, weighing, asking himself questions to which he didn't have answers. "Serena, I love you."

"And I love you too. But I understand also that this is very romantic, that it is wonderful, but it is this, Brad, that is not real. That girl, her family, they know you. You know them. That is your life. What can this really be between us? An extraordinary memory? A tender moment?" She shrugged. "This is more like 'something in a movie.' " She was quoting him. "It is nothing in real life. You can't take me home. We can't get married. She's the one you should marry and you know it." Her eyes filled with tears and she turned away as he strode rapidly toward her and pulled her into his arms.

"But what if I don't want to?"

"You have to. You're engaged to be married."

"I could break the engagement." But the bitch of it was that he wasn't sure if that was what he wanted. He loved this girl. But he had loved Pattie too. And he had been so proud, so exhilarated, so excited. Was that what he felt now? Was that what he felt for Serena? No, it wasn't excitement, it was something different, something quiet. He felt protective and tender, and sometimes almost fatherly toward her. He wanted to be there for her. And he knew also that at the end of every day he wanted her to be there for him. He had come to count on her quiet presence, her thoughtful words, her quiet moments in which she weighed all that he said. She often said things that helped him later. As he sat at his desk, tackling a problem, he would hear the soft voice beside him and move steadily ahead. She gave him a force of which Pattie knew nothing. She had survived sorrow and loss and it had made her stronger, and it was that strength that she shared with him. At her side he felt as though he could scale mountains, in her arms he found a passion he had never known before. But would it last for a lifetime? And could he truly take her home with him? These were the things he wasn't sure of. Pattie Atherton was of his world, of his culture, she was part of an already existing tapestry. It was right that they should be together. Or was it? As he stared down into the deep green eyes of Serena, he was no longer sure. What he wanted was what he had as he held her, the passion, the warmth, the longing, the strength that they shared. He couldn't give that up. But maybe he would have to. "Oh, Christ, Serena . . . I'm just not sure." He held her closer and felt her tremble. "I feel like such an ass. I know I should be doing something decisive. And the bitch of it is that you know and Pattie doesn't. I should at least tell her the truth." He felt guilty about everyone, and torn from deep within.

"No, Brad, you shouldn't. She doesn't have to know. If you marry Pattie, she need never know about me." It would be just another wartime affair, a soldier and an Italian. There were certainly enough of them around, Serena thought bitterly for a moment, and then she forced the anger from her mind. She had no right to be angry. She had given her heart to him and her self—done what she had done, knowing that there was another woman, and knowing full well that the affair might come to naught. She had gambled and probably lost. But she didn't regret the game. She loved him, and she knew that, whatever he felt for his fiancée, he also loved her. "When is she coming?" Her eyes burned into his and he took a deep breath.

"Tomorrow."

"Oh, my God." This was to be their last night, then. "Why didn't you tell me?"

"I wasn't sure exactly when she was coming until tonight. I just got another telegram." He pulled her into his arms.

"Do you want me to go now?" It was a small voice of bravado, and Brad was quick to shake his head and pull her closer still.

"No . . . oh, God, don't do that . . . I need you." And then he felt suddenly guilty again as he realized how unfair he was being. He pulled back from her slowly. "Do you want to go?" This time it was Serena who shook her head, her eyes locked into his.

"No."

"Oh, baby . . ." He buried his face in her neck. "I love you . . . I feel like such a weakling."

"You're not. You're only human. These things happen. I suppose," she sighed wisely, "that they happen every day." But nothing like it had ever happened to him before. He had never felt this confused. There were two women he wanted, and he had no idea which one was the right way to turn. "Come." Serena stood up and took his hand then. And when he looked up at her, she seemed more a woman to him than she ever had before. The idea that she was only nineteen was preposterous. She was as old and as wise as time as she stood there, smiling gently, holding out her arms to him, and slowly he stood up. "You look tired, my darling." She was aching inside, but she didn't let him see that. Instead all that she showed him was her love for him, and her quiet strength. It was the same strength that had allowed her to survive the death of her parents, her banishment to the States, and the loss of her grandmother during the war. It was the same strength that had allowed her to return, and live in the palazzo in the servants' quarters, scrubbing bathroom floors and forgetting that she had ever been a principessa. Now it was that strength that she gave to him.

She led him silently into the bedroom, stood beside her mother's bed, and began to take off her clothes slowly. It was an evening ritual between them, and sometimes he helped her and sometimes he only watched, admiring the graceful beauty of her young body and long limbs. But tonight he couldn't keep his hands from her, as the moonlight danced in her platinum hair, and his own clothes lay in a heap beside him before she was undressed, and rapidly he lifted her onto the bed and covered her body with his warm, hungry lips.

"Oh, Serena darling . . . I love you so. . . ."

She whispered his name in the moonlight, and for long hours before sunrise they forgot that there was another woman, and again and again Serena was his.

CHAPTER NINE

Major B. J. Fullerton stood looking very tall and straight and handsome at the military airport outside Rome. Only his eyes looked faintly troubled, and there were weary smudges to indicate that he had slept little, and as he lit a cigarette he realized that his hands were trembling. It seemed foolish to be nervous about seeing Pattie, but he was. Her father, Congressman Atherton of Rhode Island, had arranged for her to join a military flight over, and she was due in ten minutes. For a brief moment B.J. wished that he had had a drink before he left the house. And then suddenly he saw the plane, circling high above and then drifting lower, heading toward the runway, and finally making a graceful landing, then taxiing down the runway toward the small hastily erected building where he stood. He stood very still as he watched two colonels and a major step down the gangway, then a small cluster of military aides, one woman dressed in the uniform of a military nurse, and then he felt his heart break into a gallop as he saw her, standing at the top of the gangway, looking across the tarmac until she saw him, waving and smiling gaily, the raven hair neatly tucked into a bright red hat. She was wearing a fur coat and dark stockings, and she touched the railing, as she made her way down the stairway, with one elegant little hand neatly encased in a black kid glove. He was struck, even at this distance, by how pretty she was. That was the right word for Pattie. Pretty. She wasn't beautiful like Serena. She wasn't striking. But she was pretty, with a brilliant smile, wide baby-doll blue eyes, and a little turned-up nose. In the summer her face was lightly dusted with freckles when she went to Newport with her parents and summered at their fourteen-bedroom "cottage" with all the other friends she joined there every year. Pretty little Pattie Atherton. He felt his stomach quiver as he watched her. He wanted to run toward her as she was running toward him, but something stopped him. Instead he walked toward her with long slow strides and a wistful smile.

"Hi, pretty girl, can I show you around Rome or is someone meeting you?" He kissed her playfully on the forehead and she giggled, turning her face up toward his with her dazzling Miss America smile.

"Sure, soldier, I'd love to see Rome with you." She slipped a hand through his arm and squeezed tightly, and B.J. had to fight not to close his eyes, so afraid was he that they would show his feelings. He didn't want to do this, didn't want to play games with her or be funny. He wanted to tell her the truth as they stood there at the airport, looking at each other. . . . Pattie, I fell in love with another woman. . . . I have to break our engagement. . . . I want to marry her. . . . I don't love you anymore. . . . But was that true? Didn't he love Pattie Atherton anymore? He didn't think so as he watched her. In fact as he picked up her suitcase and followed the fur coat out of the airport, he was almost sure.

He had arranged for a car and driver, and a moment later they were sitting side by side in the backseat of the car . . . when suddenly she threw her arms around his neck and kissed him hard on the mouth, leaving a bright red imprint of the lipstick that so perfectly matched her hat.

"Hey, babe, take it easy." He reached quickly for his

handkerchief while the driver stowed her bag in the trunk.

"Why should I? I came four thousand miles to see you." Her eyes glittered a little too brightly, as though already she knew, as though she sensed something different. "Don't I get a kiss for all that?"

"Sure you do. But not here." He patted her hand and as she took off her gloves he saw the sparkle of the engagement ring he had given her only that summer. And now it was not yet Thanksgiving and he was already having second thoughts.

"All right." She looked at him matter-of-factly, and he could see shades of her domineering mother in the way her jaw set. "Then let's go back to the palace. Besides," she smiled sweetly, "I want to see it. Daddy says it's divine."

"It is." He felt a tremor pass through him. "But wouldn't you rather go to where you're staying first? Where are you staying, by the way?"

"With General and Mrs. Bryce." She said it smugly, like Congressman Atherton's daughter, and for a moment he hated her for her arrogant ways. How different she was from gentle Serena, how harsh she seemed in comparison. Was this really the pretty girl he had spent so much time with in Newport, and taken out so ardently last summer when he'd been home on leave? She didn't seem nearly as attractive now as they sat here, and he watched her out of the corner of his eye as he asked his driver to take them to his home.

He looked at the sleek waves of her bobbed hair and the expensive red wool hat. "Pattie, what made you come over here now?" B.J. had put up the window between them and the driver and now he looked Pattie straight in the eye as he sat back in his seat. He was on his guard, though he wasn't sure why. "I told you I'd try to come home at Christmas."

"I know." She attempted to look at the same time petulant and alluring, and she was almost successful. Almost. "But I missed you too much." She kissed him playfully on the neck, leaving her imprint on him once again. "And you're such a lousy correspondent." But as she looked at him there was something searching. She was asking him a question, if not with her words, then with her eyes. "Why? Do you mind my coming over, Brad?"

91

"Not at all. But I'm awfully busy just now. And"—he stared out the window, thinking of Serena, before he looked back at Pattie again with reproach in his voice and his eyes—"you should have asked me."

"Should I?" She arched one eyebrow, and again he found the resemblance to her mother striking. "Are you angry?"

"No, of course not." He patted her hand. "But, Pattie, six months ago this was a war zone. I have work to do here. It won't be easy having you around." In part it was true, but the real reason was hidden beneath. And Pattie seemed to sense that as she looked him over appraisingly.

"Well, Daddy wanted to know what I wanted for my birthday, and this was it. Of course"—she looked at him with faint accusation—"if you're too busy to see me, I'm sure that General and Mrs. Bryce will be happy to take me around, and I can always go on to Paris. Daddy has friends there too." It all sounded so petulant and so petty, and it annoyed him. He couldn't help listening to the contrast between her veiled threats of "Daddy" and Serena's solemn, whispered explanations about "my father," as she told B.J. about his conflicts with his brother, their implications, and the political pressures that had eventually led to his death. What did Pattie know of things like that? Nothing. She knew of shopping and tennis and summers in Newport, and deb parties and diamonds and El Morocco and the Stork Club and a constant round of parties in Boston and New York. "Brad." The look which she gave him was part angry, part sad. "Aren't you happy that I came to see you?" Her lower lip pouted, but the big blue eyes shone, and as he watched her he wondered if anything really·mattered to her. Only that she got her own way, he suspected, from Daddy or anyone else.

The summer before, he had found her so charming, so cute, and so sexy, and so much more amusing than the other debutantes he had known before the war. But he had to admit now that the only thing different about her was that she was a little bit shrewder and a lot smarter. He suddenly wondered if she had manipulated the engagement. She certainly had had him panting for her body on the summer porch in Newport. A diamond ring had seemed then a small price to pay for what lay between those shapely legs. "Well, B.J.?" She still wanted an answer to her question, and he had to pull his mind back to the woman sitting beside him in the car hurtling through the streets of Rome.

"Yes, Pattie, I'm happy to see you." But it had the dutiful ring of an unhappy and long-married husband. He didn't feel like a lover as he sat beside her in the car, glancing at the pretty face, the red hat, and the fur. "I think I'm just a little surprised."

"Surprises are nice though, B.J." She wrinkled her nose at him. "I love them."

"I know you do." He smiled at her more gently then, remembering how pleased she had been by all of his offerings, flowers and little presents and once a horse-carriage ride in the moonlight that he had arranged especially for her. He reminded her of it now and she grinned.

"When are you coming home again, B.J.?" The petulance was back in her voice again and he sighed. "I mean for good this time."

"I don't know."

"Daddy says he could arrange it real soon, if you'd let him." And then she winked. "Or maybe even if you don't. Maybe that could be my Christmas present to you." But just hearing her say it made him panic. The thought of being torn from Serena before he was ready filled him with dread.

He squeezed Pattie's hand too hard, and in his eyes she thought she saw terror. "Pattie, don't you ever do that. I'll handle my life in the army myself. Do you understand that?" His voice rose harshly and her eyes held him in check. "Do you?"

"I do." She answered quickly. "Maybe even better than you think." He wanted to ask her what she meant by that, but he didn't dare. Whatever she knew, or suspected, he didn't want to hear about it yet. Sooner or later he would have to talk to her. He would have to make some kind of decision, and perhaps even tell her what had happened in the past months. But not yet. In a way he knew that she was smart to have come over. If there was a way that she could have kept him, this was it. If they were truly to be married, it was good that he be reminded of her now, in person, before it was too late. But just as his thoughts began to fill with Serena, the driver passed through the palazzo's main gate. "Good heavens, B.J.!" She looked at it in astonishment. "Is this it?" He nodded, half in pride and half in amusement at the look on her face. "But you're only a major!" The words slipped from her and she clapped a gloved hand over her mouth as he laughed.

"I am glad you're impressed." He was distracted as he helped her out of the car, and he felt a wave of nervousness sweep over him. He had wanted to take her to the general's and not bring her here in the daytime. They were sure to run into Serena, and he wasn't sure that he could handle that. "I'll give you a quick tour, Pattie, and then we'll get you settled at the Bryces."

"I'm in no hurry. I slept all the way to Ireland on the plane." She smiled happily at him and walked majestically up the steps to the main hall. Here one of the orderlies swept open the enormous bronze doorway, and Pattie found herself standing beneath the magnificent chandelier. Her eye caught the grand piano and she turned to see B.J. behind her, looking amused, despite himself, at her reactions. "War is hell, huh, Major?"

"Absolutely. Would you like to see the upstairs?"

"I sure would." She followed him up the stairs, as all eyes followed. In her own way she was a very striking young woman, and none of them had seen a woman like her in a long time. Everything about her reeked of money and class. She looked like something right out of *Vogue* magazine, deposited on their doorstep, some four thousand miles from home. The orderlies exchanged quick glances. She was a looker, all right, and they had all heard that she was a congressman's daughter. If the major's old man hadn't been a senator once, and if they hadn't all known that he came from money too, they'd have wondered what he was after. But this way it seemed like they were made for each other, and as one of the orderlies whispered to another, "Jesus, man . . . just look at them legs!"

B.J. took her from room to room, introducing the men in various offices, and the secretaries, who all looked up from their work. They sat in a little drawing room where he sometimes entertained guests, looking out over the garden, and then suddenly she looked up at him, tilted her head to one side, and asked the question he'd been avoiding. "Aren't you going to show me your room?" He had whisked her quickly through his office, but he had purposely avoided the enormous room with the antique canopied bed.

"I suppose so, if you'd like that."

"I certainly would. I suppose it's as lavish as the rest of all this. Poor B.J.," she crooned jokingly. "What a hard life you live over here! And to think, people feel sorry for you, still being in Europe after the war!" But there was more than amusement and raillery in what she was saying, there was accusation now and suspicion, and resentment and anger. He began to sense all of it as he led the way down a marble hall and opened a pair of handsomely carved double doors. "Good Lord, B.J.! All this for you?" She turned to face him too quickly, and suddenly she saw him blushing to the roots of his hair. He said nothing further and walked swiftly to the long rows of windows, opened one of them and stepped onto the balcony, saying something about the view. But it wasn't the view he was seeking. He was longing for a glimpse of Serena. After all, this was her home too. "I had no idea you lived so comfortably, B.J." Pattie's voice was smoky as she stepped outside and stood beside him on the little balcony looking out over the gently rolling lawns below.

"Do you mind it?" His eyes looked deep into hers now, trying to understand who she was, and what she felt. Did she really love him, or merely want to have him? It was a question he had been asking himself now for quite a while.

"I don't mind it . . . of course not . . . but it makes me wonder if you'll ever want to come home."

"Of course I will. Eventually."

"But not for a while?" Her eyes sought other answers in his, but the slate-gray eyes were troubled and he looked away, and as he did so he saw her, sitting quietly under her tree. She sat turned so that he could see her profile, and for a moment he was mesmerized into silence, as Pattie saw her too and looked rapidly into Brad's eyes. "B.J.?" He didn't answer for a long moment. He didn't hear her. He was seeing something different about Serena, something he had never seen quite the same way before, it was a quiet dignity, a solemnity, an almost unbearable beauty, as he realized that watching her was like looking at the sky reflected in still waters, and being with Pattie was like being constantly tossed in a turbulent sea.

"I'm sorry." He turned toward Pattie in a moment. "I didn't hear what you said just then." But there was something strange in her eyes once he turned toward her, and there was something very different in his.

"Who is she?" Pattie's eyes began to smolder, and her full pouting mouth seemed almost instantly to form a thin line.

"I'm sorry?"

"Don't play that game with me, B.J. You heard me. Who is she? Your Italian whore?" A torrent of jealousy coursed through her, and without knowing anything for certain, she was almost trembling with rage. But B.J. was suddenly angry too. He grabbed Pattie's fur-covered arm in one powerful hand and squeezed it until she felt his grip.

"Don't ever say anything like that to me again. She is one of the maids here. And like most people in this country, she has been through one hell of a lot. More than you'd ever understand with your ideas about 'war work,' dancing with soldiers at the USO and going to El Morocco with your friends every night."

"Is that right, Major?" Her eyes blazed into his. "And just why is she so important to you, if she isn't your little whore?" She spat out the word, and without thinking, he grabbed her other arm and began to shake her, and when he spoke again, his voice was loud and harsh.

"Stop calling her that, damn you!"

"Why? Are you in love with her, B.J.?" And then, viciously, "Do your parents know that? Do they know what you've been doing here? Sleeping with some goddamn little Italian maid." He pulled an arm back to slap her, and then stopped himself just in time, trembling and pale, as instinctively he looked toward Serena and found her standing just below them, a look of horror on her face and tears brilliant in her eyes.

96

"Serena!" He called out her name, but she disappeared instantly, and he felt a swift slice of pain. What had she heard? Pattie's ugly accusations, her raging speech about his parents and "some goddamn little Italian maid"? He was horrified at what had happened, but only because it might have hurt Serena. He suddenly realized that he didn't give a damn about Pattie Atherton anymore. He let go of her arms and stood back carefully, with a grim look on his face. "Pattie, I didn't know this when you sent the telegram that you were coming, or I would have asked you not to, but I'm going to marry that woman you just saw there. She isn't what you think she is, but it really doesn't matter. I love her. I'm sorry I didn't tell you before."

Pattie Atherton looked at him in mingled shock and horror and began to shake her head slowly as tears sprang to her eyes. "No! You can't do this to me, damn you! I won't let you! Are you crazy, marrying a maid? What will you do? Live here? You can't take her back to New York with you, your parents would disown you and you'd embarrass everyone. . . ." She was spluttering and there were tears beginning to slide from her eyes.

"That's not the point, Pattie. This is my life, not my parents'. And you don't know what you're talking about." His voice was suddenly quiet and firm.

"I know that she's one of the maids here."

He nodded slowly, and then looked long and hard at Pattie. "I don't want to discuss this with you, Pattie. The issue is us, and I'm sorry, I made a mistake last summer. But I don't think either of us would have been happy if we'd got married."

"So you're going to ditch me, is that it?" She laughed shrilly through her tears. "That simple? Then what—bring home your little whore? Jesus, you must be crazy, B.J.!" And then, with eyes narrowed, "Or maybe I was to believe the line of crap you gave me. All that junk about how much you loved me!"

"I did . . . then. . . ."

"And now you don't?" She looked as though she would have liked to hit him, but she didn't dare.

But B.J. stood his ground. He was sure. "Not enough to

marry you, Pattie." His voice was gentle now, in spite of everything she had said. "It would be a terrible mistake."

"Oh, really." She pulled the ring from her finger and shoved it into his hand. "I think you just made a terrible mistake, buddy. But I'll let you figure that out for yourself." He said nothing, but followed her into the room, where she saw her picture, which in a moment of cowardice he had reinstalled. She walked across the room, picked up the silver frame, and hurled it against the wall. The sound of the glass shattering broke the silence between them and as B.J. watched her she began to cry. He moved toward her and put his hands on her shoulders.

"I'm sorry, Pattie."

"Go to hell!" She spun on her heel to face him. And then in a tone of viciousness, which hit him like a blow, "I hope you rot. In fact, B. J. Fullerton, if I can ever do anything to help screw up your life the way you just loused up mine, I'd be happy to help out. Anytime."

"Don't say things like that, Pattie." He felt compassion for her and wanted to believe that she didn't mean it.

"Why not? Don't you think I mean it?"

"I hope not." He looked more handsome than ever as he stood there and she hated him, as she looked at him for a last time.

"Don't kid yourself, B.J. I'm not some two-bit dago tramp. Don't expect me to fall at your feet and beg you . . . and expect me to forgive you either. Because I won't." And with that, she turned and left the room. He followed her quietly down the stairs, and in the main hallway he offered to accompany her to the Bryces', but she looked at him in cold fury and shook her head. "Just have your driver take me there, B.J. I don't want to see you again."

"Will you stay on in Rome for a few days? Maybe we could talk a little more quietly tomorrow. There's no reason why we can't be friends in a while. I know it's painful, Pattie, but it's better this way." She only shook her head.

"I have nothing more to say to you, B.J. You're a skunk, a louse." Her eyes overflowed. "And I hate you. And if you expect me to keep quiet about this, you're crazy." Her eyes narrowed viciously again. "Everyone in New York is going to know what you're doing over here, B.J. Because I'm

98

going to tell them. And if you bring that girl back with you, God help you, because they'll laugh you out of town.''

It was obvious from the way he looked at her that he wasn't afraid of Pattie, but he was angry at what she had just said. ''Don't do anything you'll regret.''

''Someone should have told you that before you ditched me.'' And with that, she walked past him and out of the door. She slammed it behind her, and B.J. stood there for a long moment, wondering if he should go after her, and knowing that he could not. The orderlies had discreetly disappeared when they heard them coming, and a moment later B.J. quietly went back upstairs. He needed a moment to himself to think over what had happened, but he knew even then that he wasn't sorry. He didn't love her. Of that he was now certain. But he did love Serena, and now he would have to make it all right with her. God knows what she had heard as Pattie shrieked at him on the balcony. As he remembered her words he suddenly realized that there was not a moment to lose in finding Serena, but as he left his office to find her, his secretary stopped him. There was an urgent phone call from headquarters in Milan. And it was two hours later before he could get away again.

He went quietly to their quarters, knocked on the door, and was answered instantly by Marcella.

''Serena?'' She pulled the door open rapidly with tears on her face and a handkerchief in her hand, and she seemed even more overwrought when she saw B.J.

''Isn't she here?'' He looked startled, as Marcella shook her head and began to cry again.

''No.'' She assaulted him instantly with a flood of Italian, and gently he stopped her, holding the old shaking shoulders in both of his hands.

''Marcella, where is she?''

''*Non so* . . . I don't know.'' And then suddenly it hit him, as the old woman cried harder and pointed to the empty room behind her. ''She took her suitcase, Major. She is gone.''

CHAPTER TEN

The major had sat with Marcella for almost an hour, trying to piece together what had happened and figure out where she might have gone. There weren't many places he could think of. She certainly wouldn't go to her grandmother's house in Venice with strangers living there, and as far as Marcella knew, there was nowhere else. She had no friends or relatives to go to, and the only thing that B.J. could think of was that she had gone back to the States. But she couldn't have done that at a moment's notice. She'd have to get another visa and make arrangements. Maybe she was staying somewhere in Rome and she would attempt to get a visa back to America in the morning. He couldn't call the American Embassy until the morning to check on that. There was nothing he could do. He felt powerless, empty, and afraid.

Brad questioned Marcella until the old peasant woman was wrung dry. Serena had run into their quarters from the door that led into the garden, rushed into her room, and locked the door. Marcella knew that because she had tried to go in when she had heard her crying, but Serena wouldn't let her in.

Half an hour later Serena had emerged, red eyed, pale, and with her suitcase in her hand. She had told Marcella simply that she was leaving, and in answer to the old woman's tears and entreaties, she had said only that she had no choice. At first Marcella thought that she had been fired, at this the old woman cast a sidelong glance of apology at the major, explaining that she had thought that it was all because of him. But Serena had insisted that it wasn't, that it was a problem that had nothing to do with him, and that she had to leave Rome at once. Marcella wondered if she was in danger, because the girl had looked so distraught that it was hard to tell if she were only upset or also frightened, and with tears, and kisses, and a last hug, Serena fled. Marcella had been sobbing hopelessly in her room for almost two hours when she heard the major's knock on the door, and hoped that it was Serena, having changed her mind.

"And that is all I know, Major. . . ." Marcella dissolved in tears again and clung to the sympathetic young American. "Why did she go? *Perchè? Non capisco . . . non capisco.* . . ." All he could do was comfort her. How could he explain any of it to Marcella? He couldn't. He would have to live with that hell himself.

"Marcella, listen to me." The old woman only sobbed more loudly. "Shh . . . listen. . . . I promise you. I'll find her. *Domani vado a trovarla.*"

"*Ma dove?*" But where? It was a hopeless wail. All those years of not seeing Serena, and now she was back and Marcella had lost her again.

"*Non so dove*, Marcella. I don't know where. But I'll find her." And then he squeezed the old shoulders and went quietly back to his own rooms. He sat in the darkness for what seemed like hours, thinking, turning things over in his mind, remembering snatches of conversation he had had with her. But no matter how deep he dug, how far into the memories, he came up blank. She had no one now except Marcella, and he realized once again how devastated she must have been to leave the old woman and the only home she had. A shaft of guilt shot through him again as he remembered the argument he had had with Pattie. He thought of what it must have sounded like at à distance, of what Serena must have thought, watching them, seeing them together, and then listening to the American woman's angry words.

After hours of painful, endless questions running around and around in his mind he gave up. There was nothing to do except wait—and wait. He went into his bedroom and stood for a long moment, staring at the bed. Tonight he had no desire to sleep beneath the blue satin of the canopy. The bed would seem painfully empty without the woman that he loved. And what if you don't find her? he asked himself. Then I'll keep looking. He'd find her if he had to comb all of Italy and Switzerland and France. He'd go back to the States. He'd do anything, and eventually he would find her, and he would tell her that he loved her and ask her to be his wife. He was entirely sure of his feelings as he lay there, and not a single thought of Pattie crossed his mind as he whiled away the hours, lying there, thinking of Serena, and wondering again and again where she could have gone.

It was only when a cock crowed in the distance at five thirty, that he suddenly shot up in bed with a look of amazement and stared out the window. "Oh, my God!" How could he have forgotten? It should have been the first place he thought of. With lightning speed he threw back the covers, ran into the bathroom, showered, shaved, and by ten minutes before six he was dressed. He left a note for his secretary and his assistants, explaining that he had been called away on a matter that was urgent, and for his secretary he left an additional note asking him to be kind enough to "cover his ass." He left all the memos where they would see them, and then slipped on a heavy jacket and hurried downstairs. He had to speak to Marcella, and he was relieved to see a light under her door when he got downstairs. He knocked softly twice and a moment later the old woman opened the door to him, at first with a look of astonishment to see him there, and then one of confusion when she saw that he was in civilian garb and not the uniform she was used to seeing him in every day.

"Yes?" She still looked startled as she stepped back for him to enter, but he shook his head and smiled with a warm look in his deep gray eyes.

"Marcella, I think I may know where to find her. But I need your help. The farm in Umbria . . . can you tell me how to get there?" Marcella looked more startled still for a long moment and then she nodded, frowning, thoughtful. She looked into his eyes again, with a hopeful gleam in her own.

She closed her eyes for a moment, remembering, and then brought him a pencil and a piece of paper, and waved him to a chair. "You write it down like I tell you." He was only too happy to obey her orders, and a few minutes later he was out the door with the paper in his hand. He waved to her one last time as he ran toward the little shed where he kept the jeep he used when he didn't have a driver, and she watched him as he drove away, with tears of hope in her old eyes.

*   *   *

The trip from Rome to Umbria was long and arduous, the roads were poor, deeply rutted, and crowded with military vehicles, foot traffic, and carts filled with chickens, or hay, or fruit. It was here that one remembered that there had been a war on not so very long ago. One still saw signs of the damage everywhere, and there were times when B.J. thought that neither he nor the jeep would survive. He had brought with him all of his military papers, and had the jeep collapsed beneath him, he would have commandeered anything he had to, to reach the farm.

As it was, it was after dark when he got there, traveling down the uninhabited, rutted road in the direction that Marcella had described to him, but he began to wonder in a few moments if he had taken the wrong turn. Nothing looked familiar according to the directions, and he stopped the car in the darkness. It didn't help him that there was even no moon by which to travel, and there were dark clouds passing through the sky as he looked up and then at the horizon beyond. But as he did so, he suddenly saw a cluster of buildings in the distance, huddling together as though for warmth, and he realized with a long tired sigh that he had found the farm.

He turned the jeep back until he found a narrow, rutted lane, and followed it through overgrown bushes in the direction of the buildings he had seen on the horizon, and a few moments later, splashing through deep potholes, he reached what must have once been a large courtyard, or a kind of main square. There was a large house facing him, barns stretching out toward the right, and an orchard both to the left and behind him. Even in the darkness he could see that it was a large place, that it was deserted. The house looked weather-beaten and empty, the doors of the barns had fallen off their hinges, there was grass growing waist high between the cobblestones in the courtyard, and what farm equipment there had once been stood rusting and broken in the orchard, which obviously had not been tended for years. He stood there for a long moment, wondering where to go now. Back to Rome? Into a village? To a nearby farm? But there were none. There was nothing here, and no one, and surely not Serena. Even if she had come here to find refuge, she could not stay here. He stared sadly at the barns in the darkness, and then at the house, but as he did so, he thought he saw something scurry into the darkness of a corner. An animal? A cat? A dream? Or perhaps someone very frightened at his intrusion. Realizing how mad he was to have come on this solitary adventure, he kept his eyes in the direction of what he had seen, and walked slowly backward toward the jeep. When he reached it, he leaned inside, and took out his pistol, he cocked it and then began to walk forward, wielding an unlit flashlight in his other hand. He was almost certain now of where he had seen the movement, and he could see a form huddled in a corner, crouched behind a bush. For an instant he realized how insane it was that he should be pursuing this encounter, that he might perhaps die, for no reason at all, on a deserted farm in the Italian countryside in search of a woman, six months after the end of the war. After all he had survived in the years before that, it seemed ironic that he could die now, he thought as he inched his way forward along the building, his heart racing.

When he had come within a dozen feet of where he had seen the movement, he pressed himself into a narrow nook, took what refuge he could find, and instantly shot one arm forward with the flashlight held aloft. He switched it on, poised at the same instant with his gun, and like his victim's, his eyes blinked for a moment in the darkness, as he realized with terror that it was not a cat at all. It was someone hunched over and hiding, a dark cap pulled low over his brow, hands held aloft.

"Come out of there! I'm with the American army!" He felt a little foolish saying the words, but he hadn't been sure what else to say, and the form, a tall angular shape in dark blue wool, moved forward and stood staring at him now, as he gave a whoop and then grinned. It was Serena. She stood wide eyed, her face white with terror and then with astonishment as he approached. "Come here, damn you! I told you to come out of there!" But B.J. didn't wait for her to move, he ran toward her, and before she could say a word, he had enfolded her in his arms. "Goddamn crazy girl, I could have shot you."

104

The green eyes were wide and brilliant in the moonlight as she looked up at him, still dumbfounded by what had happened. "How did you find me?"

He looked down at her and kissed her gently on both eyes, and then her lips. "I don't know. It came to me this morning, and Marcella gave me directions." He frowned at her then. "You shouldn't have done it, Serena. You had us all worried sick."

She shook her head slowly then and pulled away from him. "I had to. I couldn't be there any longer."

"You could have waited to talk it over." He held her hand although she stood a few feet from him now, her foot pushing a small stone on the ground.

"There is nothing to talk over. Is there?" She looked into his eyes, with all the hurt that had driven her from Rome. "I heard what she said, about me, about your family. She's right. I'm only your Italian whore . . . a maid. . . ." She didn't even flinch as she said it, and he pressed her hand.

"She's a bitch, Serena. I know that now. I didn't see things as clearly before. And what she said is not true. She was jealous, that was all."

"Did you tell her about us?"

"I didn't have to." He smiled gently at her, and they stood for a long time in the silence and the darkness. There was something eerie about being at the deserted farm alone. "This place must have been quite something before."

"It was." She smiled at him. "I loved it. It was a perfect place to be a child. There were cows and pigs and horses, lots of friendly workers in the fields, fruit in the orchards, a place to swim nearby. My best childhood memories are of here."

"I know. I remember." They exchanged a speaking look and Serena sighed. She still couldn't believe that he had found her. Things like that didn't happen in real life. They only happened in books and movies, but there they were, a million miles from civilization, together, and alone.

"Won't she be very angry that you left Rome?" Serena looked at him curiously and he shook his head slowly.

"No angrier than she was when I broke our engagement."
Serena looked shocked. "Why did you do that, Brad?" In

fact, she looked almost angry. "Because of me?"

"Because of me. When I saw her, I knew what I felt about her." He shook his head again. "Nothing. Or damn close to it. I felt fear. She's a very scary young woman, manipulative and scheming. She wanted me for something. I'm not sure what, but when I listened to her, I knew it. She wanted me to be a puppet, I think, to go into politics like her father and mine, to make her something, and to play her game. There is something incredibly empty about her, Serena. And when I saw her, I had all the answers that I'd been struggling for, for months. They were all there all along, I just didn't know it. And then she saw me look at you, and she knew it too. That was when you heard her." Serena watched him as he talked and then nodded.

"She was very angry, Brad. I was frightened for you." She looked very young as she stood in front of him in the courtyard. "I was afraid. . . ." She closed her eyes briefly. "I had to run . . . I thought that if I disappeared it would make things simpler for you. . . ." Her voice trailed off and he reached out his arms again.

"Have I told you lately that I love you?" She smiled in the darkness and nodded.

"I think that was what you meant when you came here." She looked at him pensively then and tilted her head to one side. "It is over with her, then?"

He nodded, and then smiled. "And now it can begin in earnest with us."

"It already has begun." She reached out her arms for him, and he stroked her hair with a gentle hand.

"I want to marry you, Serena. You know that, don't you?" But quietly she shook her head.

"No." It was a simple word, and he looked down at her with a smile.

"Does that mean that you don't know it?"

"No." She looked up at him again. "It means that I love you with all of my heart and I will not marry you. Never." She sounded resolute and he looked at her in dismay.

"Why in hell not?"

"Because it would be wrong. I have nothing to give you, except my heart. And you need a woman like her, of your world, of your own kind, your class, of your country, someone who knows your ways, someone who can help you if you ever do decide to go into politics one day. I will only hurt you, if that's what you want later on. The Italian war bride . . . the maid. . . .'' Pattie's words still rang in her ears. "The Italian whore . . . others will call me that too.''

"The hell they will. Serena, aren't you forgetting who you are?''

"Not at all. You're remembering what I was. I am not that anymore. You heard what Pattie said.''

"Stop that!'' He took her by both shoulders and shook her gently. "You're my principessa.''

"No.'' Her eyes never wavered from his. "I'm your upstairs maid.''

He pulled her into his arms then, wondering how he could convince her, what he could say. "I love you, Serena. I respect everything that you are. I'm proud of you, dammit. Won't you let me make my own decisions about what's right for me?''

"No.'' She smiled up at him with a look of sorrow mingled with love.

"You don't know what you're doing. So I won't let you do it.''

"Do you think we could argue about it later?'' He looked down at her with a grin, sure that eventually he would convince her, but he had suddenly realized that he had been driving for hours and he was exhausted. "Is there anywhere for us to stay? Or have you decided not to sleep with me anymore either?''

"The answer is no to both questions.'' She grinned at him sheepishly. "There's nowhere for miles. I was going to sleep in the barn.''

"Did you have anything to eat today?'' He looked at her worriedly and she shook her head.

"Not really. I brought some cheese and some salami, but I finished it this morning. I was going to walk into town tomorrow and go to the market. But I was awfully hungry tonight.''

"Come on.'' He put an arm around her shoulders and walked her slowly back to the car. He pulled open the door, helped her up into the seat, and pulled out the knapsack in which he had put half a dozen sandwiches as a last-minute thought before he left. There were also apples and a piece of cake, and a bar of chocolate.

"What? No silk stockings?" She grinned at him over the sandwich she was devouring.

"You only get those if you marry me."

"Oh." She shrugged, leaning back against the seat. "Then I guess I don't get any silk stockings. Only chocolate."

"Christ, you're stubborn."

"Yes." She nodded proudly and he grinned.

They slept in the jeep that night, their arms cast easily over each other, their legs cramped, but their hearts light. He had found her, all was well, and before she fell asleep, she had agreed to come home to Rome with him. And when the sun came up, they each ate an apple, washed at the well, and she showed him the farm she had loved as a child, when life had been so very different. And as he kissed her in front of the old barn, he promised himself that whatever it took, he would convince her and one day she would be his for good.

CHAPTER ELEVEN

When Serena returned to Rome the next day, Marcella was already sleeping. She left her suitcase in the little hall to let her know she was back, and then tiptoed upstairs with B.J. to the familiar bed. They made love as they hadn't dared to on the road, and Serena rejoiced to be back in his arms again. The pictures of Pattie were gone for good, and she felt free and happy to be alive. The next morning Marcella gave her hell for running away, and berated her at the top of her lungs for almost two hours, threatening to box her ears, shouting, insulting, and then finally bursting into tears as she clung to Serena and begged her never to go away again.

"I won't. I promise you, Cella. I'll be here forever."

"Not forever." She looked at Serena cryptically. "But for as long as you should be here."

"I should be here forever," Serena said calmly. "At least in Rome, this is my home." She had long since abandoned all thought of returning to the States.

"Maybe not for always." Marcella looked at her again.

"I don't know what you're talking about, and I don't think I want to hear it." Serena turned away to make a pot of coffee. She knew exactly what Marcella meant.

"He loves you, Serena." The voice was old and wise, and Serena wheeled to face her.

"I love him too. Enough not to destroy his life. He broke off his engagement with that American girl. He seems to think he had good reason to do it, and maybe he was right. But I will never marry him, Cella. Never. It would be wrong. And it would ruin his life. His family is very important to him, and they would hate me. They wouldn't understand anything about me. So, no matter what he tells you, or what you think, the answer is never, Marcella. I've told it to him, and I'm telling it to you. I want you to understand that. You have to accept it, just as I do, and I have accepted it, so I think you can too."

"You're crazy, Serena. His parents would be lucky to have you."

"I'm sure they wouldn't think so." She could still hear Pattie's words. She handed Marcella her coffee and went back to her own little cubicle to unpack.

After that, life was peaceful all the way through November. She and Brad were happier than they had ever been, Marcella settled down, and it was as though nothing could ever go wrong with the world. She and Brad shared a private Thanksgiving dinner. He taught her how to make a turkey and stuff it. He had commandeered some chestnuts, and some desperately rare cranberry jelly, and Marcella made sweet potatoes and peas and creamed onions for them, and together they had a rare feast. It was Serena's first Thanksgiving dinner.

"To the first of many." He toasted her happily with a glass of white wine with their dinner, while secretly she knew that this would be her last. Within the year he would surely be transferred home, and moments like this would not come again. Now and then she thought of that time and wished that she would become pregnant, but Brad was determinedly careful that nothing like that would happen, so Serena knew that when B.J. left Rome, that would be the end of it. There would be no Brad, no baby to remember him by, only memories like this one to keep her warm.

"What were you thinking about just then?" he asked her as they lay in front of the fire and he watched the brilliant emerald eyes.

"You."

"What about me?"

"That I love you." . . . And I'll miss you unbearably when you're gone. . . . She never said it, but the thoughts were always there.

"If you really loved me," he began to tease and wheedle and she grinned, "you'd marry me." It was a game they often played, but he knew he had months to convince her, at least he thought so, until the next day.

He sat at his desk, the envelope on the floor, staring at his orders, and fighting back a strong desire to cry. The idyll in Rome was over. He was being transferred. In seven days.

"You can't be." Her face had gone pale, just as his had when he read it. "So quickly? I thought they always gave a month's notice."

"Not always. Not this time. I leave for Paris a week from today." At least it was only Paris. He could come back to see her. She could come to see him. But it wasn't all that easy, and they wouldn't have the normal routine of their life anymore, their nights in the big canopied bed, the early mornings together, the constant looks and glances throughout the day, and the stolen moments when he came to her quarters after lunch just for a kiss, for a word, for a hello, a joke, just to see her and feel her and hear her . . . they would have none of that, and as he thought of it he wondered how he would live. He looked at her frankly and asked her for the ten thousandth time. "Will you marry me and come with me?" Slowly she shook her head.

"I can't marry you and you know why."

"Even now?"

"Even now." She tried to smile bravely at him. "Couldn't you just take me along as your personal maid?" He looked angry as she said it and he shook his head as though to shake off what she had just said.

"That's not even funny. I'm serious, Serena. For chrissake, realize what's happening. It's all over for us. I'm leaving. I'm going to Paris a week from today, and God knows where after that, probably back to the States. And I can't take you with me unless we're married. Will you please come to your senses and marry me so we don't lose the one thing we both care about?"

"I can't do it." There was a lump in her throat the size of a fist as she said it, and that night after he fell asleep in her arms she cried for hours on her side of the bed. She had to let him go, for his sake. She knew that she had to, if she really loved him, and she did, but she knew that it would be the hardest task of her life to peel her heart from his. She steeled herself for it daily, but when the last night came, she felt such a terror in her heart at the thought of losing him that she didn't know if she could bear it. For days Marcella had been hounding her, tormenting her, pleading with her, begging, and in his own way B.J. had been doing the same, but Serena was so certain that to marry him would ruin his life that she was unwilling to listen. She knew what she had to do, and however unbearable it was, she would do it, even if she died when he left, it wouldn't matter then. She had nothing left to live for anyway. There would never be a man that she loved as she loved B.J. And knowing that on the last night made it all the more bittersweet as she held him and stroked him, and smoothed a gentle hand across his hair, wanting to engrave the moment forever in her memory, as a way of holding on to him.

"Serena?" She had thought he was sleeping, but his voice was a whisper in the canopied bed and she leaned forward to see his face.

"Yes, my love?"

"I love you so much . . . I will always love you . . . I

111

could never love anyone else like I love you."

"Nor I, Brad."

"Will you write to me?" There were tears in his eyes as he asked her. He had finally accepted that he was going to leave Rome alone.

"Of course I will. Always." Always. Forever. The promises of a lifetime, which she knew only too well would dim in time. One day he would marry and he would forget, he would want to forget then, and it would finally be over between them. But she knew that for her it would never be over. She would never forget him. "Will you write to me?" There were tears in her eyes. There always was the threat of tears this past week, for both of them.

"Of course I will. But I'd rather take you with me."

"In your pocket perhaps, or a secret compartment, or a suitcase. . . ." She smiled down at him and kissed the end of his nose. "Paris is so pretty, you're going to love it."

"You're coming to visit in two weeks, aren't you? I ought to be able to get the papers for you as soon as I get there." She was going to spend a weekend with him in his quarters if it could be arranged, and he had made her promise that she would come often, as often as she could. And he had told her to bring Marcella. He didn't want her traveling alone on the train. But it would be impossible for both of them to leave together, she reminded him. One of them had to stay behind and work at the palazzo. He had nodded then. For Brad the past week had sped by in a fog, and by the morning of his departure he felt drained. He sat up in bed before sunrise, and looked at Serena, lying in the canopied bed, beneath a vast fan of her silky blond hair. He touched her hair and her face, and her arms and her breasts, and then gently he woke her, and they made love again, and as he held her close to him in their bed he realized that he had just made love to her for the last time in Rome. In two hours he would be leaving, and all they would have left were the occasional weekends they would share in Paris, before he would eventually be shipped back to the States. As he held her close to him she felt him swell and hunger for her again and gently she touched him, at first with her fingers, and then with her deft tongue. She had learned a great deal with Brad in their bed of love, but most of it had come from her heart, or from instinct, as she sought to bring him pleasure and to give herself to him in every possible way. And so one last time he moaned softly and ached with the pleasure of her touch, of her kiss, of their longing for each other, and he pulled himself from her mouth and entered her again. It was she who realized then what had happened, and hoped that his last gift to her would be a son.

But neither of them was thinking of anything but each other as they met for a last time in his office an hour later, and he held her and kissed her once more, as they looked out into the bleak garden and remembered how it had looked in the summer and fall. And then, gently, he turned her face toward his and kissed her for the last time.

"You'll come in two weeks?"

"I'll come." But they both knew that it wasn't sure.

"If not, I'll fly back to Rome." And then what? An abyss of loneliness for both of them over the years. She had condemned them to a difficult loss with her staunch principles about not being good enough for him to marry. And he couldn't help trying again. "Serena . . . please . . . will you reconsider . . . please . . . let's get married." But she only shook her head, unable to speak at the pain of seeing him go, her face washed with tears. "Oh, God, how I love you."

"I love you too." It was all she could say before the orderlies came to get him, and after he left the room, she let out an almost animal moan as she steadied herself against the wall and stared out into the garden. In a few minutes he would be gone . . . she would have lost him forever . . . the thought was almost more than she could bear, and she ran breathlessly down to the garden near where she and Marcella lived. She knew he would see her there as he drove away, and that way she wouldn't have to stand with the others, and only Brad and his driver would see her face contorted in sadness. As it was, when he drove past, she saw that he was crying too, his face somber and pale at the window of the car, and his face wet with silent tears as the driver pressed relentlessly forward. And then, all she saw was a face at the rear window, until finally the car that bore him away disappeared.

She walked slowly inside then, with a look of glazed pain,

and walked straight into her room and closed the door. Marcella said nothing at all to her. It was too late for reproach. She had made her decision and now she would live by it, if it killed her. And after two days of her lying there, Marcella feared that it would. By the third day Marcella was truly frightened. Serena refused to get up, wouldn't eat, never seemed to sleep. She just lay there, crying silently and staring at the ceiling. She didn't even get out of her bed the one time that he called and the orderly came to tell Marcella. She was beginning to panic and the next day she went to the orderly herself.

"I have to call the major," she announced firmly, trying to make it look as though it were official business, as she stood in the secretary's office in a clean apron with a freshly pressed scarf on her head.

"Major Appleby?" The secretary looked surprised. The new major wasn't due until the next morning. Maybe the old woman wanted to quit. They were all beginning to wonder if her niece would. No one had seen Serena since Major Fullerton had left.

"No. I want to call Major Fullerton in Paris. I will pay for it myself. But you must make the call and I wish to speak to him in private."

"I'll see what I can do." The secretary glanced at the indomitable old woman and promised that he would do his best. "I'll come and get you, if I get him on the line." As it happened, luck was with him and he got hold of B.J. less than an hour later, sitting bleakly in his new office, wondering why Serena wouldn't take his call. He didn't have good news for her anyway. Her traveling papers for a weekend in Paris had been denied. There had been some vague hint about fraternization being frowned on, and it was deemed "wisest to leave one's indiscretions behind." He had burned angrily when he had got word, and now he knew he had to tell her. All he could offer was to come back to Rome in a few weeks, when he could get away, but he had no idea yet as to when. He was sitting staring out into the Paris rain on the Place du Palais-Bourbon in the Seventh Arrondissement, when the call came in from his old secretary in Rome, and he gave a little start and smiled to hear a familiar voice. "I'm calling for Marcella, Major. She said it was important and private. I've just sent someone to fetch her. You'll have to hang on for a minute, if that's all right with you."

"It's fine." But he was suddenly very frightened. What if something had happened? Serena could have had an accident, or she could have run off to that godforsaken farm again, and this time he wasn't there to go and get her, she could fall in the well, she could break her leg, she could. . . . "Is everything all right there, Palmers?" He spoke to his secretary with concern and the junior man smiled.

"Fine, sir."

"Everyone still on board?" He was asking about Serena but didn't quite dare say her name.

"Pretty much. We haven't seen much of Marcella's niece, in fact we haven't seen her since you left, sir, but Marcella says she's sick and she'll be fine in a few days." Oh, Christ. It could have meant anything, but before Brad could give much thought to his worst fears, the secretary spoke again. "Here's Marcella now, sir. Think you can manage with her English, or do you want someone on an extension to help?"

"No, we'll manage on our own, thanks." B.J. found himself wondering how many of them knew. No matter how discreet he and Serena had been, somehow those things always got around. It had certainly got to Paris. "Thanks, Palmers, good to talk to you."

"And to you, sir. Here she is."

"*Maggiore?*" The old woman's voice came to him like a breath of fresh air.

"Yes, Marcella. Is everything all right? Serena?" In answer to his question he was pelted with a hailstorm of rapid Italian, almost none of which he understood, except the words eating and sleeping, but he wasn't sure who was eating and sleeping and why Marcella was so concerned. "Wait a minute! Hang on! *Piano!* *Piano!* Slowly! *Non capisco.* Is it Serena?"

"*Sì.*"

"Is she sick?" He was assaulted with more rapid-fire Italian, and once again begged the old woman to slow down. This time she did.

"She ate nothing, she drank nothing, she neither slept nor got up. She just cried and cried and cried and . . ." Now it was Marcella who began to cry. "She is going to die, *Maggiore*. I know it. I saw my own mother die the same way."

"She's nineteen years old, Marcella. She is not going to die." I won't let her, he thought to himself. "Have you tried to get her up?"

"*Sì. Ogni ora*. Every hour. But she doesn't get up. She doesn't listen. She does nothing. She is sick."

"Have you called the doctor?"

"She's not sick like that. She is sick for you, *Maggiore*." He was sick for her, and the damn crazy girl had refused to marry him because of her silly notions of protecting him, and now they were up the creek. "What can we do?"

He narrowed his eyes and stared out at the December rain. "Get her to the phone. I want to talk to her."

"She no come." Marcella looked more worried again. "Yesterday when you call, she no come."

"Tonight when I call, you get her to the phone, Marcella, if you have to drag her." He silently cursed the fact that there was no phone in the servants' rooms. "I want to talk to her."

"*Ecco. Va bene.*"

"Can you do it?"

"I do it. You go to Umbria to find her, now I go to bring her to the phone. *Facciamo miracoli insieme.*" She grinned in her half-toothless smile. She had just told him that they made miracles together. And it was going to take a miracle to get Serena out of her bed.

"See if you can't get her up for a few minutes first. Otherwise she'll be too weak. Wait a minute." He thought for a moment. "I have an idea. There's no one in the guest bedroom right now, is there?" Marcella thought for a minute and shook her head.

"*Nessuno, Maggiore.*" No one.

"Good. I'll take care of everything."

"You're going to put her in there?" Marcella sounded stunned. Whatever her lineage and her title, Serena was after all just an employee now at the palazzo, and a lowly one at that. No matter that she had been occupying the major's bed for all these months, that was different from moving her into

116

one of the guest rooms, like a VIP guest. Marcella was afraid there might be trouble.

"I'm going to put her in there, Marcella, whether she likes it or not. Get me Palmers. I'm going to have him carry her up there as soon as you get her ready. And an hour from now"—he looked at his watch—"I'll put through a call."

"What will I tell Sergeant Palmers?"

"I'll tell him, we can say that she is very ill and we're afraid of pneumonia, that it's too damp for her where you are, and I'm ordering all of you to bring her upstairs."

"What do we do when the new *Maggiore* arrives?"

"Marcella . . ." He didn't dare say what he was thinking. "Never mind that. Get Palmers, I want to talk to him now. You go to Serena and get her ready."

"Yes, *Maggiore*." Marcella blew him a kiss. "I love you, *Maggiore*. If she won't marry you, I will."

He chuckled at his end. "Marcella, you're on."

Just as he had known once he had seen Pattie that he knew what he wanted to do, now he knew also that all along Serena had been wrong. She was not only wrong for him, she was wrong for herself, and he wasn't going to let her do this to either of them. As he gave his orders to Palmers he was aware of an iron resolve. And if he couldn't talk sense into her over the phone, he was going to Rome. He'd go AWOL if he had to, and talk his way out of it when he got back. But before he did anything that drastic, he spoke to the military operator an hour later and had her place the call to Rome. He had already arranged with Palmers for the phone to be pulled into the guest room, and when it rang, first Palmers answered, then Marcella, then he could hear sounds of movement, of shuffling noises, muted voices, a door closing, and then in barely more than a whisper he heard her thready little voice.

"Brad? What is this? What happened? They carried me out of my room."

"Good. That's what I told them to do. Now I want you to listen to me, Serena. And I'm not going to listen to you anymore. I love you. I want you to marry me. What you've done is killing us both. You're willing yourself to die, and I feel as though I died when I left Rome. This is crazy . . .

crazy, do you hear me? I love you. Now, for chrissake, woman, will you come to your senses and come to Paris to get married or do I have to come back there and drag you out?''

She laughed softly in answer and then there was a silence, as he could almost see her weigh her thoughts. What he could not see in the silence was Serena lying back against her pillows, with tears streaming from her eyes, her hands trembling as she held the phone, fighting herself to keep from saying what she wanted, and then suddenly in a great burst of effort, she spoke up. ''Yes!'' It was still only a whisper and he wasn't sure he'd heard her.

''What did you say?'' He held his breath.

''I said I'd marry you, Major.''

''Damn right!'' He tried to sound arrogant as he said it, but his hands were trembling harder than hers, and there was a lump in his throat so large, he could barely talk. ''I'll get the papers going right away, darling, and we'll get you here as soon as we can.'' My God! My God, he thought to himself, she said yes! She said it! He wanted to ask her if she meant it, but he didn't dare. He wasn't going to give her a chance to reconsider. Not now. ''I love you, darling, with all my heart.''

CHAPTER TWELVE

The morning that Serena left Rome she stood in the garden for a long time, under her willow tree, pulling her jacket tightly around her. The sun had just come up and it was still cold, as she looked out into the distance at the hills, and then back at the white marble facade that she was leaving now for the second time. She remembered the last time she had left here, with her grandmother, to go to Venice. That time the plans had been made in a hurry, and the atmosphere had been frightening and grim. She had just lost her parents, and as she had hurried down the marble steps on the way out, she had wondered if she would ever see her home again. Now she found herself wondering the same thing as she stood there, but the atmosphere surrounding her departure was different this time. She was going to be married, and this time she felt ready to leave. After all, the palazzo was no longer hers and never would be again, it was pointless to pretend that this was really still her home. Only the tiny quarters she shared with Marcella were really theirs, and even those rooms were only on loan as long as she continued to dust and sweep and wax floors. She sighed gently to herself as she looked up at what had been B.J.'s office, her old windows, and then her eyes drifted to the balcony outside her mother's bedroom, the room she had shared with him.

"*Addio* . . ." It was a whisper in the wind as she stood there. Not *arrivederci* or *arrivederla*, until I see you again, but *Addio* . . . good-bye.

The final moments as she left the house were frantic and painful, a last hug from a crying Marcella, as they both laughed through their tears. Marcella had turned down Serena's proposal that she accompany her to Paris. Rome was the kind old woman's home and she knew her princess was now well taken care of. Serena promised to write to her often, and knew that someone would read her the letters, and if B.J. could arrange it, she would call. And moments later she was being whisked down the driveway, then passing familiar sights on the way to Termini Station, from where she would leave Rome. She caught a quick glimpse of the Fontana di Trevi, the Spanish Steps, the Piazza Navona, and then she was there in the bustle of people hurrying to catch trains, carrying suitcases and packages, looking hopeful, or tired, or excited like Serena, who suddenly looked terribly young as she took her suitcase from the orderly who had brought her to the station, and then stuck out her hand to shake his before she boarded the train.

"Thank you. *Grazie mille*." She was beaming at him. The tears she had shed with Marcella were long gone, and all she could think of now was B.J. She felt not as though she were leaving, but as though she were going home.

"Good-bye . . ." she whispered softly to herself as the train picked up speed, and she saw the familiar outline of her city begin to fade in the distance. There were no tears in her eyes this time, all she could think of now was Paris and what awaited her there.

They arrived in Paris just after noon. As they approached the city she saw the Eiffel Tower in the distance, and assorted monuments she knew nothing about and then slowly the train drew into the Gare de Lyon, and as it rolled slowly the last feet into the station, Serena stood up and pressed her face against the window, peering into the distance to see if she could find B.J. waiting for the train. There were small clusters of people waiting, but nowhere could she see him, and she began to worry that she wouldn't find him at all. It was a big station and she felt suddenly very much alone. She picked up her suitcase as the train came to a full stop, and reached for the little basket Marcella had put her provisions in, and then slowly she filed out of the compartment with the others and stepped hesitantly off the train. Once again she looked around, her eyes combing the long platform and the unfamiliar faces as her heart pounded madly within her. She knew that he couldn't have forgotten her, and she knew where to find him if for some reason they missed each other at the station, but nonetheless now the full excitement of it was upon her. She was in Paris, and she had come to meet B.J., to get married. As she stood there she knew that a whole new life for her had begun.

"Think he forgot you?" A young GI she had talked to on the train the night before looked down at her with a friendly grin, and just as Serena shook her head she saw the young GI snap to attention and salute someone just behind her. And as though she sensed him near her, she wheeled to face B.J., her eyes wide, her face filled with excitement, her throat choked with a gurgle of laughter, and before she could say anything at all, Major Bradford Jarvis Fullerton had taken her in his arms and lifted her right off the ground. The young American disappeared behind them, with a shrug of his shoulders and a smile.

CHAPTER THIRTEEN

Paris had put on all her prettiest colors for Serena that morning, a bright blue sky overhead, crisp greens here and there as they drove past pine trees, the monuments were the same familiar streaky gray they had been for hundreds of years but here and there were facades of white marble and gold leaf, and rich patinas, and everywhere the people looked happy and excited in knit caps and red scarves, their faces pink with the chill air, their eyes bright. It was almost Christmas, and however much confusion there still was in Paris, it was the first Christmas in peacetime, the first time in six years that the Parisians could truly celebrate with joy.

Hand in hand, as they rode in B.J.'s staff car, they rolled down the broad boulevards and through narrow streets, they passed the Invalides and Notre-Dame, and the extraordinary spectacle of the Place Vendôme, and up the Champs-Élysées, around the Arc de Triomphe, into the maelstrom of traffic around L'Étoile, the circular intersection where 12 main streets all met at the Arc de Triomphe and everyone raced madly for the boulevard, where they would exit again, hopefully without crashing into another car. Having safely left the Arc behind them, as Serena, wide-eyed, gazed around her, they drove sedately onto the Avenue Hoche where B.J. was quartered, in an elegant "*hôtel particulier*," a town house that looked more like a mansion, which had belonged to the owner of one of France's better known vineyards before the war. In the anguish of the days just before the occupation of Paris, the vineyard owner had decided to join his sister in Geneva, and the house had been left in the care of his servants for the remainder of the war. Eventually the Germans had appropriated it during their stay there, but the officer who had lived there had been a civilized man and the house had suffered no damage during his tenure. And now the vineyard owner had fallen ill, and was not yet ready to return. In the meantime the Americans were renting it from him for a token fee for the year. And B.J. was happily ensconced there, living not quite as grandly as he had at the Palazzo Tibaldo, but very handsomely, with two kindly old French servants who attended to his needs.

As they approached it Serena saw that the house had a handsome garden, and there was a well-tended hedge surrounding it, with a tall, ornate wrought-iron grille that closed it off from the outside. B.J.'s driver stopped the car in front of the gate, and then hurried out to unlock it before driving inside. The car stopped just in front of the house and B.J. turned toward her.

"Well, my love, this is it."

"It looks lovely." She beamed at him, not caring one whit about the house, only caring about what she saw in his eyes. And her own eyes seemed to sparkle as he gently kissed her, and then stepped out to lead her inside.

They walked quickly up the steps to another heavy iron door, which was almost instantly opened by a small, round, bald-headed man with twinkling blue eyes and a bright smile, and beside him was an equally small, and jovial-looking woman.

"Monsieur et Madame Lavisse, my fiancée, the Principessa di San Tibaldo." Serena looked instantly embarrassed by the use of her title, as she held out her hand and they both executed stiff little bows.

"We are happy to meet you." They smiled at her warmly.

"And I am very happy to meet you." She glanced just behind them at what she could see of the house. "It looks lovely." They seemed pleased at the compliment, almost as though the mansion were their own, and they offered immediately to show her around.

"It is not, we regret to say, as it once was," Pierre apologized as he showed her the rear garden, "but we have done our best to keep it intact for Monsieur le Baron." Their employer hadn't seen his home in Paris in five years, and it was possible that now ill at seventy-five years of age he would never live to, but faithful to the end, they had kept it for him, and he paid them handsomely for all that they did. Originally he had trustingly left them with a large fund for all their expenses, and now each month a check was sent to them again. In return they had cared for the beautiful home with constant love and attention, hidden the most valuable objects and the best paintings in a secret room beneath the basement, which even the Germans had not found, and now during the reign of the Americans in Paris, they were still tending the house as though it were theirs.

Like the palazzo in Rome, the halls here were of marble, but here the marble was a soft peachy rose. The Louis XV benches, set at regular intervals down the hallway, were trimmed with gilt and upholstered in a pale peach velvet. There were two exquisite paintings by Turner, of rich Venetian sunsets, a large inlaid Louis XV chest with a pink marble slab on top, and several other small exquisite pieces scattered here and there. From the hall one could glimpse the garden, visible through tall French windows, which led out onto the little paved paths bordered by pretty flowers in spring. Now the garden had little to offer, and it was into the main salon that they turned, as Serena stared in awe. The room was done in deep red damask and white velvet, there were heavy Napoleonic pieces, upholstered chaise longues in bold raspberry and cream stripes, and two huge Chinese urns beside a priceless desk. There were huge portraits of members of the baron's family, and a fireplace, large enough for the major to stand in, in which there was now a blazing fire. It was a room designed to cause one to catch one's breath in admiration and wonder, and yet at the same time it was a room that beckoned one to come inside and sit down. Serena glanced around with delight at little Chinese objets d'art, Persian rugs, and a series of smaller portraits by Zorn, of the baron and his sisters as children, and B.J. led the way into a smaller wood-paneled room beyond. Here too there was a roaring fire waiting, but the fireplace was smaller, and three walls of the room were filled with beautifully bound books. Here and there were gaps on the shelves, which Pierre pointed to with dismay. This was the only loss inflicted by the Germans. The officer who had lived there had taken some of the books with him when he left. But Pierre counted himself fortunate that nothing else had been taken. The German had been a man of honour, and had not removed anything else.

On the same floor there was also a beautiful little oval breakfast room that looked out on the garden, and a formal dining room beyond it, with exquisite murals of a Chinese village on the wall. The paper had been preserved since the eighteenth century and had been designed in England originally for the Duke of Yorkshire, but one of the baron's ancestors had bought it directly from the artist and spirited it into France. The furniture had the typical clawed feet and scroll backs of Chippendale, and there was a splendid English side-board that was waxed to a rich shine. And as Serena passed admiringly through the rooms she was reminded of her grandmother's house in Venice, but this was less sumptuous and yet more so. The Italian palazzi she had lived in had all been larger and showier than this, and yet this house was filled with such exquisite pieces that, even though it was smaller, it seemed somehow more impressive. It was more like a museum and as she wandered through it she marveled to herself and sotto voce to B.J. that they had been able to preserve everything as it was throughout the war. It was also especially touching that the old butler had trusted B.J. enough to bring out some of the really good things.

"The old boy is quite something." B.J. indicated Pierre in a whisper as they followed the old butler upstairs. Marie-Rose, his wife, had disappeared to the kitchen to get Serena something to eat. "From what he tells me, he had most of this hidden in the basement. And I get the feeling that some of the best pieces are still there." But he couldn't have hidden the furniture, Serena knew, or not all of it, and it was remarkable that none of the beautiful pieces she saw around her had been damaged or taken over the years.

Upstairs there were four pretty bedrooms. A large handsome master bedroom done in a rich blue satin, with smooth, shining woods everywhere, a handsome chaise longue, a cozy love seat, a small desk, and another fireplace. There was a pretty view of the garden below and a little peek at the rest of Paris, and there was also a small study that B.J. occasionally used as an office, as well as a dressing room, which B.J. told her would be hers. Beyond it was a beautiful bedroom done in pinks, which had belonged to the late baroness, Pierre told them, and two other bedrooms now used for guests, one in a rich green with a handsome painting of the hunt over the fireplace, and a wealth of English prints of the same sport all over the walls. The bedroom beyond it was done in gray, with toile de Jouy on the walls, showing pastoral scenes and shepherds, all in gray on a muted beige fabric that had been applied to the walls. There were handsome brass candelabra, another beautiful desk, and several other fine antique pieces.

"And upstairs is the attic." Pierre grinned at them both with pleasure. He loved showing off the house.

"It's a wonderful house, Pierre," Serena said. "I don't know what to say. It's much more beautiful than anything I've seen in Italy, or the States. Don't you think, Brad?" She looked up at B.J. gently, her eyes filled with delight. Pierre thought it made the heart light just to watch them.

"I told you she'd love the house, didn't I?" B.J. nodded and looked at Pierre.

"Yes, sir. And now if you and Mademoiselle would like to come downstairs to the library, I'm sure that Marie-Rose has prepared something for Mademoiselle." His assumption had been correct, they discovered a moment later as they walked into the library and discovered a plate filled with sandwiches, another covered with small cakes and cookies, and a tall silver jug of hot chocolate waiting for them.

B.J. could hardly wait for Pierre to leave them, which he did a moment later. Brad put his arms around his love and kissed her hungrily the moment she sat down on the couch.

"God, I never thought I'd be alone with you. Oh, baby, how I've missed you."

"And I you." For just a flash of an instant the pain of those first days without him flashed into her eyes, and she clung to him for a moment. "I was so afraid, B.J. . . . that I'd never see you again, that . . ." She closed her eyes tightly for a moment and then kissed his neck. "I can't believe that I'm here, with you, in this beautiful house . . . it's all like a dream, and I'm afraid I'll wake up." She looked around her with a happy smile, and he kissed her again.

"If you do wake up, I'll be beside you. And not only that, by the time you wake up again, you'll be my wife."

"What?" She looked startled for a moment. "So soon?"

"Why? Did you want time to reconsider?" But the young lieutenant colonel didn't look concerned as he took one of the sandwiches Marie-Rose had made them and sat back against the couch. He had been promoted when he left Rome.

"Don't be silly. I just thought it would take a little longer to organize." She looked at him in sudden realization, and a mischievous smile began to dance in her eyes. "Does that mean we're getting married today?"

"More or less. Half married, to be more exact."

"Half married?" She looked vastly amused as she sipped her hot chocolate. "You mean I'm getting married and you're not?"

"Nope, we both are. Over here you have two weddings apparently. One at *l'hôtel de ville*, like city hall, just for the record, so to speak. And the next day you do a religious service in the church of your choice. You don't really have to do the second, but I sort of thought you'd want to." He looked suddenly shy as he looked at Serena. "We could have been married by the chaplain, but there's a pretty little church near here, and I thought that maybe . . . if you'd like . . ." He was blushing like a boy, and Serena took his face in her hands and kissed him.

"Do you know how much I love you, sir?"

"No, tell me."

"With all my heart and soul."

"That's all?" He attempted to look disappointed but did not succeed. "What about the rest?"

"You have a filthy mind. The rest isn't yours until after the wedding."

"What?" This time he looked genuinely shocked. "What do you mean?"

"Just what you think. I'll go to the altar as a virgin . . . relatively!" She grinned and he let out a whoop.

"Well, I'll be. . . . Which wedding anyway? The one today, or the one tomorrow morning?"

"Tomorrow morning of course. We have the same system

in Italy that they have here." She looked prim and virginal as she crossed her long shapely legs and looked at him over her cup of chocolate.

"Well, if you aren't the most outrageous tease." And then, with determination, he set down her cup and began to kiss her, one hand sliding slowly up her leg, and the other pressing her against him.

"B.J.! Stop that!"

It was at that moment that Pierre walked in, coughing discreetly and rather loudly closing the glass doors behind him, and Serena smoothed her skirt and looked daggers at B.J., who only grinned. "Yes, Pierre?"

"The car is here, sir."

B.J. looked gently at Serena then. He had barely had time to explain and it was already about to happen. "Darling, this is it. Round One. Do you want to go upstairs for a few minutes and wash your face or something before we go?"

"Now? Already?" She looked suddenly panicked. "But I just got off the train. I look awful."

"Not to me." He smiled at her and she knew he meant it, but she stood up hurriedly and looked at him for only an instant before hurrying to the door, where she turned and looked at him distractedly.

"I'll be right back. Don't leave without me." She heard him laughing as she disappeared into the pink marble hall, and then he heard her rushing up the stairs. To him, it seemed as though she were gone forever, but in fact she was only gone for ten minutes, and when she returned, she looked lovely, and almost like a bride. The week before in Rome, Marcella had made her a simple white wool dress with broad shoulders, a plain rounded collar, short sleeves, and a tiny waist above a softly flaring skirt. The fabric was beautiful and Marcella had bought it with her savings of the past months as a gift for Serena. She had asked her to wear it at her wedding. Now, walking slowly down the stairs, her golden hair swept into a smooth figure-eight knot, her eyes bright, and the beautifully made dress swirling gently around her, she looked like a principessa to the very tips of her toes. She stood very tall as she came toward B.J., and he saw that she was wearing a single strand of pearls and matching pearl earrings in her ears, then she turned her face up toward his and he kissed her lips.

"You look beautiful, Serena." She smiled at him, wishing for only a moment that she could have had a wedding like those she had gone to with her parents years ago. Fairy princesses sweeping grandly down marble staircases in gowns that looked like white clouds, trimmed with lace and trailing behind them yards of white satin. But those were other times, and suddenly here was her wedding day and she was sure that she felt no different than those other brides. It was extraordinary to realize that when she had woken up that morning, on the train, she hadn't known that this would be her wedding day. She had known that it would be soon, but not four hours after she arrived. She looked happily at B.J. and he reached for the brown coat she had been carrying over her arm, but suddenly Pierre stepped forward discreetly and shook his head.

"No, Colonel . . . no. . . ."

"No? What no? Is something wrong?"

"Yes." The old butler nodded resolutely, held up a finger like the leader of a symphony orchestra and instructed them both. "Please wait. Just a moment. I come right back." He had disappeared then into the pantry, and a distant clattering of heels told them that he had gone downstairs. B.J. shrugged, not sure of what was going on, and Serena's heart was beginning to pound with excitement. In half an hour she would be Mrs. Bradford Jarvis Fullerton III.

"I can't believe it." Suddenly she giggled and grinned up at him like a little girl.

"What, love?" He was glancing at his watch. He hoped that Pierre wouldn't make them too late.

But Serena seemed unconcerned. "I can't believe we're getting married. It's like a fairy tale. I mean, who would believe . . ." She rattled on as they waited and then she looked up at him again. "Do your parents know?" She had just thought of that again, but she assumed that he had already let them know.

"Sure." But his answer was a little too quick, and Serena looked at him in sudden suspicion.

"Brad?"

"Yeah?"

"Did you tell them?"

"I told you, yes."

Her voice was suddenly more subdued as she sat down on one of the peach velvet banquettes. "What did they say?"

"Congratulations." He grinned lopsidedly at her and she made a face.

"You're impossible. I'm serious. Were they angry?"

"Of course not. They were pleased. And much more importantly, Serena, I'm pleased. Isn't that enough?" He looked earnestly at her, and she stood up to kiss him again.

"Of course that's enough." And at precisely that moment Pierre returned, bustling with excitement and with Marie-Rose in tow, carrying a black satin bag draped over something on a hanger. As Marie-Rose stopped talking Pierre took the cumbersome object from her, held the hanger high and unzipped the black satin bag, revealing within a sumptuous dark brown fur coat, which as it emerged from the satin turned out to be sable. Serena stared at it in silence, confused as to why it was there.

"Mademoiselle . . . Principessa. . . ." Pierre beamed at her with an official air. "This sable coat belonged to the late baroness and we have kept it with the baron's other valuables, downstairs, in the locked room, for all of these years. We think it seems appropriate . . . we would like it if you would wear it today, when you marry the colonel, and tomorrow at the church." He smiled gently at her and extended the coat as Serena almost visibly trembled.

Marie-Rose added softly from behind him, "It would look lovely with your white dress."

"But it's so valuable . . . sable . . . good heavens . . . I couldn't. . . ." And then helplessly toward her fiancé, "Brad . . . I . . ."

But he had just exchanged a long look with Pierre, and the girl's shabby brown tweed coat lay in an ugly little heap on the banquette. She was a princess, after all, and she was about to become his wife, what harm could it do to wear it just twice?"

"Go on, sweetheart. Why don't you wear it? Pierre's right, and it's a beautiful coat." He smiled tenderly at his bride.

"But, Brad . . ." She was flushed crimson, partly in

embarrassment and partly in excitement. To save time B.J. simply took the coat gently from the old butler's hands and slipped it on her. It fit perfectly over her shoulders, the sleeves were full and the right length, the coat was cut in the same flare as her dress, and instead of a collar it had a huge generous hood, which he slipped onto her head now. She looked like a fairy princess in a Russian fairy tale as she stood there, and he had to bend to kiss her as Pierre and Marie-Rose looked on with delight.

"Good luck, mademoiselle." Pierre stepped forward to shake her hand, and without thinking, she leaned forward to kiss his cheek.

"Thank you." She could barely speak, she was so moved. How much they trusted her, and how quickly, after what they had all been through in the war, it was extraordinary to be able to make these gestures, of faith and love and generosity. In a sense it was their wedding gift to her, and she was more moved than she could have told them. Marie-Rose came toward her too, and the two women hugged, as Marie-Rose kissed Serena on both cheeks.

When they arrived at *l'hôtel de ville*, at the end of the Rue de Rivoli, hand in hand they ran up the steps, and Brad held the door open for her, as she passed beneath his arm in a swirl of the sable coat. She noticed a few heads turn as she and Brad walked solemnly down a gold and mirrored hallway, stopped at an office, and he extracted a sheaf of papers from his coat pocket and handed them to a young woman who seemed to be fully up to date on the entire proceeding. He apologized to her for being late, and a moment later the young woman beckoned from a door, and Serena and Brad followed her inside. Here they were met by a heavyset clerk of some kind who asked them to sign an enormous ledger. He looked over their papers again, checked their passports, and then stamped several documents with an official-looking seal. He came around his desk then, with a harrumph and some minor adjustment to his glasses, straightened his tie, and then raised his right hand, looking as though he were about to swear them in. He muttered several banal phrases in French, and then extended a worn-out old Bible to

130

Serena, asking her to repeat after him, the following phrases, which she did with her big green eyes wide, and her face pale, and her heart beating very fast, and then suddenly it was Brad's turn, and then seconds later it seemed to be over, and the heavyset man turned and walked back around his desk and sat down.

"You may go now. And congratulations." He looked most unimpressed, and Brad and Serena looked at each other with the first hint of realization.

"We're all through?" It was Brad who spoke.

"Yes." He looked at them as though they were very stupid. "You're married."

They moved as though in a dream, holding hands all the way home, where they found the champagne Marie-Rose and Pierre had left them, and Brad toasted his wife with a tender smile.

"Well, Mrs. Fullerton, what do you think? Time to go to bed?" Brad's eyes gleamed mischievously, and Serena shook her head with a look of amusement and regret.

"Already? On our wedding night? Shouldn't we stay up for hours, or go dancing or something?"

"Is that really what you want to do?" They smiled into each other's eyes and slowly she shook her head.

"I just want to be with you . . . for the rest of my life."

"And you will, my darling, you will." It was a promise of safety and protection, which she knew he would always keep. Then he scooped the long-legged beauty into his arms and proceeded out of the living room and up the broad staircase, carrying her toward the bedroom, where he laid her gently upon the bed.

"Brad . . ." she said in a tentative whisper, and her hands were as urgent as his as she felt her husband's body and ran her hands quickly under his shirt, and then more slowly undid the trousers as she felt the huge hungry bulge in his pants.

"I love you, darling."

"Oh, Brad."

"May I?" He pulled away from her for just an instant before undoing the white dress and she nodded slowly as he unzipped it and pulled it over her head. "Oh, darling, I want you so much." His hands and his lips found her at once, and a moment later she was naked and on the big bed and so was he, the lights were dim, and the fire was bright, and outside it was suddenly nightfall, on their wedding night, as her body rose hungrily toward his, and he took her gently and fully, reveling in the knowledge that now she was his wife.

CHAPTER FOURTEEN

The religious ceremony the next morning at the little English church further down the Avenue Hoche was brief and lovely. Serena wore the same white dress she had worn the day before, but Marie-Rose had miraculously gotten her a small bouquet of white roses, and she carried them in her hand as she walked up the aisle in the dark sable coat with the hood concealing her golden hair. She looked incredibly lovely as she turned to Brad and once again said her vows, this time at the picturesque little altar, the winter sun streaming in the windows, and the little old priest smiling down on the young couple, and then giving them his blessing and pronouncing them man and wife. Marie-Rose and Pierre served as best man and matron of honor, B.J. hadn't been in Paris long enough to make any close friends, and he wanted to keep the wedding private. Within the next few days, during the official Christmas festivities that would take place around Paris, he would introduce her to everyone as his wife.

"Well, Mrs. Fullerton, do you feel married now?" He smiled at her as he held her hand on the short drive home, as Pierre and Marie-Rose sat in the front seat with the driver.

"I sure do. Twice as much as yesterday." It was extraordinary to realize that less than twenty-four hours before she had arrived in Paris, and now she was B.J.'s wife. Suddenly she thought of Marcella and wished that she could tell her, and she promised herself to write to her by that night.

"Happy, darling?"

"Very much so. And you, Colonel?" She smiled gently as she leaned forward to kiss him softly on the mouth, her face almost hidden by the sumptuous sable hood, her eyes bright as emeralds in the winter light.

"Never happier. And one of these days we'll take a honeymoon, I promise." But he hadn't been in Paris long enough to ask for any significant time off. Not that Serena cared. All their time together was like a honeymoon. She had never been happier than she was with him. "Maybe we could drive out to the country for the day, on Christmas." He looked at her dreamily. He really didn't want to drive anywhere. He wanted to stay in bed with her for the next week, and make love. She giggled then as she looked at him, almost as though she knew what he was thinking. "What's so funny?"

"You are." She leaned forward to whisper in his ear. "I don't believe a word of what you're saying. I don't think you'll drive me to the country at all. It's all a plot to keep me locked in our room."

"How did you know?" he whispered back. "Who told you?"

"You did." She chuckled again, but then smoothed the sable coat over her legs and attempted to look at him seriously. "But I have to go out to do some Christmas shopping, you know, Brad."

"On our wedding day?" He looked shocked.

"Today or tomorrow. That's all that's left."

"But what'll I do?"

"You can come with me, for part of it anyway." She smiled happily and lowered her voice again. "I want to get something for them." She indicated the front seat with her eyes as Marie-Rose and Pierre chatted animatedly with the driver, and B.J. nodded agreement.

"That's a good idea." He looked at his watch then and frowned. "After lunch I want to call my parents." Serena nodded quietly. She was nervous about the idea, but she knew that she'd have to meet them sooner or later, and it would be easier if she had spoken to them on the phone once or twice. But each time she thought of them, she found herself remembering Pattie Atherton, and all that she had said that day, in her rage, on the balcony overlooking the garden . . . you and some goddamn little Italian maid . . . your Italian whore. . . . Serena almost winced as she heard her again in her head, and Brad reached out and took her hand in his. "You don't have to worry about them, Serena. They're going to love you. And much more importantly, I love you. And then"—he smiled to himself as he thought of his family—"there are my two brothers. You're going to love them too. Especially Teddy."

"The youngest one?" She looked happily into her husband's face, trying to forget Pattie's words again. Perhaps his brothers would like her, after all.

"Yes, Teddy is the youngest. Greg is the one in between." His face clouded for a moment, "Greg is . . . well, he's different. He's quieter than the rest of us. He's . . . I don't know, maybe he's more like my father. He sort of goes his own way, and he's odd, you can influence him more easily than you can me or Teddy. We're both more stubborn than he is, and yet when he really gets something in his head that he cares about a great deal, he's like a bloody mule." He looked at her with amusement. "But Teddy . . . he's the family genius, the imp, the elf. He's more decent than any of us put together, and more creative. Teddy has"—he thought for a long moment—"soul . . . and humor . . . and wisdom . . . and looks."

"Wait, maybe I got the wrong brother."

B.J. looked at her in total seriousness. "You might have. And he's certainly more your age than I am, Serena." And then his mood lightened quickly. "But I'm the one you got, kiddo, so you're stuck with me." But it was evident, as it always was when he spoke of his youngest brother, that there was a bond of tenderness between them that reached to his very soul. "You know, after he graduates from Princeton next June he says he's going to med school, and dammit, I bet he will too, and he'll be a terrific doctor." He looked at her again with a broad grin and she leaned over and kissed him.

Back at the house on the Avenue Hoche, they opened another bottle of champagne and drank it with Pierre and

Marie-Rose, and then the elderly couple went downstairs to prepare lunch, and B.J. and Serena went upstairs to celebrate their honeymoon again, and when Marie-Rose buzzed them an hour later, they hated to get dressed and go downstairs.

Eventually Serena was dressed in a gray skirt and gray sweater, once again wearing her single strand of pearls. As he emerged from the bathroom Brad noticed that it was a very sober outfit.

"What happened to the white dress?" He had liked that, it made her waist look so tiny, and she looked lovely in white. The gray looked strangely sad for such a happy day. But it was the best skirt she owned, and the sweater was cashmere, a rarity for her too. She owned almost no clothes, except what she had brought from the convent, and what she had worked in at the palazzo. She knew she would have to buy more now that she was his wife, and she was planning to spend some of what was left of her money on that too. She didn't want to disgrace him with the ugly hand-me-downs that were mostly all that she had.

"Don't worry. I'll buy some new things." She looked embarrassed then. "Is this . . . is it very ugly?" She glanced in the mirror and realized how drab it seemed. It was a far cry from the white dress, and the borrowed sable, but this was all she had. She blushed faintly and he went to her and took her in his arms again.

"I'd love you wrapped in a blanket, you big silly. Nothing you ever wear looks ugly. You just looked pretty in the white . . . and the sable. Why don't we take you shopping this afternoon, and get you some pretty new things? My Christmas present to you."

Before she could protest, as he knew she would, he put an arm around her shoulders, and went downstairs with her, where they sat down to a sumptuous lunch. Marie-Rose had outdone herself on their behalf. There was a delicately seasoned homemade cream of vegetable soup, a tasty pâté with freshly baked bread, wonderful little roast squabs, and a puree of artichoke hearts, which B.J. especially loved. There was salad, and Brie and pears, which Marie-Rose had been hoarding for days in honor of this luncheon, and for dessert she had made a chocolate soufflé with vanilla sauce and whipped cream.

"Good God, I don't think I'll ever be able to move again." Serena stared at him almost in amazement. "I've never eaten that much in my life."

"God, it was wonderful." B.J. looked glazed as he looked up at Pierre, who offered him now a small brandy and a cigar. B.J. refused them both with regret.

And after Pierre had left them, B.J. stood up and stretched in the warm winter sunshine streaming through the long French windows, and then he went to Serena and rubbed her shoulders gently with his strong hands, as she dropped her head back and looked up at him. "Hello, my love. Are you as happy as I am?"

"Much more so. And fatter. God, after that lunch, I may never fit into my uniforms again."

"It's a good thing I wasn't wearing Marcella's white dress, I would have exploded and blown the dress to smithereens." He laughed at the vision and pulled her chair back for her, as she stood up slowly and stretched too. "I don't even feel like shopping, but I really have to."

"First"—he glanced at his watch—"we have to call my parents. It may take a while to get through, but it's important. I want to introduce them to my wife." He kissed her then and walked her into the library where he picked up the phone on the desk, dialed the operator, and began, in halting French, to give her the number he wanted in New York.

"Do you want me to do that for you?" She whispered it to him and he whispered back.

"It makes me feel competent to make myself understood in French." But he knew that his French was barely tolerable and Serena's was fluent, but nonetheless he managed, and a moment later, having given the operator all the information, he hung up.

Pierre had started a fire in the fireplace before lunch and now it was blazing along at a good clip. B.J. went to sit in front of it and beckoned to Serena, who came to sit beside him and hold his hand. She looked worried though as she came to him, and he gently stroked her hair, as though

136

hoping that that would calm her worries.

"Do you think they'll be very angry, Brad?"

"No. Surprised maybe." He was staring into the fire as he spoke. At that precise moment he was thinking of his mother.

"But you said you told them we were going to get married."

"I know I did." He turned to her then, with a quiet look in his eyes, as though he were not afraid and were very sure of what he was doing. It was in moments like that that she became aware of his strength again, and his self-confidence. Brad always seemed perfectly sure about what he was doing. It was a quality that had brought him far in his work, and that had served him well all his life. When he had gone to Princeton, he had been the captain of the football team, and he had managed that with the same quiet assurance. It had made everyone respect his word instantly, both on the team and off, and despite her worries, it made Serena feel calmer now. Just the tone of his voice was reassuring, even if she didn't quite understand what he just said. "I know I told you that I told them, Serena. But I didn't. There was no reason to. It was my decision, our decision. I wanted to wait until we were married."

"But why?" She was shocked that he had felt the need to lie to her the day before.

He sighed deeply and looked into the fire, and then back at her. "Because my mother is a very strong woman, Serena. She likes to have her way, and sometimes she thinks she knows what's best for us. But she doesn't always. If she could, she'd like to make our choices for us. I've never let her. My father always has. And she's made some damn good choices for him. But not for me, Serena, not for me." He looked as though he were thinking back over his whole life as he spoke to her. "I thought that maybe if I called her first, she'd try to put her two cents in, want to fly over and meet you first, God knows what. She'd probably tell me I was robbing the cradle. Above all, I didn't want to get you upset. You've been through enough, and I want to make things easy for you, Serena, not harder. There was no point having her come over here to look you over, tell me you

137

were terrific, and scare you to death in the bargain. So I thought we'd get our life all squared away by ourselves, and then tell her when it was a fait accompli.'' He waited a moment and then, ''Do you forgive me?''

''I suppose so.'' He made sense, but the worry had not quite left her eyes. ''But what if that makes her so angry, she dislikes me?''

''She couldn't, darling. How could she dislike you? She'd have to be crazy. And my mother is a lot of things, but not that.'' And then, as though on cue, the phone rang, and it was the French operator, announcing to him that she had his transatlantic call for him. At the other end was a nasal-sounding operator in New York who was just about to get his call on the line. He heard the phone ring three times, and then it was answered by B.J.'s youngest brother. He accepted the call and roared into the phone over the static.

''How the hell are you, old boy? And Christ, how is Paris? I sure wish I were there!''

''Never mind that. How's school?''

''Same as ever. Dull as hell. But I'm almost out, thank God, and I got accepted at Stanford Med School for September.'' He sounded like an excited schoolboy and B.J. grinned.

''That's terrific, kid. Hey, listen, is Mom around?'' He seldom asked for his father. His father had been the invisible man for thirty years. In some ways their father had a lot in common with their middle brother. Mr. Fullerton was somewhat more enterprising than Greg, after all for one term he had been in the Senate, but he had coasted more on family prestige, good connections, and lots of campaign money than on any personal charisma of his own. In truth, it was Margaret Fullerton who should have been in politics. B.J. used to tease her that she should have been the first woman president. She would have too, if she could have got away with it. But she had settled for pushing her husband, being in the circles that such people as Eleanor Roosevelt were in.

''Yeah, she's here. You okay, Brad?''

''Just great. All of you? Greg? Dad?''

''Greg got his discharge a few weeks ago.'' But it was no great shakes, as they all knew. He had served out the entire war at a desk in Fort Dix, New Jersey, spending weekends at home, or in Southampton in the summer. He had felt desperately guilty about it, as he had finally told his younger brother. But because B.J. had been so quick to get himself sent overseas and had several times had assignments in dangerous zones, their parents had been able to pull strings so that only one of their children was jeopardized. Greg had been safe in New Jersey at all times. And Teddy of course had been in college since 1941, with every intention of joining the army when he got out.

"What's he going to do now?"

"Why don't you ask him?" Teddy said with faint hesitation, and then, "Dad's going to take him into the law firm. What about you, Brad? Aren't you ever coming home?"

"Eventually. Nobody's said anything to me about it yet over here."

"Are you ready to come home yet?" There was an odd questioning tone in Teddy's voice and Brad suddenly wondered what he knew.

"Maybe not. It's damn nice over here. Ted. Listen, if I'm still here next spring when you graduate, why don't you come out to see us—me . . ." he corrected quickly with a rapid glance at Serena across the desk.

"You think you'll still be there then?" Teddy sounded disappointed. "Hell, aren't you ever going to muster out, B.J.?"

There was a moment's pause. "I don't think so, Ted. I like the army. I never thought I would. But I think this is just right for me. And . . ." He looked at Serena with tenderness in his eyes. He wanted to tell Teddy about her, but he felt he ought to tell his mother first. "Listen, I'll talk to you later. Go get Mother, Ted. And listen," B.J. said as an afterthought, "don't say anything to them, Ted. Mom's going to have a fit when I tell her I'm staying in the army."

"Brad . . ." There was that strange tone in his voice again. "I think she knows." It was as though he were warning his older brother of something.

"Anything wrong?" Brad was suddenly tense.

"No." He'd find out soon enough. "I'll go get Mom."

As it so happened, she was in the dining room having breakfast with Greg and Pattie Atherton, who had come for a special pre-Christmas breakfast with them all. When Ted went to the doorway and beckoned his mother urgently, she came quickly, with a worried frown.

"Is something wrong, Ted?"

"No, Mom, it's Brad on the phone. He called us to wish us a Merry Christmas." And as he said it he hoped that his mother would allow it to remain merry. She took the phone from her youngest son, smoothing a hand over her snowy white hair, and sat down quickly in her desk chair. She was dressed elegantly in a black Dior suit that did extremely well by her still-streamlined youthful figure. She was a woman of fifty-eight, but she could easily have concealed ten or twelve of those years, had she chosen to, which she never did. She had B.J.'s same slate-gray eyes, and the features were much the same too, but whereas on B.J. everything looked easy-going and gentle, on his mother everything looked eternally tense. One always had the feeling that she was listening for something, some superhuman, extraterrestrial whine that was audible only to her. There was always about her a kind of electric tension, and she seemed ever about to pounce, which she did frequently, mostly on her husband, and often on her sons. She was a woman one spoke to carefully and handled with the utmost caution, so as not to set her off, or "get her started," as her family called it. "Don't get your mother started, boys," her husband had always implored his sons. And in order not to himself, he hardly ever spoke, but he nodded constant agreement. When they were younger, the boys used to imitate him a lot, B.J. having perfected his father's constant noncommittal, almost mechanical "Ummmmmm. . . ."

"Hi, Mom. How's everything in New York?"

"Interesting. Very interesting. Eleanor was here for lunch yesterday." He knew she referred to Mrs. Roosevelt. "The political news these days is certainly ever changing. It's a hard time for her, for all of us really. There are a lot of readjustments going on after the war. But never mind all that, Brad darling. More to the point, how are *you*?" She said it with an emphasis that ten years before would have

140

made him extremely nervous. But he had got over being intimidated by his mother when he gave up his job in Washington and moved to Pittsburgh to suit himself. It had been a move of which she had violently disapproved, and for the first time in his life he had decided that that wasn't going to change anything for him. "Are you all right, darling? Healthy? Happy? Coming home?"

"Yes to the first three, no to the fourth question, I'm afraid. At least they don't appear to be shipping me Stateside for the moment. But I'm fine, everything's just fine." He saw Serena's expectant eyes upon him, and for the first time in a long time he realized that he was afraid of his mother. But this time he had to stand up to her, not only for himself, but for Serena. It gave him added courage as he plunged in. "I've got some good news for you."

"Another promotion, Brad?" She sounded pleased. As much as she disliked having him in the army, as long as he insisted on being in it, his frequent promotions pacified her and pleased her with their prestige.

"Not exactly, Mom. Better than that in fact." He swallowed hard, realizing suddenly what he had done. Serena was right. He should have called her first. Christ, imagine telling her like this when it was all over. He could feel a thin veil of sweat break out along his hairline and prayed that Serena wouldn't see. "I just got married." He wanted to close his eyes and gulp air, but he couldn't, not with those expectant, trusting green eyes on him. Instead he smiled at Serena and gestured that everything was going fine.

"You *what*? You're joking of course." There was a silence, but before that there had been a tight edge in her voice. He could imagine the tenseness in her face by listening to the tone of her voice. He could picture the elegant almost bony hand with the heavy diamond rings clutching the phone. "What's this all about?"

"It's about a wonderful young lady whom I met in Rome. We were married this morning, Mother, in the English church here."

There was an endless pause while he waited. At her end her face was suddenly grim, her eyes the color of the Atlantic before a hurricane. "Is there some adequate reason why you've kept this a secret, Brad?''

"No. I just wanted it to be a surprise."

His mother's voice was glacial. "I assume she's pregnant."

Slowly Brad was beginning to burn. Nothing ever changed. No matter how old they got, she still treated them the same way. Like naughty, demented little puppets. It was what had driven him away years before. He always kind of forgot that part of it and he was realizing that things were no different now.

"No, you're mistaken." For Serena's sake he went on as though all were well. "Her name is Serena, and she's blond and very beautiful." He felt faintly crazy as he said it all, and all he wanted was to get off the phone. "And we're very happy."

"How enchanting." His mother's words shot into the phone like bullets. "Do you expect me to applaud? Is it possible that this is the girl Pattie told me about in November?" His mother's tone would have cracked marble. "I believe she mentioned that the girl was a maid in the place where you lived. Or is this someone else?" By what right do you ask, damn you, he wanted to shout at her, but he controlled himself as best he could and attempted not to fly into a rage.

"I don't think that's something I want to discuss with you now. I think when Pattie was in Rome she saw things with jaundiced eyes—"

"Why?" His mother cut him off. "Because she broke off the engagement?"

"Is that what she told you?"

"Isn't that what happened?"

"Not exactly. I told her that things had changed and I wanted to call off the engagement."

"Not by the account I heard." Margaret Fullerton did not sound as though she believed her son. "Pattie said that you were having an affair with your scrub girl, and when she caught you at it, she gave back the ring and came home."

"It's a nice tight little story, Mother. The only trouble is that it's not true. The only thing true about it"—he realized that it made sense to admit at least that much to his mother,

142

in case she heard something later on—"is that Serena was working at the palazzo. Her parents owned it before the war. But her father was among the aristocracy against Mussolini, and both of her parents were killed early on in the war. It's a long story and I won't give you all the details now. She's a principessa by birth and spent the war at a convent in the States, and when she returned to Italy last summer, she found that the rest of her family had died, she had no one and nothing left, so she went back to the palazzo to see it, and was taken in by one of the maids. She's had a grim time of it, Mother." He smiled at Serena. "But that's all over now."

"How charming. A little match girl. A war bride." Her tone was venomous. "My dear boy, do you have any idea how many nobodies are wandering around Europe now pretending that they were once princes and counts and dukes? My God, they're even doing it over here. There's a waiter in your father's club who claims that he's a Russian prince. Perhaps," his mother suggested sweetly, "you'd like to introduce your bride to him. I'm sure he'd be a much more suitable companion for her than you are."

"That's a rotten thing to say." His eyes flayed. "I called to tell you the news. That's all. I think we've said enough for now." Out of the corner of his eyes he could see Serena's eyes fill with tears. She knew what was happening and it tore at his heart. He wanted to make everything right for his wife and he didn't give a damn what his mother said. "Good-bye, Mother. I'll speak to you again soon."

His mother offered no congratulations. "Before you go, you might like to know that your brother Gregory just got engaged."

"Really? To whom?" But he didn't really care now. He was too incensed about his mother's behavior and her reaction to the news of his marriage to Serena. Only one thing struck him odd before she told him, and that was that Ted hadn't said a word about Greg.

"He got engaged to Pattie." She said it with pleasure, almost with glee.

"Atherton?" B.J. was stunned.

"Yes, Pattie Atherton. I didn't write to you because I

wasn't sure, and I didn't want to cause you unnecessary pain." Bullshit. She wanted to maximize the shock. B.J. knew his mother better than that. "She began seeing him almost as soon as she got back from Rome."

"That's terrific." He marveled at what a manipulative scheming little bitch Pattie was. At least she had chosen the right brother this time. Greg would do everything she wanted him to. She had made the right choice for herself. But B.J. found himself wondering if she would destroy his brother. He hoped not, but he was almost sure that she would. He was dying to ask Ted what he thought of it, but he knew that now he wouldn't be able to speak to him again. "When are they getting married, Mother?"

"In June. Just before he turns thirty." How touching. And Pattie would be twenty-four, and the perfect bride in a white lace dress. Suddenly the mental picture of it made him almost ill. His brother devoured by that bitch. "I'm sure it would be painful for you, Brad. But I think you should be here."

"Of course. I wouldn't miss it." He felt more like himself now, but he was still awed by his mother's skill.

"And you can leave the little war bride at home."

"That's not even a remote possibility, Mother. We look forward to seeing you all then, and for now Merry Christmas. I won't bother to speak to Greg now, but give him my best." He didn't give a damn about speaking to Greg. They had never been close and they were less so now, and he had had enough of his mother and her vicious attitude about Serena. He wanted to get off the phone at all costs. He was only sorry that Serena was in the room while he spoke to his mother. He truly wished that he could tell her all that he was thinking. But he would have to do that by letter, and without delay.

"I think he's still in the dining room with Pattie. We were just finishing breakfast when you called. Pattie came by early today, they're going to Tiffany's first thing this morning to pick out the ring."

"Marvelous."

"It could have been you, Brad."

"I'm glad it's not." There was a pregnant silence.

144

"I wish it were. Instead of what you've just done."

"You won't feel that way when you meet Serena."

There was an odd silence. "I don't normally socialize with maids."

Brad wanted to explode at her reaction, but knew he could not, for Serena's sake.

"You're a fool, Brad." She rushed on into his silence. "You ought to be ashamed. A man with your connections and your chances, and look what you've just done with your life. It makes me want to weep for what you're throwing away. Do you think you'll ever make it in politics now, with that kind of woman as your wife? For all you know she's a common prostitute calling herself a princess. Pattie said she looked like a tramp."

"I'll let you judge for yourself. She's ten times the lady Pattie is. That little slut has been giving it away free for years!" He was beginning to lose his cool at last.

"How dare you speak of your brother's fiancée in those disgusting terms."

"Then don't you ever"—his voice flew into the phone like a torpedo, and at her end Margaret Fullerton was taken aback—"don't you ever speak about my wife that way again. Is that clear? She's my wife now. Whatever you think, you'd damn well better keep it to yourself from now on. She's mine. That's all. That's all you need to know. And I expect everyone in this family, including that little bitch Pattie, to treat her with respect. You bloody well ought to love her, all of you, because she's a damn sight better than any of you, but whether you love her or not, you'd better be polite to her, and to me when you speak about her, or you'll never see me again."

"I won't tolerate your threats, Bradford." Her voice was like granite.

"I won't tolerate yours. Merry Christmas, Mother." And with that, he quietly hung up the phone. When he turned to look sorrowfully at Serena, he saw that she was sitting beside the fire, her face in her hands, her shoulders shaking, and when he went to her and forced her to look up, he saw that her face was drenched with tears.

"Oh, darling, I'm so sorry you heard all that."

"She hates me . . . she hates me . . . we broke her heart."

"Serena." He pulled her into his arms and held her against him. "She has no heart, my darling. She hasn't for years. It's something everyone in the family knows, and I should have told you. My mother has a mind like a whip, and a heart of stone. She is tougher than most men I know, and all she wants is to make everyone do what she wants them to do. She has settled for pushing my father around for thirty-six years, and she's tried for years to push me around too. She has better luck with my brother Greg, and I'm not sure yet how Teddy is going to survive all this. But what she doesn't like about you is that you weren't her idea—she didn't find you, she didn't try to push me into marrying you. All she hates about you is that she has no control. I chose for myself, just like when I joined the army. That is what she can't accept. It has nothing at all to do with you. It has to do with a battle between me and her that has gone on for years."

"But Pattie . . . she told her I was the maid at the palazzo . . . what must your mother think?" Serena was still sobbing in his arms.

"Serena, my love, first of all don't ever forget who you really are. And anyway, do you think it matters to me that you were a maid or whatever you've been. The only thing that I care about is that I'm sorry you had to go through all the turmoil, and trauma, and misery and hard work. But I can tell you one thing, from now on, I'm going to make your life happy, and try to make up to you for all the rest." He kissed her damp eyes and stroked her hair gently.

"Do you think she will ever forgive us?"

"Of course she will. It's not that big a deal. She was just surprised, that's all. And she was hurt that we hadn't included her earlier." It was a gentling of the realities of the situation, but he hoped that it would do for now.

Serena shook her head sadly. "She will always hate me. And she will always think of me as the Italian maid."

B.J. laughed at that. "No, she won't, silly. I promise."

"How can you be sure?"

"I know my mother. And she knows me. She knows that

she can't run me. It's a simple fact of life. So she'll eventually accept what happened, and when she finally sees you, she'll be bowled over, just as I was, and she'll see what you are—beautiful, and gentle and lovely, intelligent, and the woman I love. They're all going to love you, Serena, even my damn mother. I promise . . . you'll see. . . ."

"But all that Pattie said—"

"Sour grapes, my love. Even my mother will recognize .that when she sees you together."

"Together?" Serena looked shocked, and B.J. looked rueful.

"She's marrying my brother Greg in June. That's an interesting development, isn't it?"

. Serena watched him closely and dried her eyes. "She's marrying your brother?" He nodded. "Do you mind?"

"Not in the way you mean. What I mind is that I think she's the worst thing that could happen to my brother. Or maybe not, maybe he needs someone to run his life. My mother can't do it forever."

"Is he really that weak?"

B.J. nodded slowly. "I hate to admit it, but he is, the poor devil. He's just like my father."

"Your father's weak too?" She looked shocked to hear him tearing his family apart so candidly. He had never done this with her before.

"Yes, my father is weak too. And my mother has more balls than an entire football team put together. I don't think it's made her happy, and at various times it has driven all of us nuts, but there it is. And all that matters, my darling, is that I love you. Now, I have done my duty, I have told my family about our marriage, I'm sorry that they didn't jump up and down with joy, but once they meet you they will, so let's not worry about that, and now let's go Christmas shopping. Is that a deal?" She looked up at him with damp eyes, and attempted a smile.

"I love you." But she almost instantly began to cry again. "I'm so sorry."

"Why? For crying all day on our wedding day, for that you should be sorry. Very sorry, especially after that terrific lunch." He handed her his handkerchief again and she blew her nose.

"No, I'm sorry because I've made your family so unhappy."

"You haven't, I promise you. You have given my mother something to think about, which won't do her any harm, and the rest of the family will probably think it's great news." And at that moment, before he could continue, the phone rang, and it was his brother Teddy, calling from the States. "What's up?" B.J. looked vaguely worried and a moment later Serena saw him break into a broad smile. "She's sensational, you're going to love her. . . . Okay . . . okay . . . I'll let you talk to her yourself." And then without further warning, he handed the phone to Serena with only the brief introduction, "My brother Ted."

"Hello, Serena, this is Teddy. I'm Brad's youngest brother, and I just wanted to congratulate you myself. I wanted you to know that I'm happy for you and Brad. And I'm sure that if my brother loves you, you must be one terrific lady, and I can't wait to meet you."

Tears filled her eyes as she murmured, "Thank you so much." She blushed and stammered then as she reached for her husband's hand. "I hope . . . so much . . . that I will not make the family unhappy. . . ." Brad could hear the terror in her voice. His poor little princess, afraid of his twenty-two-year-old brother. Poor thing, she had really been through the wringer. But never again. He would keep his mother in check when they went to New York for Greg's wedding, if they went at all.

Ted was quick to reassure her. "The only way you could make us unhappy is if you make Brad unhappy, and I can't imagine you doing that."

"Oh, no!" She sounded shocked.

"Good. Then just know how happy I am for you."

Her eyes filled with tears again and she said good-bye to her new brother and handed the phone back to Brad.

"Isn't she terrific?" Brad was beaming at her as he spoke to his brother.

Teddy sounded more serious again. "I just hope you're not as nuts as Mom said. Is she really a nice girl, Brad?"

"The best."

"You love each other?"

"Yes, we do."

"Then, I wish you the best, Brad. I wish I were there to tell you myself. I wish I'd been there to share it with you." And Brad knew that Teddy meant it.

"So do I. But we'll make up for it when we get together. What's this insanity about Greg, by the way?"

"You heard it. I guess Pattie figured that if she couldn't have you she'd have him. I'm just lucky she didn't decide to grab me, I guess."

"Luckier than you know, kid."

"I suspect as much. I hope old Greg holds up."

"So do I." They both sounded worried as they thought about Greg's impending marriage.

"Anyway, I just wanted to congratulate you both and wish you luck and tell you that I love you."

"You're a great kid, Teddy. And one hell of a fine brother. I love you." His voice was hoarse as he said the words.

"My love to you both," Ted said gently, and then said good-bye.

Brad turned to Serena with a look of great tenderness after he'd hung up. "I've got some baby brother."

"He sounds wonderful."

"He is. I can't wait for you to meet him." They held each other close then for a long moment, in the study, as Brad thought of his family so far away, and in spite of the joy of the special day he was sharing with Serena, he was suddenly homesick for the States, and his family, especially his brother Ted. "Do you want to go out now?" He looked down at his wife.

"What would you like, Brad?" She recognized that it had been an emotional hour for them both, and she felt spent, but she still wanted to buy him a gift.

But he looked at her warmly and took her hand. "I'd like to take you out and buy you everything in sight, Serena Fullerton, that's what I'd like to do." She grinned at the use of her new name. "Come on, let's go shopping."

"Are you sure?" She smiled at the anxious look in his eyes.

"Very sure. Go get your ugly coat." She had already given the sable back to Marie-Rose and Pierre. "I'm going to buy you a new one."

"Not a sable, I hope."

"Hardly." But as it turned out, he bought her a luscious blond lynx, and boxes upon boxes of new clothes. When they staggered home at six o'clock, he had bought her at least a dozen new dresses, two suits, half a dozen hats, the lynx coat, gold earrings, a black wool coat as well, shoes, handbags, scarves, underwear, nightgowns. She was totally overwhelmed by the avalanche of expensive goodies he bought her, and her own gift to him seemed so small in comparison, but it had taken almost the last of her savings. She had bought him a gold cigarette case and lighter, and later, after she gave it to him, she would have his name engraved, and the date. She planned to give it to him the following evening, on Christmas Eve.

The driver helped them deposit all their loot in the front hallway and slowly Serena and Brad walked upstairs, arm in arm, as he looked down at her with pleasure again and she turned her face up to his with a look of amazement. Who was this man she had married? Was it possible that he had such means? She had not seen such riches since before the war. It made her wonder if his family would think she had married him for his money.

"Something wrong, Mrs. Fullerton?" He was anxious that she be cushioned from the harshness of his mother's cruelty.

"No, I was just thinking how lucky I am to have you."

"Funny, I was thinking the same thing about you." He stopped her then at the top of the stairs, and picked her up gently, enveloped in her new lynx, which she had insisted on wearing out of the store, her blond hair blending with it, almost the same color, and he carried her over the threshold of their bedroom.

"What are you doing?" She said it sleepily against his shoulder. It had been a long day, filled with emotions and excitement. Their wedding, his mother, their enormous wedding lunch, all the shopping . . . it was no wonder that she was exhausted.

"I'm carrying you over the threshold. It's an American custom, to celebrate the fact that we're newly married. I can also think of other ways to celebrate the same fact." She giggled at him and he set her down on the bed and kissed her, and moments later the coat was shed, along with the rest of her clothes and they made love until they were both spent, and fell asleep peacefully in each other's arms. Marie-Rose sent up their dinner that night, on a tray on a dumb-waiter as Brad had suggested, but they never woke up after their lovemaking, or went to get the sandwiches and cocoa she had made them. They slept on like two children in each other's arms.

CHAPTER FIFTEEN

Two days later Serena awoke before her husband, and scampered quickly out of bed to find the two boxes she had concealed in her dressing room the night before. And as he looked at her, sleepy eyed and happy, stretching lazily as she came toward him, he held out both arms.

"Come to me, my lovely wife." She did so gladly, and held him for a moment, the presents still clutched in her hand.

"Merry Christmas, my darling."

"Is it Christmas?" He feigned surprise and a lapse of memory as he pulled her back into bed beside him, her warm flesh smooth against his own. "Isn't it tomorrow?"

"Oh, shut up, you know it isn't!" She was giggling at him, remembering all of the wonderful gifts he had bought her. "Here, these are for you."

This time his surprise was genuine. "When did you do that, Serena?" He had been so intent on his shopping for her that he hadn't noticed when she had purchased them at Cartier, while he bought her earrings. "You are a sneaky one, aren't you?"

"For a good cause. Go on, open them."

He kissed her first, and then slowly unpacked the first present with an enervating lack of speed. He was teasing both

her and himself and she laughed at him, until at last the
wrapping fell away and the smooth silky beauty of the gold
cigarette case lay in his hand.

"Serena! Baby, how could you?" He was shocked at the
fortune she must have spent. He hadn't even known if she
had that kind of money in her reserves. And he knew all too
well that if she did he was now holding the last of it in his
hand. But a gold cigarette case had always been, in Europe,
a standard wedding gift for a young man, and an important
one. It was the same wedding gift she would have bought
him if her parents had been alive. The difference would have
been, perhaps, sapphire initials, or an elaborate message
engraved inside. And there might have been an additional
gift of sapphire cuff links, or studs for his dinner jacket in
black onyx with handsome diamonds sparkling inside. But
Serena's gift of the simple gold case was both handsome and
impressive and B.J. was touched beyond words as he leaned
over to kiss his bride. "Darling, you're crazy!"

"About you." She giggled happily and handed him the
other gift, which he opened with equal delight.

"Good God, Serena, you spoiled me!" For a fraction of
an instant the huge green eyes looked sad.

"I wish I could have spoiled you more. If—" But he took
her in his arms before she went on.

"I wouldn't be happier than I am now. I couldn't be.
You're the best present I've ever had." And as he said it he
disengaged himself slowly from her arms and hopped out of
bed to go to his own chest of drawers in a far corner, as she
watched him with interest.

"What are you doing?"

"Oh, I don't know. I thought maybe Santa Claus may
have left something for you." He looked over his naked
shoulder with a broad grin.

"Are you crazy? After all the presents you bought me
yesterday?"

But he was walking determinedly toward her, with a small
silver-wrapped package in his hand. It had a narrow silver
ribbon, and the box was intriguingly small as he extended it
to her. "For you, darling."

She shook her head with disapproval then. "I don't
deserve more presents."

152

"Yes, you deserve the best—you are the best. Got that?"

"Yes, sir." She gave him a mock salute and her eyes grew enormous as she began to unwrap the present. Even the wrapping looked expensive, and the small black suede case looked more so, and when she opened it to reveal the shining black lining and what lay nestled on it, she could only gasp. Her hand trembled and she looked almost frightened as she saw it. "Oh, Brad!"

"Do you like it?" He took it quickly out of the box for her and reached for her trembling hand to put it on her. It was a flawless pink diamond, in an oval shape, surrounded by smaller white diamonds on a narrow gold band. The entire ring was of exquisite proportions and the color and brilliance of the ring were truly remarkable on her narrow, elegant hand.

"Oh, my God!" She was almost speechless as she stared at it. Even the size was right. "Oh, Brad!" Tears rapidly filled her eyes and he smiled at her, pleased that she was so obviously delighted.

"You deserve dozens like that, Serena. The Germans didn't leave much of that in Paris. When we get back to the States, we're going to buy what we can. Lovely things for you, pretty clothes, furs, lots of jewelry, hats, all the things that you'll enjoy. You'll be a princess—my princess—always."

It seemed to Serena in the months that ensued that she merely passed her time all day wandering in the Bois de Boulogne, going to still-half-empty museums, looking aimlessly into shops, anxiously waiting for B.J. to come home at night. All she wanted was to see him, all that meant anything to her was her husband, and B.J. discovered in her a passion he had never even begun to suspect before. They spent hours together, lying side by side in their library, staring into the fire, talking and kissing and hugging and holding, and then racing each other upstairs like two kids. But they were far from being children once they got upstairs. Their lovemaking was expert and endless, as the winter drifted into the spring.

Brad was busy with his job, but there was far less to do

now, the most pressing postwar problems had begun to be resolved, and the long-term ones wouldn't be completely taken care of for years. So what remained was a pleasant lull, a kind of easygoing limbo, in which he would actually daydream at his desk, meet his wife for lunch, go for long walks in the parks, and hurry home with her for another passionate adventure before returning to his desk.

"I can't go on meeting you like this." He grinned at her sleepily one afternoon in May, as he lay in her arms, happy and spent.

"Why not? Do you think your wife will object?" Serena was grinning. And she looked more mature now than she had five months before when she had arrived in Paris on the train from Rome.

"My wife?" B.J. looked at her, her hair tousled. "Hell no, she's a sex maniac." Serena laughed out loud. "Do you realize that I'm going to look sixty when I'm forty if we keep this up?" But he didn't look as though he minded, and Serena looked at him archly.

"Are you complaining, then?" But there was a strange gleam in her eye today, as though there were something she wasn't telling. He had thought that he noticed it when he first met her for lunch, but he had forgotten about it as they talked. Later he would press her about it. But first he had something to tell her. "Are you complaining, Colonel?"

"Not really. But I think you ought to know that I won't be able to do quite as much of this when we go back to the States." His eyes were twinkling strangely and Serena cocked her head to one side.

"Is that true?"

He nodded but looked indecisive. "Well, Americans just don't behave like this, after all."

"Don't they make love?" Serena looked mock-horrified, still with that wicked gleam in her eye.

"Never."

"You're lying."

"I am not." He was grinning at her. "Hell, we can't go on making love like this when we go back. My lunch hours won't be as long."

"Brad." She suddenly looked at him strangely. "Are you trying to tell me something?"

154

"Yes." He nodded with a grin.

"What?" But she already thought she knew.

"We're going home, princess."

"To the States?" She looked stunned. She had known that it would come eventually, but she hadn't thought it would be so soon. "To New York?"

"Only for a three-week leave. After that, my love, we go to the Presidio in San Francisco, and I become a full colonel. How do you like that, Mrs. Fullerton?" At thirty-four, Brad knew it was quite an accolade, and she knew it too.

"Brad!" She looked elated for him. "How wonderful! And San Francisco?"

"You'll love it. Not only that, but Teddy will be near us, since he's going to Stanford Med in the fall. And we'll even get home for Greg's wedding. That wraps it all up pretty nicely, wouldn't you say, my love?"

"More or less." She lay back against their pillows again, with that same mysterious grin.

"More or less? I get promoted, we get sent home, we get one of the best posts in the country, and you say 'more or less'? Serena, I ought to spank you." He mockingly pulled her toward him to turn her over his knee, but she held out a hand.

"I wouldn't do that." Her voice was oddly gentle and her eyes very bright, and something in her face made him stop pulling her toward him, as though he knew, as though he sensed it, even before she spoke.

"Why not?"

"Because I'm having a baby, Brad." She said it so gently that it brought tears to his eyes, as he moved toward her and held her.

"Oh, darling."

"I hope it's a boy." She clung happily to him, and he shook his head firmly.

"A girl. One who looks just like you."

"Don't you want a son?" She looked startled, but he was looking down at her as though she had just performed a miracle, not really concentrating on her words, just stunned by the total fulfillment he felt.

CHAPTER SIXTEEN

The car arrived to take them to Le Havre at eight o'clock in the morning. Their bags were packed and waiting in the front hall, and Marie-Rose and Pierre stood beside them, looking very starched and stiff and pale. Marie-Rose had been dabbing at her eyes ever since she had served Serena her breakfast tray that morning, and Pierre had the mournful look of a father losing his only son as he shook B.J.'s hand for a last time. It was the first time since before the war that they had cared so passionately for the people they had worked for, and the young couple who had inspired their love stood before them now, with regrets of their own. For B.J. it was the end of an era, the beginning of a whole other lifetime, as he knew only too well. During the war he had got lost, he had become someone new, found out who he was, in the anonymity of a uniform, with an ordinary name. Fullerton. It had meant nothing to anyone in the army. Fullerton? So what? But now he was going back to the States. Bradford Jarvis Fullerton III, and all that that entailed. He would see his mother, his father, his brothers, their friends, go to Greg's wedding, and attempt to explain to everyone why he was staying in the army, why it suited him, and why he no longer wanted out. He would have to justify why he didn't want to go into politics like his father, or work in the family law firm, why he was sure of his decision. And he knew as well that the silent question no one would dare ask, but which he would have to justify as well, was why he had married Serena. He felt so protective of her now as they left the safety of familiar turf in Europe. Particularly so now that she was carrying his child. But even if she hadn't been, he would have wanted to make the transition easy for her, and he knew that the first days of introduction to his mother would probably be very tense. After that he felt certain that even his indomitable mother would fall prey to

Serena's charms. But even if she didn't, he didn't give a damn. His whole heart belonged to Serena now. And after all his army years his family seemed somehow less important, less real.

But all of it weighed heavily on Brad's mind that morning as he shook hands with Pierre and stooped to kiss Marie-Rose on both cheeks, as Serena had done only a moment before.

"You promise that you'll send a picture of the baby?" It was almost exactly the same thing Marcella had said the night before on the phone from Rome.

"We'll send dozens of pictures, I promise." Serena squeezed her hand and afterward gently smoothed her own hand over the slight bulge in her lilac silk suit. Brad had already taken to feeling her stomach, to see if it had grown, almost daily, and she teased him about his fascination with his son. "My daughter," he always corrected emphatically, and Serena laughed at him. She wanted a boy to carry on his name, but he always insisted that he didn't give a damn about the name, all he wanted was a little girl that looked just like her.

The Fullertons shook hands with the couple for a last time, and waved as the car drove away, and for an instant Serena leaned her head against Brad's shoulder as they drove down the Avenue Hoche toward L'Étoile, and as she had in Rome, Serena found herself wondering when she would see these familiar sights again.

"Are you all right?" Brad looked at her with concern as he saw the serious expression in her eyes and wondered if she were feeling ill, but she nodded and smiled at him.

"I'm fine." And then after another glance out the window, "I was just saying good-bye . . . again."

He touched her hand and then held it gently in his own. "You've done a lot of that, my love." He looked into her eyes. "Hopefully now we'll settle down and have a home. At least for a while." He knew that it was possible that he might stay at the Presidio in San Francisco for as much as five years, or possibly even longer. "We'll make the house pretty for the baby and dig our heels in, I promise." And then he glanced at her again as he spoke softly. "Will you be very homesick for all this, my love?"

"Paris?" She thought for a moment, but he shook his head.

"I mean all of it, not just Paris . . . Europe."

"Yes. Brad, I was so afraid all the time, about the war, my grandmother, about ever getting back to Venice or Rome. I felt like a prisoner over there. Now everything will be different." And the truth was that she had no one in Europe anymore. Other than Marcella, the only person Serena had was her husband, and she knew that her place was with him. She had called Marcella yesterday and told her that they were leaving. She had told her about the baby too, and Marcella was so happy that she laughed and cried. But she had refused Serena's invitation to go to the States with them. Serena had Brad now, and Marcella felt that she belonged in Rome. "It's different leaving this time." She shrugged and he smiled, she looked suddenly very Italian. "I'm sad to go, but only because I know it here, because it's familiar, because I speak the language."

"Don't be silly, you speak English almost as well as I do. As a matter of fact"—he grinned at his wife—"better."

"I don't mean that way. I mean they understand my life, my spirit, my soul. It's different in the States. People don't think the way we do."

"No." He thought about it as she said it. "They don't." And he knew also that most people would not understand her background. They wouldn't even begin to guess at the beautiful things she'd been surrounded with as she grew up, the extraordinary sculptures and tapestries and paintings, the palaces in Venice and Rome that had been a matter of course to her as a child, the people she had known, the way she had lived. All of it was lost now, yet an enormous part of all that had stayed within her, woven into the fiber of her being. It made her gentle and cultured, and quiet and wise all at once, as though the beauty of all that she had known as a young girl had actually become a part of her. But B.J. had questioned for a long time how well all of that could be translated into his own culture. It was one of the reasons why he had been in no hurry to go back to the States. But now the moment had come, and in order to make the transition more gentle, he had arranged to take part of his leave on the way home. He had booked passage on the *Liberte*, which had just been awarded to France from Germany after the war, and he had arranged for a first-class cabin on one of the upper decks.

B.J. had decided against the boat train to Le Havre because he thought that the trip would be too tiring for Serena, and he preferred to have one of his orderlies drive them down quietly. That way they could stop whenever they wanted, and she would feel better when they reached the ship. As it happened, Serena had no problems on the trip down, it had been an easy pregnancy from the first, and after the first three months she felt even better than she had before. They chatted all the way from Paris, he talking to her about his old life in New York, his family, his old friends, while she told him tales about her years with the nuns. It seemed as though the trip passed very quickly, and suddenly they were at the quay, their suitcases were being taken out of the car by the driver, and a few moments later a steward was escorting them up the gangplank to their cabin, as Serena looked up at the ship in awe. This was nothing like the freighter she had taken from Dover in the company of dozens of refugee children and a handful of nuns. This was a luxury liner of the first order, and as she passed down beautifully paneled halls, glanced into red-velvet-draped staterooms, and looked at the other passengers as they boarded, she realized that this was going to be a very special trip.

Serena's eyes began to dance as she turned to her husband.

He looked at her expectantly, his own excitement showing in his eyes. He had gone to a great deal of trouble to arrange for their passage on the *Liberté* on such short notice, and it meant a great deal to him that the trip be something special for her. He wanted her entry into his world to go smoothly, and to begin happily, and he was going to do everything in his power to see that that was the case. He already knew that his brother's wedding was very possibly going to be a difficult moment, the confrontation with Pattie Atherton was not something that Brad was looking forward to, so at least before all that they would have a grand time.

"Do you like it?"

159

"Brad! . . ." She was whispering as they sedately followed the steward to their cabin, where they knew they would find the trunks they had sent ahead a few days before. "This is marvelous! It's—it's like a palazzo!" She giggled and he laughed and tucked her hand into his arm with obvious pleasure.

"Tonight I'll take you dancing." And then his face clouded quickly. "Or shouldn't we do that?"

She laughed at him as they walked into the cabin. "Don't be silly. Your son will love it."

"My daughter," he said in hushed tones, and then they both stopped speaking, because the cabin they were standing in was so spectacular that it took them both by surprise. Everything was upholstered in either blue velvet or blue satin, the walls were paneled in a deep handsome mahogany, the furniture was of the same richly burnished wood, and everywhere were small brass ornaments and fixtures, beautiful little lanterns, handsome antique English mirrors, and large airy portholes rimmed in highly polished brass. It was the perfect spot for the honeymoon they had never taken, and the whole room had an aura of comfort and luxury that made one want to stay for a year, not a week. Their trunks were already neatly placed on racks in convenient places, and their suitcases were added to them now, as the steward made a neat bow.

"The maid will be along in a moment to help Madame unpack the suitcases." He then indicated a huge bowl of fresh fruit, a plate of cookies, and a decanter of sherry on a narrow sideboard. "We will be serving lunch shortly after we sail at one o'clock, but in the meantime perhaps the Colonel and Madame would care for some refreshments?" It was all done to perfection, and they both looked enchanted as the steward bowed once more and left the room.

"Oh, darling, it's wonderful!" She catapulted into his arms and gave him a hug.

Brad looked immensely pleased. "It's even better than I thought. God, isn't this the way to travel?" He poured them both a small glass of sherry, handed her one, and lifted his in a toast. "To the most beautiful woman I know, the woman I love"—his eyes lit up in a warm smile—"and the mother of my daughter."

"Son," she corrected, as she always did now, with a grin.

"May your life in the States bring you happiness, my darling. Always and always."

"Thank you." She looked into the glass for just a moment, and then at him. "I know it will." She took a sip, and then held up her glass to toast him. "To the man who has given me everything, and whom I love with all my heart . . . may you never regret bringing your war bride home." There was something sad in her eyes as she said it, and he took her quickly in his arms.

"Don't say that."

"Why not?"

"Because I love you. And when you say things like that, you forget who you are. You can't ever forget who you really are, Serena. Principessa Serena." He smiled gently at her, and she shook her head.

"I'm Mrs. Fullerton now, not 'Principessa' anything, and I like it that way." And then after a moment's pause, "Don't you try to forget who you really are, Brad?" It was an impression she had had for several months now. She had begun to catch on to his game of anonymity, in staying both in the army and abroad. "Don't you really do the same thing I do?"

"Maybe." He looked out the porthole for a long moment. "The truth is, where and who I come from has always been a burden to me, Serena." He had never admitted that to anyone before, and it was an odd thing to admit to her now, just before they went home. "I've never quite fit. I've always been that old cliché, the 'square peg in the round hole.' I don't know why, but that's the way it's been. I don't think that either of my brothers feel that way. Teddy would fit anywhere, and Greg would force himself to, whether he did or not, but I can't do that. And I just don't believe in all that bullshit anymore. I never did. The values of people like Pattie Atherton, my mother, my father. Everything is for self-importance, for show. Nothing is ever done because it feels good, because it's what you want, because it means something. It's what looks good to

161

everyone else that counts. I can't live like that anymore."

"That's why you're staying in the army?"

"That's exactly why. Because I'm halfway decent at what I do in the army, I can live in some damn pleasant places, probably at a good healthy distance from New York, unless I get assigned to Washington at some point"—he rolled his eyes in mock horror—"and I don't have to try and play the family game anymore, Serena. I don't want to be B.J. Fullerton the Third. I want to be me, the First. Me, Brad, B.J., my own person, someone we can both respect. I don't have to go to my father's clubs or marry the daughter of my mother's friends to feel good about myself, Serena. I never did feel good about any of that, and now I know why. Because I just wasn't cut out for that. But you"—he looked at her tenderly—"you were born to be a princess. You can't run away from it, hide from it, change it, give it up, pretend it isn't there. It's you. Just like those splendid green eyes."

"How do you know that I don't dislike it as much as you dislike what you were born to?"

"Because I know you. The only thing you don't like about it is being conspicuous, showy. You don't want to appear a snob. But you don't have basic differences with your very roots, Serena. You belong in that world, and if that world still existed, I would never have taken you from it, because right now America is a place where the people don't understand the kind of world you come from. But it's the best we've got, kiddo, and all we can do is explain it to them. And if they've got any smarts at all"—he smiled gently—"we won't have to explain a damn thing. Because what you are, the beauty and the grace and the goodness and the sheer elegance of it all is written all over you, principessa or no. It wouldn't matter if you called yourself Mrs. Jones, my love, you are a princess to your very soul."

"That's silly." She was smiling and blushing faintly in embarrassment. "If I hadn't told you, you'd never have known."

"I certainly would."

"You would not." She was teasing him now and he set down his glass and took her in his arms in the beautiful blue velvet and mahogany cabin, and he kissed her hard on the mouth, and then swept her into his arms with one powerful gesture and deposited her on the room's large handsome bed.

"Don't move. I have to fix something." She smiled at his retreating back as he marched to the door of the cabin, took off the Do Not Disturb sign, opened the door, and slipped it on the knob on the other side. "That ought to take care of the maid." He turned to her with a broad grin, closed the curtains, and began to loosen his tie.

"And just what does that mean, Colonel?" She looked at him archly from the bed, every inch a princess, except that there was laughter bubbling over in her eyes.

"Just what do you think it means, Mrs. Fullerton?"

"In broad daylight? Here? Now?"

"Why not?" He sat down on the edge of the bed and kissed her again.

"Good God! I'll get pregnant."

"Terrific. We'll have twin girls."

"Oh, don't say—" But he never let her finish her sentence. His mouth was pressed down hard on hers and a moment later they had pulled back the handsome blue satin covers, to reveal white linen sheets with the monogram of the French line neatly embroidered in blue. The sheets were smooth and cool against her flesh, and his hands were warm on her breasts and her thighs as he pressed against her and she found herself hungering to feel him inside her. She moaned his name softly, and he ran his lips across her mouth and her eyes and her hair as his hands worked magic, and then suddenly, lunging toward her, he took her almost by surprise.

"Oh." It was a single prolonged sound of astonishment and then pleasure, lost in a symphony of soft murmurs and moans, as the ship slowly left the dock and they began their voyage home.

CHAPTER SEVENTEEN

The days on the *Liberté* flew too quickly. The weather was unusually good on the Atlantic, and even the usual June breezes never came up to plague them, as they lay in deck chairs side by side. Serena was only troubled once or twice by some vague queasiness before breakfast, but by the time they had eaten, taken a turn around the deck, played shuffleboard once, or chatted with some of the people they had met, Serena had always long since forgotten her malaise by then, and spent the rest of the day in total enjoyment. They usually lunched alone, retired to their cabin for a nap, and returned to the deck, before going in to change for tea, when they invariably met new people, spoke to some they had met in the days before, and listened to the chamber music. It all reminded Serena very much of her grandmother and their friends, the music they liked, the food they loved best, the grand meals, the formal dress, the gray lace dresses with pink satin underslips, with several rows of pearls and perfectly plain pumps of gray satin. It was none of it alien to her, and appeared to Serena to be part of a life she had once lived. But it was not unknown to B.J. either, and time and again they seemed to meet people whom his parents had known, or his uncles, or with whom they had mutual friends.

On the whole it was an easygoing, relaxed, delightful trip, and they were both sorry on the last night at the prospect of seeing their journey come to an end when they reached New York.

"Maybe we should just stow away and go back to Paris."

"No." She said it decidedly, propped up on one elbow in their bed after they made love. "I want to go to New York and meet your family, and then I want to see San Francisco, and all the cowboys and Indians. I think I'm going to like the Wild West."

B.J. laughed openly at the visions she conjured. "The only thing wild about it is your imagination."

"No cowboys or Indians? Not even one or two?"

"Not in San Francisco. We'll have to go to the Rockies to see cowboys."

"Good." She looked delighted as she kissed his neck. "Then we'll go there on a trip. Right?"

"And when do you plan to do all this, madame? Right up until you have the baby?"

"Of course. What do you expect me to do?" Now she looked amused. "Stay home and knit bootees all the time?"

"Sounds about right to me."

"Well, it doesn't to me. I want to do something, Brad."

"Oh, God, save me." He fell back among his pillows with a groan. "It's a Modern Woman. What do you want to do? Go out and work?"

"Why not? This is America. It's a democratic country. I could get involved in politics." Her eyes twinkled a little and he held up a hand.

"That you could not! One woman like that in my family is enough, thank you. Figure out something else. Besides, dammit"—he looked only faintly annoyed as he knit his brows—"you're going to have a baby in six months. Can't you just relax and do that?"

"Maybe. But maybe I could do something else too. At least while I'm waiting."

"We'll find you some nice volunteer work." She nodded slowly in answer, but lately she had been thinking a great deal about San Francisco. Neither of them knew anyone there, and Brad would meet people on the base, but she wanted to be doing something too. She didn't want to just sit there, with her big belly, waiting. She said as much to him a minute later. "But why not?" He looked perplexed. "Isn't that what women do?"

"Not all women. There must be women who do something more than that while they're pregnant. You know"—she looked pensive for a moment—"the poor women in Italy work, they go out and work in the fields, in stores, in bakeries, at whatever they normally do, and one day, boom, out comes the baby, and that's that, off they go with the baby under their

165

arm.'' She smiled at the thought and he laughed again at the image.

"You have a certain way with words, my love. Is that what you want to do? Boom, out comes the baby, while you're working in the fields?"

She looked at him strangely then. "I was happy when I was working with Marcella."

"Good God, Serena. That was awful, for chrissake, working as a maid in your parents' own home."

"The idea was awful, but the work wasn't. It felt good. I felt as though I accomplished something every day. It wasn't that what I was doing was important, it was that I was doing a lot, and I was doing it well." She looked like a proud little girl as she glanced at him. "I had a lot of responsibility, you know."

He kissed the tip of her nose gently. "I know you did, little one. And you worked damn hard. Too hard. I don't ever want you to have to do something like that again." He looked pleased at knowing that that would never happen. "And you won't. You're married to me now, darling. And about the only good thing about the Fullerton name is that it comes equipped with enough comfort to keep not only us but our children safe from that kind of hardship, for always."

"That's nice to know." But she didn't look overly impressed. "But I would have loved you even if you were poor."

"I know you would, darling. But it's nice not to have to worry about that, isn't it?" She nodded slowly and snuggled into his arms, before they both fell asleep. Just before she did, she thought once more of her life in San Francisco, and knew that she wanted to do something more than just have a baby. The baby was wonderful and exciting, but she wanted to do something else too. She hadn't figured out what yet, but she knew that in time she would.

At six o'clock the next morning the steward knocked on their door, to let them know that they were coming into New York. They weren't going to be docking until 10 A.M., but it was customary to enter the harbor very early. After that there were the usual formalities to be handled, and every effort was made not to inconvenience passengers by docking too early. But there was something very special about passing the Statue of Liberty at sunrise, with the golden sunlight streaking across the sky and reflecting off her arm and torch and crown. It was a sight that rarely failed to stir intense feelings, and those who got up early enough to see her always felt a special bond with their country as the ship glided into port. Serena was moved beyond words as they passed the statue lighting her way to a new life.

Even B.J. was strangely silent. The last time he had come home had been only for a brief visit, on a military flight. This time he felt as though he were coming home from the wars at last, with his wife at his side, to the country he loved. It was a feeling of well-being and gratitude that welled up inside him like a sunburst, and he knew no other way to vent it but to take Serena in his arms and hold her tight.

"Welcome home, Serena."

"*Grazie.*" She whispered softly to him as they kissed in the soft orange light of the June morning.

"We're going to have a beautiful life here, my darling." It was a promise that he meant to keep for a lifetime, hers as well as his own.

"I know we will. And our baby too."

He held her hand tightly, and they stood there for almost an hour, watching New York from the distance, as the ship hovered in the harbor, waiting for immigration officials and tugboats and clearances and red tape and all the rest of the brouhaha that always went with arrivals, but Serena and B.J. were oblivious of it all, as they stood on deck, hand in hand, thinking of what lay ahead.

At precisely the same moment Brad's mother sat in her bed on Fifth Avenue, drinking a cup of coffee, her brows knit; her eyes dark, thinking of her oldest son and the woman he was bringing home. If she could have, she would have liked to force Brad to dispose of Serena as quickly as possible, but she had not yet come up with a reasonable suggestion as to how that could be done. She no longer had a hold on any of Brad's money, there was no job he depended on his family for now. In his own way he had flown the coop and now he was hovering above them, doing just what he wanted, in his own way, with this damned Italian tramp he was bringing home. . . . His mother set down her coffee cup with a clatter, pushed back the covers, and strode out of bed with a determined air.

CHAPTER EIGHTEEN

As Serena stepped down the gangplank, walking ahead of Brad, she could feel her heart pound within her. What would they be like? What would they say? In her heart Serena held a glimmer of hope that Mrs. Fullerton—the other Mrs. Fullerton, she smiled to herself—would come around. The pressure of it all weighed on her like a thousand-pound weight as she stepped off the boat in a cream-colored linen suit, with an ivory silk blouse, and her hair done in the familiar figure-eight bun. She looked terribly young and strikingly lovely, and there was something so vulnerable and so fresh about her, like a white rose, standing alone in a crystal vase. One wanted to reach out and touch her, yet no one would have dared. Her white kid gloves were impeccable on her hands as she barely touched the railing, and she looked back once at Brad, and he could read everything in her eyes. He leaned toward her with a word of encouragement as they got closer to land.

"Don't look so worried. They won't attack you, I swear it." To himself he silently added, "They wouldn't dare," but in truth he knew that some of them would—his mother . . . Pattie . . . Greg, if he was under the influence of either of those women . . . his father? He wasn't sure. Only Teddy was someone that one could be sure of.

The steward had given her two very pretty gardenias as they left the ship that morning, and she was wearing them both on her lapel. He could smell the rich fragrance as he walked behind her. "Cheer up, kid!"

She glanced back at him again, and this time he could see

that she was pale with fear. It wasn't fair to put her through something like this, and for a moment he hated his mother. Why couldn't she have been some fat kindly old lady, instead of the sleek feline queen of the jungle that she was . . . a perfect panther, waiting to stalk her prey. B.J. could imagine her waiting, catlike and predatory, prowling the dock impatiently. He had to shake his head to rid himself of the image. But when they reached the section of the dock labeled F, in which they had to stand to wait for their trunks and meet the customs inspectors, Brad realized there was no one there to meet them. He saw neither of his parents and no familiar faces. It was a far cry from the raucous reception he had got at the airport a year before, and he felt an odd mixture of both disappointment and relief wash over him as he took Serena's hand.

"You can relax. They're not here."

Her brows knit into a worried frown. "Don't you think they're coming?" Would they shun him entirely because of her? It was what she had feared all along, why at first she had insisted on not marrying him, and had stayed on to mourn him in Rome.

"For heaven's sake, Serena, you look like someone died. Stop that. They're probably just busy as hell with the damn wedding. We'll just take a cab and go to the house." But even to him it seemed an oddly casual return after all this time.

And then he saw him, standing fifty yards away, watching them, a grin lighting up his face, making the blue eyes dance, Brad knew, without even seeing him closely. He could already imagine the little wrinkles near his eyes when he smiled. He had a way of smiling that lit up his whole face and made two deep dimples that had been his misery as a child. He was wearing white flannel slacks, a blue blazer, and a boater, and he looked wonderful to Brad as he hurried toward them. Suddenly all he wanted to do was hug him tight, but it was to Serena that Teddy was hurrying, a huge bouquet of red roses tucked into his arms, the smile Brad loved lighting up his face, and his eyes only for her, like a long lost brother or friend. He stopped dead in front of her, looking dumbstruck at her overwhelming elegance and beauty, and threw his arms around her, in a hug that took her breath away.

"Hello, Serena. Welcome home!" He said it with an emphasis and enthusiasm that brought smiles to their faces and tears to her eyes, and Serena returned his hug with equal strength as he held her. It was like being enfolded by someone one had always loved and wanted to be loved by. "I'm so glad you're both here." He looked over her shoulder at his favorite brother, and Brad couldn't wait a moment longer. He threw his arms around them both, and they stood there, laughing and crying, the three of them locked in a bear hug and standing beside the huge ship that had brought them home.

It seemed ages before Teddy let her go, and she stood back to look up at the younger brother she had heard so much about. He was even taller than Brad, and in some ways better-looking, and yet not, she realized as she looked at their faces while they chattered eagerly about everything, the wedding, their parents, the trip. Brad's features were more perfect, his shoulders broader, and he seemed a great deal more sophisticated as she looked at her husband with pride. Yet Teddy had something special, and it was impossible not to see it. It was almost a kind of glow, a kind of excitement that lit up his soul and everyone who came within his sphere. There was a joy and a warmth and a love about him that bubbled over the edges and exploded like fireworks on the Fourth of July. It was impossible not to like him, not to want to reach out and become part of his life. And Serena felt the pull of it too as she stood back and watched him, but she felt something else as well, a wave of admiration from him that was so overpowering, she wasn't sure how to react. Despite the rapid-fire conversation between the brothers, Teddy hadn't taken his eyes off of Serena since he'd arrived. And finally he spoke to her again.

"Serena, you are *so beautiful*!" He seemed knocked right off his feet and Serena could only laugh.

"Not only that," her husband added, "she's a princess. How about that!"

"She looks it." The younger brother said it with total

seriousness, and Brad watched him with tenderness and amusement.

"Now, don't go falling in love with her, kiddo, I saw her first." But there was a kind of total overwhelming awe in Teddy's face that almost made you want to look away while he gazed at Serena.

"My God, you're lovely." He couldn't take his eyes off her face, but it was Serena who broke the spell.

She whispered at him over the armful of roses he handed her after they embraced.

"Actually I'm not really Serena. I'm a girl Brad met on the ship and he asked me to take her place."

"Cute though, isn't she?" Brad put a mildly possessive arm around his bride. After all, his brother was twelve years younger than he, and only three years older than his wife, he didn't want the boy to get carried away. "By the way, how is our charming sister-in-law-to-be?"

Teddy's sunny face clouded over for a long moment. "Fine, I guess." His voice was both vague and subdued as Brad and Serena watched him. "Greg's been drunk every night for the past two weeks. I'm not sure what that's supposed to mean. Good times or terror?"

"Maybe a little of both." Brad was watching his brother's eyes.

But Teddy was always honest with him. "I don't think Greg knows what he's doing, Brad. Or maybe he doesn't want to know, which is even worse."

"Are you suggesting that someone stop this thing? Now?" Brad looked upset as he asked.

"I don't know. Mother's sure as hell not going to do it. Greg is rapidly becoming her great white hope. Ever since you've decided to become a professional soldier"—he looked disparagingly at his brother, but Brad only grinned—"and it's obvious that I'll never play the family game, it looks like Greg is it."

"Poor kid." For a moment Brad didn't say more, and then the customs officials arrived to check through their trunks and look at their passports. He asked for Teddy's as well, but Teddy quickly pulled out a special pass. One of his father's political friends had got it for him from the mayor of

New York, and it allowed him to meet friends at ships, and not have to wait until they cleared customs. It was convenient at times like this, but the customs man felt patronized by Teddy's inadvertent show of rank.

"Special privileges, eh?"

Teddy looked mildly embarrassed. "Just this once. My brother hasn't been home since the war." He waved at Brad, and the customs man's face immediately softened.

"Coming home on the *Liberté*, son? Not a bad way to travel."

"Not at all. We managed to turn it into a honeymoon."

"Your wife go over to meet you?" He had only checked the luggage. His partner had handled the passports and seen that Serena was Italian, but this man had no way of knowing. She hadn't said a word.

'No." Brad looked down at her proudly. "I met my wife over there. In Rome."

"Italian?" The customs man's eyes narrowed as he looked her over, in all her perfect ivory and golden beauty, the gardenias on her lapel, and the sun glinting on her hair, as he stood in his grayed uniform with spots on the tie and dirt under his nails.

"Yes, my wife is Italian. From Rome." Brad repeated with a smile, as the other man began to glare.

"Plenty of girls in this country to marry, sonny. Or didn't you remember? Christ, some of you young guys got over there and forgot what was back home." He glared at all three of them, and then hurried away to inspect someone else's bags. There was an angry light in Brad's eyes and blind fury in Teddy's, but Serena put a hand on each of their arms and shook her head.

"Don't. It doesn't matter. He's just an angry old man. Maybe someone jilted his daughter."

"Maybe someone ought to smash his face." Teddy was quick to volunteer but Brad looked as though he would have liked to help him.

"Never mind. Let's go home." The two men exchanged a look, Brad sighed slowly and then nodded.

"Okay, princess, you win." But he looked at her almost sadly. "This time." And then he bent to kiss her. "I don't ever want anyone saying things like that around you again."

"But they will." It was only a whisper. "Maybe it'll take time."

"Bull," Teddy spoke and she laughed at him then, and they hailed a porter and began the final leg home.

CHAPTER NINETEEN

Teddy had left his parents' chauffeur waiting patiently outside the pier area in the midnight-blue Cadillac limousine his father had bought for his wife's use the previous Christmas. But most of the time Margaret Fullerton still preferred driving her own car, a handsome bottle-green convertible Lincoln Zephyr, which she drove almost every day. To her sons' delight however, that left the Cadillac and the elderly chauffeur free for their use, and Greg made free use of the car, except when Teddy beat him to it, as he had today. His mother had had a meeting of the Board of the American Red Cross, final details to attend to for the rehearsal dinner the next day, and a luncheon with another board she was on, all of which had kept her from meeting Brad and Serena at the ship. And Greg had had an important meeting downtown with his father, which had left only Teddy to meet B.J. and his bride, in the elegant midnight-blue car.

"My, my, is this new?"

"Yup. A Christmas present from Pop."

"For you?" Brad looked stunned.

"Hell no." Teddy grinned. "For Mother."

"Oh, well. That figures. Get to use it much or only for state occasions?"

"Only when Greg's not around?"

"That figures too."

But before they could say more, the old chauffeur had got out of the car and was hurrying toward them. He pulled off his cap, and a smile lit up his face from ear to ear. He had worked for the Fullertons since Brad had been a little boy.

"Hi, Jimmie!" B.J. clapped him on the shoulder and the old man chortled with delight and hugged him.

"You look good, boy. Good to see you back!"

"It's good to be back." There was genuine pleasure between the two men. "Jimmie, I'd like you to meet my wife." He turned to Serena with obvious pride and the old man almost dropped his jaw when he saw the blond beauty.

"Pleased to meet you, Mrs. Fullerton." He mustered it almost shyly, and she shook his hand warmly, with her gentle smile that extended deep into the emerald eyes.

"Brad has told me a great deal about you."

"Has he?" Jimmie looked immensely pleased. "Welcome to America." He narrowed his eyes. "You speak very good English. Have you been here before?"

She nodded. "I was here during the war. In Upstate New York."

"That's a good thing." Jimmie smiled warmly.

Serena gave him an answering smile and he waved them all inside the car. "I'll take care of this mess. You kids relax." But only Teddy and Serena got inside the car, and Brad stayed out to help his old buddy sort through their assorted trunks and belongings.

Inside, Teddy still seemed unable to take his eyes off Serena. "How was the trip over?" He wasn't quite sure where to begin, and it was so odd being alone with her. He just wanted to reach out and touch her, but it was different now with Brad not there with him. He wanted to touch the creamy skin, the extraordinary golden hair, and then suddenly he felt a mad urge to kiss her, but not as a brother, or even as a friend. As the thought crossed his mind he flushed deeply and a thin veil of perspiration broke out on his forehead.

"Are you all right?" Serena was looking at him strangely. "Are you ill?"

"No . . . I . . . I'm sorry . . . I don't know . . . I just . . . I think it's just excitement. Seeing Brad back, meeting you, Greg getting married, graduating last week." He wiped his brow with a white linen handkerchief and sat back beside

174

her. "Now, where were we?" But all he could think of was that face, those eyes. It was almost as though they bore through him. He had never seen a woman as lovely as this.

But Serena was looking at him gently, her face riveted with concern and unspoken understanding. "Please . . ." She faltered for only a moment. "You're upset about me, aren't you? Is it so great a shock? Am I so different really?" She sounded almost consumed with distress and guilt.

But Teddy nodded slowly. "Yes, you are. But not in the way you think. Serena," he sighed and reached for her hand. What the hell. Brad wouldn't kill him. "You're the most beautiful woman I've ever seen, and if you weren't my brother's wife, I'd ask you to marry me right this minute!" For a moment she thought he was joking, and then she saw something almost heartbreaking in his eyes. Her own eyes widened in surprise as she looked at him.

"Making time with my wife, little brother?" B.J. opened the door of the elegant limousine and hopped inside with a casual look of unconcern, which belied the faint tremor he had felt while he busied himself outside. Teddy had always been the best-looking of the brothers, and he was certainly more her age, but that was crazy thinking and he knew it. Serena was his wife, she loved him, and she was having his child.

But Teddy only laughed and shook his head as he ran a hand through his hair. "I think you just saved me from making a total ass of myself, Brad."

"Want me to get out so you can try again?"

"No!" Teddy and Serena said it in unison, and with that they looked at each other, and both of them began to laugh, like hysterical children, and the uncomfortable moment was broken. They laughed half the way home, suddenly began teasing each other and Brad, and the friendship began in earnest that morning.

Teddy gave them a brief rundown of what the wedding would be like, what was expected of them, and who was coming to the rehearsal dinner. Brad already knew that he was going to be the best man, and Teddy was an usher. In addition there were to be ten other ushers, eleven bridesmaids and a maid of honor, two children as ring bearer and flower girl, and the ceremony was to be at St. James Church on Madison Avenue, with an enormous reception at the Plaza Hotel, immediately thereafter. It was expected to be a grandiose affair and the Athertons were spending a fortune.

The rehearsal dinner, on the other hand, was being given at their father's club, the Knickerbocker, and there were to be a mere forty-five guests, in black tie, for a formal dinner.

"Oh, Christ." Brad groaned aloud. "When's that again?"

"Tomorrow."

"And tonight? Can we have some time to ourselves, or do we have to perform some other tribal dance with the whole troupe?"

"Mother's planning a small family dinner. Just Mother and Dad, Greg and I, and of course Pattie." A flicker of worry showed in Teddy's eyes.

"That ought to be cozy." The last time Pattie had seen Serena she had called her a whore, and he had broken their engagement, and not even a year had gone by since then.

A moment later they pulled up in front of the awning of their building, and the doorman rushed forward to open the door, as Jimmie stepped out to take over.

"Is Mother upstairs?" Brad wanted the meeting over with. His eyes bored into Teddy's, as if trying to take support and energy from his younger brother to help protect and buffer his wife.

"Not yet. She won't be home till three. We'll have the place to ourselves, while Serena gets acquainted." It was a kind of blessing. Serena meekly followed her husband and brother-in-law inside, into a richly paneled, tapestry-hung lobby, with high ceilings and marble floors, immense plants, and a chandelier worthy of Versailles twinkling down at them.

Brad and Ted whisked her into the elevator and up to the top floor, where the hallway led to a single apartment, the penthouse overlooking Central Park, where all three boys had grown up, and which sent a little shiver of excitement down Brad's spine now as Teddy unlocked the door and stood aside for them to enter. Two maids in black uniforms with lace aprons and caps were frantically dusting the main hallway. It was paneled in extraordinarily beautiful Japanese screens, the floors were a harlequin black and white marble, and here again was a beautiful chandelier, but this one much more so than the one in the lobby. It was a Waterford piece, over two hundred years old, and a work of art in itself, which matched the elaborate sconces along the walls. The whole entrance reminded Serena of a brilliantly lit ballroom. The maids were quick to welcome Brad home, and they went off to report to the cook that he was back, and he promised to go out to the kitchen to see her in a minute. But first he wanted to show Serena the apartment where he had grown up.

In its own way it reminded her of the palazzo. It was smaller of course, and it was after all an apartment, yet it had a grandiose quality to it more typical of a house, and the way it was decorated looked not unlike the assorted homes in which she had grown up. There were delicately shaded Aubusson rugs, damask drapes, and rich brocades, a grand piano in the library, as well as three walls of rare books, and in the dining room there was an impressive collection of family portraits. The living room was subtle and lovely and very French. There were two Renoirs and a Monet, a great deal of Louis XV, rivers of white silk and gray damask, accented with a little dusty rose, and vast quantities of gilt and marble. It was certainly not a ''little apartment'' by anyone's standards, and its main virtue in Serena's mind was that it gave her the impression she had already seen it before. It was just like all the palazzi she had known as a child. It was in better condition, and there were some very fine things, some even lovelier than what she had seen in Venice, and yet it had that familiar ring that one finds in Paris and London and New York and Rome, Munich or Barcelona or Lisbon or Madrid, the look of a vastly expensive home filled with priceless things, the rich gilts of Louis XV, the needlepoint scenes of Aubusson, the shapes and the colors and the smells that all looked so familiar. It was almost as though she wanted to sigh in relief and say, ''It's all right, I've already been here.'' Teddy had noticed the look of relief on her face and immediately teased her.

"What did you expect? Lions and tigers and a woman with a whip and a chair?"

But Serena laughed at him. "Not quite, but . . ." There was teasing in her face as well.

"Close, huh? Well, you're in luck. We only feed the Christians to the lions on Tuesday. You're two days late."

"It's a beautiful place."

Brad was looking around him as though seeing it for the first time, and he smiled at them both. "You know, I'd forgotten how nice it all is." It had been ten months since he'd been home on leave, and that had been so hectic that he'd never really noticed his home the whole time he was there.

"Welcome home, Big Brother."

"Thanks, kid." He squeezed his younger brother's shoulder, and put an arm gently around his wife. "You all right, sweetheart? Not too tired?" Just the way he said it warned Teddy of something.

"Something wrong?" He looked at them both worriedly and Brad shook his head with a smile, but there was a look in his eyes that Teddy had never seen there before, a look of tenderness and pride and excitement. "What's up? Or am I being nosy?"

"I guess not. I wanted to tell everyone tonight. But I'd like to tell you first." He had a right now to hear this first. B.J. reached for Serena's hand and smiled at Teddy. "We're having a baby."

"Already?" Teddy looked stunned. "When?"

"Not for another six months, or six and a half, to be exact." Brad looked teasing. "It's decent. We've been married for six months now."

"I didn't mean that." Teddy looked embarrassed and then glanced at Serena. "It just seems so soon."

"It is soon, and I'm glad. I'm not as young as you are. I don't want to waste any time, and Serena's happy too." He beamed at her again and Teddy smiled as he watched them.

"I think I'm sick with jealousy, but the weird thing is, you know, I'm not even sure I mind."

B.J. laughed at the candor of his younger brother and all three of them chuckled together. Something very odd had happened between the three of them that day. A new bond had formed between two people who had already loved each other all of their lives and they had managed to include in it a whole other person. It was as though the three of them stood within a magic circle, and they knew it.

"Boy, I'm gonna be an uncle!" He began to whoop, Serena laughed, and B.J. tried futilely to get him to quiet down.

"Don't tell the whole household yet, for chrissake. I want to tell Mother first. Think she's ready to be a grandmother yet, Teddy?"

There was a long silence as the two brothers exchanged a pointed glance. "I'm not sure."

Only Serena had said nothing in the past few minutes, since they had begun to talk about the baby. "Are you feeling all right, Serena?" Now suddenly Teddy shared B.J.'s concern, and she laughed at them both.

"Yes, I'm fine. Perfect. Terrific."

"That's good," and then with another mischievous dimpled grin, "Too bad you can't wait two years to have it, I might be able to deliver the baby."

"That's a thrill we can live without," Brad filled in quickly. "But at least you'll be out there to share the big moment with us." It pleased Brad to know that his little brother would be living in San Francisco too, or very near it. For four years he was going to Stanford University Medical School, and he hoped that they would see a lot of each other. He told him so now, and Teddy nodded his head emphatically.

"Especially now. I want to come and see my nephew."

"Nope." Brad looked strangely firm.

"Nope?" It was Teddy's turn to look surprised. "I can't see him?"

"You can see *her*. It's a niece."

"A niece? You want a girl?" He looked shocked. "That's unnatural! Aren't men in our family supposed to be all worked up about continuing the name?"

"Yup, and I'm going to have a daughter and she's going to marry a guy named Obadiah Farthingblitz and I'm going to be happy as hell for her at her wedding."

"You're nuts. In fact"—he looked from one to the other—"I suspect that you both are. Which may be your salvation. You know, I think we're going to have some damn fine times in California, guys."

"Will you come and see us often, Teddy?" Serena looked at him warmly.

"As often as you'll let me. I'll be out in September for med school. Meanwhile I'm going to Newport this summer to do whatever damage I can do there. I'm stopping in Chicago on the way out, and I should reach you by the last week in August. I'll come and stay." He said it with the assurance of family, and Brad laughed.

With that, the three of them swept into the kitchen, greeted the cook, stole some cookies, tasted some asparagus, sniffed at a mysterious stock that Brad swore smelled like turkey, and moments later they departed and took refuge in Brad's old study. It now belonged to Teddy, and they reminisced as they ate narrow little watercress sandwiches on delicate white bread and drank lemonade. It was a pleasant way to while away the afternoon, waiting for the rest of the family to return, and shortly after lunch Serena fell asleep on the couch. Both men were happy she slept, tense as both knew the next hours would be for everyone. Something had already told Brad, now that he was back on home turf, that none of it was going to be easy. Before he had come back to this house, he had been able to vacillate about what he thought would happen, how his mother would behave. He had tried to play a game with himself that he could no longer play here. His mother's very strength made itself felt so clearly in this house that it was impossible to delude oneself about her for a moment. This was not going to be easy in any way. What Margaret Fullerton had wanted Brad to bring home as his wife was a girl like the thousands of debutantes he had met over the years, a girl more or less like Pattie Atherton, she didn't want a principessa from Rome as her daughter-in-law. She didn't give a damn about that. She wanted the daughter of one of her friends at the Colony Club, someone who went to the same places they did, knew the same people, did the same things. And there was one undeniable thing about Serena that Brad knew would never sit well with his mother: Serena was totally different. It was what he loved about her, what had already captivated Teddy in only a few hours. She was not an ordinary sort of girl in any way. She was extraordinary in every possible way. She was spectacular, beautiful, smart as hell, but she wouldn't fit into the New York, Stork Club, 21, Colony Club mold. And more than ever, as he looked at his peacefully sleeping aristocratic Italian bride, Brad realized to his very gut that there was going to be trouble.

CHAPTER TWENTY

Margaret Fullerton came home that afternoon at exactly three fifteen, looking precisely as she had when she left the house that morning. Impeccable and elegant, in a pearl-gray silk suit from Chanel with a dusty-rose silk blouse and matching lining in her jacket. She wore delicate gray kid shoes, gray stockings, a small gray lizard bag, and her smoothly coiffed white hair looked as perfect as it had at eight o'clock that morning. As was her usual routine, she came in, greeted the servants, set down her handbag and gloves on a large silver tray in the front hall, glanced at the mail carefully laid out by one of the maids, and walked into the library.

There, she would, as a matter of course, either ring for tea, or make some phone calls in answer to the list of messages always neatly left on her desk by the butler. But this afternoon she knew that Brad was coming home. She wasn't entirely sure if they were back yet or not, and she was sorry that she had been unable to meet him, but she sat in the library now, looked at her watch with a feeling of anticipation, and rang for the butler. He appeared in the doorway a minute later with a look of expectation.

"Yes, ma'am?"

"Is my son here, Mike?"

"Yes, ma'am. Two of them. Mr. Theodore is here, and also Mr. Bradford." Mike had been with them for almost thirty years.

"Where are they?"

"Upstairs. In Mr. Theodore's den. Should I call them?"

"No." She stood up quietly. "I'll go to them. Are they alone?" She looked hopeful. As though Serena might already have been disposed of. But the butler carefully shook his head.

"No, ma'am. Mrs. Fullerton—Mrs. Bradford Fullerton," he explained, "is with them." Margaret Fullerton's eyes raged, but she only nodded.

"I see. Thank you, Mike. I'll go up in a moment." She had to think now, just for a minute, of what she was going to say and how she was going to say it. She had to handle it right or Brad would be lost to her for good.

She also knew that Teddy would have to be kept in the dark. She had already made the mistake of telling him what she had in mind. It had been a stupid thing to do and she knew it, her youngest son had a warm heart and dreamy eyes, and his philosophies about life belonged in a romantic novel, not in a real world filled with opportunists and fools, and little Italian tramps after her son's fortune.

Margaret Hastings Fullerton had been orphaned at twenty-two, when both her parents had been killed in a train collision abroad. They left her with an enormous fortune. She had been well counseled by the partners in her father's law firm and a year later she had married Charles Fullerton and merged her fortune with his. Hers had been born of the country's steel mills, and had been sweetened over the years with important land holdings and the acquisition of numerous banks. Charles Fullerton, on the other hand, was of a family whose money had been derived from more genteel sources. They had made a fortune in tea in the previous century, had added to it enormous profits from coffee, had huge holdings in Brazil and Argentina, England and France, Ceylon and the Far East. It was a fortune that had boggled even her mind, and Margaret Hastings Fullerton didn't boggle easily. She had always had a remarkable understanding of the financial world, a fascination with politics and international affairs, and had her parents lived, her father would probably have seen to it that she married a diplomat or a statesman, possibly even the President of the United States. As it was, she met Charles Fullerton instead, the only son of Bradford Jarvis Fullerton II. Charles had three sisters, all of whose husbands had gone to work for Charles's father. They traveled extensively and constantly throughout the world, managed the companies well and satisfied the old man in all possible ways, except one. They were not his sons, and Charles was, but Charles had no interest whatsoever in inheriting his father's throne at the head of the empire. He wanted a quiet life, to practice law, to travel as little as possible, and to reap the fruits of all that his father and grandfather had created. It was Margaret who found the Fullerton investments fascinating, who wanted him to join the others, and eventually take over the firm. But she knew within months of their marriage that there was no hope of that. She was married to one of the country's richest men, and he didn't give a damn about the excitement of how that fortune had been created. Her plans for him, as well as his father's, went awry, and he had his own way in the end. He joined several friends from law school, formed his own firm, and practiced law in his own quiet way. He had none of the flamboyance or ambition of his forebears. Nor did he have the steely drive of his wife, who in truth was much like his father. She and the old man had got along famously until he died, and it was she who had truly mourned when the empire was sold off bit by bit. Gone were the vast holdings in exotic countries, gone the dreams that one day Charles would change his mind and take his place in charge of it all, gone her hopes of being the force behind the throne.

She had turned her ambitions then from international business to politics. And here, for a brief time, she had succeeded. She had managed to convince Charles that what he wanted most in life was a seat in the Senate. It would enhance his career, help his law firm, delight his wife and friends, and she assured him that it was everything he wanted. In truth, he had found it tedious and boring, he had disliked spending time in Washington, and he had refused to run again when his term came to an end. With relief he had returned to his law firm in New York, leaving Margaret with no illusions and few dreams. He had carved a niche for himself that he wanted, a quiet spot behind a desk in New York, and he wanted nothing more. If it was not enough for her, it was nonetheless more than adequate for him. All that remained for Margaret Fullerton was to turn her hopes toward her sons.

Bradford was certainly the most enterprising of her sons, but like his father, he was intractable and did exactly as he wished. None of the jobs he had had so far had been what Margaret would have called important, he refused to use the connections he had, and although he had some interest in politics, she was beginning to doubt that it was enough ambition in that direction to make him alter the course of his life. What he wanted, not unlike his father, Margaret had often thought with dismay, was a life that was "pleasant" and meant something to him. He had no interest in power, as she saw it, industry or commerce on a grand scale, or an empire like that of his ancestors. Greg, on the other hand, was a great deal more malleable. Though he was not as bright as Brad, in him she saw more hope, and by marrying a congressman's daughter, he would certainly be in the right circle to pursue politics if that was the direction in which he was pushed. And Margaret knew that she could count on Pattie to get Greg moving.

Teddy was another matter entirely, and Margaret had known that about her youngest child, almost from the day he was born. Theodore Harper Fullerton moved at his own pace, in his own time, in precisely the direction he wanted. He had his mother's drive, but in none of the same veins. And now he was about to pursue his career in medicine with the same kind of energy and determination that she would have had, if she had had a career of her own. One couldn't help but respect Teddy, but she steered clear of him too. He was not someone she could influence, or even move at times, and it was with him that she locked horns constantly. They disagreed about everything, from politics to the weather. Particularly this recent business about Brad's little harlot from Rome. She had told the entire family exactly what she thought about that nonsense, and more specifically she had told her husband precisely what she thought needed to be done. It was a shame that nothing could be done before he brought her to New York, but with Greg's wedding coming so quickly, she didn't have time to go to Paris to see them. She would just have to take care of it when they came to New York. And she was sure that there would be no problem. It was obvious that the girl was after his money, from what Pattie had said, but it still wasn't too late to buy her off. They would pay her passage back to Europe, give her a handsome sum to unload her, and the annulment proceedings would be begun at once. If she was smart and willing to cooperate, Brad didn't even have to know about their arrangement. All she had to tell him was that she had changed her mind about everything and was going home.

As Margaret made her way upstairs now to Teddy's den, she thought about the papers in her desk downstairs. It would all be so simple. She had thought about it again all that morning, and it was a relief to know that the matter was almost at an end. Her intense desire to get rid of Serena had eclipsed almost all else lately. She had scarcely thought about the wedding, and it had taken some of the joy away from the thrill of seeing Brad home. It was part of why she hadn't gone to the ship to meet him. She just wanted to unload Serena, and then she could enjoy having her oldest boy home. She was already planning a trip to San Francisco in the fall to see him. She wanted to visit Teddy at Stanford, and she could see Brad at the same time, in his new post at the Presidio. Besides, she had old friends there, and knew that she would have a pleasant time. The thought of the prospective trip warmed her, as she stood silently for a moment, as though girding her strength, and then with a small determined smile, she knocked on the door.

"Yes?" The voice was Teddy's, and there was laughter within. She could hear a woman's voice, and Brad's deep voice and soft laughter as she answered.

"It's me, dear. May I come in?"

"Of course." The words were spoken as Teddy pulled open the door, looking down at his mother, a smile still lighting his eyes. But the smile faded quickly once he saw her. He felt an immediate tension pass between them, and he felt an instant desire to protect Serena. "Come in, Mother. Brad and Serena are here." He made a point of including her too. "We've been waiting for you to arrive."

She nodded, stepped swiftly into the room, and, an instant later, stood facing her oldest child. She stopped and didn't move toward him, but there was obvious emotion in her eyes. "Hello, Brad."

Without any sign of strain he moved toward her and gave her a warm hug. "Hello, Mother." She clung to him possessively for just a moment, and then stepped back, with a mist of tears in her eyes.

"My God, it's good to have you home safe and sound."

"Yup, here I am, all in one piece. Home from the wars at last." He grinned cheerfully at her, and then stepped aside and with a single loving gesture he waved to the tall, graceful blond woman standing just behind him in the ivory silk suit, with the enormous emerald eyes. "I'd like you to meet my wife, Mother. Serena, this is my mother." He executed a stiff little bow, and for an instant there was no movement whatsoever in the cozy room. There was total and absolute silence, as though everyone were holding his breath while the two women met, but it was Serena who broke the ice. She came forward very quickly, with a graceful hand extended and a nervous but friendly smile.

"Mrs. Fullerton, how do you do?" She looked exquisite as she stood there, and the older woman's eyes seemed to narrow as she looked Serena over carefully from head to foot. "I'm very happy to meet you."

Margaret Fullerton put forth her hand, with a look of ice. "How do you do? I hope you had a pleasant trip." There was no suggestion that this was her daughter-in-law she was meeting for the first time. She was a total stranger, and Margaret intended to see that nothing changed that. "Sorry not to meet you at the ship, Brad." She turned toward her son with a smile. "I got bogged down with things, and I thought I'd leave that honor to Teddy. But we'll all have dinner together tonight. And tomorrow." She ignored Serena completely in her description of their plans. "And then of course on Saturday there's the wedding. You've got a rehearsal for it tomorrow, and half a dozen other things.

You'll have to stop in to see your father's tailor in the morning. He used your old measurements for a cutaway and striped trousers, but you'd better let him check you over quickly tomorrow, while he can still make some changes before it's too late.''

"Fine." There were fine lines of tension around Brad's eyes. He didn't give a damn about the cutaway and striped trousers. He wanted his mother to give some sign that she had accepted his wife. "What about the three of us having lunch tomorrow, quietly somewhere?"

"Darling, I can't. You can imagine how mad everything is just before the wedding." Her eyes gave nothing away, but Brad felt his whole body go tense.

"Isn't all of that supposed to be the Athertons' problem? I thought the bride's mother was the one with all the headaches."

"I have the rehearsal dinner to arrange tomorrow night."

"Well, then afterward we'll spend some time together." He wasn't pleading, but he was asking, and as he listened to his older brother, Teddy began to ache inside. He could see exactly what his mother was doing. Just as she had managed not to go to the boat, now she was avoiding them again. What in hell was she doing? he wondered. Trying to pretend that Serena didn't exist, or was there a reason for her behaving this way? Teddy had an unpleasant feeling that something they would all regret was about to happen.

"I'll do my best, dear." His mother's voice was non-committal. "Have you seen your father?"

"Not yet." It had occurred to Brad as well that no one except Teddy had put himself out to welcome him back and meet Serena, and he was slowly sorry that he had made the time to come home on their way to San Francisco. They could have gone to Rome to say their good-byes there, or wandered around Europe for a couple of weeks before flying home and merely changing planes in New York.

But maybe he should give them more of a chance, he decided. It was a hectic time for them all, and he couldn't expect everyone to drop what they were doing just for him. But it was not for himself that he cared about it, it was for Serena. Already he could see something wary in her eyes as he glanced at her.

187

"You'll be at dinner with us tonight, won't you, Brad?" His mother gazed at him, as though he were the only one included in the invitation.

"Yes." He looked at her pointedly. "We both will. And which room do you want us in, by the way?"

For only an instant his mother looked annoyed. He was forcing her to deal with the issue of Serena, and it was the last thing she wanted to do at that point in time. But she realized that, for the moment at least, there was no avoiding it. "I think the blue room would be fine. How long are you staying, dear?" She looked only at her son and never once at the girl.

"For two weeks, until we leave for San Francisco."

"That's marvelous." She turned then, glanced searchingly at Serena, and then looked back at Brad. "I have a few details to take care of, darling. I'll see you in a little while." And then, unexpectedly, she looked back at Serena and spoke to her with great care. "I think perhaps it would be a good idea if you and I spent a little time together. If you could come to my boudoir for half an hour before dinner, I think we might speak alone." Serena nodded immediately and Brad looked surprised. Maybe the old girl was making an effort after all, he decided, perhaps he had wronged her.

"I'll show her where it is, Mother." For an instant Brad looked pleased, but unnoticed by the others, there was terror in Teddy's eyes.

Their mother left them a few minutes later and Teddy looked strangely worried. Brad teased him about it, and Serena sat down with a long nervous sigh, staring at them both.

"Why do you suppose she wants to see me alone?" Serena looked worried, and her husband smiled.

"She just wants to get to know you. Don't let her intimidate you, love. We've got nothing to hide."

"Should I tell her about the baby?"

"Why not?" Brad looked proudly at her and they exchanged a smile, but Teddy was quick to intervene.

"No, don't." They both looked at him, startled, and he blushed.

"Christ, why not?" B.J. looked almost annoyed. He had

only been home for a few hours, and he was already feeling unnerved by his family. What odd people they were, he remembered now, and all the intrigues and plots and tensions and insults. His mother always kept them all at fever pitch, and it annoyed him severely to become a part of that again now. "Why shouldn't Serena tell her?"

"Why don't you tell her together?"

"What difference does it make?"

"I'm not sure. But she might say something to upset Serena." Brad thought about it for a moment and then nodded.

"All right. Anyway"—he looked pointedly at his wife—"don't let the old bag push you around, love. Just be yourself and she won't be able to resist you." He bent down to give her a hug and thought that he could almost feel her tremble. "You're not afraid of her, are you?"

Serena thought about it for a moment and then nodded at him. "Yes, I think I am. She's a very striking, very strong woman." She had also been much prettier than Serena had expected, and much tougher. Serena had never met anyone quite like her. Her grandmother had been a strong woman, but in a much purer sense. Her grandmother had had quiet strength and determination. Margaret Fullerton had something different. One sensed instantly about her that she used her strength to get what she wanted, and perhaps in ways that were occasionally ugly. There was something that ran just under the surface of Margaret Fullerton that was as cold as ice and as hard as nails.

"There's nothing to be afraid of, Serena." He said it gently as he pulled her off the couch and prepared to take her to the blue room, where his mother had said they would be staying, and as Teddy followed them upstairs he was praying that his brother was right.

189

CHAPTER TWENTY-ONE

As it turned out, Brad was still in the tub at the hour of Serena's appointed meeting with his mother. And the butler led the way downstairs, down a hall with walls covered with small exquisite paintings, three tiny Corots, a small Cézanne, a Pissarro, two Renoir sketches, a Cassatt. The paintings were beautifully framed and hung as though in an art gallery, with excellent lighting, against wonderfully draped taupe velvet walls. The carpeting beneath her feet was thick and of the same pale mocha color, it was in sharp contrast to the marble floors she was so used to in Rome and Venice and Paris. The softness of the carpeting beneath her feet in the Fullertons' apartment felt as though she were walking on clouds. The furniture was all handsome and quiet, there was a great deal of Queen Anne, some Chippendale, some Hepplewhite, and a few quiet Louis XV pieces, but everywhere were rich woods and subdued colors. There was none of the gilt and marble of the richer Louis XV pieces or the Grecian-inspired Louis XVI. The Fullerton apartment was done in excellent taste, with the best of everything in evidence in rich abundance, but none of it was showy. Even the colors Margaret had chosen for her home were soft beiges, warm browns, ivory shades, and here and there a deep green or a restful blue. There were no peaches or rubies or brilliant greens. It was a whole other look than the Renaissance splendors of the palazzi Serena had known, which she had to admit that she still liked better. Yet this had a certain warmth to it, and it was all as elegant and restrained as Margaret Fullerton herself.

When the butler stopped at her boudoir door, he stepped aside for Serena to knock, and then bowed rapidly and disappeared as Serena entered. She found her mother-in-law sitting in a small room at a beautiful little oval table, a butler's tray from the era of George III, with a drink in her hand, and a heavily carved crystal decanter and another glass on a silver tray, waiting for Serena's arrival. There was a large portrait over the small ivory couch on which she sat, and the man in it wore a huge mustache and pince-nez, over dark turn-of-the-century clothes, and his eyes seemed to leap out of the portrait and ask a thousand questions.

"My husband's grandfather," she explained as Serena felt his eyes on her and glanced toward the painting. "He is responsible for almost everything that your husband has." She spoke pointedly, as though Serena would understand her, and to the young Italian girl standing before her, it seemed a very odd thing to say. "Please sit down." Serena did as she was told, and sat very primly on the edge of a small Queen Anne chair, in the black velvet dress she had chosen for dinner. It had a low square neckline and broad straps, a slim skirt, and over it she wore a short white satin jacket. It was a suit that Brad had bought her just before they left Paris, and Serena knew that she wouldn't be able to wear it for much longer. Her ever growing waistline would soon refuse to be restricted by the small waist of the dress. But for tonight it was perfect, and she wore it with pearl earrings and her pearl necklace, and she looked very grown-up and very pretty as Margaret Fullerton looked her over again. Even she had to admit that the girl was pretty, but that wasn't the point. The fact was that if she didn't go back to Europe she was going to destroy Brad's life. "Would you care for a drink?" Serena shook her head quickly. The baby had made it almost impossible, in recent weeks, to even so much as sniff wine.

While Margaret poured herself a drink, Serena studied her. She was an amazingly distinguished-looking woman, and tonight she wore a rich sapphire-colored silk dress, set off by a handsome necklace of sapphires and diamonds, which her husband had bought her at Cartier's in Paris after the first world war. Serena's eyes were held for a long moment by the necklace, and then her glance shifted to the enormous sapphire earrings, and the matching bracelet on her arm. With an assumption of understanding, Margaret Fullerton nodded and decided that it was time to make her move. "Serena, I'm going to be very candid with you. I don't think that there's any reason for us to mince words. I understand from—from friends"—Margaret Fullerton hesitated for only a moment—"that you met Brad while you were working for him in Rome. Am I correct?"

"Yes, I—I got the job when I came back to Rome."

"That must have been a fortunate circumstance for you."

"At the time it was. I had no one left in Rome, except"—she struggled for a way to explain Marcella—"an old friend."

"I see. Then the job at the palazzo must have been a godsend." She smiled, but her eyes were frighteningly cold.

"It was. And so was your son."

Margaret Fullerton almost visibly flinched, as the young woman sat very straight in her chair, the pretty ivory face framed by the collar of the white satin jacket, her eyes bright, her hair brushed until it shone. It was difficult to find fault with Serena, but Margaret was not to be fooled by appearances. She already knew exactly what she thought of this girl. She went on now with a look of determination.

"That was exactly the impression I had, Serena. That you needed Brad's help, and he came to your rescue, perhaps in getting you out of Italy. All of which is quite admirable of him, and perhaps even very romantic. But I think that getting married may have been carrying things more than a little bit too far, don't you?" For an instant Serena didn't know what to say, and whatever came to mind, Margaret did not give her the chance to say it. "We all know that men sometimes get involved in unusual situations during wartime, but"—her eyes blazed for a moment as she set down her glass—"it was mad of him to bring you home."

"I see." Serena seemed to shrink visibly in her chair. "I thought that perhaps . . . when we met—"

"What did you think? That I'd be fooled? Hardly. You're a very pretty girl, Serena. We both know that. But all that nonsense about being a princess is precisely that. You were a charwoman working for the American army, and you latched onto a good thing. The only unfortunate thing is that you weren't smart enough to know when to let go." For an instant Serena looked as though she had been slapped. There were tears in her eyes as she sat back in her chair, and

Margaret Fullerton stood up and went to her desk. She returned a moment later with a small folder, sat down again on the small couch, and looked at Serena squarely. "I'm going to be frank with you. If what you wanted was to get out of Italy, you've done that. If you want to stay in the States, I'll see to it that that is arranged. You can settle yourself anywhere in this country, except of course where Brad lives, which means neither San Francisco, nor here. If you want to go back to Europe, I will arrange for immediate passage back. In either case, after you sign these papers, annulment proceedings will be initiated by his father's law firm at once, and you will be rewarded handsomely for your trouble." Margaret Fullerton looked matter-of-fact and not the least bit embarrassed by what she had just said to Serena.

But Serena seemed to be sitting even straighter in her chair, and the emeralds in her eyes had suddenly caught fire. "I'll be rewarded?"

"Yes." Margaret looked pleased. She was obviously on the right track. "Quite handsomely. Brad's father and I discussed it again last night. Of course you must understand that once you sign these papers you will have no right whatsoever to attempt to sue for more. You'll have to take what you get, and leave it at that."

"Of course." Serena's eyes blazed, but now she too sounded matter-of-fact. "And for precisely what price are you buying your son back?"

For an instant Margaret Fullerton looked annoyed. "I don't think I like your choice of expression."

"But isn't that what you're doing, Mrs. Fullerton? Buying him back from an Italian whore? Isn't that how you view it?"

"How I view it is entirely immaterial. What you have done, snagging my son as you did while he was overseas, is liable to affect his entire future, and his career. What he needs is an American wife, someone of his own class, his own world, who can help him."

"And I could never do that?"

Margaret Fullerton laughed and spread her hands in the small elegant den. "Look around you. Is this your world?

The world you come from? Or is this only what you wanted? What exactly did you plan to give him, other than that pretty face and your body? Have you anything to give him? Position, connections, resources, friends? Don't you understand that he could have a career in politics? But not married to an Italian charwoman, my dear. How can you live with what you have done to his career . . . his life?'' The tears stood out once again in Serena's eyes and her voice was husky when she answered.

"No, I have nothing to give him, Mrs. Fullerton. Except my heart.'' But she answered none of the other questions. It was none of the woman's business what she came from. In truth, she came from something far grander than this, but who could explain that now? It was all over. Gone.

"Precisely.'' Margaret went on. "You have nothing. And to be blunt, you are nothing. But I suspect that you want something. And I have what you want.'' *Do you; you bitch?* Serena silently raged. . . . *Do you have love . . . and patience and understanding and goodness and a lifetime to give me? Because that's what I want to give him.* But she said nothing.

Without saying another word, Margaret Fullerton opened the folder she had brought from her desk, and handed a check to Serena. It was made out in the amount of twenty-five thousand dollars. "Why don't you have a look at that?'' Out of curiosity Serena took it from her, and glanced at the numbers in disbelief.

"You would give me that to leave him?''

"I would and I am. In fact we can have this business over within a matter of minutes, if you will simply sign here.'' She pushed a single typewritten document toward Serena, who stared at it in amazement. It said that she agreed to divorce Bradford Jarvis Fullerton III, or obtain an annulment, as soon as possible, that she would either leave the country or reside in another city, and would never, at any time, discuss any of this with the press. She would fade out of Brad's life immediately, in exchange for which she was to be paid the sum of twenty-five thousand dollars. Furthermore, the paper went on, she swore that at this moment in time she was not pregnant and would attempt to make no

194

future claim on Brad for paternity of any child she subsequently had. When she saw that, a smile broke out on her face and a moment later she began to laugh. They had thought of everything, those bastards, but suddenly now it seemed funny.

"Apparently you find something amusing here?"

"I do, Mrs. Fullerton." There was still a green blaze in Serena's eyes, but now she felt mistress of the situation at last.

"May I ask what amused you? This document was very carefully prepared." She looked furious at Serena's reaction, but she didn't dare let the girl know.

"Mrs. Fullerton." Serena smiled at her sweetly and stood up. "Brad and I are having a baby."

"You're *what*?"

"I'm pregnant."

"And when did *that* happen?"

"Two months ago." Serena looked at her proudly. "The baby is due in December."

"That certainly adds a new dimension to your schemes, doesn't it?" The older woman was almost overwhelmed by fury.

"You know"—Serena looked at her, with one hand on the door—"you may find it very hard to believe, but I have no schemes about Brad, and I never have, right from the first. I know that you think I am a poverty-stricken little tramp from Rome, but you're only partly right. I have no money. That is all. But my family was quite as illustrious as yours." Her eyes strayed to the portrait on the wall. "My grandfather looked not unlike that man. Our house"—she smiled at the older woman—"was far grander than this one. In fact all three of our houses were. But the important thing, Mrs. Fullerton, is that I want nothing from your son. Except his love and our baby. The rest I don't want, not his money or your money or his father's money, or that check for twenty-five thousand dollars. I will never take anything from any of you except," she spoke very softly, "my husband's love." And with that, she slipped quietly out of the room and closed the door, as Margaret Fullerton stared at it with sheer fury, and an instant later anyone passing her boudoir would have heard the shattering of breaking glass. She had thrown her glass of sherry at the fireplace. But as far as she was concerned the battle wasn't over. Before Brad left New York for San Francisco, she would see to it that Serena was gone, baby or no baby. And she had two weeks in which to do it. And she knew she would.

CHAPTER TWENTY-TWO

The family dinner that night was an event of intriguing auras and currents. Margaret sat at the head of the table in her sapphire-blue silk looking beautiful and charming. There was no sign of what had come before the meal, and if she avoided any conversation with Serena throughout it went unnoticed. At the opposite end of the table sat Charles Fullerton, pleased at having all three of his sons home at once, which was a first since the war, and he toasted all three of them handsomely, as well as the two young women, who were "new additions" to the family, as he put it. Greg seemed unusually expansive at dinner. Brad realized after the first course that his brother was drunk, and he looked searchingly at Teddy, wondering why. Was it the excitement of the impending wedding? Nerves? Or was he uncomfortable around Brad, because he was marrying Pattie? Pattie herself chattered incessantly and was playing her "adorable" role, flirting with her big blue eyes and managing to take in all the men in the family each time she told a story. She was nauseatingly deferential to her fiancé's mother, and she managed to ignore Serena completely. Only Teddy really paid any attention to Serena. Brad was seated too far from her to be of much help. She was seated between Teddy and Charles, and his father offered little conversation throughout the meal, so it was left to Teddy to make her feel welcome, which he was glad to do. He leaned toward her and spoke to her quietly, made her laugh once or twice, but mostly he noticed that she was far more withdrawn than she had been that afternoon in his study. He wanted to ask her how the private interview had gone with his mother, but he was afraid that someone might overhear him.

"Are you all right?" he finally whispered halfway through the meal. She had been staring into her wineglass and saying nothing.

"I'm sorry." She apologized to him for being so dreary, pleaded exhaustion from the emotions of their arrival, and managed not to convince him.

"I think something's wrong, Brad." Teddy looked at him with concern after dinner as they walked quietly into the library behind the rest of the family.

"I'll say there is. Greg is plastered out of his mind, Pattie is all caught up in playing Scarlett O'Hara, you look like you've just been to a funeral, and Mother's so busy running the show that Dad can't get a word in." Brad looked discouraged by his first night back home.

"You mean you remembered it different?" Teddy tried to look amused. "Or were you hoping it had changed in your absence?"

"Maybe a little of both."

"Don't hold your breath. It can only get worse over the years." As he said it he glanced at Greg and Pattie. "Has she said anything to you at all?"

"Only thank you when I congratulated her and Greg." And then, as he knit his brows, "She didn't say a single goddamn word to Serena at dinner, and neither did Mother."

"I didn't expect Pattie to, but Mother . . ." Teddy looked troubled and then touched his brother's arm. "Brad, something was wrong with Serena at dinner. I don't know if she just wasn't feeling well because of the baby or what, but she was awfully quiet."

"Do you think it was Mother?" The two brothers exchanged a glance.

"You'd better ask her. Did you see her after she was with Mother before dinner?"

"No. I didn't see her until we were all at table."

197

Teddy nodded thoughtfully, with a worried look in his eyes. "I don't think I like it."

But Brad smiled at the look on his younger brother's face. "Come on, old man, you worry more than all of us put together. Why don't you have a drink and relax for a change?"

"Like Greg?" Teddy looked at him pointedly in annoyance. "How long has he been doing this number?"

"Two or three years now." Teddy spoke in an undervoice and his older brother looked shocked.

"Are you kidding?"

"Nope. Not a bit. He started drinking when he went in the army. Dad says it's boredom. Mother says he needs a more challenging job now, like something in politics maybe. And Pattie is pushing him to go to work for her father."

Brad looked chagrined, and then met his wife's eyes and forgot what his little brother was saying. "I'll be back in a minute, Ted. I want to make sure Serena is all right." He was standing beside her a moment later, and leaned down to whisper in her ear. "You feeling okay, sweetheart?"

"Fine." She smiled up at him, but it was not the usual dazzling smile that left him aching to kiss her and almost breathless. There was something very subdued about her tonight and he knew that his brother was right. Something was wrong with Serena. "I'm just tired." She knew that he didn't believe her. But what could she tell him? The truth? She had promised herself that she wouldn't do that, as soon as she had left his mother's room. She wanted to forget what the woman had told her, and shown her, the check, the paper, the unkind words, the accusations, all of it. For a moment, as she had left the boudoir, she had felt like a tramp, just from the assumptions that had been made. Now she wanted to forget it and put it behind her.

"Do you want to go upstairs?" he whispered to her, still with the same worried frown.

"Whenever you're ready," she whispered back. In truth, it had been a very depressing evening. Mr. Fullerton was precisely as Brad had described. Weak—a man with no spine. She had been literally unable to look at his mother, Pattie had filled her with terror as she had chirped and flirted her way through the evening, and Serena had been frightened that she would create a scene and call her some of the things she had called her from the terrace in Rome. Greg had been pathetic, drunk before the first course, Brad had been seated too far away to be of much help, and only Teddy had helped her get through the evening. Suddenly she had to admit that she felt drained, and for a moment as she sat there in her chair in the library, looking out over the park, she felt as though she might faint, or burst into tears. She had been through too much in the past three hours and she suddenly felt it.

"I'm taking you upstairs." Brad had seen it too, and standing close enough to overhear him, Teddy nodded his approval.

"She looks beat."

Brad nodded and offered her his arm, which she took with a grateful look as he made his excuses to the rest of the group, and a moment later they were on the stairs, and at last in their room, and as Brad closed the door behind them Serena lay down on the bed and burst into tears.

"Baby . . . Serena . . . honey . . . what happened?" He looked stupefied as he stood staring at her. It took a moment to register what had happened and then he was instantly beside her, lying on the bed, cradling her gently, and stroking her hair. "Serena . . . darling . . . tell me. What is it? Did someone say something to you?" But she was determined not to tell him. She only lay there and sobbed, shaking her head and insisting that it was a combination of pregnancy and exhaustion. "Well, in that case"—he looked at her in growing concern when at last she stopped and wiped her eyes—"you're staying in bed tomorrow."

"Don't be silly. I'll be fine after a night's sleep."

"Nonsense. And if I have to, I'll call the doctor."

"What for? I'm fine." The prospect of being trapped in bed in his mother's house depressed her still further. What if Margaret came upstairs to torment her some more, or press her with another paper? But that was unlikely, Serena knew, what could she do now, now that she knew they were having a baby? "I don't want to stay in bed, Brad."

"We'll discuss it in the morning." But that night he held

her tightly in his arms and she had cried out in her sleep several times, and by the morning he was genuinely worried. "That's it, no discussion. I want you in bed today. We still have the rehearsal this evening, and the rehearsal dinner after that. You have to rest up and get your strength." Emotionally if not physically he was right, but the prospect of staying in bed still depressed her. "I'll come home this afternoon right after I see the tailor, and I'll keep you company."

"Promise?" She looked like a beautiful child as she sat up in their bed in the sunny room.

"Absolutely."

He kissed her before he left, and she lay in bed with her eyes closed for half an hour, just letting her mind drift, remembering their walks in the garden in Rome, moments in Paris, the day they got married, and she was so intent on her pleasant imaginings that she didn't even hear the knock on the door just before lunch.

"Yes?" She suspected that it might be Teddy, and when the door opened, she was already expecting him, with a warm smile. But her smile faded quickly when she saw that it was Margaret. She was wearing a perfectly simple black silk dress and she looked ominous as she stood there.

"May I come in?"

"Certainly." She hopped quickly out of her bed and put on the pink silk robe Brad had bought her in Paris. Margaret said nothing as she watched her put on the wrapper, and waited until the girl was standing before her, nervous and expectant. She knew that her mother-in-law hadn't just come to see her to see how she felt. She could feel her heart pounding within her, and she indicated the two comfortable chairs at the far end of the room. "Would you like to sit down?"

Margaret nodded, and a moment later they both sat down. She looked at Serena inquiringly then. "Did you tell Brad about our little conversation?" Serena shook her head silently. "Good." Margaret regarded that as hopeful. Surely it meant that Serena wanted to make some arrangement with her. If she were a decent girl, Margaret assumed, she would have been shocked and would have told Brad. "I have just spent two hours with my lawyer.''

"Oh." Almost without warning, there were tears in Serena's eyes, but it happened to her a lot lately. The doctor had told her that crying easily wasn't uncommon in the first months of pregnancy, and neither she nor her husband should take it seriously. Until the day before she hadn't, nor had Brad. But suddenly she felt very different. She felt as though this woman was single-handedly out to destroy her. And she was right.

"I'd like you to read over some papers, Serena. Perhaps we can come to some agreement after all, in spite of the child." She spoke of it like a handicap, and Serena began to hate her in earnest. She quietly shook her head and held out a hand as though to stop Margaret physically, if she couldn't stop her words.

"I don't want to see them."

"I think you will."

"I don't." The tears began to spill onto her cheeks, and without saying a word, Margaret took the papers out of her handbag and handed them to Serena.

"I know this must be very difficult for you, Serena." It was the first humane thing she had said. "I'm sure there are even some emotions between you and my son. But you must think of what's best for him, if you love him. Trust me. I know what's best for him." Her voice was deep and power-ful as she attempted to cast her spell over Serena, and in amazement Serena read what Margaret had handed her. It was extraordinary and like something in a nightmare, that this woman was so desperate to separate her from her son. It was worse than the very worst she had expected. She had expected tears, hysterics, names, accusations, but not this cold-blooded series of papers and contracts and dollar signs, in order to end their love. This time Margaret had come up with several alternatives. For one hundred thousand dollars, she and her unborn child were to relinquish all claim on Brad, and never to see him again. In addition there would be support in the amount of two hundred dollars a month until the child reached the age of twenty-one, which equaled an amount of fifty thousand four hundred dollars, the paper informed her. Or she could have an abortion for which they would pay, in which case she could have one hundred fifty thousand dollars immediately, all cash. Of course she'd have to, again, give up Brad. Margaret felt that that was the best plan, she told Serena, as Serena stared at her in disbelief.

"Do you really mean this?" She was stunned.

"Of course I do. Don't you?"

Quietly Serena handed her the papers. "I was so shocked last night that I didn't say very much, but I thought that you understood that I would never do anything like this. I would never give Brad up, like this, for money. If I did give him up, it would be for his own good, not for any 'reward' to me, as you put it. And"—she almost choked on the words— "I would never . . . never . . . dispose of our baby." Tears spilled onto her cheeks as she said it. She looked up at Margaret Fullerton then, her eyes open and green and candid, filled with hurt and something very much akin to despair, and for an instant Margaret Fullerton was ashamed. "Tell me, why do you hate me so much? Do you really think I want to hurt him?"

"You already have. Thanks to you, he's staying in the army. He knows there's nowhere else for him now. Except the army, with crude men and their war brides, and their half-breeds. Is that the life you want for him if you love him?" Serena choked on her sobs and Margaret went on. "If it weren't for you, he'd have a magnificent life, a great career, and he'd be married to Pattie."

"But he didn't want her." Serena sobbed again, almost unable to control herself now. "And I will make him happy."

"Physically perhaps." His mother withdrew into her shell. "But there are other more important things."

"Yes, like love, and children, and a good home, and—" Margaret Fullerton waved an impatient hand. She wanted to get the business done before Brad returned from downtown.

"You're a child, Serena. You don't understand. Now, we have some business to attend to, don't we?" She tried to sound forceful, but Serena stood up, her whole body shaking, and her voice choked with tears.

202

"No, we don't. You can't take him from me. I love him. And he loves me."

"Does he? Don't you think he's just infatuated, Serena? And what will you do in a year or two if he grows tired of you? Will you divorce him, or let him divorce you? And what will you do then? You'll try and get the money you won't take from me now."

"I will never want money from him." She was shaking so hard, she could barely speak now, but the old woman had thought of this contingency too.

"Prove it. If you don't ever want money from him, Serena, prove it."

"How? By running away? By killing my baby?" Serena was sobbing almost hysterically.

"No. By signing this." She took another paper out of her handbag and handed it to Serena, who clenched it in her trembling hand and did not read it. She only stared at the woman she had come to hate so much in only two days. "It says that if Brad leaves you, or dies intestate, that you relinquish all right to any money from him, or from his estate, for you or any children you may have. What it basically says is that if you don't have him you don't want his money either. Will you sign that?" Serena looked at her with unveiled hatred. The woman had thought of everything.

But this time Serena nodded. "Yes, I will sign it, because if he leaves me, I don't want his money anyway. I only want him."

"Then sign it." It wasn't what she had wanted. She had wanted to get rid of the girl for good, but failing that, at least this way she knew that Brad was protected, and in time she could work on him. He couldn't stay married to the girl forever, no matter how pretty she was. For the moment she was young, but in a few years he would tire of her. And perhaps by then he would be tired of the army too. It wasn't too late after all, he was only thirty-four. And in the meantime she had Greg to take care of. She had time to wait for Brad to get rid of this girl. As she watched, Serena signed the paper with trembling fingers, and handed it back to her mother-in-law. A moment later Margaret Fullerton left the room and before she went, she turned to Serena with a look of determination. "This paper is legal, Serena. You won't be able to overturn it. As long as you're not married to him any longer, either widowed or divorced, you won't get a dime from him, or from us. Even if he wants to give you something. I'll have this, and that will stop him. You can't take anything from him now.'

"I never wanted to."

"I don't believe that." And with those words, she turned and closed the door.

Serena almost stumbled to the bed, and lay down on it, and once again, as they had the night before, the sobs came and shook her whole body until she lay in bed feeling spent.

When Brad returned from downtown, he was horrified at how pale and exhausted Serena looked. Her eyes were swollen from crying, and she was obviously feeling very ill.

"Sweetheart, what happened?" As she had the night before, she had decided not to tell him. It seemed the final betrayal to her to tell him about what his mother had done. It was something between her and Margaret Fullerton. She would never tell Brad.

"I don't know. Perhaps it's the change of water or climate. I've been feeling very ill."

"You've been crying?" He looked upset.

"Only because I didn't feel well." She smiled wanly at him.

He shook his head slowly, dismayed at how worn she looked. "I think I should call the doctor."

"Brad, don't." He gave in to her finally, but he was still distressed half an hour later when he went downstairs to make her a cup of tea himself and he found Teddy in the kitchen, making himself a sandwich.

"Can I make you one too?" Brad shook his head as he put the kettle on to boil. "What's up?"

"I'm worried about Serena. She hasn't looked right since last night."

Teddy suddenly looked worried too. "Something happen today?"

"Not that I know of. But I just got back from lunch, and she looks awful. She looks like she's been crying since I left, and she's pale and shaky." He smiled sheepishly at his

204

brother. "You don't know enough about all that yet to tell anything by taking a look at her, do you? I wanted to call Mother's doctor for her, but she won't let me. I'm afraid she might have a miscarriage or something."

"Is she having cramps?"

"She didn't say so. Do you suppose that's why she's been crying? Maybe she knows something's wrong and she doesn't want to tell me." He looked suddenly panicked, as the water for her tea started to boil. "I'm going to call the doctor."

"Now, calm down." Teddy took the kettle from him and set it back on the stove. "Why don't you ask her first. Find out if she has cramps or she's had any bleeding."

"Oh, Christ." Brad looked pale at the thought. "If something ever happened to her or the baby . . ." He didn't dare finish the thought, but Teddy put a hand on his arm.

"Nothing is going to happen to Serena, or the baby either, most likely. So just stop getting yourself worked up. Why don't you go upstairs and see how she's doing, and I'll bring her tea up in a second. All right?" Brad looked at him with immeasurable affection.

"You know something, you're even better than you were as a kid. You're going to be some doctor, Teddy."

"Shut up. You're embarrassing me. Now go take care of your wife. I'll be right up." But a few minutes later, on his way up, Teddy ran into his mother in the hallway.

"Where are you off to? And drinking tea? Good Lord, that's a new one!" She smiled at him in amusement.

"It's for Serena. Brad says she doesn't feel well." He had been about to make light of it, but as he said the words he saw his mother's face.

"Well." He decided not to stall any longer. "I'll let you know if she needs to see a doctor."

"Do that." But she had asked not a single question as to how Serena was.

Teddy knocked on the door of their bedroom, and Brad pulled it open quickly and stepped aside.

"Something wrong?" He could see the look in Teddy's eyes, but the younger brother only shook his head and covered his own concern with a smile.

"No. Nothing. How's she feeling?"

"Better, I think. Maybe she's right. Maybe she's just exhausted." He lowered his voice, she was combing her hair in the bathroom. "She says she hasn't had cramps or bleeding, so maybe she's all right. But Christ, Ted, I'd swear she'd been crying all morning." The conversation was cut short as Serena emerged from the bathroom, looking radically different than she had half an hour before. Her hair was combed, her face washed, her eyes were bright, and she was smiling at Teddy, with her pink satin robe wrapped around her, and little fluffs of pink slippers peeking beneath the hem.

"My God, Serena, you look gorgeous." He kissed both her cheeks, took her hands, and sat down next to her on the foot of the bed. "Brad said you weren't feeling so hot, but you look terrific to me." And then with an almost professional air that made his brother smile, remembering when he had been a nine-year-old terror breaking windows, "Are you feeling all right, Serena? You have us both worried."

"I'm fine." She shook her head emphatically, but as she did so her eyes filled with tears, and a moment later, as though she couldn't stop herself, she reached out to Brad and sobbed in his arms. She was mortified at the scene she was creating, but she was unable to stop, and he looked at his brother over her shoulder in desperation, until at last the sobs subsided and she blew her nose in the handkerchief Teddy handed her. He patted her hand gently with a smile and looked into her eyes when she turned toward him.

"It happens to everyone sometimes, you know, Serena. You've had a lot of new experiences in the past few days, a lot of new people, it's a lot to handle. Even if you weren't pregnant, I think it might wear you out."

"I'm sorry." She shook her head and dried her tears again. "I feel so stupid."

"You shouldn't." He handed her the cup of tea, then Teddy looked up at his older brother, cocked his head to one side, and gave him a boyish grin. "If I promise not to play doctor with her, do you think you could leave us alone for a minute, Big Brother?" But he had such a disarming way of asking that there was no way Brad could resist. He nodded after a moment, and slipped out the bedroom door, promising to be back in a few minutes with two more cups of tea. Teddy waited until he knew his brother would have reached the stairs and then he turned toward Serena again. He took her hand in his own and looked into her eyes. "I want to ask you something, Serena, and I'd like to know the truth. I swear I won't tell Brad." He had already guessed that if what he suspected was true she wasn't going to tell him. "Will you tell me the truth?"

She nodded slowly. She felt no need to be on her guard with Teddy. Even more so than with Brad, whom she wanted to protect.

"Does my mother have anything to do with your being upset?"

She hesitated and bumbled, and blushed furiously as she pulled her hand away from his and began to walk around the room. All of her actions gave her away at once as he watched her.

"Did she come to see you today, Serena?"

"Yes." She turned to him quickly. "But just to see how I felt before she went out to lunch."

She was playing the same game as his mother and he knew it, but he decided to call Serena's bluff. "She didn't go out to lunch today, Serena. And she told me that she hadn't seen you at all. So both of you are lying." He looked at her pointedly, but without accusation. "Why?" It was a simple open question, and when she saw the look in his eyes, she began to cry again.

"I can't tell you."

"I already told you that I wouldn't tell Brad."

"But I can't . . . it would—" She sat down on the bed and began to sob again and this time it was Teddy who took her in his arms. She felt so soft and warm and delicate against him that it almost took his breath away as he held her. For a mad moment he wanted to tell her that he loved her, but he remembered all too quickly that this wasn't why he was holding her in his arms.

"Serena . . . tell me . . . I swear I'll help you. But I have to know."

"There's nothing you can do. It's just that—" She paused and then blurted it out. "She hates me."

"That's ridiculous." He smiled into her hair. "What makes you think that?"

And then suddenly, for no reason except that she trusted him, she decided to tell him about the confrontation the night before, the awful contract, and finally the paper she had signed.

"You signed it?"

She nodded. "Yes. What difference does it make? If he leaves me, I don't want his money anyway. I'll take care of the baby myself."

"Oh, Serena." He gave her a hug. "But that's crazy. You'd have a right to support for you and the child. And if he dies—" Serena stopped him with her eyes. She wouldn't even hear about it.

Teddy wanted only to ease her pain. "He'd never leave you and the baby unprovided for. But what a stinking thing to do." He stared miserably at Serena. "Welcome to the family, love. Sweet, isn't it? Christ." He looked at her again and then put his arms around her. "Poor baby." And then with a serious look in his eyes he looked down at her gently with an odd smile. "If anything ever does happen to him, Serena, and he doesn't have a will, I'll take care of you and your children, I promise."

"Don't be silly . . ." And then with a little shudder, "Don't talk about that." She looked at him gently then. "But thank you."

"I do think you should tell Brad though."

"I can't."

"Why not?"

"It would make him furious with his mother."

"As well he should be."

She shook her head again. "I can't do that, to either of them."

"You're crazy, Serena. She deserves it. That was a stinking, sick, rotten thing to do." But he didn't have a chance to go any further, Brad had just opened the door and came in carrying a tray with three fresh cups of tea.

"How's my wife? Any better?"

"Much." She answered before Teddy could. "And your brother is going to make an excellent doctor. He took my pulse and just from that, he told me I was pregnant.''

"What's the prognosis?''

"At least twins. Possibly triplets.''

But Brad could still see that his brother was worried, and despite the bravado and the gaiety it was obvious that Serena was still troubled. A moment later, when she went to the bathroom, he looked at Teddy. "Well? Do you think I should call the doctor?''

"You want to know what I think? I think that the minute Greg marries that little bitch tomorrow, you two should get the hell out of New York and go somewhere healthy and pretty and just take it easy. She's been through a lot just getting here, from what you've said, and from what I gather from her. Just get her out of New York, away from the family, and go relax with her somewhere before you settle down in San Francisco.''

Brad looked thoughtful. "That might be good advice. I'll think about it, Teddy.''

"Don't think about it. Do it. And my other advice is not to leave her alone for a second.''

"You mean in New York?'' Brad looked surprised.

"I mean even in this apartment. She needs you every minute. She's in a strange country, with strange people, and she's more scared than she lets on. Besides which, she's pregnant, which is emotionally difficult for some women in the beginning. Just be there with her, Brad. All the time. I think that's what happened today. She just got upset, and you weren't around to turn to.''

It sounded unusual for Serena, but Brad was willing to buy it. She had certainly fallen apart radically that morning in his absence, and there was no other way to explain it.

"What are you two plotting?'' Serena emerged again with a suspicious look directed at Teddy, but from the look in his eyes and the obvious calm on Brad's face she knew that he hadn't betrayed her.

"I was telling your husband to take you on a honeymoon right away, like tomorrow.''

"I don't think I'm eligible anymore.'' She looked at her stomach and pretended to pout and her husband pulled her toward him and sat her on his lap.

"You're going to be eligible for a honeymoon with me for the next ninety years, lady. Would you like that? I thought Teddy had a good idea?" She nodded slowly.

"Don't you want to stay here?" She looked thoughtful as she asked him and he shook his head.

"I think we'll both have had enough by the wedding."

"Why don't you think about it before you decide." But Teddy burst into the conversation with a direct look at Serena.

"I think it's bad for you to be here, Serena. You need fresh air and rest, and you won't get that in New York. How about it? Are you going?" He looked at them both and Brad laughed.

"Christ, one would think you're trying to get us out of here."

"I am. I have friends coming to town next week, and I need the guest room." He grinned impishly.

"Where shall we go, Serena? Canada? The Grand Canyon? Denver on our way west?" None of it was familiar to Serena, but Teddy looked at Brad thoughtfully.

"What about Aspen? I spent a few weeks there, visiting a friend last summer, and it's fabulous. You could drive there from Denver."

"I'll check it out." Brad nodded, and then looked at his wife. "Now, let's settle something else. I want you to stay in bed tonight for the rehearsal dinner."

"No." She shook her head quietly. "I'll come with you."

"Shouldn't she stay in bed?" Once again the elder brother turned to the younger, and both were amused.

"I'm not a doctor yet, B.J., but I don't think she has to." He looked quietly at Serena then. "But it might be a lot smarter." He knew that she would know what he meant. But suddenly Serena knew that she would not give up another battle to that woman. She had got at least one of her papers signed and she was assured that Serena would not leave Brad and attempt to run off with the family fortune, but as for the rest of it, she would not be beaten yet again. If they hated her, she had to learn to live with it. But she wouldn't be shunned and forced to stay in her room like some dismal little mouse whom everyone had rejected. They thought that she was a tramp and a harlot and a maid and Lord knew what else, and if she didn't show up, everyone would think that Brad was ashamed of her. Instead she would go, and stand at his side, and make everyone look at him with envy. Her eyes danced as she thought about it, and she looked at her husband and her brother-in-law with a look that managed to combine both mischief and hauteur.

"Gentlemen, I'm coming."

CHAPTER TWENTY-THREE

When Serena came down the stairs of the apartment before the rehearsal dinner, it was easy to believe that she was a principessa. For the glimmer of an eye, even her mother-in-law looked slightly awed. She was wearing a shimmering white silk dress, woven with threads of gold, draped over one shoulder and falling in a gently draped cascade of shimmering folds. The dress fell straight from her shoulder to her feet, and didn't show her slowly enlarging waistline. She looked like a goddess, as she stood beside her husband, with a white flower in her hair, gold sandals on her feet, and her lovely face made up to perfection.

Teddy whistled and even Greg looked more than a little stunned.

The group left together a few minutes after they had assembled in the front hall, the three brothers, their parents, and Serena. Pattie and her parents were meeting them at the club, where a private room for the rehearsal dinner had been arranged.

The groom's mother was wearing a floor-length red satin dress with a little cape in the same fabric, which she had ordered from Dior, and her white hair looked startling in contrast, as she swept into the car, with Greg and Teddy on either side. Her husband chose to sit on one of the jumpseats in the limousine, and Brad and Serena sat in front, which at least kept Serena away from Margaret, a fact for which Teddy was thankful, as he attempted to maneuver things that way from the first. He had promised himself that he would do all he could to make Serena's evening bearable. Since her husband didn't know what agony his mother had caused, the least Teddy could do was be there for her. Serena was deeply grateful to him once again, as their eyes met, and she knew he understood and would not betray her. It was extraordinary to realize that she had only finally met him the day before and they were already fast friends. It was as though he were her brother too, and always had been, as she glanced into the back seat and caught his eye and he grinned at her.

"Flirting with my brother?" Brad whispered it in her ear in the front seat and she shook her head with a little grin.

"No. But it's like I have a real brother."

"He's a good kid."

"So are you." She beamed up at him, and he kissed her gently on the tip of her nose, as she wondered if his mother was watching. It was odd, and unpleasant, to think of oneself always observed, always hated, always resented, even now that she had signed one of those papers. It was incredible to think that that woman had actually tried to get her to sign a paper giving up not only her husband but her child as well. She grew quiet again as she thought of it.

"Are you feeling all right?" Brad was quick to ask her.

"I'm fine. You don't need to worry. I'll be fine tonight."

"How do you know?" He was only half teasing.

"Because you're here."

"Then I'll see to it that I am every minute."

But later in the evening, that was less easily arranged. His mother had placed him at a table with the rest of the wedding party, and since he was the best man, he was sitting on Pattie's left, and Teddy was also at the same table. Serena was put at a table with several older couples and a number of very homely girls, all of whom had known each other for years and spoke almost not at all to Serena. And she couldn't even see Brad or Teddy directly from where she was sitting. She felt as though she were stranded in the midst of strangers, and where he was sitting, Brad felt exactly the same way. He was particularly annoyed at the seating, which had been arranged by his mother. Sitting him next to Pattie seemed a tactless thing to do, but traditionally, as he was the best man, no one could really find fault with his sitting next to the bride. The maid of honor was seated next to Greg, and all of the other bridesmaids and ushers were seated down the sides of the table. On the whole it was a very convivial evening, and Brad managed to talk a great deal to the girl on his left, a tall girl with red hair who had gone to school with Pattie at Vassar, and she had just returned from a long stay with friends in Paris, so at least they had something in common and something to say. She had also spent several years in San Francisco as a child, so she knew that city, and she told him some of the things she thought he needed to know before moving out there, about parts of town that were more or less foggy in case he didn't want a house on the base, ideal spots to spend a day on the beach, places to fish, favorite parks, wonderful places to go with children. None of it was very serious conversation, but it gave them something to talk about and it relieved him at least of having to talk to Pattie, until he suddenly found himself alone with her right after the dancing started, the redheaded girl having been claimed by the usher on her left, and Greg having gone off with the matron of honor. It left Brad, next to Pattie, with almost all of the others on the dance floor, and it suddenly seemed very uncomfortable to be seated next to her alone.

He glanced to his right, and found that she was looking at him, and somewhat ruefully he smiled at her, trying not to think of what had happened in Rome. "Looks like we've been deserted." It was a dumb thing to say, but he couldn't imagine what to say to her. She turned her little heart-shaped face toward him, her mouth in a familiar pout.

"Does that bother you, Brad?"

"No." Which was a blatant lie. He was finding it damn awkward.

She sat there as though expecting something from him, like a kiss or an arm around her shoulders. Everyone knew that they had been engaged the year before, and now suddenly here she was, about to marry his brother, and they were sitting alone at the main table, side by side. Everyone must have been wondering what they were saying.

"Don't you want to dance, Brad?" She looked at him petulantly and he blushed and nodded quickly.

"Sure, Pattie. Why not?" At least she wasn't making a scene, or reminding him of what had happened between them. He stood up next to her chair, took her hand, and they went directly to the dance floor to dance a merengue. She was an expert dancer, and he was suddenly reminded of their nights at the Stork Club, when he'd been on leave after the war, and a little drunk on the excitement of Pattie. She was a damn pretty girl, but in a whole other style from Serena. Serena had elegance and grace, a face that people turned around to look at, and a kind of perfect beauty that took one's breath away. Pattie had something very warm blooded and sexy about her, until one knew her well, and then one knew that beneath the cuddly mannerisms lay a heart of ice. But at any rate she was a good dancer, and she was about to become his sister-in-law, so he was making the best of their moments on the floor. The merengue led into a samba, which became a fox-trot and eventually a waltz, and no one seemed to change partners, so neither did Brad. He kept her out there, much to her delight, and when the waltz became a tango, they stuck with it, until finally Pattie looked at him with her Kewpie-doll smile, fanning her face with her hand.

"Aren't you ready to die from the heat?"

"I'm getting there."

"Want to get some air?"

He hesitated for only a fraction of a second, and then felt that he was being unnecessarily ungracious. What was wrong with going out for some air, after all? "Sure." He glanced over the dance floor, looking for Serena, but he couldn't find her. So he followed Pattie out of the private dining room and down the stairs to the street, where the June air was almost as hot and heavy as the hall.

"I'd forgotten how well you dance." He looked at her as he took a cigarette from his gold case, Pattie glanced at it, and then at his face quickly.

"There's a lot you've forgotten about me, Brad." He said nothing to her in answer, and she reached for the cigarette he had lit, took a long drag, and then put it back between his lips with traces of her deep cherry lipstick on it. "I still don't understand what you did. I mean why?" She looked straight at him and he was sorry they had come out for air. "Did you do it just to get at me? Was that it? I mean, why her? She may be pretty, but she's nothing. And how long will you want that, Brad? A year? Two? And then what, you've ruined your life for that little harlot?"

He was about to go back inside, but he stopped dead in his tracks at her words, and his voice was like ice when he spoke to her. "Don't ever say anything like that to me again, you little bitch. From tomorrow on, for better or worse, you and I will be related. You'll be my brother's wife, and I'm still not sure what that means to you, but from where I sit that means that I'll do my damnedest to respect you." He exhaled his cigarette slowly, and looked down at her with displeasure. "That, however, is going to be quite a challenge."

"You didn't answer my question." She looked suddenly angry, and the pout had become more of a sneer. "Why did you marry her, Brad?"

"Because I love her. Because she is a remarkable woman. Because she's special. And dammit, what business is it of yours?" He didn't have to explain anything to Pattie. "Speaking of which, I might ask you the same thing. Or more to the point, do you love Greg, Pattie?"

"Would I marry him if I didn't?"

"That's an interesting question. You might try answering that one too. Or is it just the family name you wanted, and one Fullerton is as good as another. Was Teddy next in line?" Suddenly, as he stood there, he realized that he hated her. She was spoiled, strident, and vicious, and he wondered now how he had ever even considered marrying her.

"You're a son of a bitch, do you know that?" She narrowed her eyes and stood glaring at him as though she would have liked to slap him.

"That's all you deserve, Pattie. You sure as hell don't deserve my brother."

"That's where you're wrong. I'm going to make something of him. Right now he's nothing." For a horrifying instant she sounded like his mother.

"Why don't you just leave him the hell alone?" Brad's eyes blazed into hers. "He's decent guy. And he's happy as he is." Or was he? Would he be drunk all the time if he was happy?

"Greg needs direction."

"Toward what? A political career he doesn't want? Why don't you just stay home and have kids, instead of pushing him?" But at his words something ghastly happened to Pattie's face and she grew pale.

"That's not in the cards."

"Why not?" Brad watched her eyes, there was something strange there that he didn't understand.

"Your brother can't have children, Brad. He had syphilis when he was in college, and now he's sterile." For a long moment Brad was shocked into silence.

"Do you mean that?"

"Yes." There was something deeply unhappy in her eyes. "But he didn't bother to tell me, until last month, when everyone knew we were engaged. And he knew that I wouldn't go through another broken engagement. Christ." She laughed a brittle little laugh. "Everyone in town would laugh till their sides split, poor little Pattie Atherton, dumped by another Fullerton."

"That's not the same thing. . . ." Brad reached out and touched her arm. "I'm sorry, Pattie. He should have told you before. That was a lousy thing to do."

"I thought so too." And then in a soft distant voice, "He'll pay for that in the end."

"What the hell do you mean?" Brad looked shocked.

She shrugged. "I don't know." And then she looked up at Brad, with a grim little smile. "I wanted to marry him to get back at you. I guess you could say I used him. But the funny thing is that he used me. He got the last laugh. He got me to say I'd marry him, and then he tells me he's sterile a month before the wedding."

"Would you have married him if you'd known?"

216

She shook her head. "No. I guess he knew that. That's why he didn't tell me."

Brad looked thoughtful as he looked down at this woman he had once thought that he knew, but he realized now that he didn't know her at all. She was manipulative and vengeful, and yet she had her vulnerabilities too—needs that spurred her to hurt others. He was deeply sorry for his brother. In her own way she was actually much worse than their mother. "It was wrong of Greg to hide that from you." It startled him to see that side of his younger brother. "Maybe in the end this will be for the best. You'll be able to devote yourselves to each other."

She didn't answer at first. "Wouldn't it matter to you if your wife couldn't have children, Brad?"

"Not if I really loved her."

"But she can, can't she?"

He hesitated for a long moment and then decided that he had better tell her. She'd find out soon enough, and he wanted to be honest. "Serena is pregnant, Pattie." But as soon as he said the words, he knew he'd made a mistake, there was a look of viciousness in her eyes that was almost frightening.

"Knocked her up quick, didn't you? Is that why you married her?" If it were, maybe she'd feel better. Maybe he'd had to marry her. . . . But her hope was stillborn.

"No, it's not." His eyes met hers squarely, and after a long silence she turned on her heel and walked away. And a moment later Brad went back inside, and immediately ran right into Greg.

"Where's Pattie?" There was a look of nervous suspicion in his eyes and it was obvious that he was drunk again as he lurched slightly toward his brother.

"She's here somewhere. We went out for some air, and she just came back in. Maybe she's in the ladies' room."

Greg stared at Brad. "She hates your guts."

Brad nodded slowly, watching Greg's eyes, and for the first time he realized how little he knew him. "She wasn't right for me, Greg. I would have broken it off when I got back anyway, even if I hadn't met Serena." He was sure of that now. "We'd have made each other miserable." But he wasn't sure that she and Greg would do better. "Are you happy, Greg?" He wanted to tell him that it wasn't too late to change his mind, that he'd be better off, but he wasn't sure if he should tell him.

"Hell, yes, why not?" But he didn't look like a happy man. "She'll keep me on my toes." For a moment he looked malevolently at his brother. There was jealousy there too, even more than he had seen in Pattie's eyes. "She's a firebrand in bed, but you know that. Or have you forgotten?"

"I never knew." It seemed the only thing to say as he cringed at his brother's remark.

"Bullshit. She told me."

"Did she? Maybe she just said that to make you jealous."

Greg shrugged as though he didn't really care, but it was plain he did. All his life he had come in second best to his brothers. He knew what he was, and what he wasn't. "I don't really care. Virgins are the shits. I didn't even like them when I was in college."

"Apparently." Brad wanted to bite out his tongue for what he had just said, and his eyes instantly met Greg's.

"She told you, didn't she? The bitch. Why the hell did she have to tell you?"

"You should have told her before." It was an almost fatherly reproach.

"And maybe you should mind your own goddamn business. I don't see you running your life so smoothly either, Brad, marrying your little Italian piece of ass. Christ, I'd expect you to have the brains to leave that where you found it."

"Stop it, Greg!" Brad's voice was low and gruff.

"The hell I will. If you'd done what Mother expected you to, she wouldn't be on my back. You'd be in politics where you belong and I could do what I want. But no, Big Brother has to play independent, leaving me holding the bag. And me, what do I get out of all that? I get a royal pain in the ass and a gun to my head. Now I'm the hope of their hearts and I get stuck with all their expectations. Looks to me like you got off easy, as usual." He sounded more drunk than he had

218

before, and infinitely more bitter.

"You don't have to do what they want. You can please yourself, for chrissake." Brad was actually sorry for him. And at the same time he knew that Greg didn't have the guts, not to face up to their mother, or Pattie.

"The hell I can. And now there's Pattie. She expects me to go to work for her father."

"If you don't want to, don't."

Greg looked at him with bitter amusement, and his face broke into a wintry smile. "Brave words, Brad. There's only one problem."

"What's that?"

"I'm not a brave man." And with that, he drifted off, leaving Brad feeling desperately sorry for him.

CHAPTER TWENTY-FOUR

The next morning Serena tiptoed downstairs to make herself a cup of tea and get a cup of coffee for Brad, when she ran into her mother-in-law in a blue satin dressing gown in the kitchen.

"Good morning, Serena." She said it so icily, it was worse than if she had snubbed her totally, and Serena felt instantly both rejected and subdued.

"Good morning, Mrs. Fullerton. Did you sleep well?"

"Relatively." She gazed at Serena, and did not ask her the same question. Her eyes were calculating and very, very cold. "I've been thinking that it might be wiser if you declared yourself ill today, rather than go to the wedding. You have the perfect excuse at your disposal." She was referring of course to the baby. But Serena looked shocked. She had no desire whatsoever to go to the wedding, but she knew it would cause talk if she didn't go.

"I don't know if Brad—"

"Of course it's up to you. But in your shoes, I would think that you'd be grateful to spare yourself the embarrassment. This is Pattie tie's day after all, you might think of that, and not cause her more pain than you already have." Serena wanted to give in to her urge to cry but instead she nodded in silence.

"I'll think about it."

"See that you do that." And with those final words, she left the kitchen. The servants were bustling about somewhere else, and Serena let herself down into a chair and blew her nose softly. After she'd pulled herself together, she poured Brad his coffee, made her cup of tea, put both on a tray, and walked slowly upstairs, trying to decide what to do, and when she reached their room, she knew that she had no choice. If her mother-in-law wanted her to stay away from the wedding, then she wouldn't be there. And perhaps it was better that way.

As she let herself into their room with the tray, she heaved a small sigh, and Brad looked up as he heard her.

"Something wrong, love?"

"No . . . I—I have a terrible headache."

"Do you?" He looked instantly worried. "Why don't you lie down? It must have been all the dancing last night."

Serena smiled at him. "It's not that. I'm just tired." And then, as she lay down on the bed, she looked up at him. "You know, I feel awful saying it, Brad, but . . . I don't think I should go."

"Do you feel that ill?" He looked surprised, this morning she·wasn't even pale, and she had drunk her tea very quickly, something she didn't do, he had noticed, when she wasn't feeling well. "Do you want me to call the doctor?"

"No." She sat up in bed and kissed him. "Do you think your brother will forgive me?"

"Yes. If you want to stay home, I won't push you."

"Thank you." She watched him get ready a little while later, and her heart felt heavy, not because of what she was missing, but because of the reason she was. Margaret Fullerton was ashamed of her and wanted to do everything possible to keep her away. It made Serena feel shut out and unwanted. No matter how much Brad loved her, it hurt not to have his family accept her too.

"You okay, love?" He glanced at her on the bed as he put his top hat in place and pulled on his gloves. He looked very dashing in the cutaway and striped trousers, the gray top hat, and gray gloves. It was going to be a very elegant wedding, and Serena was suddenly sorry to miss it. Teddy knocked on the door a moment later, wearing the same costume and holding a sprig of lily of the valley for Brad to put in his lapel.

"They'll think I'm the groom, I can't wear that." He made a face.

"No, they won't, his is bigger." And then he looked startled as he looked from Serena to Brad and then back to the bed again. "What's the matter, aren't you going?"

"I don't feel well."

"You didn't feel well last night either and you went. What's up today?" He was instantly suspicious. It was as though he had fine antennae for the subtlest of lies, especially those that related to his mother.

"I feel worse." But she said it a little too easily, as she sat up in bed and crossed her arms.

"I don't believe you." He looked at Brad. "You two have a fight?"

"Hell no. Serena just said she didn't feel well enough to go, and I didn't want to force her."

"Why not?" Teddy smiled as he sat down on the bed beside her. "Do you really feel sick, Serena?"

She nodded. "I really do."

"I'm sorry. We'll miss you." But as he said the words two huge tears sprang from her eyes. She felt left out again, and now she wanted to go with them. If only Mrs. Fullerton hadn't put it to her so harshly. She felt as though she really couldn't go. It was as though she shouldn't go, if she had any decorum, or respect for her mother-in-law at all. "What's wrong?" Teddy was looking at her searchingly and she shook her head, trying unsuccessfully not to cry.

"Oh, I hate being pregnant, all I ever do is cry!" She laughed at herself, and Brad came over to stroke the soft blond hair that fell past her shoulders and onto the pillow.

"You just take it easy today, and I'll be back as soon as I

can." He left the room then, to go check on Greg. He was nervously getting ready in his own room down the hall. He had had his own apartment for years, but for his last night as a bachelor he had come home and slept in his old room. He knew that way, no matter how drunk he got the night before, he wouldn't be allowed to oversleep on his wedding day.

But as soon as Brad had left the room, Teddy narrowed his eyes and looked at her. "What really happened?"

"Nothing." But she didn't look directly at him and he knew something was wrong.

"Don't lie to me, Serena. Why won't you go?"

It was uncanny the way this man could make her talk, and how much she trusted him. She told him things she wouldn't even tell Brad. But she also knew that he had kept her confidence the day before, and so now she let go, as the tears filled her eyes once again. "Your mother thinks I shouldn't go. But don't tell Brad. I don't want him to know."

"She told you that?"

"She said that it would be unkind to Pattie, and if I had any decency, I wouldn't go, that I had done enough to Pattie already." Serena looked woeful, and Teddy almost jumped off the bed.

"What a lot of crap. God damn it, Serena. If you don't stand up for yourself, my mother is going to push you around for the rest of your life. You can't let her!"

"It doesn't matter. She doesn't want me there. I think she's afraid I'll disgrace all of you."

"Serena." Teddy looked at her pointedly. "Everyone last night wanted to know who you were, I mean who you *really* were. There was talk all over the restaurant about your being a principessa, and it probably annoyed the hell out of Mother. All that garbage about your being a nobody, and somebody's maid, nobody will buy any of that crap after last night. You look every bit what you are: a beautiful, aristocratic lady. I don't know what the hell is eating my mother, except that Brad did something he wanted and made the decision for himself. But if what she wanted was Pattie Atherton as a daughter-in-law, then she's getting that too. One of these days she's going to get over her feelings

222

about you, Serena, and you can't give in to her all the time before she does. What she did to you yesterday is not only outrageous but immoral, and the truth is that Brad should know, but if you insist, then I won't tell him. But what she's doing today is the last straw, dammit, it's indecent." It crossed his mind for only a moment that his mother was jealous. Perhaps she couldn't bear all that Serena was, and that Brad had found her for himself, won her, and planned to keep her. Maybe she had wanted to lose him to someone she could manipulate, some girl she could push around, which she seemed to think she was going to do with Pattie. "But you can't let her keep doing this to you, dammit. It's not right."

"What's not right?" Brad stood in the doorway, looking at them both, and there was sudden tension in his face as he searched their eyes. "There's something I'm not being told, and I don't take kindly to secrets in my own family." He looked at his wife. "What is it, Serena?" Serena looked down, away from his gaze. He held up a hand. "No tears this time. Just tell me." But she couldn't and she wasn't going to. It was Teddy who spoke first.

"She doesn't want to tell you, Brad, but I think you ought to know."

Serena almost leaped off the bed at him, her arms outstretched as though she could stop him, but he had just said something to her with his eyes. Instinctively she almost shouted "No!"

"I'm going to tell him, Serena." Teddy spoke quietly and Serena burst into tears.

"For chrissake, what is it?" Their little melodrama was making him extremely nervous, and he was already unnerved. He had just come from Greg's room, he had got so drunk the night before that the butler was still trying to revive him. "What the hell is going on?"

Teddy stood up and faced him. "Mother doesn't want Serena to go to the wedding." Serena looked as though she had been given an electric shock, and her husband looked as though he had been at the other end of the electric current.

"Mother *what*? Are you crazy?"

"No. She had the unmitigated gall to tell Serena that she

owes it to Pattie not to be there. Serena ran into her in the kitchen, and she suggested that Serena develop a diplomatic illness and stay home."

"Is that true?" He looked at his wife in unadulterated outrage, as she nodded. He walked toward the bed then and she could see that he was trembling. "Why didn't you tell me?"

"I didn't want you to be angry at your mother." Her voice shook and she was obviously fighting back tears.

"Don't you ever do that again! If anyone ever says anything like that to you again, I want to know it! Is that clear?"

Brad looked both pained and thoughtful. He stood for a long moment then, and finally pointed to his brother. "Get out of here, Teddy." And he pointed at his wife. "And you get out of bed. I don't give a damn what you wear, but I want you dressed in ten minutes."

"But, Brad . . . I can't . . . your—"

"Not a word!" This time he roared it. "I'm the best man at my brother's wedding, and you're my wife. Is that clear? Do you understand that? You're my wife, that means you go everywhere I do, and you are accepted by the same people who love and accept me, whether that means my friends, or my family, or the people I work with. And if anyone does not accept you, and does not accord you the appropriate courtesy due you, I want to know it. Immediately next time. Not through the kind offices of my brother. Is that clear, Serena?"

"Yes." She murmured softly.

"Good. Because I want that to be clear to you, and to my mother, and to Pattie and Greg, and anyone else who seems not to understand it. I'll explain it to my mother next, and while I'm doing that, you are to get your ass out of that bed and into whatever you were supposed to wear to this bloody farce of a wedding. And don't you ever do this again. Don't ever pretend to be sick, or hide something from me. You tell me. Is that clear?" She nodded, and he walked over and pulled her roughly into his arms and kissed her. "I love you so much, dammit. I don't ever want anyone to hurt you. I promised to love, honor, and protect you as long as we both shall live, at least give me a chance to do that, baby. That's what I'm here for. And don't you ever, ever take shit from my mother again.'' She was both touched and shocked at his rancor toward Margaret. He studied her. ''Did something like this happen to upset you yesterday, Serena?'' He watched her eyes as she answered, but she only shook her head. ''Are you sure?''

''Yes, Brad, I am.'' She couldn't tell him that his mother had made her sign a paper. He would never speak to his mother again, and she didn't want to be responsible for that. This was bad enough.

He walked rapidly toward the doorway, and stood there for a moment, smiling at her. ''I love you, Mrs. Fullerton.''

''I love you, Colonel.'' She blew a kiss at him and he disappeared, trying to steel himself for the confrontation about to occur.

He found Margaret in her boudoir, dressed in a beautiful beige silk dress she had ordered from Dior for the wedding. They had all of her measurements in Paris, and all she had had to do was select a sketch and approve the swatch of fabric. She was also wearing a hat they had designed for her, made of delicate feathers of exactly the same beige. It swept low over one eye, and then lifted in the back to make room for an elegant twist of her thick white hair.

''Mother, may I come in?''

''Of course, darling.'' She smiled pleasantly at him. ''This is an important day. Have you seen your brother yet?''

''In both cases, yes.''

''I meant Greg. How is he?''

''Almost comatose, Mother. The servants are trying to bring him around. He got very drunk last night.'' He wanted to say ''As usual,'' but he didn't.

''Pattie will straighten him out.'' Margaret exuded a confidence that Brad could not quite bring himself to feel.

''Maybe. But first, speaking of Pattie, I'd like to straighten you out about something.''

''I beg your pardon.'' His mother looked shocked at his tone, and he did nothing to soften it as he continued.

''You should beg my pardon, Mother. Or rather, Serena's. And I want to make something clear to you once and for all. Serena is my wife, whether you like that fact or not. Apparently you asked her not to come to Greg's wedding. That you would dare do such a thing astounds me and hurts me. If you'd like us both not to come, that would be fine, but if you'd like me to be there, then you'd best know that I'm bringing Serena." There were tears in his eyes now as he went on. They were tears of anger and fury and disappointment. "I love her with all my heart, Mother. She's a wonderful girl, and in a few months we'll have a baby. I can't make you accept her. But I won't let you hurt her. Don't ever do anything like this again."

With a hesitant step his mother walked toward him. "I'm sorry, Brad. I—I misunderstood . . . I'm afraid this has all been very hard for me too. I just never expected you to marry someone . . . different. I thought you'd marry someone here, someone we knew."

"But I didn't. And it's not fair to punish Serena for it."

"Tell me." His mother looked at him with interest. "Did she tell you this herself?"

"No, you see, Serena loves me too much to put herself between you and me. She confided in Teddy, and he told me."

"I see. Did she say anything else?"

He looked at his mother strangely. "Is there more to tell?" Could his mother have done more? Had he been right to worry about Serena's obvious upset the day before? "Is there something I should know?"

"No, not at all." With relief she realized that Serena hadn't told him, not that it would have changed anything. She wouldn't have given that paper up to anyone now. The paper Serena had signed was already in her vault. She was still convinced that Serena was after his money, and years later when she left him and tried to soak him, his mother would save the day with the paper she had had the foresight to force Serena to sign. One day he would thank her.

He had one more thing to tell her. "I think, under the circumstances, that it will be better if we leave today, after the wedding. I'll try to get a compartment on the night train to Chicago, and if I can't, we can stay in a hotel and leave in the morning."

"You can't do that." Suddenly her eyes blazed.

"Why not?"

"Because I want you here. You haven't been home for any decent amount of time in years."

"You should have thought of that before you declared war on Serena."

Her eyes were angry and cruel and bitter. "You're my son, and you'll do what I tell you."

Brad's voice was oddly quiet. "I'm afraid you're wrong. I'm a grown man with a wife and family of my own. I am not your puppet. Father may be, and my poor weak brother, but I'm not, and don't you ever forget it."

"How can you talk to me this way? How dare you!"

Brad took a careful step toward her. "Mother, stay out of my life or you'll regret it."

"Brad!"

But he said nothing as he turned and walked out of the room, slamming the door behind him.

CHAPTER TWENTY-FIVE

Serena was sedately led to her seat by her brother-in-law Teddy, in St. James Church on Madison Avenue, in New York, at exactly ten minutes before eleven. The church was filled with towering trees of white flowers and everywhere there were garlands of fragrant white blossoms, lily of the valley, freesia, white roses, tiny spicy white carnations, with mists of white baby's breath intertwined among the larger flowers. There were white satin ribbons threaded between the trees, and a long white satin runner down the aisle. But the atmosphere in the church was solemn more than festive, and on either side of the aisle were elegantly dressed women and men in dark suits or striped trousers, there were large flowered hats and bright colors, and old people and young faces, as the organ began to play softly. Serena had been placed in a pew by herself, and a few moments later two imposing-looking dowagers joined her. One wore an elaborate crepe dress in deep purple, with amethyst brooches, and a huge rope of pearls, and a lorgnette through which she frequently glanced at Serena. The lady with her was more somberly dressed, but her quiet gray silk suit was highlighted by several very large diamonds. Here and there Serena saw familiar faces from the rehearsal dinner, and at frequent intervals she found herself glancing at Teddy, as though for comfort. She had only known him for a few days, and yet she already thought of him as someone she loved and could depend on. He stopped near where she was sitting once, squeezed her shoulder gently, and went back to his duties.

And at exactly one minute to eleven the huge front doors were closed, the organ began to play more loudly, and there was a sudden hush in the church, unbroken even by whispers, and as though by magic the ushers and bridesmaids began to appear, in a solemn procession of cutaways and striped trousers and organdy dresses in palest peach. There were picture hats to match, and the dresses were so lovely that Serena gazed at them in fascination. They had enormous Victorian sleeves and high necks, tiny waists, and full skirts with elegant little trains. Each bridesmaid carried a bouquet of tiny roses in the same color, and when the last of the bridesmaids had passed by and the flower girl appeared, she was wearing a miniature version of the same dress, except that the sleeves were tiny round puffs and there was no train over which she could fall. She carried a silver basket filled with rose petals, and she had an angelic face, as she giggled at her brother who wore a short black velvet suit and solemnly carried a velvet cushion on which lay both rings. Serena smiled at the children with damp eyes, and then turned to see who came behind them, and as she did she caught her breath at the vision that stood there. It was a fairy princess in a dress of lace so magnificent that Serena thought she had never seen anything like it. It was obviously an heirloom. A gasp and a murmur ran through the church as Pattie stood there in the high-necked full-sleeved gown of her great-grandmother. The dress was well over a hundred years old. There was a short necklace of exquisite diamonds that she wore at her neck, a tiny tiara that had been made to match, and pearls and diamonds glittered in her ears, and all around her hung a cloud of veil that seemed to sweep behind her for miles, covering her train and most of the aisle as she marched regally by on her father's arm. It was impossible not to feel dwarfed beside her, her dark beauty in sharp contrast to the soft white, and Serena was absolutely certain that she was the most beautiful bride she had ever seen. It was impossible to associate, even for a moment, this totally perfect scene with all that Brad had told her about Pattie. This couldn't be the same woman, Serena found herself thinking. This was a goddess, a fairy princess. It was she who looked like a principessa, Serena mused as she sat there. And then with a heavy heart she realized that it was she who could have been Brad's wife. He could have been the groom at this wedding, married to the striking little dark-haired beauty from his own world. Had he done that, there would have been no strife, no anger, no problem with his mother. And as she thought of it all she felt guilt pour over her for all that she had done to disrupt B.J.'s life. Her eyes wandered back to the altar, where she saw Greg standing stiffly beside his bride. And just behind them stood Brad and the maid of honor, and as Serena watched her, a distinguished-looking girl with red hair, which somehow blended well with the peach dress and large picture hat, she wondered if Brad was regretting what he had lost when he married her. He could have had the redhead, or any of the pretty blondes with their bright, freckled, American faces. He could have names that everyone recognized, whose aunts and grandmothers and fathers they had known. He could have lived the life his mother wanted for him, keeping his family intact. Instead he had married a stranger to this world, and he would become an outcast. As she thought of it the tears filled her eyes and ran slowly down her cheeks. She felt a grief beyond measure at what she had done to him. Oh, God, what would happen if he ended up hating her for it?

She sat solemnly through the rest of the wedding, and watched the procession file sedately past her on the way out, and when it was over, she went through the reception line like any other stranger, shaking hands with the twenty or so bridesmaids and ushers, until suddenly she reached Teddy, and he grabbed her by the arm.

"What are you doing here, silly?"

"I don't know." She looked suddenly embarrassed. Had she done the wrong thing? She felt foolish and he put an arm around her with a grin.

"You don't have to be so formal. Want to stand here with us?" But Serena knew that their mother would undoubtedly have a fit.

"I'll just wait outside." She stood there for a moment beside him, and suddenly Pattie saw her and stared angrily.

"This is my wedding, Serena, not yours, or had you forgotten?"

Serena flushed to the roots of her hair, stammered something, and she began to back away. But Teddy was quick to grab her. He knew how much she had already been through, and he wanted to slap Pattie for what she had just said. "Can't you just shut your damn mouth for once, Pattie? If you don't watch it, you'll end up looking like a shrew, even in that dress." With that, he left the line, his arm around Serena, and signaled to Brad to meet them outside. Margaret was looking daggers at them, and Pattie had gone white, but only one or two people had overheard them, and a moment later they were safely outside.

"Well, at least I have you to make things even."

"Hmm?" She was still looking upset and distracted as they stood in the bright sunshine.

"I've got one wonderful sister-in-law and one bitch." Serena laughed in spite of herself and saw Brad coming toward them.

"Something happen in there?" he was quick to ask, and Serena shook her head, but Teddy waved a finger and frowned.

"Don't lie to him, dammit." He smiled at his brother. "Our brand-new sister-in-law is just being herself."

"Was she rude to Serena?" Brad began to smolder.

"Of course. Is she ever anything but rude, except to those she is trying to impress? Christ, I don't know how Greg is going to stand her." He said it sotto voce so only his brother heard him, but they both knew the answer to that one, and neither of them liked it. Most likely Greg was going to stay drunk for the rest of his life. That morning, in his still-besotted state, he had told his older brother that he was marrying her because she had been Brad's fiancée, and everyone knew that Brad was terrific so she had to be a terrific girl. In a moment of madness Brad had tried to dissuade him from getting married, but Greg was too frightened to alter his course only hours before the wedding, and all morning in church Brad had remembered Serena's question: "Are you going to be the one to stand up and object at the wedding?" He had wanted to, but he hadn't dared.

A few minutes later the entire wedding party disappeared into six limousines and moved on to The Plaza, where the Grand Ballroom had been reserved. Here again the flowers were lavish, and the orchestra struck up the moment they arrived.

Serena was once again seated with strangers at a table far from the others, and it seemed ages before Brad came to find her. She looked tired from the strain of making polite conversation, and she was a little overwhelmed by the crowds around her.

"Are you all right, love?" She smiled and nodded. "How's my daughter?"

"He's fine." They chuckled at each other, and he led her onto the dance floor in a slow waltz a moment later. Teddy sat at the bridal table and watched them circling slowly together. They were truly the perfect couple. His tall, handsome blond brother, and the graceful golden-haired woman in his arms. Their faces met at precisely the right angle, their smiles would have lit the room, they looked so happy that they should have been the bride and groom, and not the nervous, high-strung little brunette drinking too much and talking too loudly, sitting beside the man she had just married, who sat staring straight ahead, as Teddy watched them. Greg had no sparkle in his eyes, instead there was a dull glaze as he finished his Scotch on the rocks and signaled the waiter for another.

It was only a few moments later that Brad and Serena

came to find Teddy. Brad leaned down to his brother's ear and whispered that they were leaving.

"Already?"

He nodded. "We want to catch the train tonight, and I want Serena to rest for a while. We have to pack—" He faltered for a moment, and his younger brother laughed at them. Maybe he did want her to rest, and they did have some packing to do, but it was apparent that B.J. had other things on his mind as well. If they had been alone, Teddy would have teased him. "We'll see you in San Francisco, kiddo. When exactly are you coming?"

"I'm leaving New York on the twenty-ninth of August, so I should arrive in San Francisco on September first."

"Give us the details when you write and we'll come to meet you." Brad held his shoulder for a long moment and looked into his brother's eyes. "Thank you for everything. For making Serena feel so welcome."

"She is welcome." His eyes moved over to his new sister. "I'll see you out West, Serena." And then he grinned. "By then you'll be as big as a whale." The three of them chuckled.

"I will not!" She tried to look offended, but didn't. Instead she put her arms around him and kissed him on both cheeks. "I'll miss you, litte brother."

"Take care of each other."

The two men shook hands, Teddy kissed Serena again, and a moment later, after Serena had said a polite farewell to the bride, shaken her parents-in-law's hands, and congratulated the almost incoherent groom, they left the party. It was an enormous relief to have the wedding behind them. As they left The Plaza hand in hand Brad pulled off his tie, dropped it with his gloves into his top hat, and hailed a hansom cab to take them home to the apartment on Fifth Avenue.

Serena was enchanted as they clip-clopped into the park behind the horse, and he put an arm around her. It was a hot sunny day, the summer had begun, and by nightfall they would be on their way to their new life in California.

"Happy, darling?" He looked down at his wife, his pleasure at finally being alone with her shining in his eyes.

"How could I be anything but happy with you?" She reached up to kiss him and they held each other for a long moment, as they drove slowly down Fifth Avenue to the apartment.

CHAPTER TWENTY-SIX

They left the apartment before the others returned, and for a moment Brad stood in the front hall and looked around him with regret, and almost sorrow.

"You'll come back." She said it softly, remembering how she had felt when she left Rome, but he shook his head as he looked down at her.

"That isn't what I was thinking. I was thinking that I wanted this to be so nice for you. I wanted you to have a wonderful time in New York . . . I wanted them to be wonderful to you. . . ." His eyes were bright with tears and she took his hand and kissed it.

"*Non importa.*" It doesn't matter.

"Yes, it does. To me."

"We have our own lives, Brad. Soon we will have the baby. We have each other. The rest matters, but not so much."

"It does to me. You deserve to have everyone be good to you."

"You are good to me. I don't need more than that." And then she smiled, remembering Teddy. "And your brother."

"I think he's head over heels in love with you." He smiled at his wife. "But I can't really blame him. So am I."

"I think you're both silly." She sighed as she thought of her brother-in-law. "I hope he finds a nice girl at Stanford. He has so much to give someone."

Brad was quiet for a moment, thinking of how much he owed Teddy. Then he said, "Ready?" She nodded assent, and he closed the door behind them. Downstairs a cab was already waiting. Their luggage was piled up on the front seat and in the trunk, their smaller bags were tucked in around them.

The ride to Grand Central Station passed quickly. A few minutes later they got out, found a skycap, and threaded their way through the crowded station. Serena looked around her in fascination, there were armies of people shuffling around beneath the enormously tall ceilings. Everywhere around her were advertisements and posters and billboards and announcements. She looked like a little girl as she trundled along beside her husband, and he almost had to shoo her out of the main lobby to get her to the platform area where they would find their train.

"But it's wonderful, Brad!"

He grinned at her delight, and tipped the porter as he unloaded their bags onto the train.

"I'm glad you like it."

But she liked the train even better. It was far more luxurious than any of the postwar trains in Europe. In Italy and France nothing had as yet been completely restored from the condition it had been left in by the armies of occupation. Here mahogany-skinned white-coated porters with stiff caps assisted them into their tiny but impeccable quarters. They had a velvet banquette, immaculate linens, thick rugs beneath their feet, and a tiny bathroom. In Serena's opinion it was the perfect honeymoon suite, and the prospect of spending three days there with Brad enchanted her.

Their actual plan was to spend two days on the train until they reached Denver, to leave the train there, rent a car, drive to Aspen, and then return to Denver, and take the train on to San Francisco. Brad had taken his brother's suggestion, and the young couple could hardly wait. But first they had to take the train to Chicago, where they would spend the day and change trains, then continue their journey.

Half an hour after they had boarded, the train inched out of the station and hurtled through New York. As Serena watched the city disappear behind them, Brad was silent beside her.

234

"You're so quiet. Is something wrong?" She looked at him inquiringly as they rolled along.

"I was just thinking."

"What about?"

"My mother."

For a moment Serena said nothing, and then she raised her eyes slowly to her husband's. "Perhaps she will come to accept me in time." But the memory of what Margaret had tried to do told Serena that her mother-in-law would never come to love her. There was no trust, no understanding, no compassion, and no interest. There was nothing but bitterness and resentment and hatred. She had tried to buy Serena off in the most venal of ways. To think she had wanted her to abort her own grandchild. What kind of woman was Margaret Fullerton?

"It kills me that she was so unfair." And he didn't even know the whole.

"She couldn't help it." Serena found herself thinking back to the morning's wedding. How strange to think that it could have been Brad's wedding and that Pattie could have been sitting at that very moment on the train. The very thought sent a chill through her, and she reached for his hand and held it tightly.

"It doesn't matter, love. We have our life now. And you're going to love San Francisco."

But before she loved San Francisco, she loved Denver, and she loved Aspen even more. They stayed in the town's only hotel, a quaint Victorian affair with high ceilings and lace curtains. The meadows were covered with wild-flowers, the mountains were still capped with snow. It looked just like the Alps to Serena when she looked out the window every morning, and they went for long walks beside streams, and lay in the sunshine on the grass, talking about their respective childhoods and their hopes for their own children.

They spent almost two weeks in Aspen, and they hated to leave when the appointed day came for them to return to Denver and resume their journey on the train. But they once again boarded the train heading west from Chicago, and this time they only had to travel for a single day, and the Rockies were too soon left behind them. The day after they had boarded, they awoke to see hills in the distance and flat land around them, and a little while later Serena was enchanted to catch a glimpse of the bay. The train station was located in a singularly ugly part of the city, but as soon as they got a cab and made their way north into the heart of town, they saw how lovely a city it really was. To their right lay the bay, shining and flat, dotted with boats, and rimmed with hills. All around them were the steep hillsides, with Victorian houses built on them, there were tiny pastel-colored houses and handsome brick mansions, stucco Mediterranean villas, and delightful English gardens. It was a city that seemed to combine the charm of a dozen countries and cultures, with blue skies overhead and clouds that looked as though they had been painted. And as they approached the Presidio they could see the Golden Gate Bridge, leading majestically into Marin County.

"Oh, Brad, it's so lovely!"

"It is, isn't it?" He looked pleased, and in his heart he felt something stirring. He knew that they had come halfway around the world together, and that this would be their first real home. San Francisco. Their first child would be born here, and perhaps others. He looked at her as she gazed at the bay and the bridge, and gently he leaned over and kissed her.

"Welcome home, my darling."

She nodded, with a tender smile, and looked around her, feeling the same things that he had.

The taxi drove in through the Presidio Avenue Gate in Pacific Heights, and followed the steep curving road down the hills beneath the huge trees growing in the Presidio, and a moment later they were parked in front of the Headquarters Building, where Brad hopped out, put on his hat, and saluted his wife smartly. He had worn his uniform for their arrival, since officially he would be reporting for duty, and he stepped into the main building with his hat under his arm, and disappeared while Serena waited and looked around her. The influence of the architecture seemed to be mostly Spanish, the view of the bay and the bridge were superb, and some of the houses on the base looked very handsome.

236

She was amazed at how quickly Brad emerged from the building, with a broad smile, and a set of keys in his hand, which he dangled at her. He gave the driver instructions, and they wound their way back up another hill, through the woods, and stopped when they reached a point that seemed to float above the entire setting. Here there was a cluster of four houses, all very large and quite solid, in the same Spanish style, and Brad pointed to the one at the end of the cluster.

"For us?" Serena looked stunned. The house was splendid.

"Yes, ma'am." Serena was impressed at how well they treated a colonel, but he was grinning at her oddly as he opened the door and carried her inside. "Do you like it?"

"It's so lovely!"

They wandered around their house then. Someone had had the foresight to leave them some towels and sheets. Serena realized that they would have to go out and buy furniture, but the house itself was lovely. It had a big Spanish-style kitchen, which someone had redecorated in blue and white Mexican tile. There were overhead hooks for plants, huge windows that looked out over the bay, and a door that opened into the garden. There was also a handsome formal dining room, with a domed ceiling, a small chandelier, and a fireplace; a living room, which also had a splendid view of the Bay, and an even larger fireplace. Upstairs there was a cozy wood-paneled den, and three very pleasant bedrooms, all of them with views of the water.

It was perfect for them, the baby, and even gave them a room for Teddy. Serena was quick to point that out, and Brad looked at her, as though he had never been as happy.

"It's not your palazzo, my darling, but it is pretty."

"It's better," she said, smiling at him, "because it's ours." At least for the duration. But she knew that they could be there for years, and the Presidio was considered a choice post in the American army.

They slept on the cots that had been provided for them for that night and went downtown the next day to buy some basics, a large double bed of their own, two small French nightstands, a Victorian dressing table for Serena, and a beautiful fruitwood dresser, chairs, tables, fabrics for curtains, a rug, and a wealth of kitchen equipment. And they began to live a married life together—waiting for their child.

And in late August the house really looked as though they had lived there for years. There was a warm, welcoming quality about it that delighted Brad every time he stepped into the front door, and the colors Serena had chosen always rested him and always made him happy that he was back. She had done the living room in rich woods and dull red, and a soft raspberry color. There were handsome English prints on the wall, always a profusion of flowers on all the tables, and she had made the curtains herself from a beautiful French fabric. The dining room was formal and a soft ivory white, filled with orchid plants and a view of the profusion of flowers she had planted in the garden. Their own bedroom was all done in soft blues, "like the bay," she had teased him, Teddy's room, as she called it, was done in warm browns, and the baby's room was all done in bright yellows. She had worked hard all summer to get it ready, and the day Teddy arrived she looked around as they left to pick him up and decided that she was proud of what she had done.

"Forget something?" Brad questioned her from the doorway as he watched her waddle toward him. She was five months pregnant and he loved to see her shape as she lay in bed beside him or emerged from the shower in the morning. She looked full and ripe and wonderful to him, her whole body as graceful as it had been, and yet the full weight of their child swelling her belly. He loved to touch it and feel the baby kick, and now he smiled and patted her tummy gently as she stood before him. "How's our little friend?"

"Busy." She smoothed the plaid overblouse over her navy blue skirt and smiled at her husband. "He's been kicking all morning."

Brad looked concerned. "Maybe you did too much getting ready for Teddy." But Serena shook her head.

"No, I didn't." She looked over her shoulder as she closed the door. "The house looks nice, doesn't it?"

"No. It looks wonderful. You did a great job, darling."

She blushed, but she looked pleased. For a girl of twenty,

238

she had come a long way and done a great many things. Sometimes he had to remind himself of how young she was. He had just turned thirty-five that summer. "I'm glad that Teddy's coming."

"So am I." He started their dark blue Ford and looked at his watch. It seemed like only days before that they had arrived themselves, and when they found Teddy, just stepping off the train at the station, Brad felt as though they had only just left New York. The two brothers shook hands and clapped each other on the shoulder, as Serena hurtled herself into Teddy's arms, and they squeezed each other hard, and then laughing, he stepped back and patted her protruding stomach.

"Where'd you get the beachball, Serena?"

She looked at him primly. "Brad gave it to me as a present." All three of them laughed, and Teddy followed them to the car. He only had one bag with him. The rest of his things had been sent directly to Stanford several weeks before.

"How do you like it out here, you two?"

"We love it. But wait till you see what she's done with the house." Brad looked at his wife proudly. "You'll see why we love it." And as soon as Teddy stepped inside, he knew what his brother had meant. Serena had created an atmosphere of well-being that touched everyone who entered. One wanted to unravel on the couch, stare at the bay in peaceful silence, and never leave again.

"You did a beautiful job, Serena." She looked pleased, and then jumped up to bring him tea and sandwiches and little cookies. "Will you please sit down?" He went after her, but she shooed him back into the living room with his brother, who looked at them both, like two children, happy to be playmates again.

"How's Greg?" Brad didn't wait long to ask the question, and there was concern in his eyes as he asked.

"About the same."

"Which means what?"

Teddy hesitated and then shrugged, with a small sigh. "I'll be honest with you, I don't think he's happy with Pattie. He's drinking even more than he was before."

"He couldn't possibly." Brad looked upset.

"Well, he's sure as hell trying. I don't know." He ran a hand through his hair, as he looked at his brother. "I think she pushes him all the time. She always wants him to do something different than he's doing. She wants a bigger house, a better life, wants him to have a better job. . . ."

"All in three months?"

"Sooner if possible. She bitched for two months about their honeymoon. She thought he should have taken her to Europe. But he wanted to go to Newport instead, which she didn't consider a honeymoon. The house he had rented for her for the summer wasn't as fancy as the one her brother-in-law had got her sister, and on and on it went."

"No wonder he drinks." Brad looked dismayed at what he was hearing. "Think he'll stick with it?"

"Probably. I don't think he even considers any other option." Certainly no one in their family had ever got divorced, but in the face of what he was hearing from Teddy, Brad would certainly have considered it. And one thing was sure, and that was that he was glad he hadn't fallen into Pattie's trap. The tragedy was that Greg had.

But the strangest thing of all was hearing all of the news so distantly from his brother. When he had been in Europe, everyone had made a point of staying in touch. They had written as often as they could, especially his mother. And now, since he and Serena had come to California, there was a measurable difference. Greg no longer wrote at all, feeling uncomfortable toward Brad perhaps, about his sudden marriage to Pattie. Or maybe, in light of what Teddy had just said, he was just desperately unhappy. Brad had heard from his father only once, but from his mother never. He had called her a few times at first, but her voice had been so chill, her remarks about Serena so cutting, that he no longer called her, and she never called him. And he hated to admit it, but he missed hearing from them. It was as though, in an odd way, he and Serena had become outcasts from an old familiar life.

CHAPTER TWENTY-SEVEN

Teddy had expected to be totally devoured by his studies when he got to Stanford. But as things turned out, it wasn't quite as ferocious during the first semester as he had feared. And although he had a mountain of reading to do most of the time, he still managed to come into town to see them, particularly at the end of Serena's pregnancy. He wanted to be there if something momentous happened. He had already told Brad that when the time came he wanted to be around. Brad had promised to call him at Stanford in case she went into labor, and they both assumed that Teddy would have time to come into town on the train and walk the halls with his brother for as long as it took the baby to arrive.

On the third weekend in December, Teddy was on vacation from school and staying with them, and Serena's due date was still four days away. Brad was gone for the day on mock-war maneuvers in San Leandro, and Teddy was upstairs studying for exams. Serena was in the baby's room, folding tiny white nightgowns and checking things over for what Teddy accused her of being the four hundredth time. She was just putting the nightgowns back in the drawer when she heard a strange sound almost like a pop, and then suddenly felt a gush of warm water run down her legs, and splash onto the shiny wood floor. She stood there for a moment, looking startled, and then walked slowly into the baby's bathroom, to get some towels so that the fluid wouldn't stain the floor. She felt an odd sensation of cramping both in her back and low in her stomach and knew that she had to call the doctor, but first she wanted to take care of the floor. He had already explained to her that at the first sign of pains, or if the bag of waters ruptured, she was to call him, but she knew that from that time it would still take many hours. She wasn't even worried about Brad being in San

241

Leandro. He would be back in time for dinner, and there was nothing he could do after he drove her to the hospital anyway. They wouldn't let him see her while she was in labor, and at least this way he would be spared some of the pacing with Teddy. There was no reason at all why Teddy couldn't take her to the hospital and then come back later with Brad.

She felt a sudden surge of excitement as she realized that the time had come and in a few hours she would be holding her baby and she laughed to herself as she knelt on the floor with the towels, but the laughter caught in her throat and she had to clutch the chest of drawers to keep from screaming, a cramp had seized her so brutally that she could barely breathe. It seemed hours before it had ended, and there was a damp veil of sweat on her forehead when at last it had passed. It was definitely time to call the doctor, she realized, and she was a little startled to discover that the first contraction could be so painful. No one had warned her that it would start with such vehemence. In fact the doctor had told her that at first she probably wouldn't even know what the pains were. But there was no mistaking this, or the next one, as it brought her to her knees halfway back to the bathroom with the damp towels, and she suddenly felt a pressure so sharp and so heavy that she fell to all fours on the floor. She held her stomach and moaned both in pain and terror, and in his room Teddy thought he heard a strange sound like an animal moaning, but after a moment he decided it was the wind and went back to his studies, but a minute or so later he heard it again. He picked up his head and frowned, and then suddenly he realized that it was someone groaning and he heard the sound of his own name. Frightened, he stood up, not sure of where it had come from, and then realizing that it was Serena, he ran out into the hall.

"Serena? Where are you?" But as he stood only a few feet away around a bend in the hallway, she was in the grips of yet another pain so forceful that she was unable to breathe or speak his name again. "Serena? Serena? Where are you?" A terrible moan met his ears, and he hastened toward it, coming through the door of the baby's room and finding her in the bathroom doorway, crouched on the floor. "Oh, my God, what happened?" She was so pale and in such obvious pain that he felt his own knees tremble. "Serena, did you fall?" Instinctively he reached for her pulse and found it healthy, but as he held the delicate wrist in his fingers, he saw her face contort with a pain so terrible that he winced as he watched and tried to take her in his arms as she screamed. But she fought to keep him away from her, as though she needed every bit of air and each touch was painful, and it was fully two minutes before her face relaxed and she could speak to him rationally again.

"Oh, Teddy . . . it's coming . . . I don't understand . . . it just started . . ."

"When?" He was desperately trying to gather his wits about him. He had only seen one childbirth, although he had already carefully studied all the chapters in his textbook on the subject, but he didn't feel at all equal to the task of delivering his own niece or nephew and he knew that he had to get her to the hospital at once. "When did it start, Serena? I'll call the doctor."

"I don't know . . . a few minutes ago . . . ten . . . fifteen . . ." She was still trying to catch her breath and was sitting propped against the wall, as though she no longer had the strength to move.

"Why didn't you call me?"

"I couldn't. My water broke, and then it just hit me so hard, I couldn't even"—her breath began to come more quickly—"speak . . . oh, God . . . oh, Teddy . . ." She clutched at his arm. "Another . . . pain . . . now . . . ohhh . . ." It was a terrible groan of pain, and he held her hands in his own and watched her helplessly. Instinctively he had glanced at his watch when it began, and he saw with utter amazement that the contraction was over three and a half minutes long. He recalled what the textbook had said, when he read it only a few days earlier, that in general, contractions lasted from ten to ninety seconds, and it was only in rare cases that they extended past that, and that when they did, it was frequently in unusual labors, with frequent, prolonged, and violent contractions, which generally shortened the labor process by several hours. The more brutal the pains, the quicker the baby would be born.

With a look at Serena he ran his handkerchief across her

243

forehead as the pain ended. "Serena, I want you to lie here. I'm going to call the doctor right now."

"Don't leave me."

"I have to." He was going to ask for an ambulance, he was sure that she was about to have the baby, and before he even left the room, he could see that she was having a contraction again. But he knew that he had to call the doctor, and he did so as quickly as he could. An ambulance was promised, and the doctor told him to stay with her. Teddy told him that he was a first-year med student, and the doctor explained how, if the ambulance came before he did, Teddy should hold and clamp the cord. He said that under the circumstances he wanted to ride to the hospital with her. He had a feeling, as Teddy did from watching her, that the baby was going to come in record time. And by the time Teddy returned to the bedroom, he found Serena hunched over on all fours and crying. She looked up at him miserably as he came in, and he wanted to cry with her. Why did it have to be so difficult this first time, and where was Brad, and why the hell was it all happening so fast?

"Serena, the doctor's coming, just take it easy." And then he had a thought. "I'm going to put you on the bed."

"No . . ." She looked terrified. "Don't move me."

"I have to. You'll feel better if you lie down."

"No, I won't." She looked suddenly frightened and angry.

"Trust me." But the conversation was interrupted by another roaring pain. And when it was over, without saying another word, he scooped her into his arms and deposited her gently on the canopied bed in the baby's room. He pulled back the pretty yellow quilt and the blanket, and let her lie on the soft cool sheets, her enormous belly thrust into the air, and her face pale and damp, her eyes huge and afraid. He had never seen anyone look so vulnerable, and for an instant he was terrified that she might die. As though from his very soul the words sprang from him. "You're going to be all right, my darling. I love you."

It was as though he had to tell her, just this one time, to get her through. He had never seen anyone in so much pain. She smiled at him then and clung tightly to his hand, and he found himself praying for the ambulance to come. But his prayers were not answered. Almost at the same moment he saw the searing anguish leap across her face and in a single gesture she pulled herself up and grabbed his shoulders, clutching him as though in terror as she tried not to scream.

"Oh, God . . . oh, Teddy . . . it's coming . . ."

"No, it isn't." Oh, please no. . . . Together, without knowing it, they began to cry. They were two children, lost on a desert island, and all they had was each other, and she was holding so tightly to his shoulders that the grip of her hands hurt him. "Lie down. Come on. That's it." He lay her down again as the pain ended, and she seemed to be breathing even faster, and before her head had even touched the pillow she was writhing again, and this time when she grabbed for him, she could not restrain the scream.

"Teddy . . . the baby . . ." She was pushing at the bed, and then holding her belly, and as though in a single instant, Teddy found himself watching her not like a frightened schoolboy but a man. He knew just from his textbooks what was happening, and it would do her no good if he let himself be as frightened as she was. He knew that he had to help her. Without saying a word, he pulled gently at her skirt and quietly undressed her. He went to the bathroom and found stacks of clean towels. "Teddy!" She began to panic.

"I'm right here." He stuck his head out and smiled at her. "It's going to be all right."

"What are you doing?"

"I'm washing my hands."

"Why?"

"Because we're going to have a baby."

She started to say something, but another pain stopped her. He rushed through his scrubbing, grabbed his towels, and went back to the bed, where he draped her carefully with the towels, and then he took two extra pillows and propped her legs up, and she said nothing. She was too involved with the pains, and too grateful that he was with her. And then suddenly with the next pain she seemed to lift off her pillows again and instinctively he went to her shoulders and supported her as she began pushing. "It's okay, Serena, it's okay . . ."

"Oh, Teddy, the baby . . ."

"I know." He lay her back on the pillows when it was over, and looked between the draped towels on her legs, and then suddenly, as she began to push through another pain, he gave a shout of excitement. "Serena, I can see it . . . come on . . . keep pushing . . . that's it . . ." She groaned and fell back on her pillows but only for a moment. She was panting and breathless and he held her hand as he watched, but there was nothing for him to do now except watch as the baby crowned and then he reached down gently and turned it, wiping the tiny face gently with a soft towel, and then suddenly as though it objected to having its face washed, the baby gave a gurgle and then began crying, and Teddy looked up into Serena's face and they began crying too. Her face was wet with tears as she heard the baby.

"Is it all right?"

"It's just beautiful." Teddy was laughing and crying and when another pain came, he freed the shoulders, and a minute later Serena gave a shout first of pain and then of exultation and the baby lay in her uncle's hands and he held her up to show her mother. "It's a girl, Serena! A girl!"

"Oh, Teddy." Serena lay on her pillows with her eyes streaming, and she reached out to touch a tiny hand and at the same moment they heard the doorbell.

Teddy began to laugh as he set the baby down on the bed beside Serena. "It must be the doctor."

"Tell him we already have one." She smiled at him and reached for his hand before he could leave her. "Teddy . . . how can I ever thank you? I would have died without you."

"No, you wouldn't."

"You're terrific." And then, remembering what she had heard him say earlier. "I love you too. Don't ever forget that."

"How could I?" He kissed her gently on the forehead and went to answer the doorbell. It was indeed the doctor, and the ambulance arrived just as Teddy pulled open the door. Dr. Anderson hastened upstairs and marveled at the baby and Serena, congratulated Teddy on a fine job on his first delivery, soundly knotted the cord, and directed the ambulance drivers to put mother and child carefully on the stretcher.

The cord would be cut at the hospital, and both of them would be carefully checked out. But it looked to the doctor as though everything had gone very smoothly. He looked at his patient with a grin and checked his watch.

"Just how long were you in labor, young lady?"

"What time is it?" She smiled at him. She was tired, but she had never been so happy.

"It is exactly two fifteen." He glanced at Teddy. "What time did the baby come?"

"Two oh three."

Serena chuckled. "It started at one thirty."

"Thirty-three minutes on a first labor? Young lady, next time we're going to park you in the hospital lobby for the last two weeks." The three of them laughed, and the men carried mother and daughter out on the stretcher, and Teddy looked at the room for a moment before he left it. He would never forget sharing this moment with her, and he was suddenly glad that they had been alone.

When Brad got back from maneuvers that evening, he found his brother sitting nonchalantly in the kitchen, eating a sandwich. "Hi, kid. Where's Serena?"

"Out."

"Where?"

"Having dinner with your daughter." It took a moment for it to sink in, as the younger brother grinned.

"What the hell does that mean?" Brad felt his heart begin to race. And then suddenly he understood. "Did she . . . did . . . *today*?" He looked stunned.

"Yup." His brother answered coolly. "She did. And you have a beautiful baby girl."

"Have you seen Serena? How is she?" He was instantly flustered and even looked a little afraid.

"She's just fine. And so is the baby."

"Did it take very long?"

Teddy grinned. "Thirty-three minutes."

"Are you kidding?" Brad looked shocked. "How the hell did you get her to the hospital in time?"

"I didn't."

"What?"

Teddy laughed, and gave his brother a warm hug, but

247

there was suddenly something more grown up about him, even Brad had noticed it when he came in. It was as though in a single afternoon there was something different about Teddy, as though in some subtle way he had changed. "Brad, I delivered the baby."

"What? Are you crazy?" And then he grinned. "Crazy kid. For a minute I believed you. Big joke, very funny. Now tell me what happened."

Teddy grew serious as he looked into his brother's eyes. "I mean it, Brad. I didn't have any choice. I found her on the floor of the baby's room, already in hard labor. The water had just broken, and she went right into labor at an incredible clip." He sounded strangely official, and Brad's eyes almost fell out of his head. "She was having three- and three-and-a-half-minute contractions every thirty seconds, and by the time I came back from calling the doctor and the ambulance, she was starting to push. It was all over pretty quickly. And the doctor and the ambulance got here about ten minutes after the baby."

"Oh, my God." Brad let himself slowly down into a chair, and for an instant Teddy wondered if he was angry. Maybe it upset him that his own brother had delivered his wife's baby, but it wasn't that that Teddy saw in Brad's eyes as he looked at him. "Can you imagine what would have happened if I'd been alone with her? I'd have panicked."

Teddy smiled and touched his arm. "I almost did for a while there. For a minute or two it was pretty scary, but I knew that I had to help her, Brad . . . there was no one else." The brothers looked into each other's eyes for a long moment, and Brad put out his hand with tears in his eyes.

"Thank you, Teddy." He wanted to tell him then that he loved him, but he didn't know how, and the tears were too thick in his throat.

Twenty minutes later he was standing beside Serena, and she looked almost exactly as she had that morning when he had left for San Leandro. She looked pretty and fresh, bright eyed and cheerful. The only difference was that the belly was gone. And no one would have suspected from her look of jubilation that only a few hours before she had been through so much pain. "How was it, baby? Was it really awful?"

248

"I don't know." She looked faintly embarrassed to admit to him how much it had hurt her. "For a little while I thought I couldn't stand it . . . but Teddy . . . he was right there with me . . . and he was so good. . . . Brad"—her eyes filled with tears of joy and emotion—"I would have died without him."

"Thank God he was there."

The nurse put her in her wheelchair then so that they could go to see the baby, and Brad laughed at the tiny pink bundle with the screwed-up face and swollen eyes. "See, I told you! A girl!" They named her Vanessa Theodora. Vanessa was the name they had agreed on before, and Theodora for her uncle, the doctor.

And that night Brad called his mother to tell her. His voice was still vibrant with excitement when he placed the call, and it seemed to take forever for his mother to come on the line. He spoke to his father first, who offered his eldest son the appropriate congratulations. But there was no warmth in Margaret's voice when she spoke to him.

"It must have been a dreadful experience for Teddy." Her voice hit Brad like a cold shower.

"Hardly, Mother. And I would think that if he's going to be a doctor he'd do well not to find that kind of experience 'dreadful.' " But that wasn't the point and they both knew it. "He said it was the most beautiful thing he'd ever seen." There was an awkward silence as Brad fought with his own sense of disappointment at his mother's reaction. He was too happy for her to spoil it for him, but she dampened his spirits nonetheless.

"And your wife is well?"

"She's wonderful." A smile began to grow on his face again. Maybe there was hope after all. At least she had asked after Serena. "And the baby is beautiful. We'll send you pictures as soon as we have some."

"I don't think that's necessary, Brad." Necessary? What did she mean "necessary"? Christ. "I don't really think you understand how your father and I feel."

"As a matter of fact, I don't. And don't bring Father into this. This is your war with Serena, not his." But they both knew that Margaret ran the show, and where she led, her husband followed. "And I think it stinks. This is the happiest day of my life and you're trying to spoil it for us."

"Not at all. And I find it very touching to hear you sounding so paternal. But that doesn't change the fact that your marriage to Serena is a tragedy in your life, Bradford, whether you acknowledge that yet or not. And the addition of a child to further embellish an already disastrous union is not something I can celebrate with you. The whole affair is a tragic mistake, and so is that baby."

"That child is no mistake, Mother." He was seething. "And she is my daughter and your first grandchild. She's part of our family, not just my family, but yours, whether you accept that or not."

There was a long silence. "I do not. And I never shall."

He bid his mother good-night then and there were tears in his eyes when he hung up the phone, but it only made him love Serena and the baby more. His mother would have been furious if she had known that.

CHAPTER TWENTY-EIGHT

The years in San Francisco were happy ones for Brad and Serena. They lived in their own happy little world, in the pretty house overlooking the bay. Brad loved his work at the Presidio, and Serena was never bored with Vanessa. She was an enchanting golden-haired child who seemed to combine the best of both her parents. In truth she looked a great deal like Brad, but she had the easy laughter and grace of her mother.

Teddy came as often as he could. He called Vanessa his fairy princess and read her endless stories. He could never see them as often as he wanted to anymore, because his studies at Stanford were so demanding. It was only during holidays that he could really relax and spend some time with them. Whenever Teddy could get over, he took Vanessa to the zoo, and on special outings, and by the time she was three, she would stand at the door when she knew he was coming, and watch every passing car, until she saw him, and then she would scream with delight and shout. "He's coming! He's coming! It's Uncle Teddy!"

Other than her parents, he was the only family she really knew. She had only met her other uncle twice, when Pattie and Greg had come through San Francisco on their way to the Orient. Pattie had stared hungrily at the child, and several times been rude to Serena. Greg seemed not to see her at all, as he sat in his usual stupor between drinks. And Pattie had made a point of telling Serena how much their mother-in-law hated the baby without ever having seen her.

It was Pattie's idea to go to Japan for a vacation. Traveling had become her latest passion. But other than that, Serena and Brad had had no contact with the family back East. Ever since his mother's candid rejection of Vanessa, Brad had had minimal contact with his mother and when his mother had once come to San Francisco to visit Teddy, she had refused to see Brad with Serena, and Brad had refused to see his mother without her, so she had stubbornly left town in the end without seeing Brad, or Serena, or Vanessa. Teddy had been heartbroken about the family rift and had begged her to change her mind, but she wouldn't. If anything, she was more determined than ever.

Whatever her grandparents' feelings were about her, it mattered not at all to Vanessa. She was a constantly happy, sunny child, with an even disposition and almost no ill temper. And she was so passionately loved by both her parents and her uncle that the absence of others to adore her never mattered.

It was shortly after her third birthday that Serena and Brad told her that she was going to have a little brother or sister, and she clapped her hands with delight and hurried upstairs to draw the new baby a picture. She made a picture of an elephant, which looked more like a dog, and Serena framed it and hung it in the nursery. This time the baby was due in August. And Teddy was already teasing her about it. He was graduating from medical school in June, and by then she would be seven months pregnant.

"And if you think I'm going to run off the stage at

commencement and deliver a baby, lady, you're crazy. Besides, my rates have gone up since last time." It was a family joke now that he had delivered her first baby, and she was only a little nervous that this time the baby might come as quickly. The doctor had warned her that it could happen, and she had promised to stay close to home, and the phone, in the last two weeks of July and into the beginning of August.

Teddy was going back to New York in July after a brief trip around the West, and in August he was beginning his internship at Columbia Presbyterian in New York.

But the graduation itself was causing a great deal of excitement in the family. Everyone was coming out, his mother, and Greg and Pattie. His father had suffered a stroke and was too ill to be moved now, but everyone else would be there to see him get his diploma.

"Well, Doctor, excited?" Brad looked at his brother in his cap and gown the morning of the graduation and Teddy beamed. He was twenty-six now, and Brad was thirty-eight, but they both looked almost the same age. Brad still had a boyish quality about him, and Teddy had matured immensely at Stanford.

"You know, I just can't believe it. I'm actually—finally—going to be a doctor!"

"I knew that almost four years ago." Together they smiled at each other in a few private moments during the tense family gathering at the ceremony. Margaret Fullerton had actually refused to acknowledge Serena at all, and Pattie was delighted. The only one unaware of the obvious hostility was Vanessa, and Teddy looked at her now with a familiar glow of pleasure.

"I love that kid so much."

Brad smiled. "This time maybe she'll have a little brother."

"You sure like to call the shots, don't you?" His brother teased and then Brad remembered something.

"Yeah. By the way, I'd like you to do me a favor."

"Sure. What's up?" Teddy looked casually at his brother. It was rare that Brad asked him anything at all.

"I'm going overseas in a few days, just for a little advisory mission in Korea. I'd like you to keep an eye on the girls for me. You know, after last time I'm always afraid that if I leave for work and forget to call home she'll have had the baby in twenty minutes on her way in with the groceries.''

"Nah, give her half an hour.'' Teddy grinned for a minute, and then looked at his brother more seriously. "Will this mission be dangerous?'' He had a sudden odd feeling about it. Brad was being unusually offhand, but he could see that his eyes were worried.

"I doubt it. We've had advisers over there for a little while. I just want to see how they're handling it. We're not really getting involved. We're just watching.'' But watching what?

"For how long, Brad?'' Teddy looked worried.

"I'll just be gone a few days.''

"I didn't mean that. I meant how long will we just be watching over there?''

"Awhile.'' Brad sounded noncommittal, and then looked at his brother. "I have to be honest with you, Teddy. I think we're going to find ourselves in a war there. A damn strange one, I have to tell you, but that's what I think. I'm going to be reporting to the Pentagon on my findings.''

Teddy nodded. "Just take care, Brad.'' The two brothers exchanged a long glance, and Brad patted his arm before going to tell Serena. "Not to worry, kid. Not to worry.''

But when he told his wife, he was startled at her reaction. Unlike her usual acceptance of whatever he did, this time she begged him not to go to Korea.

"But why? It's only for a few days, and the baby's not due for another two months.''

"I don't care!'' She had shouted at first and then cried. "I just don't want you to go.''

"Don't be silly.'' He had brushed it off as pregnancy nerves but that night he heard her crying in the bathroom, and she begged him over and over again not to go and clung to him near hysterics. "I've never seen you like this, Serena.'' He was actually worried. Maybe something else was wrong and she hadn't told him. But she insisted that wasn't the case.

"I've never felt like this. I can't explain it.''

"Then forget about it. Teddy'll be here, and I'll be back before you know it." But Serena was panicked. She had a premonition that filled her with terror.

CHAPTER TWENTY-NINE

The morning that Brad left for Seoul, Serena felt unusually nervous. She had funny little cramps in her left side, the baby's feet had jabbed her all night. Vanessa had cried repeatedly at breakfast, and just before Brad left, Serena had to fight an almost overwhelming urge to burst into tears again, as she had ever since he had told her he was leaving. Again she wanted to beg him not to go, but surrounded by orderlies and assistants, and sergeants and brass, and Vanessa and Teddy, she didn't feel she could do it. He knew how she felt, and he had insisted he was going.

"Well, Doctor." He shook hands with his brother. "Take care of my girls for me. I'll be back in a few days." He was playing it down, after all the hysterics with Serena.

"Yes, Colonel." Teddy's eyes were teasing, but nonetheless he looked worried. There was something about Brad going to Korea that made him desperately uncomfortable too. But like Serena, he felt that this was neither the place nor the time to discuss it.

Serena kissed Brad longingly on the mouth, and he teased her about her big belly. She was wearing a big flared blue gingham dress and sandals, and her soft blond hair hung down her back. She looked more like Alice in Wonderland than an expectant mother. Vanessa waved to her daddy as he went up the ramp, and a moment later the plane was high in the sky, and Teddy ushered them to the gate and drove them home. Serena took Vanessa upstairs for her nap, and came down a few minutes later, her eyes worried, her face strained, as it had been for days now.

"You okay?" She nodded, but she was strangely quiet, and then she decided to confide in Teddy.

"I'm so nervous, Teddy."

He looked at her for a minute, wondering if he should tell her that he was too, but he decided against it. "I think he'll be fine."

"But what if something happens?" Tears sprang to her eyes again and Teddy took her hand with an air of quiet confidence.

"He'll be fine. I just know it."

But when the phone rang the next morning, Teddy had an eerie premonition as he sprang to answer it. He moved almost by reflex, as he did whenever he was called to the wards in school, but now as he held the phone he had a sudden urge to slam it down before he could hear anyone speak.

"Hello?"

"Is Mrs. Fullerton there?"

"She's still sleeping. May I help you?"

"Who is this?"

There was a pause. "Mr.—Doctor"—he smiled—"Fullerton. I'm Colonel Fullerton's brother." But the smile had already faded. He had a terrible feeling in the pit of his stomach.

"Doctor." The voice sounded grave. "I'm afraid we have bad news." Teddy held his breath. Oh, God . . . no. . . . But the voice went relentlessly on, as Teddy felt nausea overwhelm him. "Your brother has been killed. He was shot down north of Seoul early this morning. He was in Korea in an advisory capacity, but there was a mistake—"

"A mistake?" Teddy suddenly shouted. "A mistake! He was killed by mistake?" And then in terror, he lowered his voice.

"I'm terribly sorry. Someone will be coming out to see Mrs. Fullerton later."

"Oh, Jesus." Tears were pouring down his face and he could no longer speak.

"I know. I'm very sorry. They'll be bringing his body home for burial in a few days. We'll bury him here, with full military honors, at the Presidio. I imagine his family will want to come from back East." They had just come for Teddy's graduation, and now they would be coming back for Brad's funeral. As the realization hit him Teddy slowly hung up and the tears began to roll down his face. He dropped his face into his hands and sobbed silently, thinking of the big brother he had always looked up to, and of Vanessa and Serena. And then as though he sensed something, he looked up and saw her standing in the doorway.

"Teddy?" She looked terribly pale and she stood very still, as though her whole body were tense and straining.

For a moment he didn't know what to do or say. It was not unlike the moments before he had delivered her baby. And now, as he had then, he pulled himself together, and walked quickly to where she stood, put his arms around her, and told her, "Serena . . . it's Brad . . ." He began to sob. His big brother was gone. The brother he loved so much. And now he had to tell Serena. "He's been killed." Her whole body was tense and then he felt her slump against him.

"Oh, no . . ." She stared at Teddy in total disbelief. "Oh, no . . . Teddy . . . no." He led her slowly to a chair and eased her into it as she stared at him. "No!" And suddenly she put her hands to her face and began to whimper, as Teddy knelt before her, tears streaming down his face as he held her. When she looked up at him again, he had never seen eyes so bleak. "I knew it . . . before he left . . . I felt it . . . and he wouldn't listen." Sobs racked her as they cried, and then suddenly he saw her stiffen as her eyes went to the doorway. He turned to see what she saw, and there, watching them, in her nightgown, was Vanessa.

"Where's Daddy?"

"He's still away, sweetheart." Serena wiped her tears with her hands and held her arms out to her daughter. But as the child climbed onto her lap with a look of concern, Serena was overcome and Teddy couldn't bear to watch them.

"Why are you and Uncle Teddy crying?"

Serena thought for a long moment, her eyes flowing freely, with the child in her arms, and then she gently kissed Vanessa on the soft golden curls and looked at her with wisdom and sorrow. "We are crying, my darling, because we have just had some very sad news." The child watched her mother with wide, trusting eyes. "And you're a big girl so I'm going to tell you." She took a deep breath, and Teddy watched her. "Daddy isn't coming back from his trip, my darling."

"Why not?" She looked shocked, as though they had just told her that Santa Claus was gone forever. And for Serena and Vanessa, he was now.

Serena steeled herself and attempted to speak calmly. "Because God decided that he wanted Daddy with Him. He needed Daddy as one of his angels."

"Is Daddy an angel now?" Vanessa looked amazed.

"Yes."

"Does he have wings?"

Serena smiled, as fresh tears sprang to her eyes. "I don't think so. But he's up in heaven with God, and he is with us all the time now."

"Can I see him?" The child's eyes were enormous as she asked and Serena shook her head.

"No, my darling. But we will always remember him and love him."

"But I want to see him!" She began to cry and Serena held her tight, thinking the same words . . . and they would never see him again . . . never . . . he was gone forever.

Later that morning several officials came to see her. They gave her all the details she didn't want, made a formal little speech about how he had died in the service of his country. They explained about the funeral and told her that she could stay at the Presidio for another thirty days after that, as Serena tried to understand what they said and felt that she understood nothing.

"Thirty days?" She looked at Teddy blankly. And then it dawned on her. The Presidio owned their home, and now she no longer belonged to the army. She would get a small pension, but that was all, she had to go out into the big world and learn to live like a civilian. Gone the protected little dream world of the forests of the Presidio, hanging over the bay, and being protected by her husband. It was all over for her now. And the real world was waiting out there to devour her. She remembered also, as did Teddy, the paper that her mother-in-law had made her sign at the very beginning, and by the next morning Teddy had discovered that his brother had died intestate. He had left no will, so that everything he had reverted to his family. There would be nothing for Serena, or Vanessa, or the new baby. The implication of what lay before her was so overwhelming that Serena lay awake for two nights, staring at the ceiling. He was gone . . . he was never coming back . . . Brad was dead. She repeated it to herself over and over and over. She opened the closet doors and saw his clothes there, there were even shirts in the cupboard downstairs that needed ironing. But he was never coming back to wear them, and as the realization hit her again, she knelt on the laundry room floor, clutching his shirts and sobbing. Teddy found her there and led her slowly upstairs, where they discovered Vanessa looking tiny and stricken, hiding in Brad's closet. She had climbed into Teddy's lap and with big sad eyes had asked him, "Now will you be my daddy?" They were all aching with the strain and the misery, and by the third day Teddy noticed a total change in Serena. She moved as though she were in a daze, not understanding, barely thinking, and suddenly mid-morning he heard her give a shout of pain. Almost as if he sensed what had happened, Teddy ran in to find her in her bedroom. Her water had broken. She was already doubled over on the floor in unbearable pain. But this time was different from when she had had Vanessa. This time there were no breaks in the pains at all, and by the time she reached the hospital, she was hysterical. The baby had not come in half an hour. Teddy had run Vanessa to a neighbor, and he had watched Serena closely before the ambulance came, and on the ride to the hospital. This time her pulse was thready, her breathing tortured, her eyes glazed. She went into shock in the hospital, and an hour later her son was stillborn. Teddy sat in the waiting room for several hours until he could see her, and when he did, he was overwhelmed by those once emerald eyes, now a deep sea filled with pain. She was so deep in her own misery that she didn't even hear him call her name.

"Serena." He reached for her hand. "I'm here."

"Brad?" She turned glazed eyes toward him.

"No, it's Teddy." Her eyes filled with tears and she turned her face away.

She was still like that the next morning, and two days later when they discharged her. And that morning they had to bury her son in a tiny white coffin, which they lowered slowly into the ground as she fainted. The next day they brought home Brad's body, and she had to go to headquarters and sign papers. Teddy thought she would never make it. But somehow she did, as she signed the forms with a look of horror that almost overwhelmed him.

And through it all there was Margaret Fullerton to contend with too. Serena had insisted on calling her herself, and there had been no scream of anguish from Brad's mother. There had been only unbridled fury and a sense of revenge, as she blamed Serena for what had happened. If he hadn't married her, he wouldn't have stayed in the army, and he would never have gone to Korea. With a voice trembling with rage she vented her grief by attempting to destroy Serena, and at last she reminded her venomously of their contract.

"And don't think you'll get a dime from me, for you or your child. I hope you both rot in hell for what you did to Bradford." She slammed down the phone, and Serena cried inconsolably for two hours. And it was then that Teddy felt the same hatred for his mother that he knew Brad had. All he wanted to do was protect Serena, but there was nothing he could do to change what had happened. Brad was gone, leaving no will, and even if he had left one, it would have been small comfort to Serena. She wanted her husband back. She didn't want the money.

When Margaret Fullerton arrived from New York, she brought Pattie and Greg with her. Brad's father was still too ill to make the trip, and in any case, under doctor's advice, they hadn't told him the awful news.

Teddy picked up the threesome at the airport. His mother looked rigid and grim, Greg seemed in a haze, and Pattie nervously chatted on the way in from the airport. The only thing his mother said on the drive into town was "I don't want to see that woman." Teddy felt his guts seethe.

"You're going to have to. She's been through enough without you torturing her further."

"She killed my son." Her eyes were filled with hatred.

"Your son was killed in Korea on a military mission, for God's sake, and Serena just lost a baby."

"Just as well. She couldn't have afforded to support it now anyway."

"You make me sick."

"You'd do well to stay away from her, Teddy, unless you want trouble with me."

"I won't do that." Nothing more was said and he left them at the hotel and went back to Serena.

At the funeral the next day Margaret stood with Pattie and Greg, and Teddy stood between Vanessa and Serena. Vanessa seemed not to understand what was going on, and her mother kept a clawlike grip on Teddy's hand throughout the military honors. At the end they handed her the folded flag, and slowly Serena turned, walked to where Margaret stood, and held it out, with trembling hands, to Brad's mother. There was a moment's hesitation as their eyes met and held, and then the older woman took it from her, saying not a single word of thanks. She handed it to Greg and then turned and walked away, her face concealed by a black veil as Serena watched her.

Teddy drove Serena and Vanessa home after that and he glanced at his sister-in-law as she blew her nose.

"Why did you do that?" She knew he meant the flag. "You didn't have to."

"She's his mother." Her eyes filled with tears as they met his, and suddenly she put her head on his shoulder and she sobbed. "Oh, God, what am I going to do without him?" He stopped the car and then took her in his arms and held her as Vanessa watched them.

CHAPTER THIRTY

"Serena?" He came up softly behind her as she sat in the fog in the garden, listening to the foghorns. In the past week she had become a kind of ghost—a haunted person. It was painful to see, as if she were slipping away.

"Yes?"

"You've got to be all right, Serena. You have to."

"Why?" She looked at him blankly.

"For me, for yourself, for Vanessa . . ." His own eyes filled with tears. "For Brad."

"Why?"

"Because you have to, dammit." He wanted to shake her. "If you fall apart, what will happen to that child?"

"You'll take care of her, won't you?" She looked suddenly desperate, and with a sigh he nodded.

"Yes, but that's not the point. She needs you."

"But will you?" Her eyes searched his face and they both remembered the paper. "If I die, will you take care of her?"

"You won't die."

"I want to."

He shook her then. "You can't." And with that, they both heard a little voice from the doorway.

"Mommy, I need you." She had had a bad dream, and at the sound of her voice Serena began to awake from hers. The following week Teddy helped Serena find an apartment, and she packed up all of their beautiful things and moved to Pacific Heights. It was a two-bedroom flat with a view of the bay, which she could just manage on her pension, and if they wanted to eat too, she realized that she was going to have to get a job.

"Maybe I should go downtown and start selling my body?" She looked cynically at Teddy and he did not look amused. But the thought, however sarcastic, sparked an idea for Serena, and the next day she went downtown and inquired at all the large department stores. By noon the next day she had been hired, and she returned to tell Teddy that she was employed. "I got a job today."

"Doing what?" He worried about her all the time. She had been through so much, the loss of her husband, her baby, her home. How much could she stand? He asked himself that question often.

"As a model for seventy-five dollars a week."

"And who will take care of your daughter?"

"I'll find someone." There was a look of determination on her face as she said it. She refused to be beaten by life, no matter how hard it tried to defeat her. She had survived the loss of her parents, and the war. Now Brad. But she was determined to get through it. For Vanessa.

He shook his head. "I don't want you to do that. I want you to let me help you." But she wouldn't. She had found a job, and she was going to support them. If it killed her, she was going to make it. She owed that much to Brad. It had been only three weeks since he had been killed in Korea, and now the United States was at war—it was as if her private war was becoming public.

She looked at Teddy now in sudden fear. "How soon are you going back to New York?" She knew he was due to start his internship in August and it was almost July. But he was shaking his head slowly.

"I'm not."

"You're staying?" For a moment she looked thrilled.

"No." He took a deep breath. He had been dreading telling her. "I enlisted in the Navy. I want to go to Korea."

"What?" She screamed the word at him and unconsciously grabbed his shirt. "You can't do that! Not you too . . ." She began to sob quietly as she clutched him and he pulled her into his arms with tears in his own eyes.

"I have to. For him." And for her, he thought to himself. To get away from the feelings he had that threatened to spill over at any moment.

"When do you leave?"

"A few days. A few weeks. Whenever they call me."

"And what about us?" She looked suddenly terrified.

"You'll be all right." He smiled at her through his tears. "Hell, you have a job."

"Oh, Teddy, don't go." She held him close to her, and nothing more was said, as they stood there, holding on to the last shreds of what was no more, would never be again. Just as her childhood had ended as Mussolini's bullets had ripped into her parents long ago, now another era was over. She would never again be Brad's wife, never feel his arms around her. And now there wouldn't even be Teddy. They had all grown up. In three short weeks. The early days were over.

Book Two

SERENA:
THE
SURVIVAL
YEARS

CHAPTER THIRTY-ONE

At six o'clock in the morning, on a foggy day in late July, Serena stood at the pier in Oakland, hugging Teddy for the last time. The weeks had flown by so quickly, she couldn't believe that he was already leaving. She had begged him to change his mind at first, and then finally she had accepted his decision. And it was obvious from the way things were going in Korea that sooner or later he would have to go. He had got a commission in the Navy, and would get his training as an intern somewhere in Korea. It certainly wasn't what they had been planning. But then again, ever since Brad's death what was?

For Serena the whole world had turned upside down in less than two months. Now she was a widow, alone with Vanessa, working. And as she looked at Teddy in his uniform she realized that the last human being she could depend on was going to be gone. She clung to him for a long moment, fighting back tears as she closed her eyes.

"Oh, God, Teddy . . . I wish you weren't going."

"So do I."

And then, trying to be a brave sister, she smiled gamely. "But be a good kid and wear your galoshes, write to me on Sundays . . ." And then in a hoarse whisper, "Don't forget us. . . ."

"Oh, Serena . . . don't say that!" He pressed her tightly against him, and anyone watching would have thought that she was saying good-bye to her husband, not her husband's brother, as he wiped the tears from her cheeks, hugged her again, and then stood back to look at her for a last time.

"I'll be back. Soon too. So you take care of yourself and Vanessa for me." She nodded, the tears streaming from her eyes, as others hurried past them to board the ship that was to sail in an hour. God, how he wanted to stay with her, he

267

thought to himself as he looked at her. Yet he knew that he had to go. It was something that he had to do for himself and his brother, no matter what anyone said. His mother had flown out from New York in a fury, threatening to pull strings, use connections, and get him kicked out of the service. But he was so vehement about his decision that in the end even she capitulated. One had to respect his motives and his way of thinking. What was terrifying was the possibility that he might be killed.

Serena tried not to think about it as she reached out to touch him just one last time. They had an extraordinary bond between them, had had from the beginning, and it had strengthened when he had delivered Vanessa. But in the past two months there had been something more, being with Teddy was like holding on to a part of Brad. It allowed her to hold on to him in some distant, melancholy way. And now she was losing Teddy too. But hopefully not forever.

"Serena . . ." He started to say something, and then stopped as the boat horn sounded, blotting out everything else that anyone said. It bleated three more times, and a gong sounded. It was time to go, and Serena felt a rush of panic, as he grabbed her, pulled her toward him, and held her tight. "I'll be back. Just know that."

"I love you." Her eyes filled with tears and she shouted it in his ear as she clung to him. He nodded, picked up his bag, and moved onto the ship with the others. It was several minutes before she saw him again, standing high above her, on the deck, waving slowly, and she couldn't fight back the tears. They streamed down her face unrestrained, until at last the horns bleated again, in concert with the foghorns in the distance, and the ship began to pull out slowly. She felt as though it were pulling her heart with it, and when the ship was swallowed up entirely by the fog, she turned away slowly and went back to her car with her head down, and tears still pouring from her eyes.

When she returned to San Francisco, Vanessa was waiting with a baby-sitter and she wanted to know how soon Uncle Teddy was coming home. It took all of the strength that Serena could muster to explain to her again, that Teddy would be gone for a long time, but he would come back to them as soon as he could. They had a lot of nice things to do together, Serena encouraged, like going to the zoo, and the rose gardens in the park, the Japanese tea garden, the circus when it came to town . . . but before she could finish, there were tears in her eyes again and she was holding her daughter and squeezing her tight.

"Will he be like Daddy and never come back?" Vanessa's eyes were huge in her grief-filled face and Serena shuddered at the thought.

"No! Uncle Teddy will be. back! I told you that." She wanted to shout at the child for voicing the terrors she was wrestling with herself. But Serena's voice trembled as she said it, and as she had a thousand times in the past weeks, she found herself longing to turn back the clock. If only she could close her eyes and go back to the days she had shared with Brad, of knowing that he would protect her, that he would be there for her . . . back to the golden days they had shared at the Presidio . . . or in Paris . . . or the first days in Rome. Weeks ago she had written to Marcella, to tell her the news. And the answer, dictated to one of the new maids who worked under her, had been desolate. She offered Serena her sympathy as well as her prayers. But she needed more than that now. She needed someone there to hold her hand, to reassure her that she would make it.

There were times in the ensuing months when she really wondered if she would survive. Months when she could barely pay the rent, when bills were overdue, when they ate peanut butter and jelly sandwiches or only eggs. She had never known this kind of poverty before. During the war the nuns had kept her safe, and at the palazzo in Rome after that, she and Marcella had been well provided for, but now there was no one to turn to, no one to help her, no one to lend her money when she only had two dollars left and wouldn't get paid for another three days. Time and again she thought of the agreement she had signed with Margaret Fullerton. If she had never been forced to sign that damned piece of paper, at least she and Vanessa would have been able to eat. Vanessa would have had pretty clothes to wear and more than just one beat-up pair of little shoes. Once, in desperation, she almost turned to them for help, but she couldn't, and in her heart of hearts she knew it wouldn't have done any good. Margaret Fullerton was so vehement and irrational in her hatred of Serena that there was nothing Serena could say or do to change her mind. It was a hatred so broad and deep that it even reached out to envelop Vanessa, her only grandchild. Margaret didn't give a damn if they did starve. Serena suspected that she probably hoped they would.

Only the joy of finding Vanessa at the end of a day kept her going. Only the letters from Teddy warmed her heart. Only the money from her modeling at the department store kept them alive. There were days when she thought she would drop from exhaustion and when she wanted to cry with despair. But day after day, six days a week, she went downtown to model, to wander around the floors in the latest creations, to hand out perfume samples, to stand near the front door in a striking fur coat, to model in the fashion shows when they had them. It wasn't until the second year that she was promoted to the designer salon. And then she modeled for special customers, or in the big shows. She wore only their finest designer dresses from New York or Paris, and she was rapidly learning the tricks of her trade, how to do her hair in half a dozen flattering styles, how to do her makeup to perfection, how to move, how to smile, how to sell the clothes just by weaving a kind of spell. And whereas she was beautiful before, with the new skills she was learning, she was even more remarkable looking than she had been before. People talked about her in the store, and often people stared at her. The women customers looked at her in envy, but more often with a kind of fascination, as though she were a work of art. Their husbands stared at Serena, utterly awed by her beauty, and it wasn't long before the store's advertising agency saw her, and they made her their main model for the store. Every week her photograph was in the papers, and by the end of her second year at the store people began to recognize her around town. Men asked her out. She got invited to parties by relative strangers, but her answer was always the same. Without exception she declined. Her only interest was in returning home to Vanessa, to play with the little golden-haired child

270

who looked so much like B.J., to sing silly songs with her at the little piano Serena had bought at an auction, to read her stories, and to share their dreams. Serena told her that one day she would be a beautiful, famous lady. . . .

"Like you, Mommy?"

Serena smiled. "No, much prettier than I am, silly. Everyone will stop to stare at you in the street, and you will be successful and happy." Serena would stare into space for a moment, thinking of her own dreams. Was that what she wanted? To be stared at? To be successful? For her, modeling had been the only answer, but it was a strange life, making her living by how she looked, and often she felt foolish and unimportant, like the mannequin she literally was. But none of that mattered—she couldn't afford to have doubts about it. She had to survive.

It was a painfully empty life. She had the child, and her work, and their apartment. But other than that, she had nothing at all. No man, no friends, no one to talk to or to turn to. There seemed to be no room in her life for anyone but the child. And at night she would sit and read, or write letters to Teddy. They took weeks to reach him in the distant outposts of Korea. He was a resident now, and wrote to her long sorrowful letters about what he thought of the war. To him, it all seemed a senseless carnage, a war they couldn't win and didn't belong in, and he longed to come home or be transferred to Japan. There were times when she would read his letters over and over, holding them in her hand, and then staring out at the bay, remembering his face the day she had met him . . . the way he had looked in his cutaway at Greg's wedding . . . the day he had delivered Vanessa . . . at his graduation at Stanford. It was odd how often now, in her mind, she confused his face with her husband's. It was as though over the past two and a half years they had got confused in her mind.

And on their third Christmas alone Serena and Vanessa went to church and prayed for his safety, as they did each Sunday, and that night Serena lay in her bed and cried. She was aching with loneliness and exhaustion, from the years alone, the endless hours of hard work at the store, and all that she poured out to Vanessa. It was as though she had to give it all, and there was no one to replenish her strength for her. Week after week she waited anxiously for Teddy's letters. They were what kept her going. It was in writing to him that she poured out her own soul. In a sense it was her only real contact with a grown-up, and her only contact with a man.

At work she spoke to almost no one. Word had got out at one point that she had been an Italian princess before her marriage to an American soldier, and everyone decided that she was arrogant and aloof, and they were frightened by her beauty. After a while no one even tried to make friends with her. They had no way of knowing how lonely she was behind the cool facade of the princess. Only Teddy knew when he read her letters, her pain and loneliness and the still-fresh grief for her husband were obvious between the lines.

"It's amazing to see," she wrote to him after Christmas, "how they all misunderstand me. They think me cold and snobbish, I suppose, and I let them. It's easier, and safer perhaps, than allowing them to know how much I hurt inside." She still missed Brad but it was more than that now. She missed someone. Someone to talk to and to share with and to laugh with, and go for walks on the beach with. She couldn't bear to do the things she had done with Brad, or even with Teddy, they only made her feel more lonely, and reminded her of how alone she was. "I feel at times as though this will go on forever. I will always be alone, here, with Vanessa, night after night and year after year, in this apartment, working at the store, and no one will ever know me. It frightens me sometimes, Teddy. It is as though you are the only one left who has truly known me. . . ."

There was of course Marcella, but it had been years since she had seen her, and Marcella was part of another life now. The letters that she dictated to someone else to be sent to Serena were always stilted and awkward, and left an empty chasm there too. In effect there was only Teddy, thousands of miles away in Korea, and it was only in the last few months of the war that they both began to realize what had happened. After two and a half years of writing letters, baring their souls to each other, holding each other up across the miles, she finally understood why there had been no one

272

in almost three years. She was waiting for him.

The morning that she heard the news that the war was over, she was working at the store, and wearing a black velvet evening suit with a stiff white organdy collar, and she stood in the middle of the designer salon with tears streaming down her face.

A saleswoman smiled at her, and others chattered excitedly among them. The war in Korea was over! And Serena wanted to give a whoop of joy. "He's coming home," she whispered, but someone overheard her. "He's coming home!"

"Your husband?" someone asked.

"No." She shook her head slowly, with a look of amazement on her face. "His brother." The woman looked at her strangely and Serena suddenly knew that an important question was about to be answered. When the years of letters suddenly ended, what would Teddy be to her?

CHAPTER THIRTY-TWO

Teddy returned from the Far East on August 3, and as he set foot on land in San Francisco, he was officially discharged from the Navy. His residency had been completed in the heat of the war, he was trained as a surgeon, as few had been in the States, and he was on his way to New York to train for another year with a great surgeon. But none of that was on his mind as he stepped off the plane at the airport. His blond hair glinted in the sunlight, his face was tanned, and he squinted at the horde of people waiting. How different it was from the day he had left on the ship in Oakland. And how different he felt. He had been gone for three years, and he had just turned thirty.

And he felt as though in three years of war everything about him had changed. His interests, his needs, his priorities, his values. On the long flight over from Japan he had wondered again and again how he was going to fit in. For almost three years he hadn't seen his family. His mother's letters had been newsy, but he had always felt light-years away from home. Greg had only managed one or two letters a year. His father had died the year before. And most of his friends had eventually stopped writing, except Serena. His main contact with civilization had been with her, and now suddenly he was back, in the midst of a world no longer familiar, looking for a woman he hadn't seen in three years.

His eyes searched the crowd, and he wandered slowly toward where the visitors were gathered. Signs waved, bunches of flowers were held aloft, tears streamed down faces, frantic hands reached out to husbands and sons and lovers who had been gone for years. And then suddenly he saw her, so staggeringly beautiful that he felt his heart lurch. She stood very tall, and wide eyed and quiet, in a red silk dress that hung straight and narrow on her body, with her silky blond hair loose on her shoulders, and the emerald-green eyes looking straight at him. Like her, he was oddly silent, there were no wild gestures, no running, he just walked steadily toward her, and then as though they both knew, he pulled her into his arms and held her with all his might, as tears ran down both their cheeks, and then forgetting the years that had drifted between them, he kissed her full on the mouth, as though to ease away all the years of loneliness and pain. They held each other that way for long moments, and then at last pulled apart and looked at each other, but her eyes were full and sad as they reached up to his. Teddy had come to her, she knew now, but Brad never would. It was as though in the past three years, waiting for his return, she had fooled herself that it was Brad in Korea and not Teddy. But she understood now, almost like a physical blow, that her husband was lost forever. In all the years of letters it had been as though she were reaching out to Brad as well as Teddy. The two men had somehow merged as one in her mind. And now she had to face the truth again, as her heart plummeted within her and she tried not to let her grief show in her face.

"Hello, Serena."

She smiled now, over the first shock, and then simultaneously they both looked down at the little girl beside her. It was here that they both saw the three lost years most clearly. Vanessa was almost seven, and she had been three and a half when Teddy left.

"Good Lord, princess!" He knelt down in the hubbub to talk to Vanessa. His eyes were a bright dancing blue, and his face lit up in a gentle smile. "I'll bet you don't remember your uncle Teddy."

"Yes, I do." She tilted her head to one side, and when she smiled, he saw that both her front teeth were missing. "Mommy showed me your picture every night. Yours and my daddy's, but he's not coming home too. Mommy told me. Just you."

"That's right." A little knife of pain cut through both Serena and Teddy at once, but he was still smiling at the little girl. "I sure have missed you." She nodded seriously as she looked him over.

"Are you really a doctor?" She looked worried as he nodded. "Are you going to give me a shot?" He chuckled and shook his head as he lifted her up to his shoulder.

"I certainly am not. How about an ice cream cone instead?"

"Oh, boy!" They began drifting through the crowd toward the main terminal. He had to pick up his bag, and then they could be on their way, back to the apartment he had helped her find before he left, to the place he had remembered every night and day as he sat in the jungles of Korea, remembering Serena's face. And now, as he glanced at her, he saw that she had changed. He didn't say anything to her about it until they were back in the apartment on Washington Street, and they were sitting in the living room together, drinking coffee and looking out at the bay.

He eyed her for a long searching moment, seeing the sadness still there, and the seriousness, and at the same time something tender, and he reached gently for her hand as he set down his cup. "You've grown up, Serena."

"I hope so." She smiled at him. "I'm twenty-seven now."

"That doesn't matter. Some people never make it."

"I've had a lot of reason to grow up, Teddy." She looked toward the other room, to where Vanessa was playing, and then back at him. "So have you."

He nodded slowly, remembering things he didn't even want to. "Sometimes I didn't think any of us would survive it." And then he forced a smile. "But we did. And I suppose the experience will be worth something." And then, seeing all that was in her face, and unable to restrain himself from asking, "You still miss him, don't you?"

She nodded. "Yes, I missed you both."

"And you only got one of us back." He looked at her strangely as he said it. He had understood everything he had seen in her face when he first saw her at the gate. "Maybe it never sinks in that someone isn't coming home. I don't know." He shook his head. "At times I'd wonder for a minute when I'd get a letter from you why there was no news of Brad, and then I'd remember."

She nodded understanding. "He had only been dead for two months when you left. I don't think either of us had had time to absorb it." And she knew now more than ever how true that was.

"I know." He looked at her searchingly. "And now?" He was asking her a serious question and she knew it.

"I think maybe today I finally understood." She sighed softly. "In a way I've hidden from the truth a lot. All I've done is work and take care of Vanessa." He knew that from her letters.

"At twenty-seven, that isn't much of a life." And then, with a gentle smile, "You know, you look different."

She seemed surprised. 'Were you disappointed?" But at this Teddy laughed and shook his head.

"Oh, Serena . . . haven't you looked in the mirror in the last three years?"

This time she laughed at him. "Too much! That's all I've done."

"Well, whatever you've done, you're even more beautiful than you were when I left here."

She squinted at him in amusement. "Has the war perhaps affected your eyesight, Lieutenant?" But they both laughed together.

"No, princess, it hasn't. You're the most beautiful woman I've ever seen. And I thought that was true when I first met you in New York."

"Ah." She waved a disparaging hand at him. "Now it's all fakery and makeup."

"No." It was something more. Something difficult to describe. Something in her face, in her eyes, in her soul. It was maturity and gentleness, wisdom and suffering, and all of the love that she had lavished on Vanessa. It was something more that she had become in addition to her physical beauty. It was something that made one want to stare at her, something one sensed as well as saw. He looked at her then and asked her a question. "Serena, are you serious about modeling?" He had never given it a thought in all the years in Korea. He just assumed that it was something she did to pay the rent. But now that he saw her, the way her bones had begun to stand out, the way she looked, the way she did her hair and her face, the way she moved now, he knew that if she wanted to she could have a tremendous career. It was the first time the thought struck him, as they sat on the couch. But Serena only shrugged.

"I don't know, Teddy. I don't really think so." She smiled and looked like a very young girl again. "Why would I want to do that? Except maybe to pay the rent." That was still a month-to-month struggle for her. Even now.

"Because you're so beautiful, and you could make a lot of money." He looked pointedly at her. "And since you won't take anything from me, it might be a thought. Have you thought at all about going to New York to model?" She had said nothing about it in her letters, but now he wondered, and he began to like the idea more and more, not for entirely unselfish reasons.

"I don't know. The thought of New York scares me." She looked worried. "I might not be able to find work in New York." And yet it was an appealing prospect and maybe a way to make more money than she had in the last three years.

"Are you kidding, Serena?" He look her by the hand and walked her to the mirror. "Look at that, love." She looked embarassed and she blushed as she glanced at herself and the handsome blond man standing behind her: "That face would find work as a model anywhere in the world. Principessa Serena . . . The Princess . . ." As they stared at her together he suddenly realized that something magical was happening, as though they were seeing each other for the first time.

"Teddy, no . . . come on . . ." She pulled away from the mirror, embarrassed, and he turned her slowly to face him, and kissed her, and when he did, he was suddenly overwhelmed with desire for this woman he had secretly loved for seven years. But just as he was about to touch the beautiful body, he felt her stiffen in his arms, and he made himself stop.

"Serena . . . I'm sorry . . ." He looked suddenly deathly pale, and he could feel his whole body tremble. "It's been a long time . . . and—" He faltered, and she took his face gently in her hands, her eyes filled with tears.

"Stop it, Teddy. You have nothing to be sorry about. I knew this was coming. We both did. We've been pouring our souls out to each other for three years." And then she dropped her hands from his face, hugged him close, and nestled her face in his shoulder. "I love you as a brother, Teddy. I always have. I was wrong in thinking that there could be something more. For the last year I'd begun to wonder, without really admitting it to myself, but I was hoping that you could come home and"—she choked on her tears—"replace . . . him." She felt guilty even saying it, and she pulled away from Teddy at last. "It's not fair to expect that of you. It's just not the same thing. It's funny." She smiled through her tears. "You're so much like him, but you're *you*. And I love you, but I love you as a sister, not as a woman, or a lover, or a wife." They were cruel words and they hit him like rocks. But they were words he needed to hear. He had deluded himself for too many years.

She was watching him closely and he took a deep breath and looked at her with gentle eyes. "It's all right, Serena. I understand."

"Do you?" She was quiet and firm and more beautiful than he had ever seen her, as she stood before him in her narrow silk dress. "Do you hate me for not being able to give you more?"

"I could never hate you. I love you too much. And I respect you too much."

"For what?" Her eyes were empty and sad. "What have I done to deserve that?"

"You've survived—under rotten circumstances, thanks to my mother—you're a terrific mother to Vanessa, you've knocked yourself out working and supporting her. You're an amazing woman, Serena."

"I don't feel amazing." She gazed at him with enormous eyes. "I feel sad. Sad at what I can't be to you."

"So do I. But maybe it's better this way." He hugged her again, praying that his desire for her wouldn't betray him. He pulled away again after a minute. "Just promise me one thing, when you fall in love again one day, and you will, make sure he's a terrific guy."

"Teddy!" She laughed and the agony of the past half hour began to lighten a little. "What a thing to say!"

"I mean it." And he looked as though he did. "You deserve the best there is. And you need a man in your life." He knew from what she had told him in her letters of her celibate life just how long it had been.

"I don't need a man." She was smiling now.

"Why not?"

"Because I have the best brother in the world." She slipped an arm around his waist and kissed his cheek. "You." And as he felt her next to him he felt his whole body tingle, but they had come a long way from the past in a few hours and now he knew where he stood.

CHAPTER THIRTY-THREE

The next day Serena had to go to work, and instead of leaving Vanessa with the sitter, she left her with Teddy, and after lunch they came to visit her at work. They found her on the second floor, in a magnificent lilac taffeta ballgown, and as they got off the elevator Teddy saw her, and he stopped for a moment just to watch her, as he caught his breath. What a magnificent woman she had become in his absence. She had grown into her full promise and more. Even Vanessa seemed to sense something remarkable in her mother and she looked at her with awe. Serena looked like someone in a priceless painting as she swept into a chair and held out her arms in opera-length white kid gloves.

"Hi, sweetheart. Oh, you look so pretty!" Teddy had dressed her in a blue organdy dress and black patent-leather shoes with white knee socks and a blue satin ribbon in her silky blond hair. And then Serena's eyes found Teddy.

"Hello." She smiled. "How are you managing?"

"I'm loving it." And then as Vanessa wandered away for a moment, his eyes held her close to him for just a fraction of a second, and then the brotherly look came back to his eyes.

"What are you and Vanessa doing this afternoon?"

"Going out for ice cream. I told her I'd take her to the zoo tomorrow."

"Don't you want some time for yourself?" She looked troubled. What would they do when he was gone? But perhaps he would come out and visit. They had talked about it this morning over breakfast, but everything but the present seemed very remote. "I'll be home at five thirty. I'll take over then."

He chuckled softly. "Seeing you in that outfit, I can't imagine you doing anything except maybe going to the opera."

280

"Not exactly, love." She grinned at him. "I have to do the laundry tonight. This is all make-believe."

"You could have fooled me." He laughed softly, still somewhat in awe of her looks. And as he gazed at her Vanessa came scampering back to show her the lollipop one of the saleswomen had given her.

"And now we're going out for ice cream!" She looked happily at Teddy.

"I know all about it. Have a good time, you two." It was an odd feeling, watching them leave hand in hand. She always felt so terribly responsible for Vanessa, as though there were no one who could ever take her place, but as she watched the child with her uncle, she suddenly felt as though she could relax. If something had happened to her at that very moment, Vanessa would have been safe and well cared for. Just knowing that took a thousand-pound weight off her back.

That night the three of them cooked spaghetti, and Teddy read Vanessa stories in bed, while Serena cleaned up. She wore slacks and a black turtleneck sweater, her hair wound high on her head, and she looked very different from the magical creature who had worn the lilac taffeta ballgown only that afternoon, as Teddy mentioned with a grin when she came in and told them that it was time to turn off the lights.

"You know, I was serious last night when I asked you about your modeling." He looked at her intently as she finished up in the kitchen and he munched a handful of grapes. "You have the makings of a great model, Serena. I don't know a damn thing about the business, but I know what you look like, and there's nothing like it in this country. I bought some magazines when I was out with Vanessa today." He pulled them out of a bag on one of the kitchen chairs and showed her, flipping through them. "Look at that . . . baby there's no one like you."

"Maybe they like it like that." She refused to take him seriously. "Look, Teddy." She looked almost amused at his faith in her. "I got lucky, I got a job here at the store, they use me a lot because they need me and I look all right in their clothes. But this is a small town, this is not like New York, or where there's a lot of competition. If I went to New York, they'd probably laugh in my face."

"Do you want to try it?" He looked intrigued at the idea, and Serena shrugged.

"I don't know. I have to think about it." But her eyes had begun to light up, and then she looked at Teddy seriously for a moment. "I don't want you to pay my way to New York though."

"Why not?"

"I don't take charity."

"How about justice?" He looked annoyed. "I'm living off your money, you know."

"How do you figure that?"

"If my brother had had enough sense to make a will, you'd have got his money and none of this would even be an issue. Instead, thanks to my charming mother, it reverted to his brothers. I got half of Brad's money, Serena, and in truth it belongs to you."

She shook her head firmly. "If it belongs to anyone, then maybe Vanessa." Her eyes lifted to his. "So when you make a will, perhaps one day . . ." She hated to say the words, but he nodded.

"I did that before I went to Korea, because you were so damn stubborn you didn't take anything from me."

"I'm not your responsibility, Teddy."

He looked at her soberly. "I wish to hell you were." But she didn't answer. There was no question of that. She would never have accepted anything from him.

She was independent now, and intent on taking care of herself and her own. "Why don't you ever let me help you?"

Her eyes were serious as she answered. "Because I have to take care of myself and Vanessa, there's no one else who's going to be there for us all the time, Teddy. You have your own life. You don't owe us anything. Nothing. The only person I ever counted on was Brad, and now that's over, he's gone."

"And you don't think that anyone will ever take his place?" It hurt him to ask her the question, especially after what had happened between them the night before.

"I don't know." And then she sighed softly. "But I do know one thing, and that is that no matter how much I may love you or need you, Teddy, I will never let myself be dependent on you.''

"But why? Brad would have wanted you to."

"He knew me better than that, scrubbing floors in my parents' palazzo. Besides, I made a deal with your mother.''

Teddy's eyes were instantly angry. "A deal that cost her nothing and has cost you three years of hard work.''

"I don't mind that. It's been for Vanessa.''

"And what about you? Don't you have a right to more than that?''

"If I want more, I'll get it for myself.''

He sighed then. "You don't suppose you'll ever get smart and marry me, will you?''

"No.'' She smiled gently at him. "Besides, I tore one Fullerton away from his family''—her eyes clouded as she said it—"I couldn't do that to you too.'' And it was unlikely that Margaret Fullerton would ever let her. She'd see Serena dead first. And Serena knew it.

"You know, what my mother has done to you makes me sick, Serena.'' His face was sad and serious as he spoke to her.

"It doesn't matter anymore.''

"Yes, it does, who are you kidding? And one day it could matter a lot to Vanessa.''

Neither of them spoke for a long moment. And then Serena looked at him with worried eyes. "If I go to New York, do you think she'll come after me?''

"What do you mean?'' He looked shocked.

"I'm not sure. Drive me away somehow, hurt my career if she can . . . do you think she would?''

He wanted to say no, but as he thought of it he wasn't certain.

"I wouldn't let that happen.''

"You have your own life, and God only knows how she'd do it.''

"She's not that powerful, for chrissake.''

'Isn't she?'' Serena looked at him pointedly, knowing full well just how vengeful his mother was.

And softly Teddy whispered, "I wish to hell she weren't.'' But she was. They both knew she was.

CHAPTER THIRTY-FOUR

"You'll write to me?" Her eyes were bright with tears, but she was smiling, and he kissed her for a last time.

"Better than that, I'll call you. And I'll come out to visit you both as soon as I can get away."

Serena nodded, and Teddy reached out once more to Vanessa. "Take care of your mommy for me, princess."

"I will, Uncle Teddy." And then with a sad little wail, "Why can't we come too?" His eyes instantly sought Serena's, and she felt as though there were lead weights in her heart. For Vanessa it was like losing the past all over again. And more than that, Teddy had once again become an important part of her present.

They kissed him one last time, and a moment later he boarded the plane, and Serena and Vanessa stood at the airport, waving at the plane as it took off down the runway and then, hand in hand, they went home, feeling as though a part of their souls had left them.

He called them from New York a few days later, and reported that all was well. He was starting work at the hospital in a few days. He was going to be working with one of the country's leading surgeons, polishing up what he had learned in Korea. He mentioned in passing that he had contacted the wife of an old friend, because she worked in a modeling agency. He had hand-delivered Serena's photographs the previous morning, and he'd let her know what the response was as soon as he heard himself. But after the phone call Serena felt an even greater void than she had before she spoke to him. It was almost a physical ache as she thought of how far away he was and how long it might be before she saw him again. And aside from Vanessa he was the only family she had.

But four days later he called her. He was laughing and

excited and almost stammering into the phone as she tried to sift out what had happened. He sounded as though he had won the Irish Sweepstakes.

"They want you! They want you!"

"Who wants me?" She was still confused as she stared at the phone.

"The agency! Where I took your pictures!"

"What do you mean, they want me?" She suddenly felt a thrill of excitement race through her.

"I mean they want you to come to New York. They want to represent you. They already know of half a dozen potential jobs they would send you out for, just for a start."

"But that's crazy!"

"No, it isn't, dammit. You are. Serena, you are the most beautiful woman I've ever seen, and you're out there hiding in some damn department store. If you want to be a model, for chrissake, then come to New York and really be one! Will you come?"

"I don't know . . . I have to think . . . the apartment . . . Vanessa . . ." But she was laughing and smiling, and her head felt all in a whirl.

"School hasn't started yet, this is only August. We'll get Vanessa into a school here."

"But I don't know if I can afford it." She felt equal parts of excitement and terror. "I'll call you back. I have to think." She sat staring in amazement at the bay outside her windows. Modeling in New York . . . "the big time," she grinned to herself . . . why not? But then suddenly once again she grew frightened. She couldn't. It was crazy. But then again so was sitting in San Francisco, leading no life at all, going to work every day. But what if the Fullertons harassed her? Or was Teddy right? Maybe she should take a chance on going, no matter what. She was still mulling it over the next morning when he called again.

"All right. You've had all night. When are you coming?"

"Teddy, stop pushing!" But she was laughing as she looked at the phone. Still, deep inside she knew that she was resisting.

"If I don't push you, you'll never get off your ass to do it."

He was right and they both knew it. "Why are you doing

this to me?'' The fear in her voice was easy to hear now.

He paused for a moment and then answered. ''I'm doing it for two reasons. Because I want you here, and also because I think you could have a terrific career.''

''I don't know, Teddy. I have to think about it.''

''Serena, what in the hell is the problem?'' And then as he waited he instinctively knew before she told him. It wasn't just San Francisco, it was Brad. ''It's Brad, isn't it? You feel close to him there.''

That was exactly it. He had just delved to the heart of the problem. ''Yes.'' It was a single anguished word. ''It's as though when I leave here I'll finally leave him.'' Tears sprang to her eyes as she said the words, and at his end Teddy sighed.

''Serena, he's already gone. You have to think of yourself.''

''I am.''

''No, you're not. You're hanging on to the city where you lived with him. I understand it. But it's a lousy reason to give up a career. What do you think he'd say?''

''To go.'' She didn't hesitate for a second. ''But that's not so easy to do.''

''I'm sure it isn't.'' His heart went out to her again. ''But maybe you have to force yourself to do it.''

''I'll think about it.'' It was all he could get out of her that day, and late that night she lay in bed, thinking over every possible aspect of the decision. On the one hand she was dying to go, on the other it tore at her heart to leave San Francisco. She was safe there and she had lived there with him, but how long could she hold on to a ghost? She was well on her way to doing it for a lifetime and she knew it. There had been no men in her life for three years, and her entire existence centered around Vanessa. In New York she'd have a chance for a whole new life now. As she lay awake at 5 A.M., thinking it all out, she felt gripped by a surge of excitement, and suddenly she turned over in bed, reached for the phone, and called Teddy. It was 8 A.M. in New York, and he was standing in the kitchen, drinking a cup of coffee.

''Well?'' He smiled when he heard her voice.

286

She closed her eyes tight in the darkness of her room, held her breath for an instant, and then let it out with a whoosh. "I'm coming."

CHAPTER THIRTY-FIVE

The apartment that Teddy found her in New York was tiny. She had given him the limit of what she could afford, and he had come as close to it as possible without finding something absolutely god-awful. He had found her a tiny one-bedroom walk-up on East Sixty-third Street between Lexington and Third. The neighborhood was halfway decent, the Third Avenue elevated train still trundled by at frequent intervals, but Lexington Avenue was fairly pleasant, and Park Avenue, only a block west, was lovely. The apartment itself faced south and was bright and sunny, the bedroom was very small, but the living room was pleasant.

When Serena saw the apartment, she was enchanted. The furniture was simple and unpretentious, freshly painted white wicker chairs, a bright hooked rug, bright prints on the walls, and a handsome quilt on Vanessa's bed, which she later discovered was a present from Teddy. It looked like a cozy guest apartment in someone's house, instead of an entire apartment. The kitchen was barely bigger than a closet, but it was furnished with just enough pots and pans to put a meal together for herself and Vanessa, and as she closed the last cupboard and looked around, she looked at Teddy with a delighted smile and clapped her hands like a child. Vanessa was already busy with the dollhouse from Uncle Teddy.

"Teddy, it's wonderful! I like it even better than our apartment in San Francisco."

He smiled at her apologetically. "I wouldn't exactly compare the view." He peered out at the other narrow buildings crowded onto Sixty-third Street, and could well imagine it all with snow and slush and soot in a few months. He turned around to face her then, with a gentle look in his eyes. "Serena, I'm glad you're here." He knew that for her it had been an act of enormous trust. What if she didn't find work here? What if he had been wrong? There was no certain knowing.

"I'm glad too. Frightened out of my wits," she said, smiling. "but happy." The very tempo of the town had filled her with excitement on the way in from the airport.

He spent the rest of the evening explaining to her how to get around the city, what was where, where not to go, and what were the safest areas. And the more she listened, the more she liked it. She had to go to the agency for her first interview the next day, and she was so excited, she could barely stand it.

When Serena appeared at the Kerr Agency the next morning, she was startled at what she found there, gone were the easygoing, relaxed people she had run into modeling in San Francisco. Here everything was business, it was quick-fire, high pressure, rushed, and hurried, and there was no fooling around. No casual air surrounded this business, it was an office filled with well-dressed, well-made-up women sitting at desks, speaking on phones with stacks of composites piled up before them, file cards referring to jobs pinned up on boards in front of them, and telephones ringing every time one turned around. Serena was ushered to one of the desks in a businesslike way, and she found herself being looked over by an attractive dark-haired woman. The woman at the desk was wearing a crisp beige wool suit, a matching silk skirt, her hair was impeccably combed in a shoulder-length pageboy, and hanging over the silk blouse was a thick rope of pearls.

"I saw your photographs a few weeks ago," she told Serena. "You're going to need new ones, probably a whole book, and a composite." Serena nodded dumbly, feeling terribly stupid and almost too inarticulate to speak. "Have you got anyone who can do that?" With wide eyes she shook her head. She had worn a pale blue sweater, a gray skirt, a simple navy-blue cashmere blazer she had bought at the store in San Francisco, and her long graceful legs seemed endless as she crossed them and the woman noticed the black Dior pumps. Her hair was carefully knotted, and in each ear she had worn a simple pearl. She looked more like she was going to tea with a friend in San Francisco than going to a modeling interview in New York. But she was so nervous about what to wear that she decided to dress simply. Whatever she had on they probably wouldn't like anyway, so what the hell. She had gone to the interview almost rigid with fear, and now she sat staring at this woman, wondering what she was thinking of her. Probably they would never use her, Teddy had been crazy. Whatever made her think that she could model in New York? But the woman in the beige suit was nodding, and wrote down a name on a card that she handed across the desk. "Make an appointment with this photographer, put the photographs of your past jobs in order, get your hair cut, have your nails done a deep red, and come back to see me in a week." Serena sat there staring at her, wondering if there was really any point, and as though the woman could see what she was thinking, she smiled at her. "It'll be all right, you know. Everyone's nervous at first. It's not the same here as it was in San Francisco. You're from out there?" She suddenly looked kindly and interested, and Serena tried desperately not to seem so ill at ease.

"I've been living there for seven years."

"That is a long time." And then she cocked her head, as though hearing an accent. "Where were you from before that?"

"Oh," Serena sighed, feeling uncomfortable, "that's a long story. My husband and I moved there from Paris. We were in Rome before that. I'm Italian." The woman's eyebrows raised.

"Was he Italian too?"

"No, American." She almost said facetiously that she was a war bride, but there was no reason to be nasty to this woman. She seemed genuinely interested in Serena.

"Is that why you speak such good English?"

Serena shook her head slowly. In two minutes this woman had got more out of her than anyone had in years. In the years she was married to Brad, she was so wrapped up in him and Vanessa and Teddy that she had made no close friends on the base, and afterward, when she was modeling, there was no room in her life for anyone but her child. And now suddenly this woman had extracted much of her life story. There was nothing left to tell her except the nightmare of losing her parents to Mussolini and how her husband had died. But she still had the woman's question to answer. "I was here during the war. My family sent me over."

The woman seemed to be calculating something as she looked down at Serena's file card again. "What was your name again?"

"Serena Fullerton."

The other woman smiled. "It sounds too English. Couldn't we make it more exotic? What was it before you got married?"

Serena looked at her hesitantly. "Serena di San Tibaldo." She said it with the full lilt of the Italian.

"That's lovely . . ." She grew pensive. "But it's so long . . ." She looked up at Serena hopefully. "Did you have a title?" It was an odd question to ask, but she was in the business of selling people, beautiful faces with exotic names. Tallulah. Zina. Zorra. Phaedra. This was not a business for Nancy or Mary or Jane. She looked at Serena expectantly, as Serena seemed to hold back.

"I . . . no . . . I . . ." And then she suddenly thought what the hell, what difference did it make? Who cared anymore? There was no one to be shocked or raise an eyebrow or object. Her whole family was dead, and if a title mattered so much, why not give them hers? If it meant that much more money for her and Vanessa, so what? "Yes." The woman's eye narrowed, wondering if Serena was telling the truth. "Principessa."

"Princess?" The woman in beige looked genuinely shocked.

"Yes. You can check it out. I'll give you my birthdate and all that if you want."

"My, my." She looked very pleased. "That ought to look very pretty on your composite . . . Princess Serena . . ." She squinted, again looking at the paper on which she wrote

it, and then Serena again. "Sit up straight for a minute."
Serena did. Then she pointed to the far corner, past some
other desks. "Walk over there and come back." Gracefully,
her head held high, Serena did so, and as she returned, her
green eyes flashed. "Nice, very nice. I've just thought of
something. I'll be right back." She disappeared into an
inner office, and it was a full five minutes before she came
back. When she came back, she brought someone with her.

"This is Dorothea Kerr," she announced simply. "The
head of the agency." It was unnecessary to explain that.
Serena stood up quickly and extended her hand.

"How do you do?" But the tall spare woman with gray
hair pulled sharply back and sharp spectacular cheekbones
wedged in at an extraordinary angle beneath huge gray eyes
said nothing to Serena. She merely looked her over, like a
horse she was buying, or a very expensive car.

"Is your hair natural?"

"Yes."

She then turned to the woman in beige. "I'd like to see
her without all those clothes on, and then I think we ought to
send her to Andy. Don't mess around with any of the
others." The woman in beige nodded and made a rapid
note. "I want to have something on her in the next two
days. Can you do that?"

"Of course." It would mean everyone working overtime,
including Serena, but if Dorothea Kerr wanted "something
on her" in two days, they would move heaven and earth to
see that it was done. "I'll call him right away."

"Fine." Dorothea nodded at Serena then and walked
away quickly. The door to her office closed almost instantly,
and Serena's head began to spin. A minute later, as she
listened to the conversation, she realized that Andy was
Andrew Morgan, the most important fashion photographer
on the East Coast. An appointment was made for later that
morning, and before that she had to go to the hairdresser for
a trim.

"Do you know how to find it?" The anonymous woman
in beige looked sympathetic and then patted Serena's hand.
"You know, she really liked you. She wouldn't have wanted
shots on you in two days if she didn't have something big in

mind for you." But Serena still found it all very baffling and a little hard to believe. "Are you excited?"

Serena looked at her and felt her hand tremble as she took the note with the hairdresser's address. "I think so. So much has happened in the last five minutes that I'm not sure what I feel."

'Well, enjoy it. Not everyone gets their first shots done by Andy Morgan." *Andy* Morgan? *Andy?* For an insane moment Serena wanted to laugh. It was almost impossible not to be overwhelmed by what was starting to happen. It couldn't be. It wasn't real. It was crazy. But she glanced at the clock and knew that she had to get moving.

"Do I have to wear anything special for the photographs?"

"No, Dorothea said she'd have everything sent over. She particularly liked the idea of your being a princess. I think she's going to have him play that up in the shots." For an instant Serena felt acutely nervous, perhaps she shouldn't have told them. But it was too late to stop them now. The woman in beige explained once again all the places where she was expected, wished her luck, and then went back to the stack of composites and file cards on her desk.

She arrived at Andrew Morgan's studio at exactly eleven thirty, as she had been told. And she didn't leave it again until almost nine o'clock that night. He shot black and white and color, he did head shots, candid, high fashion, evening dresses, tennis clothes, bathing suits, ermine, chinchilla, sable, Balanciagas, Diors, Givenchys, and jewels. He did her hair up and down and her makeup subtle and heavy and wild and crazy. She had had more clothes and furs and jewels and different outfits on in nine hours with Andrew Morgan than she had worn in all of the years she had worked in San Francisco. He was a tiny elf of a man, with a wonderful smile that lit up his black eyes, horn-rimmed glasses, and a shag of silvery gray hair that fell constantly in his eyes, he wore a black turtleneck sweater and black slacks and soft kid jazz dance shoes, and he seemed to leap through the air as he took the pictures. He reminded her constantly of a dancer, and she was so totally enamored of him, that she did all that he told her to do. More than that, he seemed to cast a kind of spell as he worked. She worked tirelessly with him for hours, and it wasn't until she walked in her front door that she realized how exhausted she was. Vanessa was already asleep. She had wanted to wait up to see her mommy, but Teddy had explained that they were taking beautiful pictures of her mother, and he had told her how beautiful her mother was, and how this was something very important for her. By the time Vanessa fell asleep, he had won her over again, and he read her two stories and sang her three lullabies, and halfway through the third one she fell asleep.

Exactly two days later Dorothea Kerr called her herself and requested her to come into the office that afternoon.

When Serena arrived, her knees were almost trembling, her hands were damp, and she was feeling excessively grateful that Teddy had had another of his rare free afternoons. She had already found an agency for baby-sitters, but even they couldn't work miracles at short notice. But when she saw the photographs taken by Andy Morgan, she knew that he could. Each one was like a work of art, something to hang in a museum, and as she looked at herself she felt that she barely knew whom she was looking at. Even she had to admit that he had captured something extra-vagant and striking and regal, and she couldn't believe that she could look so beautiful, certainly not in real life. She looked up from the photographs and met the eyes of Dorothea Kerr, hard and gray on her own, and Dorothea leaned back in her chair and gnawed on a pair of glasses as she stared at Serena some more.

"Well, we have what we need here, Serena. What about you? Just how interested in all this are you? Very, a little? Enough to work your tail off? Do you just want a job or do you want a career? Because I want to know now before we waste our time on someone who doesn't give a damn about the job."

"I care very much about the job." She sounded sincere and she was, but for Dorothea it wasn't enough.

"Why? Are you in love with this business? Or with yourself?"

"No." Serena faced her squarely. "I have a little girl."

"And that's the only reason?"

"It's part of it. This is the only way I know to make a living, and it's a good living. I like the work." She looked at Dorothea with a sparkle in her eyes. "To tell you the truth, I'm anxious to try my luck in New York." Her excitement was beginning to show and the older woman smiled.

"You're divorced?"

"I'm a widow, with a small pension from the army. That's it."

Dorothea looked intrigued. "Korea?" Serena nodded. "What about your family, don't they help?"

"They're all dead."

"And his?"

Serena began to look unhappy, and Dorothea was quick to pick up on where not to tread. "Never mind. If you say you need it for your little girl, then obviously you need it. I just hope the kid has a big appetite, to keep you wanting to go out and work." She gave Serena one of her very rare smiles, and then she looked serious again. "What about the title?" She sighed softly. "I did a little research on it, and I gather it's genuine, Serena. How do you feel about using it? Does it go against the grain?"

Serena smiled softly. "Yes, but that doesn't matter. I came here to do something with you. As you put it, for a career, not a job. If that makes a difference"—she almost gulped thinking of her grandmother—"go ahead, use it."

"It should help us create an image. Princess Serena. 'The Princess.' " She looked thoughtful for a moment. "I like it. I like it very much. What about you? How does it feel?"

"It sounds a little silly to me now. I've been Serena Fullerton for a long time, and I never really used the title. It seemed more a part of my grandmother."

"Why?" Dorothea looked at her squarely. "You look like a princess, Serena. Or don't you know that yet?" In truth Serena did not, as Teddy knew only too well. She had no idea how lovely she was, and in a way that was part of her charm. "In any case wait till you start seeing your pictures all over town, you'll know it then. And"—she gnawed at a pencil and then grinned—"since you are a princess, we will ask a royal price. One hundred dollars an hour for Princess Serena. We'll give them the impression that you don't need it, that this is all a lark, and if they want you, they'll have to pay through the nose. A hundred an hour." Serena was breathless at the thought. A hundred an hour? Would she get any work? "Okay, we'll put your book together for you. You come back tomorrow, Serena. Get plenty of rest, do your hair and nails and face to perfection. Wear something simple and black, and be here at nine thirty. Tomorrow we send you out with your book, and you start work. But I warn you, we're only going to use you for the big jobs, at a hundred dollars an hour, you're going to be bypassing a lot of the less important work. What that means is that you're stepping in at the top, you're in the big leagues, and you're going to have to be perfect. Anything less and they'll laugh both you and me right out of this town."

"I'll do my very best." The green eyes were filled with terror, and she felt twenty-seven going on two. "I promise."

"Don't promise. Just do it." Dorothea Kerr's eyes hardened as she stood up. "If you don't, princess or no, you'll be canned." And with that, she turned on her heel and left the room.

CHAPTER THIRTY-SIX

It was a month later when Margaret Fullerton saw the first ad. A full page in *The New York Times* for a new line of cosmetics. They had done a rush job to get Serena in on the shoot, but it was a sensational picture. Margaret Fullerton had the page folded on her desk the next time Teddy came to dinner. She didn't say anything until coffee was served in the library downstairs, and then gingerly she took the newspaper page off of her desk, touching it as though it might be poisoned.

Her eyes raised slowly to her son's, and she looked at him for a long moment with slowly simmering anger.

"You didn't tell me she was in town. I assume you know?" Her eyes drove into her son's. She knew that he had remained in touch, and that he was excessively fond of Vanessa. Many times he had tried to soften Margaret toward the child, but to no avail, and Margaret was sure that Serena would have let him know she was in New York. "Why didn't you tell me?"

"I didn't think you cared." It was something of a lie, but his eyes didn't waver.

"The child is here too?"

"Yes."

"Are they living here?"

"They are."

And then, with a look of disdain, "As I suspected, the tramp is still incredibly vulgar."

Teddy looked momentarily stunned. "Mother, how in God's name can you say that? She's not only gorgeous, she's elegant as hell, and aristocratic. Look at that picture."

"She's nothing but a whore and a model. This, my dear boy, is all artifice, and in an extremely vulgar profession." But she had noticed with some interest that the line of cosmetics was owned by a company for which she served on the board of directors. "I assume you've seen her."

"I have." His heart was pounding with restrained anger. "And I plan to see her again, her and Vanessa, as often as I can. That child is my niece and Serena is my brother's widow."

"Your brother had eminently regrettable taste in women."

"Only in the one previous to Serena." Match point. Pattie had all but destroyed Greg, and he was now an obvious alcoholic. "You know." He glared down at his mother as he stood up. "I really don't think I want to sit here while you do a hatchet job on Serena."

"Why? Are you sleeping with her too? Undoubtedly you and half of New York by now."

"My God!" It was a roar from Teddy. "What do you have against her?"

"Everything. She destroyed my son's career, and indirectly she killed him. Isn't that enough? Your brother is dead because of that woman, Teddy." But there was no grief in her eyes, only fury and vengeance.

"He was killed by the war in Korea, for chrissake, or doesn't that count? Are you so hellbent on your vendetta that you can't admit the truth? Haven't you done enough to her? If it were up to you, she would have starved after Brad died. She has supported that child for almost four years alone, worked herself to the bone, and you have the nerve to look down on her, and if it's any of your goddamn business, she's still faithful to my brother."

"How would you know that?" The older woman's eyes narrowed with interest.

But Teddy was beyond wisdom or control. "Because I've been in love with her for years. And do you know what? She won't have me. Because of Brad, and because of you. She doesn't want to come between us. Christ"—he ran a hand through his hair—"I wish she would."

"Do you? I'm sure it could be arranged. And in the meantime, my boy, I suggest you open your eyes. The reason she won't have you most likely is because she knows I'm too smart for her and she knows there would be no profit in it."

"Do you think that's why she married Brad?"

"Without a doubt. I'm sure she had every confidence that, if need be, she could overturn our little contract."

"Then why didn't she try?" His voice was still uncomfortably raised, and his mother looked at him with an expression of annoyance.

"I suppose her lawyers advised her not to."

"You make me sick."

"Not nearly as sick as I'll make you if you don't stay away from that woman. She's a cheap little trick, and I won't have her using you the way she used Brad."

"You don't run my life."

"Don't be so sure. How do you think you got appointed for training with your fancy surgeon?" He looked at her with horror and almost visibly cringed.

"Did you do that?"

"I did." For a moment he felt ill, and he made an instantaneous decision to quit the next day, and then knew almost as quickly that he would be giving up the opportunity of a lifetime. For the first time in his life his mother had him by the balls, and he hated her for it.

"You're a despicable woman."

"No, Theodore." Her eyes were hard and cool, like highly polished marbles "I am a powerful and intelligent woman. You'll admit that it makes an interesting combination. And a dangerous one. Keep that in mind, and do stay away from your little friend."

He stared at her for a moment, bereft of words, and then turned on his heel and left the room. Margaret Fullerton heard the front door slam less than a minute later.

It was not unlike the sound Serena heard the next morning at the agency as she waited outside Dorothea Kerr's office. The door slammed, the walls shook, and suddenly Dorothea stood before her. "Get into my office." She almost shouted it at Serena, who looked utterly stunned as she followed Dorothea into her office.

"Is something wrong?"

"You tell me. That cosmetics ad you did that ran in *The New York Times* . . . the ad agency received a call from the parent company, telling them that if they ever used you again they'd lose the account. Now how would you explain that? You seem to have come to New York not with a clean slate but with some old scores to be settled. And frankly I don't want your goddamn wars interfering with my business. Now what the hell is going on?"

Serena looked totally amazed as she sat and stared, and then suddenly the light dawned. "Oh, my God . . . no . . ." Her hand flew to her mouth, her eyes filled with tears. "I'm so sorry. I'll resign from the agency at once."

"The hell you will." Dorothea looked even angrier. "I have eighteen bookings for you in the next two weeks. Don't play virgin in flight, just tell me what I'm dealing with. Then let me decide whether or not to kick you out. I make the decisions around here, and don't you forget it." Serena looked awed by the woman's harsh words, but had she looked closer, she would have seen that there was concern in Dorothea's eyes. She was well aware that Serena was more than a little naive, and she had an overwhelming urge to protect her. Despite her brutal ways she had felt that from the first, although she hadn't confided her feelings to Serena. "Okay, start talking, Serena. I want to hear what this is about."

"I'm not sure I can discuss it." The tears were pouring slowly down her cheeks in little black mascara-filled rivers.

"You look like hell. Here, use this." She handed her a box of tissues and Serena blew her nose and took a deep breath as Dorothea poured her a glass of water, and then the tale came out, all of it, from the beginning. Of losing her family in the war, of how she had met Brad and how much she had loved him, the broken engagement to the debutante from New York, and the rage of Brad's mother. She even told her about the contract Margaret had made her sign, and then she told her of Brad's death, and the baby she had lost, and the last three years of working to support Vanessa.

"That's all of it." She sighed deeply and blew her nose again.

"That's enough." Dorothea was more than touched by the story—she felt a fury, a call to arms. "She must be an incredibly evil woman."

"Do you know of her?" Serena looked bleak, there was no way she could defeat Margaret Fullerton. And after five weeks in New York, Serena knew her mother-in-law was already out to get to her. She had been afraid of her when she had decided to come to New York, but she had lulled herself into the false hope that her fears were unfounded.

"I only know her by name. But by God, now I'd like to meet her."

Serena smiled a small wintry smile. "You'd regret it. She makes Attila the Hun look like a sissy."

Dorothea looked her new model straight in the eye. "Don't kid yourself, sister, she's just met her match."

"There's a difference. You're not rotten." She sat back in her chair, looking exhausted. "The only thing for me to do is quit and go back to San Francisco."

"If you do"—Dorothea's eyes didn't waver from her face—"I'll sue you. You signed a contract with this agency, and like it or not, I'm going to hold you to it."

Serena smiled at the older woman's way of protecting her.

"You'll lose all your clients if I stay."

"She doesn't own every major corporation in New York. And as a matter of fact, I want to check out her tie-in with that line of cosmetics."

"I just don't think—"

"Good. Don't think. You don't need to. Go put on a fresh face, you have a go-see in twenty minutes."

"Mrs. Kerr, please . . ."

"Serena." The head of the agency came around her desk and, without saying another word, put her arms around Serena. "You have had more rough breaks than anyone I've ever heard of. I'm not going to let you down. You need someone to protect you." Her voice gentled almost to a whisper. "You need a friend, little one, let me at least do that for you."

"But won't it do your agency harm?" Serena was once again seized with terror.

"It'll do us more harm if you leave, but that's not why I want you to stay. I want you to stick it out, because I want you to beat those bastards. Serena, the only way you'll do that is if you stand your ground. Do it for me . . . for yourself"—and then she played her trump card—"do it for your husband. Do you really think he'd want you to run away from his mother?"

Serena thought it over before she spoke. "No, he wouldn't."

"Good. Then let's fight this one out side by side. I'll put the old bitch back in her place, if I have to go and see her myself." And Serena knew she would.

"Don't do that."

"Any good reason why not?"

"It'll create an open war."

"What do you think you've already got? She called a cosmetics company and an ad agency and had you canned. I'd say that's pretty open." Serena smiled in dismay. "Just leave all that to me. You do your job. I'll do mine. It isn't often I get to fight for someone I like, and I like you." The two women exchanged a smile.

"I like you too. And I don't know how to thank you."

"Don't. Just get your ass to that go-see. I'll call and tell them you'll be late.'' She shooed Serena out of her office, but just before she reached the door, she turned again with a smile and whispered, ''Thank you.''

Dorothea's eyes were damp when the door closed, and ten minutes later she was on the phone, arranging a meeting with Margaret Fullerton.

The meeting between Dorothea Kerr and Margaret Fullerton was short but not very sweet. When Margaret discovered what the meeting was about, her eyes went icy. But Dorothea didn't give a damn. She told her to stay out of Serena's career, or without a moment's hesitation Dorothea would sue her.

''Am I to understand that you are her representative?''

''No, I am the president of her modeling agency. And I mean what I say.''

''So do I, Mrs. Kerr.''

''Then we understand each other.''

''May I suggest that your client change her name. She no longer has any right to it.''

''Legally, I believe she does. But that's of no importance. She's not using your name, she is using her own title.''

''Characteristically vulgar.'' Margaret Fullerton stood up. ''I believe you've said everything you came here to say.''

''Not quite, Mrs. Fullerton.'' Dorothea stood to her full height. She had once been a very tall and very beautiful model. ''I want you to know that I have hired an attorney for Serena, as of this morning. He will be made fully aware of your harassment, of your already costing Serena one job, and if there is any further problem, the press will have a field day. Won't your fancy friends just love reading about you in the *Daily News*.''

''I believe that is an empty threat.'' But it was obvious that Margaret Fullerton was livid. She had never been threatened before, and she had seldom met her match, certainly not in another woman.

''I wouldn't try my luck if I were you. I mean every word I say. Serena is going to be the most successful model in this town, with or without your interference, so you'd better adjust yourself to it.'' And then as she turned in the doorway before she left, she looked scornfully over her shoulder.

"I would think you'd be embarrassed after all you've done. You know, sooner or later those things get out. And I suspect you won't like it."

"Is that a threat?" Her hands were trembling as she stood and glared at her opponent.

"As a matter of fact," Dorothea said, smiling sweetly, "yes." And then she was gone, leaving Margaret Fullerton wanting to kill her.

Margaret spoke to Teddy that night and put it to him plainly. "I forbid you to see that woman."

"You can't forbid me to do anything. I'm a grown man. What will you do—have *me* fired?" Serena had already told him the story.

"I can change my will at any time."

"Be my guest. I've never given a damn about your money. I'm a physician. I can make my own way. In fact I'd prefer to."

"Perhaps you'll have to. I mean every word I've said."

"And so do I. Good night, Mother." He had hung up on her then, and she burst into tears. For the first time in her life she knew what it meant to feel powerless. But not for long. Margaret Fullerton was a woman of ingenuity and determination. And she'd be damned if Serena Fullerton—or whatever she called herself—would win the next round.

CHAPTER THIRTY-SEVEN

For the next month Vanessa almost never saw her mother. She saw baby-sitters and her uncle Teddy, and her mother came home exhausted every night at seven or eight or nine o'clock, too tired to eat, or talk or move. She would sink into a hot bathtub, and sometimes go directly to bed. Teddy was himself enormously busy at the hospital, spending five and six

302

hours a day in surgery, and he had to be up at four o'clock every morning. But nonetheless he found time to help Serena out. It was the least he could do to counterbalance his mother's continuing subtle efforts to destroy her. She never did quite enough to be sued by Dorothea Kerr's attorneys, but whenever she could, she put a spoke in Serena's wheels. She had even insinuated to the press that Serena was not a princess but a charwoman from Rome, who had scrubbed floors in a palazzo, from whence she had adopted her title. She failed to mention, of course, that the palazzo had once belonged to Serena's parents. And it seemed useless to Serena to try to tell them the true version. Besides, she was too busy to care, and every night when she came home she was exhausted. She had lost fourteen pounds in two months from hard work and worry. But the photographs that were daily being shot of her were the most striking Teddy had ever seen. She seemed to get more beautiful and more skilled with each job she did, and it was impossible to believe that she hadn't been doing this in New York and Paris and London for years. There was nothing of the novice about her. She was good at what she did, and she worked hard. Even Dorothea Kerr said that The Princess was a pro. She was known around town now by her title, and from the very first moment no one even flinched at her fee. She had already put aside a very tidy sum of money, and she had been proud that she had been able to pay Vanessa's tuition at a wonderful little private school on Ninety-fifth Street. It was run in a totally European manner, and all of the classes were taught in French. Already in two months Vanessa had become bilingual, and it reminded Serena once again that one day she wanted to teach her Italian too. But now she had no time. She was too busy working. And Teddy was filled with admiration for her.

"Well, famous lady, how does it feel to be the hottest model in New York?"

"I don't know." She smiled at him as she sat next to Teddy on the floor one Sunday with the paper. "I'm too exhausted to feel a thing." And then she looked at him with an impish smile. "It's all your fault, you know, Teddy."

"Nah, it's all because you're so ugly." He leaned over to

kiss her on the cheek and then a question came into his eyes. "Have you had any dates?"

She wondered why he asked, but she was noncommittal. "I haven't really had time." And then she decided to be honest with him. He was her best friend, after all. "But I'd like to. I think I'm finally ready. Why, do you have anyone in mind?" It was the first time he had ever asked her.

"To tell you the truth," he said, looking a little shy, "I have a friend who's a surgeon who's been begging me to introduce you to him. If doctors had lockers, his would be plastered with pictures of you."

She laughed at the image. "Is he nice?" Lately she really had been wishing to meet a man. It had taken her four years to get over Brad, but suddenly she led a different life now. In San Francisco her life was too reminiscent of him, but in New York everything was different. "Would I like him?"

"Maybe. He's divorced. And he may be a little too quiet."

Serena laughed. "Are you telling me I'm loud?"

"No." He grinned at her like a brother. "But you've got awfully glamorous, kid. Maybe you'd want someone more flamboyant."

"Have I really changed that much?" The thought shocked her. Brad hadn't been flamboyant. He had been loving and solid and strong. That was what she still wanted now, but on the other hand she wasn't the same girl Brad had married. She had been nineteen then and it seemed an aeon ago, those years after the war when she was so dependent on him. She wasn't dependent on anyone now, except, in a very relaxed way, Teddy. "Why don't you arrange a dinner with your friend?" It was obvious that she was interested, and it was there that Teddy saw the greatest change in her. Six months before she would have refused instantly.

But as it turned out, the dinner never came to be. Serena's schedule was impossible to rearrange. In truth, she didn't have time to have dinner with Teddy's friend. After trying a few times to arrange it, Teddy finally gave up, not quite sure of his own reasons, still uneasy about the depth of his feelings for her. The agency kept her going at fever pitch. Even Vanessa complained about it sometimes. "I never see you anymore, Mommy." But on her daughter's seventh birthday Serena had gone all out and taken her and four of her friends to the circus. It had been a grand event, and Vanessa had forgiven her for the chaos of the past few months.

But things did not improve after Christmas. She had literally one day off for Christmas, and spent it with Vanessa and Teddy, but the next morning she was running through the snow in a bathing suit and a fur coat for Andy Morgan, leaping into the air with her blond mane flying straight up. Two weeks later she was sent to Palm Beach for a shoot there, then to Jamaica, back to New York, off to Chicago. She managed to take Vanessa with her each time she went, which wreaked havoc with the child's schoolwork, but she worked on it with Vanessa every night when she finished work, and she was so happy doing what she did that somehow it made everyone forgive her for the long hours that she was busy.

By the following summer Kerr had raised her rate to two hundred dollars an hour and "The Princess" was the talk of New York and a prize for every photographer in the country. Dorothea Kerr kept a close watch on her career and controlled everything she did with an iron hand, which pleased Serena. She valued the older woman's guidance and they had become friends. They seldom saw each other outside business hour, but they spent long hours talking in Dorothea's office, and the advice she gave Serena was always excellent. Particularly in regard to Margaret Fullerton, who for the moment had stopped being a problem. Serena was just too successful for her slanderous reports to have any effect. And Dorothea was pleased for her.

"I hope you're enjoying this, Serena, because it's fun while it lasts, but it doesn't last forever. You'll make a bundle of money. Put it away, do something sensible with it"—Dorothea had started her own agency, but Serena had no ambition in that vein—"and realize that it's only for a time. You have your day and then it's someone else's turn." But she had been impressed from the first with the way Serena handled it. She was an intelligent girl, with a sense of direction, and she didn't fool around. She worked hard and

305

she went home, and whatever else she did no one ever knew. Dorothea was tired to death of models who got drunk and arrested, who caused disturbances, bought sports cars and cracked them up, got involved with international playboys, and then attempted suicide in the most public manner possible, and then of course failed. Serena wasn't like them. She went home to her little girl, and Dorothea always suspected that there were few men in her life, and even at that, only very circumspect dates, there hadn't been anyone serious since her husband.

That summer Serena had been in New York for a year, and she was so busy that she could barely spend a minute with Teddy. Fortunately for her, Vanessa was in camp for two months.

By the middle of August Serena was so booked up with jobs every day that she asked Dorothea to stop scheduling so many. She needed some time off and she had decided to give herself at least a week before Vanessa came back.

"Can't you put them off for a couple of weeks?" She looked pleadingly at Dorothea.

Dorothea looked at the waiting list of people begging for Serena, and smiled at her with a knowing look. "You're a lucky lady, Serena. Just look at this." She handed the list briefly to Serena, who shook her head and groaned as she fell into a chair. She was wearing a white linen skirt, a little red and white striped halter, and red sandals, with red and white bracelets all up and down one arm. She looked like a peppermint stick as she stood there, all fresh and blond and young and groomed to perfection, and it was easy to see why half the photographers in town wanted to use her, not to mention at least a dozen in Italy, France, Germany, and Japan. "You know, I almost envy you. I'd like to think it was like this for me. But I'm not sure it was. On the other hand"—she smiled again—"you have a much better agency than I had in my day." Serena laughed and ran a hand through her hair.

"So can you get me a break in the next couple of weeks, Dorothea? I really need it. I haven't been away all year." Teddy had fled to Newport a few days before, and she really envied him his time at the seashore. He had offered to take

her to the Cape, but ever since Vanessa had gone, she had
been doubly busy, and she hadn't been able to get away.
Now at least, if she could have some time to herself, she
could go out to the Hamptons, or even stay in town and,
luxury of luxuries, stay in bed for a few days!

"I'll see what I can do." She mused over the list again.
"The only one I actually don't think I can change is Vasili
Arbus." She glanced at the name.

"Who's that?"

"You don't know him?" Dorothea looked surprised.

"Should I?"

"The British think he's another Andy Morgan. He's half
English, half Greek, and totally crazy, but"—she thought
about him for a moment—"he does extraordinarily good
work."

"As good as Andy?" After a year in New York Serena
knew them all, and Andy Morgan had also become a friend.
She occasionally met him for lunch at the studio between
jobs, and when they had a shooting together, they stayed on
after hours to talk about work. There was nothing physical
about the relationship, but she was very fond of him as a
friend and a colleague.

Dorothea was still pondering the question. "I don't
know. He's awfully good. His work is different. You'll see."

"I have to do him?" Serena looked annoyed.

"We have no choice. He booked you three months ago,
from London, for a job that he knew he had coming up over
here. He's only here for a few weeks to service some of his
American accounts, and then he'll go back to London. I
hear he keeps a house there, another in Athens, an apartment in Paris, and a villa in the South of France."

"Does he only travel or does he also work?" For some
reason the very sound of his name annoyed her. He sounded
spoiled, and she had already met a few of his genre.
International playboys hiding behind cameras, using it as a
new and interesting way to pick up girls. And that she did
not need. As Dorothea said, she was a pro, and she worked
like one. Vasili Arbus didn't sound like her cup of tea.

Dorothea looked at her over her glasses. "Why not give
him a chance?" And then she added with thoughtful

deliberation, "As a photographer. Not as a man. He's charming as hell, but Vasili Arbus is not someone to get involved with. Not that you would." She smiled at Serena, who looked amused.

"I must be known in this business as The Ice Maiden." Serena grinned, but Dorothea shook her head.

"I don't think so, Serena. I think most of the guys just know that you don't fool around. It makes you easier to work with, I suspect. There are no expectations other than the obvious professional ones."

"Well, I'll just see that Mr. Arbus understands that."

Dorothea couldn't repress a smile. "With him, I must admit, you may have a little more trouble."

"Oh?" Serena arched an aristocratic eyebrow. She never had trouble with anyone she worked with, because she chose not to.

"You'll see. He's just like a big charming child."

"Terrific. I want to go on vacation, and you stick me with working for a childlike playboy." Dorothea mused for a moment, Serena had inadvertently come up with the perfect description of Vasili. That was just what he was—a childlike playboy. "Anyway, see what you can do. If you can't cancel him, I'll do it. Just so he does the work quickly, and I can get the hell out of town for a rest while the rest of my family is still away." She had two weeks before Vanessa came back from camp and Teddy returned from Newport.

"I'll do what I can."

But the next morning Dorothea informed her that she had been able to shift everything around except Vasili Arbus, and he expected her to come to his studio at two o'clock that afternoon.

"Any idea how long he'll be shooting?"

"He thought maybe two days."

"All right," Serena sighed. Two days she could handle, and then she could go somewhere for a few days and relax. She couldn't join Teddy in Newport of course, because of his mother, but she didn't even mind that. She knew that his life there was a round of parties, and when she went away, she didn't even want to comb her hair.

She got the address of the studio Arbus was using, checked

her supplies, makeup, hair spray, mirrors, an assortment of brushes, four pairs of shoes, a bathing suit, some shorts, stockings, three different brassieres, and a little simple jewelry. You never knew what you were going to need when you went to work.

She reported to the address she'd been given at exactly two thirty and was led into the studio by his assistant, a very attractive young man. The boy spoke English with an accent, it was not quite a lisp, and not quite a slur, he had dark brown hair and olive skin, big black eyes, and a boyish air about him, and Serena guessed correctly that he was Greek.

"We've seen a lot of your work, Serena." He looked at her admiringly. "Vasili likes it very much."

"Thank you." She smiled pleasantly at him, wondering how old he was. He looked about nineteen, and she felt like his grandmother at twenty-eight.

"Would you like some coffee?"

"Thanks. Should I start working on my makeup?" She also wanted to know how they wanted her to do her hair, but the young man with the black eyes shook his head.

"Just relax. We're not shooting this afternoon. Vasili just wants to meet you." At two hundred dollars an hour? He was paying just to meet her? Serena looked a little surprised.

"When do we start working?"

"Tomorrow. The next day. When Vasili's ready." Oh, Jesus. She could see her vacation flying out the window as they got acquainted.

"Does he always do this?" To Serena it seemed foolish. If there was work to be done, she wanted to do it and go home.

"Sometimes. If the client is important and the model is new. It means a lot to Vasili to know his models."

"Oh, really?" There was an edge to Serena's voice and she hoped that it didn't mean too much to him. She was not there to play with Vasili. She was there to do her work before the camera and that was it. But just as she began to say something else to the assistant, she felt a presence behind her, and she turned to see a man looking into her eyes with such magnetic power that she caught her breath. He had startled her, standing so close to her, but everything about him was startling. His hair shone like onyx, his eyes were like black gems, sparkling at her with barely hidden laughter, he had a broad angular face and high cheekbones, a rich, sensuous mouth, and a suntan that gave him almost honey-colored skin. He was tall and broad shouldered, with narrow hips and long legs. He actually looked more like one of his own male models than a photographer, and he was wearing a red T-shirt and jeans and sandals.

"Hello. I am Vasili." He had a distinct but subtle accent, an interesting mixture of both British and Greek. He held out a hand to her and she shook it, and for an instant she was spellbound, and then suddenly she laughed in embarrassment, feeling foolish to have been so taken with the way he looked.

"I'm Serena."

"Ah." He held up a hand as though to command silence. " 'The Princess.' " He bowed low, and then stood up with a broad grin, but even as he teased her his eyes seemed to caress her, and one felt an almost irresistible pull toward the broad chest and powerful arms. "I'm glad you could come here today to meet us." Either he spoke in the royal we, or he was referring to his assistant, and Serena smiled.

"I thought we were going to be shooting."

"No." He held up the imperious hand again. "Never. Not on an important job like this one. My clients always understand that I must get acquainted with my subjects." She couldn't help thinking that it was costing them a fortune, but apparently that didn't matter to him.

"What are we shooting?"

"You." Obviously, but the way he said it made her feel unusually important, as though she were there as herself, not just a model to make a dress or a car, or a set of towels, or a new brand of ice cream look good.

She tried a different tack, as his eyes gripped her. He never seemed to let go of her once with his eyes. It was almost as though she could feel him touch her, and she felt an odd stirring deep within. It was a stirring that she resisted, a feeling she pretended not to have, and yet for an instant she sensed that Vasili Arbus was going to become an important part of her life. It was almost as though she had a premonition, and

310

she didn't have any idea why that should be. She forced her thoughts of him from her mind and returned to the questions about the sitting. "Who's the client?"

He told her and she nodded. They were going to be photographing her with children, two male models, and alone, in an important ad for a new car. "Can you drive?"

"Sure."

"Good. I don't have an American license. You can drive me out to the beach and we'll shoot there." For two hundred dollars an hour she wasn't usually asked to play chauffeur, but with him everything seemed so easy and natural and friendly that one wanted to go along with whatever he said. He looked at her with interest, and she knew that he was probably studying the planes of her face for the shooting, but she felt oddly naked as he watched her. She was used to arriving for a job, getting ready, and going to work in an almost anonymous fashion. It was odd and a little uncomfortable to be moving along at such an easy pace. It made her feel conspicuous as he looked at her, as though he was seeing her and all that she was and was not. Not just "The Princess," the creation of the Kerr agency, but someone real. "Have you had lunch?" She looked instantly startled. In her year of modeling in New York no one had ever asked her if she was tired or hungry or sick or exhausted. No one had ever cared if she'd had lunch or not.

"I . . . no . . . I was in a hurry. . . ."

"No." He wagged a finger at her. "Never, never rush." And then, with a deliberate air, he set down his cup of coffee, said something in Greek to his assistant, and picked up a bright green Shetland sweater off a chair. "Come." He held out a hand to her, and without thinking, she took it. They were halfway out the door before she remembered her things.

"Wait . . . my bag . . . I forgot it. . . ." And then, nervously, "Where are we going?"

"To get something to eat." His smile dazzled her with its snowy perfection. "Don't worry, Princess. We'll come back."

She felt foolish being so nervous around him, but his informal manner threw her off, and she didn't know what to expect from him. Downstairs was a silver Bentley with a chauffeur. He hopped in nonchalantly and spoke to his driver, this time in English, directing him to a place that Serena did not know. It was only when they crossed the Brooklyn Bridge that Serena began to worry.

"Where are we going?"

"I told you. To lunch." And then he narrowed his eyes as he looked at her. "Where are you from?"

She hesitated for a moment, not sure what he was asking. "New York . . ." and then, "the Kerr Agency." But he laughed at her.

"No, no. I meant where you were born."

"Oh." She giggled nervously at him. "Rome."

"Rome?" He looked at her, startled. "You're Italian?"

"Yes."

"Then the title—it's real?" He looked astounded, and she nodded. "Well, I'll be damned." He turned in his seat to smile at her. "A real princess." And then, in Italian, *"Una vera principessa."* He held out his hand to her in formal Italian greeting. *"Piacere."* He kissed her hand then and looked amused. "My English great-grandfather was a count. But his daughter, my grandmother, married beneath her, she married a man with an enormous fortune and no aristocratic connections at all. He made a great deal of money buying and selling factories, and in trade in the Far East, and their son, my father, must have been a bit of a mad man. He patented a series of extraordinary gadgets that related to ships, and then got involved in shipping in South America and the Far East. Eventually he married my mother, Alexandra Nastassos, and managed to kill both himself and my mother in a yachting accident when I was two. Which"—he leaned toward her and spoke in a whisper—"is probably why I'm a little crazy too. No mother and no father. I was brought up by my mother's family, because my father's parents were both dead by the time my parents died. So I grew up in Athens, went to Eton, in England, because they thought my father would have liked that. I got kicked out of Cambridge," he said proudly, "moved to Paris, and got married. And after that it all became very boring." The dazzling smile shone at her like a noonday explosion. "Now tell me about you."

"Good Lord. In twenty-five words or less?" She smiled at him, more than a little awed by what he had just told her. The Nastassos name alone was enough to startle anyone. They were one of the biggest shipping families in Greece. And now that she thought of it, she vaguely remembered hearing about him. He was the black sheep of the family, and she thought she'd heard that he'd been married several times. The third time he had married it had been on the front page of the paper in San Francisco, he had married a distant cousin of the queen.

"What were you thinking?" He looked at her in a child-like, open fashion, in the enormous silver car, with the chauffeur staring stolidly straight ahead.

"I was thinking," she said, looking at him honestly, "that I think I've read about you."

"Have you?" He looked amused. "Let's see, you wouldn't have read about my marriage to Brigitte, she was my first wife and we were both nineteen. She was the sister of a boy I knew at Eton. But my second wife perhaps, Anastasia Xanios." She loved the way his tongue slipped over the words, his accent was delicious. "You might have read about her, or perhaps Margaret"—he looked at her with his big black eyes—"the queen's cousin." He was so outrageous that she laughed.

"How many times have you been married?"

"Four." He answered her honestly.

She counted backward in her head and looked at him with a grin that matched his own. "Then you left one out."

He nodded, but the smile dimmed. "The last one."

"Which one was she?" Serena had not yet understood that this was not like the others.

"It was . . . she was French. She was a model." And then he looked at Serena with dark, tragic eyes. "She died from an overdose last January. Her name was Hélène."

"Oh, I'm so sorry." She reached out and touched his hand. "I really am. I lost my husband too." All she could think of was what he must have felt when his last wife had died. She still remembered the incredible pain of losing B.J. and it had been more than four years.

313

"How did your husband die?" Vasili was looking at her now gently.

"In Korea. He was one of the first casualties, just a few days before war was declared."

"Then you've been through it too." He looked at her oddly. "It's so strange. Everyone jokes about it . . . married four times . . . another wife. But each time it's different. Each time . . ." He looked at Serena and she almost wanted to cry. "Each time I love as though it were the first time . . . and Helene, she was only a child. Twenty-one." Serena didn't ask why she had done it. She assumed that the girl had committed suicide with sleeping pills, it was the only kind of drug overdose she could imagine. He shook his head then and held tightly to Serena's hand. "Life is a strange place sometimes. I very seldom understand it. But then again"—he cocked his head to one side with a boyish smile—"I no longer try. I live my life from day to day." And then he sighed softly. "I have my work, my friends, the people I work with. And when I'm behind the camera, I forget it all."

"You're lucky." Serena knew only too well that hard work dulled the pain. "You don't have any children, Vasili?"

"No." He looked sad and then shrugged with a small smile. "Maybe I haven't met the right woman yet. Have you children, Serena?"

"One. A little girl." His eyes lit up at her answer.

"What is her name?"

"Vanessa."

"Perfect. And she is blond and looks exactly like you?" His eyes danced.

"No. She is blond and looks exactly like her father." Serena laughed.

"He was handsome?" Vasili looked intrigued.

"Yes." But it all seemed very far away now. Four years was a long time.

"Never mind, little one." He leaned over and kissed her cheek and she had to remind herself that he was not a friend but a photographer she was going to work with. But it seemed hard to believe that she hadn't known him for years.

314

She felt oddly comfortable with him now, and captivated, as though he had flown her to a foreign land. He might as well have, she realized as the car stopped a few minutes later and they got out. They were at a seafood restaurant at Sheepshead Bay. It looked fairly scruffy, but inside was the rich smell of steamed clams and melted butter, fish cooked in herbs, and fresh bread being warmed. They had a marvelous lunch, undisturbed by anyone, and it was close to five o'clock when they emerged.

"That was absolutely divine." Her stomach felt full, she felt comfortable and relaxed. She would have liked to stretch out somewhere for a nap, as Vasili put an arm around her shoulders and swung his sweater in the air. It certainly didn't feel like an afternoon when she should have been working. She looked at him with a warm smile, and he stood aside with a bow, as the chauffeur opened the door and she got back into the car. Once ensconced beside her, he leaned forward and gave the driver instructions, and she realized a few minutes later that they were not going home. "Is this another adventure?" After all, Sheepshead Bay was not her usual luncheon fare. But Vasili only smiled secretively and took her hand. She could no longer bring herself to feel pressed about the time, or agitated. She had nowhere to go except home, and there was no one there. "Where are we going?" She leaned back against the comfortable upholstery with a smile.

"To the beach."

"At this hour?" She looked surprised but not alarmed.

"I want to see the sunset with you, Serena." It seemed an odd idea but she didn't really want to object. She was more comfortable with this man than she had been with anyone in years. And more than that, she was happy. He suffused her with a kind of joie de vivre that she hadn't remembered in a very long time, if ever.

The driver knew exactly where Vasili wanted him to go, and he drove through assorted ugly little suburban communities, until he reached the right one, and drove the enormous Bentley sedately up to a small pier. There was a ferry boat tied up and bobbing in the water, and their timing had been perfect, there were already half a dozen people aboard.

"Vasili?" For the first time Serena looked worried. "What is this?"

"The ferry to Fire Island. Have you been there before?" She shook her head. "You will love it." He looked so sure about what he was doing that she was no longer unnerved. "We won't stay long. Just long enough to see the sunset and walk on the beach, and then we'll come home." For some reason she trusted him, everything about him seemed to suggest to her that she would be safe with him. He had a way of imparting the impression that he was totally in control and one could rely on him.

Hand in hand with Vasili she boarded the ferry, and they set off for Fire Island. The ride took half an hour, and they got out on the island on a narrow little pier, and then he walked with her straight across the island to a beach that took her breath away, it was so lovely. It stretched out for miles, a narrow sandspit in the ocean, perfect white sand, and soft waves for almost thirty miles.

"Oh, Vasili, it's incredible."

"Isn't it?" He smiled. "It always reminds me of Greece."

"Do you come here often?"

He shook his head slowly, his black eyes burning into hers. "No, Serena, I don't. But I wanted to come here with you." She nodded, and then turned away, not sure of what to say. She didn't want to play games with him. But he was so open and so appealing, and he had a magnetic quality about him that drew her to him. They walked on the beach for a while, and then sat down to watch the sunset, and they sat that way for what seemed like hours, in the growing dusk, his arm around her shoulders, each of them listening to his own dream. At last he stood up slowly and pulled her to her feet, she had her sandals shoved into her pockets, her hair was loose and blowing softly in the wind, and he touched her face with his hand, and then very gently he leaned toward her and kissed her, before walking slowly down the beach with her, and then back to the pier. They said little on the ferry ride home, and she was astonished to realize that in the last few minutes of it she fell asleep with her head on his shoulder. But he was that kind of man. He teased her about it once they were back in the Bentley, and they laughed and joked on the rest of the ride home. An hour after they had stepped off the boat from Fire Island she was in front of her door on East Sixty-third Street, and it was difficult to explain what had happened in the past eight hours. It was just after ten o'clock, and she felt as though she were returning from a magical journey with this extraordinary black-eyed man.

"See you tomorrow, Serena." He said it very gently, and did not try to kiss her again. She nodded, with a smile, and waved as she unlocked the outside door and disappeared into the building, and as though in a dream she drifted up the stairs.

CHAPTER THIRTY-EIGHT

As relaxed and magical as the day before had been, the day of working with Vasili at the studio was a day of grueling devotion to his work. He shot unrelentingly for hour after hour, in the studio, in the car, with the male models, with the children, head shots of Serena, and shots of the car alone. She watched him work and realized that even Andy Morgan hadn't worked that hard when she was photographed by him. There was a kind of manic excitement about Vasili, a physical electricity that filled the room, and when the day ended, everyone in the studio was drained. Vasili himself was drenched with perspiration, his navy-blue T-shirt stuck to him like wallpaper, and he used a towel to wipe his face and his arms, and then sat down with a broad grin. The smile that exploded in his eyes seemed to be just for Serena, and she felt herself drawn to him as she had been again and again, and she sat down beside him with a warm smile.

"You should be very pleased." Her voice was gentle, and his face was very near to hers.

"So should you, Princess. You were fantastic. Wait until you see the shots."

"I assume we're through." There was disappointment in her voice as she said it, and she looked amazed when he shook his head. "We're not? You can't really mean to shoot more, Vasili. We got everything imaginable today."

"No, we did not." He attempted to look outraged, but his laughing eyes would not play the game. "We only did studio work today, tomorrow we work outdoors."

She grinned at him. "Where?"

"You'll see."

And the next day she did. He had found a series of hills and a rugged little canyon in New Jersey, and she drove the car, hopped out of it, lay on the hood, pretended to change a tire for him, did everything but overhaul the engine, and at the end of the day, she was even amused. Not only did he get to know his subjects but he apparently got to know his objects too. She teased him about it as they drove back to the city together, and he congratulated her again on her style.

"You know, Princess, you're damn good."

She looked at him happily as she flung back her mane of blond hair, and longed to touch his. "So are you."

He dropped her off at her door that night, and two days later he called her. "Come and see what we've done."

"Vasili?"

"Of course, Princess. I have the proofs and the contact sheets to show you." It was unusual for the model to see them before the client, but he was so excited about what he'd shot that he wanted her to rush right over to the studio, and she did. The photographs he had got of her were sheer genius, prizewinning quality, truly remarkable photographs, and he was ecstatic, and when she saw them, so was she. As was Dorothea Kerr at the agency, and the client, and everyone involved with the job. And by the following week Dorothea Kerr had scheduled them again together four more times.

"Look who's here!" She teased as she walked into the studio for the third time. "Not tired of my face yet, Vasili?" She had wanted a vacation, but after working with him, she had given up the idea. It was more exciting to work with

Vasili, and she knew that he wouldn't be in the States for very long. Besides which, there was still that odd magnetism about him, and she was always haunted by the memory of the sunset they had shared on Fire Island. Whenever they worked together, she remembered those moments, and when she had slept on his shoulder on the ferry. The memories suffused her face with a gentle quality that showed in the photographs later, and the work they did together was like ballet or fine art.

"How's my princess today?" He leaned over to kiss her on the cheek, and then he smiled at her. The job they had to do was a quickie, and this time they were finished in a few hours. They knew each other so well that it was easier and easier to work together, and after the shoot was over, he pulled on a fresh T-shirt and looked over his shoulder at Serena. "Want to go out for dinner somewhere, Princess?"

She didn't hesitate for a moment. "I'd love it." And this time he took her to Greenwich Village, to his favorite bar. They ate spaghetti and mushrooms and a giant salad, white wine, and afterward they wandered through the streets and ate Italian ice.

"Don't you ever miss Italy, Serena?"

She hesitated for a moment and then shook her head. "Not anymore." She told him then about all that she had lost there, her parents, her grandmother, both palazzi. "I belong here now."

"In New York?" He looked surprised, and she nodded. "Wouldn't you be happier in Europe?"

"I doubt it. I haven't been there in so long. I lived in Paris for a few months with my husband, but it all seems so long ago now."

"How long is it?"

"Eight years."

"Serena." He looked at her squarely then, his black eyes brilliant with a kind of fire. "Would you work with me in Paris or London? I'd like to work with you again, and I don't spend that much time here."

She thought about it for a moment. He was wonderful to work with, and together they created something very rare. There was an extraordinary undercurrent between them, she wasn't quite sure what it was, but it appeared in the photographs every time. "Yes, if I could make arrangements for my daughter."

"How old is she?"

"Almost eight."

He smiled at Serena. "You could bring her along."

"Maybe. If it was only for a few days. She has to go to school."

He nodded. "Let's think about it."

"Are you leaving soon?" Serena looked disappointed, and she glanced at him as they passed through Washington Square and left the Village.

"I don't know." He looked at her strangely. "I haven't decided yet. But I've almost finished all the jobs I came here to do." And then he shrugged again, like a remarkably beautiful schoolboy. "Perhaps I should try to drum up more work." Serena laughed. They had only been working together for a week, but their hours together had been so long and intense and filled with hard work and feeling that it was difficult to believe that they hadn't worked together at least a hundred times before. "What are you thinking?"

She looked at him with a smile. "That I like working with you, and that I'll miss you." And then, almost shyly, "I've never become involved with any of the photographers before."

"That was what Dorothea told me." He looked at her teasingly. "She said that you are a pro, and that I wasn't to try any of my tricks on you."

"Aha! Do you usually use tricks?"

She was teasing, but he was not when he answered. "Sometimes. Serena . . ." He seemed to hesitate and then decided to tell her. "I am not always the most circumspect person." But that much was apparent about him. "Does that matter to you?"

"I don't think so." She answered quickly, but she wasn't entirely sure what he meant. All photographers were a little wild sometimes. He wasn't the only one. The only thing different about him was that he had been married four times.

"You know." He stopped walking and turned to face her.

320

"You are such an unusual woman that sometimes I don't know how to tell you what I'm thinking."

"Why not?" She frowned, afraid that she had seemed stiff or perhaps stuffy. If they were to be friends, he should have been able to be himself. "Why can't you tell me what you think?" Her eyes clouded and he moved toward her and gently kissed her.

"Because I love you." Time seemed to stand still as they stood there. "That's why. And you're the loveliest woman I ever met."

"Vasili . . ." She lowered her eyes and then raised them again to look at him, but he didn't let her continue.

"It's all right. I don't expect you to love me. I've been a crazy man all my life. And one pays a price for that." He sighed as he said it and smiled a sad little smile. "It makes one quite unsuitable for anyone decent."

"Don't be silly."

But he held up a hand again. "Would you want a man who had had four wives?" His eyes bore into her as he asked her.

"Maybe." Her voice was soft as satin. "If I loved him."

And his voice was as soft as hers. "And do you think you could love such a man . . . perhaps . . . if he loved you very, very much . . .?"

As though the gesture were made by someone else, she felt herself nodding, and the next thing she knew she was crushed in his arms. But she found as she stood there that that was all she wanted. She wanted to be with him, to be his, to stand beside him forever, and when he kissed her this time, she felt her whole heart go out to him with her kiss.

He took her home to her apartment that night and left her outside her doorway. He kissed her as passionately as he had before, but he forced himself to leave her at the door. He was back again though the next morning, with fresh coffee and croissants, a basket of fruit, and an armful of flowers, and she opened the door to him sleepily in her nightgown and was astounded as he stepped inside. What began after that was an old-fashioned courtship. They were together every minute of the day. He had finished his work, and she took her vacation from the agency at last. They went to the beach and the park and the country, held each other and kissed and touched, and it wasn't until the end of the week that she went to his hotel room at last. He was staying uptown at the Hotel Carlyle, in a huge beautiful suite overlooking the park. He took her there just to show her the view, and then once again he kissed her, but this time neither of them could hold back anymore. He held her in his arms with such an aching of desire that she could hardly bear it, and she knew then that there was no fighting what had to be. They needed and wanted each other too badly to try to stem the tides anymore, and they took each other with such unbridled passion that Serena wondered once or twice if they would live through the night. But when morning came, they were spent at last, lovers to their very souls, and she felt as though she belonged to him forever. She was Vasili's now, to her very core.

The agony of it was that he was leaving for Paris on the following morning, and Teddy and Vanessa were due back in two days.

Serena sat looking serious after their first cup of coffee. "It's all right, darling. I promise you. You'll meet me in London."

"But, Vasili . . ." He made it sound so simple. She had Vanessa, a child she couldn't easily leave and didn't want to, and then there was Teddy, she hated to leave him too. He had been a brother and a friend to her for so long, and such a constant presence in her life in New York, that it was difficult to imagine being without him. She looked at Vasili now and felt sorrow well up within her. She didn't want him to leave the next day.

"Then come with me."

"But I can't . . . Vanessa—"

"Bring her along. She can start the school year in Paris or London. She speaks French, so it can't be a problem." And then with a grin, "It's only as complicated as you make it."

"That's not true. I can't just uproot her so I can run around chasing after a man."

"No." He looked at her seriously then. "But you can bring her with you if you choose to marry that man." Serena said nothing. She only stared at him. "I mean that.

I'm going to marry you, you know. The only question is when it will suit you. I think that we settled the rest of the question last night." Serena blushed furiously and he kissed her. "I love you, Princess. I must have you for my own."

But who really was Vasili? Serena felt sudden panic well up in her. How could she do this? What was she doing? But it was as though Vasili could read her mind. "Stop worrying, my darling. We will work everything out." But how from three thousand miles across the ocean? She got up from where she sat and wandered slowly toward the window, her long beautifully carved ivory body looking like a white marble statue in motion, and it filled Vasili with desire again. "Serena." He said it so softly that it was barely more than a whisper.

"Will you marry me?"

Her eyes filled with tears. "I don't know." But she already knew that she had embarked on an ocean she could not control. She wanted this man more than she had wanted anyone since Brad. Just as he seemed to feel about her, she also felt that she had to have him, but it was a kind of breathtaking roller-coaster whirl. There was nothing calm or peaceful about this. It was raw passion and a constant riptide of desire. He walked toward her now, fully erect and with his black eyes blazing.

"Will you marry me, Serena?" It wasn't a menace, but it was a wonderful growl, and he swept her into his arms, as she caught her breath and he held her. "Will you?"

Slowly, hypnotically, she nodded. "I will." And then he took her on the floor of his hotel room, and she cried out with her own desire.

And when it was over, he looked down at her with a small victorious smile. "I meant what I said, my beloved princess. I want you to be my wife. Did you mean what you said?"

She nodded slowly. "Then, say it, Serena." He pinned her to the ground and for a moment she thought she saw madness in his eyes. "Say it. Say that you will be my wife."

"I will be your wife." She repeated it as she watched him.

"Why?" But as he asked her his whole face seemed to melt and once again he became gentle. "Why, Serena?" It was a tender whisper.

"Because I love you." Her eyes filled with tears and he took her in his arms and made love to her again and again, telling her all the while how much he loved her.

CHAPTER THIRTY-NINE

The next morning Vasili left for Paris, and Serena stood at the airport, staring after his plane. It had all been like a dream, and she felt as though she were still in a trance as she got back into the Bentley and rode back to her apartment. Did he mean what he had said? Was he serious about marrying her? How could she know so soon? She barely knew him. Now that he was gone, she felt slightly less under his spell. And there was Vanessa . . . the child had never even met Vasili. Serena's heart pounded at what she had done. She wanted to reach for the phone and confide in Dorothea, but she was ashamed to admit that she had fallen so easily for Vasili's charms.

As she sat and stared out the window that night, the phone rang. It was Vasili, in Paris, he already missed her and wanted to know how she was, and his voice was so gentle and so sexy that she found herself swept off her feet again. By the next morning the apartment was filled with flowers. There were four baskets of white roses for his princess, and by noon she had received a box from Bergdorf Goodman, containing a spectacular fur coat.

"Oh, my God." She stood staring into the mirror, in her nightgown and the mink coat, wondering how she would explain it, and once again the full force of what she had done came to mind. In two hours she had to pick up Vanessa at Grand Central Station, and she knew that Teddy would be back from Newport late that night. She wanted to tell him something, but she felt strange explaining Vasili to him. It had all happened so quickly and with such force. She was pensive and a little nervous as she stood there debating, but the phone rang again and it was Vasili. He wanted her to meet him in London for a few days the following week. And it seemed to her that if she did that, it would at least give her another chance to evaluate how she felt. She accepted quickly, thanked him profusely for the coat, said that she really couldn't accept it, but he insisted. And after they hung up, she put it back in the box and hid it in a suitcase.

When she picked up Vanessa at Grand Central, the child was filled with her adventures at camp. She introduced her mother to all of her friends before they tearfully parted at the station, and on the way home she didn't stop once to catch her breath. Serena was grateful that nothing was required of her, all she had to do was ooh and ahh, and make the appropriate affectionate gestures, but she felt as though her mind were already crammed full with her own confusion, and there was no room for anything else, not even Vanessa.

It wasn't until after eleven o'clock that night when the doorbell rang that she really knew how anxious and confused she was. She opened the door to tall, blond, deeply suntanned Teddy, he held out his arms to her and she looked vague and a little embarrassed.

"You sure don't look too happy to see me." He teased her with a broad grin, and she laughed nervously as she kissed him.

"I'm sorry, love. I'm just so damn tired."

He frowned at her in consternation. "I thought you were going to take a vacation."

"I was . . . I did . . . I mean I meant to . . . I don't know. There's just so much work from the agency right now."

"That's crazy." He looked annoyed. "You promised me you'd rest."

"Well, I did. Sort of." But how could she tell him? She knew that she couldn't, at least not yet. But she decided to leap into some of it very quickly, otherwise she knew she'd never have the courage to say anything at all. "I'm going to London next week, by the way."

"You are?" He looked startled. "They're really pushing you these days, aren't they?"

She nodded. "Can you stay here with Vanessa?" It made her feel awkward to ask him, but she didn't know anyone else she trusted Vanessa with as much as Teddy. He nodded pensively.

"Sure. What kind of a shoot is it?"

Serena busied herself with some papers. "I don't know yet."

By the time she left she was feeling very nervous. She cried when she said good-bye to Vanessa. Her guilt made her feel convinced she'd crash on the plane, she was sure that the whole trip would be a disaster, and she really didn't want to go. Yet, something drove her to do it, and by the time she was halfway to Shannon Airport for their first stop, she was so excited, she could hardly breathe. All thought of the loved ones she had left behind had almost vanished, and all she could think of was Vasili, waiting for her at the other end. When she saw him in London, it was a jubilant reunion. He took her to his little mews house in Chelsea and made love to her in the beautiful little blue and white bedroom on the second floor. The shoot, it turned out, had been canceled. But instead he had scheduled a round of parties, and was taking Serena to all of the most important social events. Much of the London season wasn't in full swing yet. It was still early in September, but Serena thought that she had never been to so many parties in so few days. He introduced her to everyone he could think of, took her on long romantic walks in the park, shopped with her in Chelsea and at Hardy Amies and Harrods, took her to cozy places for lunch and dinner. He seemed proud to introduce her to everyone in sight, and on her second day there, there was an item in the paper about them. "And who is Vasili Arbus's spectacular new romance? They say the ravishing Italian blonde is a princess, and she certainly looks the part. Don't they make a handsome pair!" On the third day someone had matched up her photographs with her name from some fashion shots they had previously seen, and the papers boldly speculated. PRINCESS SERENA, VASILI ARBUS'S NUMBER FIVE? It was a headline that made Serena nervous, remembering how often items from London were picked up in New York. But by the end of the week she had grown used to the gossip, and it seemed as though she had always been part of his life. She brought him coffee and croissants in the morning, he gave her long sensuous massages at night. They talked until all hours of the morning, and she watched his friends with a sense of intrigue. For the most part they seemed a racy crew, but she thought that perhaps in time one could find a few people among them who were worthwhile. She couldn't truly say that she disliked his life. His studio was enormous and very efficient, his house was enchanting, and the man himself had wit and genius, tenderness and humour and taste. He was, in many ways, all that one could want in a man. But she still felt that she hadn't known him for a very long time. And yet, overwhelming everything was his obvious love for her and their passion. They seemed to spend endless hours making love, and again and again he urged her to marry him quickly. And although she thought she should hold off for a while, she really didn't want to. She wanted to be with him every hour of the day, every moment. Peeling her body away from his was almost painful. And they were always together. She could no longer imagine a life apart from his and he wanted to marry her by Christmas. Serena still had occasional doubts and fears about getting married so fast and perhaps upsetting Vanessa, but he pooh-poohed them.

"I don't want to wait. I don't see why we should. I want us to have a life together. To spend all our time with each other, working, having fun, with our friends." He looked tenderly at her. "We could have a baby, and, Serena, I'm thirty-nine. I'm in a hurry to have you be all mine forever."

"Let me try to work it out when I get home. I have to break this to Vanessa."

"Do you still want to marry me?" He looked suddenly crushed, and she leaned forward and kissed him on the lips.

"Of course. I just don't want to startle her by doing it so quickly." And then there was Teddy she would have to explain it to. She wondered what would be his reaction. But Vasili was always insistent.

"When it's right, you have to grab the moment." It was not unlike what Brad had said nine years before, which

327

somehow gave his urge to rush into marriage a little more respectable credence.

"I'll work it out." Her voice was very quiet.

"When?" He was pushing and it drove her crazy. She was already torn between reason and passion.

"As soon as I go home."

When she got off the plane at Idlewild Airport in New York, Teddy was waiting. He looked strangely serious, and Serena saw almost right away that his eyes were sad. He kissed her as he always did, and when at last they had picked up her bags and got into his car, he turned toward her. "Why didn't you tell me why you went over there?"

A knife of guilt cut through her. He already knew. "Teddy . . . I went for a shoot, and the shoot was canceled."

"But you went to see a man too, didn't you?" Her eyes glued to his, she nodded. "Why didn't you tell me?"

She sighed deeply then and shook her head. "I'm sorry, Teddy. I don't know. I just didn't know where things stood. I thought I'd tell you when I got back."

"And?" He looked deeply hurt that she hadn't told him. He had seen a small item in the papers. It mentioned Vasili Arbus by name, and that Serena was staying with him.

She took a deep breath then and looked into his eyes. "I'm getting married." She wasn't sure why but she felt as though she had to defend herself to him.

"Already?" He looked shocked. "To Vasili Arbus?"

"Yes, to both questions." She smiled then. "I love him very much. He's brilliant and wonderful and creative and a little crazy."

"So I've heard." He stopped to look at her then. "Serena, do you know what the hell you're doing?"

"Yes." But she still felt a little flutter of fear. It had all happened so quickly.

"How long have you known him?"

"Long enough."

"Serena, do whatever you want, live with him, go to London, but don't marry him. Not right away. . . . I've heard a lot of strange things about that man."

"That's not fair, Teddy. It's not like you." She looked upset. She wanted Teddy to approve of what she was doing.

"I'm not saying that because I'm jealous, I'm saying it because I love you. I've heard that—that he killed his last wife." He looked terrified and pale in the car, and Serena's eyes grew bright with anger.

"How dare you say something like that! She died from on overdose!"

"Do you know of what?" His voice was strangely quiet.

"How the hell do I know?"

"Heroin."

"So she was a junkie, so what? That's not his fault, and he didn't kill her."

"Oh, God, Serena . . . please be sensible, you have so much at stake, yourself and Vanessa." And dammit, he thought to himself as he voiced his objections, I still love you. "Why don't you just give it time?" But he was forcing her to dig in her heels.

"I know what I'm doing. Don't you trust me?"

"Yes." His voice was very quiet. "But I'm not sure I trust him."

She shook her head and looked out the window. "You're wrong, Teddy. He's a good man."

"How do you know that?"

"I feel it." She looked steadily at Teddy. "And he loves me. And we're in the same business. Teddy . . ." Her voice grew very soft. "It's right."

"How soon are you going?"

"As soon as I can."

"What about Vanessa?"

"I'm going to tell her when I get home." And then she looked searchingly at the man who had been her brother-in-law and dearest friend for years. "Will you come to see us?"

"Anytime you let me."

"You'll always be welcome. You're the only family I have, other than Vanessa. That better not change now."

"It won't." But he drove her into the city in silence, trying to recover from the shock of all she'd said. For the first time in a long time he wanted to tell her that he loved her. He wanted to stop her madness, to protect her.

CHAPTER FORTY

"But why do we have to move to London?" Vanessa was looking plaintively at her mother.

"Because, darling, I'm getting married and that's where Vasili lives." Serena felt very odd as she tried to explain it to Vanessa. All of the things that she was doing wrong seemed even more difficult to explain. It was wrong that she was moving so quickly, that she was giving up her career in New York, that she was leaving Teddy, that Vanessa hadn't met Vasili.

Vanessa looked at her now. "Can't I just stay here?" Serena felt as though she had been slapped by her daughter.

"Don't you want to come with me, Vanessa?" Serena had to fight back tears.

"But who'll take care of Uncle Teddy?"

"He will. And you know, one of these days he might get married too."

"But don't you love him?" Vanessa looked more than ever confused, and Serena looked distraught.

"Of course I do, but not that way—oh, Vanessa, love is complicated." How could one explain to a child about passion? "Anyway, now this nice man has come along and he wants you and me to come and live with him in London. And he has a house in Athens, and an apartment in Páris, and . . ." She felt like a complete fool trying to convince her daughter. Vanessa was just a child, not yet eight, and yet she knew when her mother was doing something wrong. Dorothea Kerr had been a great deal more blunt about it.

"Frankly I think you're stark-staring crazy."

"I know, I know. It sounds nuts." Serena was constantly having to defend what she was doing and it was exhausting. "But, Dorothea, this is special. I don't know how to tell you. He loves me, I love him. Something magical happened between us when he was here."

"So he's good in bed. So what? So go sleep with him in London or Paris or the Congo, but don't marry him. For chrissake, the man has been married four or five times."

"Four." Serena corrected soberly.

"And just what do you think will happen to your career? You won't stay on top forever, kid. Some new face will come along."

"That's going to happen anyway, and I can work in London." There was no convincing her, but by the time she left New York, three weeks later, Serena's psyche was exhausted. She was tired and pale and hadn't slept in weeks.

Teddy took them to the airport, and all three of them cried as though it were the end of the world. He was quiet and restrained, but the tears flowed down his face as he kissed Vanessa, and Vanessa clung to him like her last friend. Serena felt as though she were destroying the family she cherished, and at the end she held Teddy in her arms and she couldn't even speak. All she could manage to squeeze out just before they boarded was an anguished "I love you." And then with a last wave they were gone. The flight over was bumpy and Vanessa cried most of the way, and by the time they reached London, Serena was almost ready to turn back. But as she stepped off the plane she saw him, and her eyes filled with tears as she laughed. Vasili looked like a balloon vendor at a fair, as he stood with at least fifty helium-filled balloons in one hand, and an enormous doll stuck under his other arm.

"Is that him?" Vanessa stared at him with interest, and it struck Serena again how much she looked like Brad.

"Yes. His name is Vasili."

"I know." Vanessa glanced disparagingly over her shoulder at her mother and Serena grinned at what an able grown-up she could be sometimes.

The doll was wearing a fancy blue satin dress, a small white fur cape, and an old-fashioned hat. She looked like a little girl of a hundred years before.

Vasili came slowly toward them, the balloons held aloft, as people smiled "Hello, could I sell you a balloon, little girl?" Vanessa laughed. "And I also happen to have this dolly." He pulled the big handsome doll out from under his arm and handed her to Vanessa. "Hello, Vanessa. My name is Vasili."

"I know." She stared at him, as though sizing him up, and he laughed. "I'm glad you came to London."

She looked at him honestly. "I didn't want to come. I cried a lot when I left New York."

"I can understand that." He spoke to her gently. "When I was a little boy, I lived in London, and then I had to move to Athens, and that made me very sad." Serena recalled as he said it that he had been two when his parents died, and he couldn't possibly remember, but at least it sounded good to the child. "Do you feel better now?" She looked up at the balloons and nodded. "Shall we go home?" He held out a hand to her and she shook it, and then for the first time he stood up and looked into Serena's eyes. "Welcome home my darling." Her heart melted as she looked at him. She wanted to thank him for how wonderful he had been to Vanessa, but she knew that this wasn't the time. She could only tell him what she felt with her eyes.

At the little house in Chelsea he had prepared everything for Serena and Vanessa. There was a dollhouse in the little blue and white guest room. There were dolls on the bed. There was a chair just Vanessa's size. And all over the house were enormous bouquets of beautiful flowers. He had hired a new maid to take care of Vanessa. And there was champagne cooling in a silver bucket in their bedroom, when at last Serena sat down on the bed with a sigh.

"Oh, Vasili . . . I thought I'd never survive." She thought back over the past weeks and almost shuddered. For hours on the plane all she had been able to think of was Teddy, looking so bereft when they left, and his begging her not to get married right away. She had cried when she said good-bye to Dorothea Kerr too, and she already felt a twinge of nostalgia for the life she had left behind in New York. And yet this was going to be so much better, and she knew that this was right for her. But all her life she had been saying good-bye to beloved people and places, and each time she did so again, it brought back some of the sorrow of the past.

"Was it very rough?"

She looked at him a little sadly. "In a way, but I kept thinking that I was coming home to you." And then she smiled tenderly at him. "I had a hard time convincing people that we aren't crazy." She looked at him with a bittersweet smile. "Doesn't anyone believe in love anymore?" Yet even in her own heart she knew that she had done something crazy, or impetuous at best.

"Do you believe in love, Serena?" He looked at her as he handed her a glass of the chilled champagne and she took it from him.

"I wouldn't be here if I didn't, Vasili."

"Good. Because I love you with all my heart." He toasted her quietly. "To the woman I love . . . to my princess. . . ." He linked his arm in hers and they took the first sip, and then his eyes danced as he looked into hers. "How soon is the wedding?"

She smiled tiredly at him. "Whenever you like."

"Tomorrow," he teased.

"How about giving us a little time to adjust?"

"Two weeks?" She nodded. "In two weeks then, Mrs, Arbus. Until then you remain my princess." He smiled gently at her then and took her face in his hands to kiss her, and moments later her body was entwined with his on the enormous bed, and Teddy and Dorothea and New York were all but forgotten.

CHAPTER FORTY-ONE

The wedding was pretty and festive and conducted at the home of one of his friends in Chelsea. There were about thirty people present, and no members of the press. Serena looked magnificent in a beige silk dress that hung to the floor, with tiny beige cymbidium orchids in her hair.

A minister performed the ceremony. Three of Vasili's other four weddings had been only civil, so the minister had been willing to perform this one for them, after some discussion with both the bride and groom. Vanessa stood beside her mother at the wedding, holding tightly to her hand and glancing at Vasili. In the past two weeks she had begun to like him, but he was still a stranger to her, and she didn't see him very often. He was at the studio most of the time in the daytime, and every night they went out.

Serena herself was exhausted by their hectic schedule. She was trying to adjust to it all, but she never seemed to catch up. They went to parties, balls, concerts, the theater, parties after parties after parties, and were frequently not yet in bed when the sun came up over London. How he managed to work as hard as he did was a mystery to Serena. By the end of two weeks she had circles under her eyes and she was exhausted. The only prospect of relief in sight was a week at his house in Saint-Tropez, where they were going to spend their honeymoon. But Vanessa was already complaining about that. She didn't want to be left alone with the maid, and she wanted them to take her with them. Vasili wanted to be alone. And Serena felt as though she were being torn in half. After lengthy discussions with Vanessa, they did manage to leave the day after the wedding, and as they took off in the plane Serena sat back in her seat with an enormous sigh.

"Tired?" He looked surprised and Serena laughed at him.

"Are you kidding? I'm ready to drop. I don't know how you do it."

"Easy." He grinned at her with his boyish grin, and pulled something out of his pocket. It was a small vial of pills, she saw a moment later. "I take whites."

"Whites?" She looked startled as she glanced from him to the bottle and then back to his eyes. "You take pills?" He had never told her and he nodded.

"They allow me to keep going night and day. Want one?"

"No, thanks. I'll wait till Saint-Tropez and get some sleep." But deep within she was shocked. She remembered suddenly what Teddy had told her, that Vasili's last wife had died of a heroin overdose.

"Don't look so worried, love." He bent toward her with a kiss. "They won't kill me. They just keep me moving at a speed that I like."

"But aren't they bad for you?"

"No." He looked amused. "They don't do any harm. And if I take too many, I just take something to counteract it. Not to worry." He suddenly sounded like a pharmacist and Serena was startled to realize that he took pills. She hadn't been aware of it before, and it underlined to her again how little she knew of him. At times she felt as though they had been together forever. At other times she felt as though she scarcely knew him at all. "For God's sake, Serena." He looked at her expression again with obvious annoyance. "You look as though you've just discovered I'm an ax murderer. For chrissake . . ." He got out of his seat and walked to the front of the plane. He returned a few minutes later with half a bottle of wine for them both. "Or do you object to that too?"

"I didn't object to the other. I was just surprised." She looked hurt. "You didn't tell me before."

"Do I have to tell you everything?"

"You don't *have* to do a damn thing, Vasili." She looked angry and declined the wine.

But he was looking at her more gently. "Yes, I do have to do something."

"And what's that?" She still looked annoyed.

"I have to kiss you, that's what." She grinned at him then,

and a little while later the tension had worn off.

Their stay in Saint-Tropez was everything a honeymoon should be. They walked naked on their private beach, swam in the gentle swell of the Mediterranean, drove around the Maritime Alps in a Maserati, went to the casino in Monte Carlo, saw few of Vasili's friends, and were mostly alone. They spent late mornings in bed, stayed up till all hours making love, and were only in the newspapers once, when one of the French papers made a fuss about their arrival at the Carlton for drinks: "Vasili Arbus and his new bride, honeymooning in Cannes . . . she was a princess and a model, now she's his queen . . ." He read it to her the next morning over breakfast.

"How did they know that you're my queen?" He smiled happily at her.

"Someone must have squealed."

"You know what I'd like to do next week?"

"What, my love?" She smiled at her husband. It was something very different than she had shared with Brad. But she was almost ten years older now. she felt very much a woman with Vasili, and she loved the heady feeling of being his wife.

"I'd like to go to Athens for a few days." But her face clouded over. "Wouldn't you like that?"

"I ought to get back to Vanessa."

"She'll be fine with Marianne."

"That's not the same." Vanessa was in a new environment and she wanted her mother. It had been hard enough to convince her that they really needed their one-week honeymoon alone.

"Then why don't we stop off in London and pick her up on the way?"

"What about school?" Serena felt exhausted just thinking of how complicated that would be. Sometimes it was difficult following in his wake. He did precisely what he wanted, when he wanted, and he wasn't used to all the considerations that were a normal part of Serena's life.

"Can't she skip school for a little while?"

It would be easier than arguing with Vasili, or trying to make him understand. "I suppose she could."

"Fine. I'll call my brother and tell him we're coming."

"You have a brother?" She looked amazed. He had said nothing about any siblings.

"I most certainly do. Andreas is only three years older than I am, but he's much more serious." He seemed amused. "He has four children and a fat wife and he lives in Athens and runs one of the family businesses. I've always preferred life closer to my English relatives. Andreas, in his soul, is entirely Greek."

"I can't wait to meet him."

"And I'm sure he can't wait to meet you."

It was easy to believe when the three of them got off the plane in Athens the following week. Andreas was waiting at the airport with a huge bouquet of roses for Serena, a doll and an enormous box of chocolates for Vanessa, and his own children had arranged a little party for her at their house in Athens. His youngest child was fifteen and his oldest was twenty-one, but they were all delighted to meet Vasili's new stepchild. He had never before married anyone with children, and they were intrigued by this new wife of his, with the golden hair. She was so beautiful and so graceful, and even Andreas was taken with her. Serena instinctively liked him. He seemed kind and generous and thoughtful, and much more serious than Vasili, who constantly accused him of being stiff. But he wasn't really. He was a man of great substance and responsibility, in contrast to Vasili's more whimsical nature. And Andreas was enchanted with his new niece, whom he escorted around Athens with great seriousness, as he showed her sights he thought would amuse her, while his own children went to school and Vasili and Serena disappeared for their own tours. Vasili had a thousand things he wanted to show Serena, and Vanessa was happy with Andreas. She liked him even better than her new stepfather, who still seemed a little odd to her and was guilty of depriving her too frequently of her mother. But Andreas reminded her a little of Teddy, and she thought him better-looking than Vasili. As she beat him for the fourth time in a row over the checkerboard, she fell head over heels into her first crush.

They stayed in Athens for more than a week, and when it

was time to return to London, Vanessa was bitterly disappointed. She wanted to go on playing checkers forever with Andreas, whom she had come to love, but both Serena and Vasili said that they had to get back to work. Vasili had several jobs waiting for him at the studio in London, and Serena had already made an appointment with an agency to come in and show them her book. For the next several weeks the whole family was busy, Vasili and Serena with their work, and Vanessa at school, it seemed as though everyone had settled back into real life. Until one night when Serena was waiting for Vasili to come back from the studio, he still hadn't showed up two hours after they were expected at someone's house for a formal dinner. Serena was waiting for him in a spectacular gold dress she had just got from Paris, and her calls to the studio had been to no avail. She hoped that nothing was wrong, but when he arrived at the house, she was shocked. He looked filthy and disheveled. His hair was all askew, there were deep circles under his eyes, his shirt was covered with spots, his pants were unzipped, and he was walking unsteadily toward her at a much too rapid pace, as though he were operating on the wrong speed.

"Vasili?" He looked as though he had been mugged. She had seen him leave for the studio that morning, in the same pale blue shirt, camel-colored corduroy slacks, and a tweed jacket that he had just bought. Now the tweed jacket had disappeared. "Are you all right?"

"Fine. I'll be dressed in a minute." He sounded normal, but he looked anything but, and Serena was deeply worried as she followed him upstairs. He turned around to stare at her, and she saw that he was weaving. "What the hell are you following me for?"

"Are you drunk?" She was staring at him. But with that, he threw back his head and laughed.

"Am I drunk? Am I drunk?" He repeated it again and again. "Are you crazy?" She knew then that he was, but he didn't really look drunk, as she followed him into the bedroom, hoping that Vanessa hadn't heard them.

"Vasili, we can't go . . . you're in no condition." As she approached him she saw that his eyes looked almost crazy, and his mouth moved differently as he mimicked all that she said. "I'm not going." There was a frantic tone in her voice. This was a man she had never seen before, and it frightened her to see in him a stranger.

"What's the matter? Are you ashamed of me?" He walked toward her belligerently, and she stepped back, frightened. "You think I'd hit you?" She didn't answer but she was very pale. "Hell no, you're shit beneath my feet." She was shocked at what he was saying, and she turned quickly and left the room. He found her in Vanessa's room a few minutes later, making an excuse as to why they had changed their minds about going out.

"Vasili doesn't feel well," she said gently.

"Doesn't he?" It was a roar from the door. "Yes, he does. Your mother is lying, Vanessa." Both mother and child looked shocked as he advanced into the room. He was steady on his feet again but the same mad light was still in his eyes.

Serena hurried toward the door and gently pushed him through it. "Please come upstairs."

"Why should I? I want to talk to Vanessa. Hi, baby, how did your day go today?"

Vanessa said nothing and her eyes looked enormous in her face. Vasili reeled toward Serena then, still standing in the doorway.

"What did you do? Tell her I was drunk?" He spat the words at her and Serena's eyes began to blaze.

"Aren't you?"

"No, you asshole, I'm not."

"Vasili!" Serena was shouting now. "Get out of Vanessa's room!"

"Why, afraid I'll do something that will make you jealous?"

"Vasili!" It was the growl of a mother lion and he wheeled and left the room. He went down to the kitchen then, raided the icebox, and returned to their bedroom again, like an animal on the prowl.

"Want to fuck?" He looked at her over his shoulder as he picked at a plate of cold potatoes he had found in the icebox. The question seemed more rhetorical than real and Serena wanted to shake him.

339

"What in God's name is wrong with you? Did you take more pills?"

He shook his head. "Nope. What about you? Did you?" It was impossible to talk to him, and a few minutes later she locked herself in Vanessa's room with the child, and spent the night there.

The next morning he slept until almost noon, and when he finally came downstairs, it was evident that he was both ashamed and ill.

"Serena . . ." He looked at her, overwhelmed with remorse. "I'm sorry."

"You should be." She looked at him coldly. "And you owe an apology to Vanessa. Just what exactly happened to you last night?" It was as though he had gone crazy.

"I don't know." He hung his head. "I had a few drinks. They must have reacted strangely. It won't happen again." But it did. In almost precisely the same manner, once the following week, and twice the week after that. On Vanessa's birthday he was the worst he had ever been, and two days later that he disappeared for an entire night. It was as though he had gone totally berserk in the past month, and Serena couldn't understand it. He was like a totally different man than the one she had first met. He was angry, hostile, gloomy, vicious, and the mood came upon him more and more often. He spent the night at his studio now and then, and shouted at her when she asked for an explanation. And it made her more frantic yet when two days before Christmas she went to the doctor to discuss several minor problems she was having, which included nausea, vomiting, dizzy spells, headaches, insomnia, and all of it, she knew, was due to her nerves. It was exhausting to try and shield Vanessa from what was happening, and she was seriously thinking about going home to the States.

"Mrs. Arbus," the doctor said, looking at her kindly, "I don't think your nerves are the problem."

"They're not?" Could it be serious, then?

"You're pregnant."

"Oh, my God." She hadn't even thought of that.

That night she sat looking distracted and unhappy, staring into the fire in their den. Vasili was home and he was

340

strangely subdued, but she didn't want to tell him.
Abortions weren't totally impossible in London, and she
hadn't decided what should be done.

"Tired?" He had been trying for half an hour to strike up
a conversation, and she only nodded.

"Yes." She still wouldn't look at him, and at last he came
and sat next to her and touched her arm.

"Serena, it's been awful, hasn't it?"

She turned huge sad eyes up to his and nodded. "Yes, it
has. I don't understand it. It's as though you're not
yourself."

"I'm not." It was as though he knew something she
didn't. "But I'll change that. I promise. I'll stay here with
you and Vanessa until Christmas, and then I'll go somewhere and straighten out. I swear." His eyes were as sad as
hers.

"Vasili . . ." Serena looked at him hauntingly. "What
happened? I don't understand."

"You don't need to understand. It's something that never
has to be a part of your life." She wanted to ask him then if
it was drugs but she didn't dare. "I'll take care of it, and I'll
be the man you met in New York." He nuzzled her neck
gently and she wanted to believe him. She had missed him so
much and she had been so frightened. "Do you want to do
something special for Christmas?" She shook her head. He
hadn't even been aware enough to notice how ill she was
feeling.

"Why don't we just stay home?"

"What about Vanessa?"

"I've already got something planned for her."

"What about us? Do you want to go to some parties?"

She shook her head, disinterested, withdrawn, unhappy,
and it killed him to see her like that. "Serena, darling . . .
please . . . everything will be all right." She looked at him
then, more confused than ever. He was so loving, so gentle,
so understanding. How could he turn into that other man?

"Why don't we go to bed? You look exhausted."

She sighed softly. "I am." But after he thought she was
asleep, he was in the bathroom for hours, and when she got
up again to go to the bathroom once he had finally come out

341

of it, she walked in and let out a scream. On the sink, next to a blood-stained ball of cotton, lay a hypodermic needle, a match, and a spoon. "Oh, my God!" She wasn't even sure what she was seeing, but she knew that it was something awful, and little by little, as she stood there, the light dawned. She remembered what Teddy had told her about Vasili's last wife . . . heroin . . . and she suddenly knew that that was what she was seeing.

And suddenly she sensed also that he was standing right behind her, she could almost hear him breathing, and when she turned around, he was leaning against the wall, almost falling, his eyelids drooping, with a look of pallor that made him look as though he were about to die. Terrified, she began to whimper and shrank from him, as he lurched toward her, muttering at her about what the hell was she doing, snooping. Terrified, she ran out of the room.

CHAPTER FORTY-TWO

The morning of Christmas Eve Serena sat across the dining table from Vasili, and with a pale face and shaking hands she set down her cup. They were alone in the dining room and the doors were closed. Vasili looked as though he had been embalmed only that morning, and he did not attempt to meet her eyes.

"I want you to know that I'm going back to the States the day after Christmas. I'd leave tonight, except that it would upset Vanessa. Just stay away from me until I go, and everything will be fine."

"I understand perfectly." He actually hung his head in shame, and she wanted to hit him for what he had done, for what he was doing, to himself as well as to her. She couldn't even think of what was happening in her own body. She hadn't had time to think of it all day. She'd have to make arrangements for an abortion when she got back to New York, maybe Teddy would even help her, but she didn't want to waste time here. She just wanted to go home.

She got up from the table then, and suddenly, as she walked toward the door, the whole room spun around her, and a moment later she awoke lying on the floor. Vasili was kneeling beside her, looking at her in terror, shouting at the maid for a damp cloth to put on her head. "Serena! . . . Serena! . . . oh, Serena . . ." He was crying as he knelt beside her and Serena felt tears spring to her own eyes as well. She wanted to reach up and hold her arms out to him, but she couldn't do it. She had to be strong. She had to leave him, and leave London, and get rid of their child. "Oh, my darling, what happened? I'll call the doctor."

"Don't!" Her voice was still weak and the room spun as she shook her head. "I'm all right." It was a whisper. "I'll get up in a minute." But when she did, she looked sicker than he.

"Are you ill?" he asked her in despair, wondering if he had done that to her, but she only shook her head.

"No, I'm not."

"But it's not normal to faint like that."

She looked at him unhappily as she stood in the doorway at last. "What's been happening around here isn't normal either. Or maybe you hadn't thought of that."

"I told you last night I would stop it. Day after tomorrow I'm going into the hospital for a few days, and then I'll be myself again."

"For how long?" she shouted at him. "How often has this happened before? Is that how your wife died? Were you both shooting up drugs and she overdid it?" Her voice trembled and tears poured down her face.

But now he began to cry too as he spoke in an agonized whisper. "Yes, Serena . . . yes . . . yes! . . . I tried to save her, but I couldn't. It was too late." He closed his eyes then, as though he couldn't bear the thought.

"You make me sick. Is that what you expected from me? To find a friend you could use drugs with?" She shook as she shouted at him, and neither of them saw Vanessa come down the stairs. "Well, I won't. Do you hear me? And I

343

won't stay married to you either. I'm going back to New York and the minute I get there I'm having an abortion and—'' She stopped, realizing what she had just said. And he came instantly toward her.

"What did you say?'' He grabbed her shoulders, his eyes wide.

"Nothing, dammit . . . nothing!'' She slammed the door to the dining room behind her and ran toward the stairs where she found Vanessa crying softly. Vasili was upon them a moment later, and the three of them sat on the stairs in tears. It was a grim scene, for which Serena hated both herself and Vasili. Vasili apologized again and again for what he had done to both of them, Serena clung to Vanessa, and Vanessa screamed at Vasili that he was killing her mother. It seemed a hopeless tangle, and at last it was Vasili who led them both upstairs. Nothing more was said about the baby. But when at last Vasili was alone with Serena again, after they had left Vanessa calmer with the maid, he asked her if what she had said was true.

"So you're pregnant?'' She nodded and turned away. He came to her slowly then and touched her shoulders with his hands as he stood behind her. "I want you—no, I *beg* you to keep my child, Serena . . . please . . . give me a chance . . . I will be clean again in a few days. It will be as it was before. I don't know what happened. Maybe it was the adjustment between us, the responsibility of pleasing Vanessa. I went crazy for a little while. But I'll stop it. I swear it. Please—''His voice cracked and she turned around to see her husband dissolved in tears. "Don't kill my baby . . . please . . .'' Even Serena couldn't resist him, and she opened her arms and held him close.

"How could you have done it, Vasili? How could you?''

"It won't happen again. If you want, I'll go into the hospital tonight. I won't even wait until after Christmas. I'll go now''

She looked at him strangely and nodded. "Do it. Do it right away.'' He called the hospital ten minutes later, and she drove him there within the hour. She kissed him good-bye in the lobby and he promised to call her that night. When she left him, she drove directly home and climbed into her bed, and Teddy called her half an hour later, allegedly to wish them both a merry Christmas, but a few minutes later he asked if everything was all right. She had to fight to control her voice as she spoke to him, and she said nothing about coming home. But when she handed the phone to Vanessa, the child cried so hard that she almost couldn't speak. Serena sent her back to her room a few minutes later and Teddy confronted her then.

"Are you going to tell me what's going on there, or do I have to come over to see for myself?" The thought of confessing her mistake to Teddy made her cringe, but she was too unhappy to fool him, and in a rush of tears she told him what was going on. "Oh, my God. You've got to get out."

"But that's not fair. He just went into the hospital for detoxification. Maybe I owe it to him to give him a chance. He says he'll be himself again when he comes out."

"That's not saying much."

Serena wiped away her tears and sniffed. "That's a rotten thing to say."

"He's a rotten man. Face it, dammit. You've made a terrible mistake. And you can't drag Vanessa through this, or yourself."

"But what if he comes back from the hospital all right?" And now she was having his baby. She began to cry again, thinking of all the problems and decisions she had on her hands. "Oh, Teddy . . . I don't know what to do."

"Come home." He had never sounded as firm before. "I mean it. Get your ass on a plane tomorrow and come back to New York. You can stay with me."

"I can't leave now. He's my husband. It's not right." All her torment and conflict surfaced at once and she resisted Teddy's suggestion with all her might.

"Then send Vanessa until you're sure he's cleaned up."

"And be away from her at Christmas?" Serena started to cry again.

"Oh, for God's sake. Serena, what in God's name is happening over there . . . what's happening to you?" She felt crazier than Vasili as she tried to answer his question.

"I'm so unhappy and frightened, I can't think straight."

"That much I know."

But the rest he didn't. "I'm pregnant."

He whistled softly. "Holy shit." And then after a thoughtful pause, "Look, get some rest. I'll call you tomorrow." But the next day when he did, all hell had broken loose in New York. Someone at the hospital where Vasili was detoxing had fed that little item to the press, and it had gone over the AP wires before morning, appearing in a small but nasty news article in the States. Margaret's clipping service had sent the article over by messenger. She was furious and at the same time almost victorious.

"It's not bad enough that she uses our name to flaunt herself, all over New York, now she's married to that miserable café-society junkie. For God's sake, Teddy, what next?" She had called him at eight o'clock in the morning "Do you still speak to that woman?"

"I called her last night."

"I don't understand you."

"Look, dammit, she's my sister-in-law. And she's having a rough time." But this time even he was having difficulty defending her. She had made a poor choice. It wasn't her fault, of course, but the press was not inclined to be kind, and the little piece was certainly an embarrassment to the family and to Vanessa, which was more important. For once his mother was right. About Vasili, if not his wife.

"She deserves a rough time. And may I remind you that she is not your sister-in-law. Your brother is dead. And she is married to that trash."

"Why did you call me, Mother?" There was nothing else to say. He didn't want to defend Vasili; and he didn't want to discuss Serena with her.

"I wanted to know if you'd seen the item. As usual, I've been proven right."

"If you mean that you're right in your opinion of Vasili Arbus, I completely agree. As for Serena, let's not discuss it. You haven't made sense on that issue in years."

"I'm amazed you manage to keep any patients, Teddy. I think you're demented. On that subject at least. She must be quite spell-binding, judging by you and your brother."

"Is there anything else?"

"No, except that you can tell her that if anyone ever uses

346

our name in relation to her, to describe her, or her previous unfortunate alliance to my son, I will indeed sue her. That witch Dorothea Kerr no longer enters into it. I assume 'The Princess' ''—her voice was scathing—''is retired.''

''For the moment.''

''I suppose whores can always take their trade up again.'' At that he hung up on her, and called Serena. It was early afternoon in London and she sounded better than she had the night before. She had spent the whole morning calming Vanessa, and she said that when she spoke to Vasili at the hospital, he sounded a little more himself.

''Then you're not coming home?'' Teddy sounded agonized at his end.

''Not yet.''

''Keep me posted at least and if I don't hear from you, I'll call back in a few days.'' After the call Serena went back to Vanessa's room, to hear another diatribe about Vasili. It had been an excruciating few days.

''I hate him. I wish you had married Teddy, or Andreas.'' She remembered Vasili's brother in Athens.

''I'm sorry you feel that way, Vanessa.'' Serena's eyes filled with tears again. She was always being pulled between them, and Vanessa was looking at her strangely now.

''Are you really having a baby?''

Serena nodded. ''Yes, I am.'' That was going to be a problem too. Nothing was easy anymore. It was hard even to remember when it had been. ''Does that upset you very much?''

Vanessa thought about it for a minute and then looked at her mother. ''Couldn't we just leave and take it back with us to the States?'' It was what Serena had thought of doing, but then she would have had an abortion.

''It's Vasili's baby too,' she said gently.

''Does it have to be? Couldn't it just be ours?''

Slowly Serena shook her head. ''No, it couldn't.''

CHAPTER FORTY-THREE

A week later Vasili came out of the hospital, and he appeared to be almost angelic. They led a quiet life, stayed home much of the time, he was kind and thoughtful and loving with Vanessa. It was as though in his last rash act of self-indulgence he had finally seen the light. He explained to Serena that he first tried heroin ten years earlier, as a kind of lark, to see what it was, and within weeks he had got hooked. Andreas had ultimately arrived from Athens, seen the condition he was in, and put him immediately in a clinic to clean up. After that, he had stayed away from it for a year and then someone had offered it to him at a party, and he had fallen off the wagon again. For the next five years he had been on and off it, and then he had stayed totally clean until he met his last wife. Shortly after their marriage he had discovered that she used it—"chipped," he called it—and she had wanted him to use heroin with her, so she "didn't feel so lonely," she had told him pouting, and stupidly he had tried it again. Their relationship had apparently been a catastrophe of using dope together, and in the end she had died. That had sobered him again, until now he had tried it again. But this time he was certain that it was the last. Serena, however, found it discouraging to learn that he had been in and out of the hospital to clean up so many times.

"Why didn't you tell me?" She had looked at him sadly, feeling as though she had been cheated.

"How do you tell someone that? 'I have been a heroin addict.' Do you know how that sounds?"

"But how do you think I felt when I found out, Vasili?" Her eyes showed him how great was her pain. "How could you think I wouldn't know?" The tears began to flow again then.

"I didn't think I'd get hooked again."

She closed her eyes and lay back among her pillows.

"Serena, don't . . . darling, don't worry."

"How can I not?" She looked at him with anguish. "How do I know you won't start again?" She didn't trust him now. She didn't trust anything about his life.

He held up a hand solemnly. "I swear it."

For the next five months he was as good as his word. He was absolutely exemplary and he spoiled Serena rotten, doing everything he could to make up to her the pain he had caused her and to assuage her fears about his using again. He was thrilled about the baby, told everyone he knew, talked endlessly to his friends, his clients, his models, everyone knew about the baby, and of course he called his brother Andreas first of all. Andreas had sent them the biggest teddy bear Serena had ever seen, and it already sat in what would later be the baby's bedroom. He sent Vanessa an antique bride doll at the same time.

They were days of tenderness and gentle loving between Vasili and Serena. The boyish charm he had had in the beginning emerged again, and they spent long hours going for walks hand in hand. He took her to Paris twice, they spent Vanessa's Easter holiday in Athens, with Andreas and his wife and children, and then Vasili and Serena stopped in Venice on their way home, and she showed him her grandmother's house and all her favorite places. They had a wonderful time, and she thought that she had never been happier when they came home. The baby wasn't due until the first of August, and in early June Serena settled down to do the baby's room. She had bought beautiful little quilts and some wonderful old children's paintings of storybook characters in watercolors and oils. She herself was going to paint a mural, and Vanessa had been giving up dolls and stuffed animals, anticipating that she'd have a real doll soon. As June drew to an end she was excited about the baby. Serena was eight months pregnant, and it seemed incredible that the time was almost here. Vanessa had been invited to cruise the Greek Islands with Andreas and his family, but she wanted to stay near her mother to see the baby, and she still felt uneasy about going away alone. She didn't want to leave Serena, not even to visit Teddy, who had offered her a vacation in the States with him. "After the baby comes" was her answer to everyone, and Serena laughed when Vasili said the same thing to all invitations.

The pregnancy had been surprisingly easy, and the only thing that worried her now was that the same thing might happen with this baby as had happened with Vanessa, and if she started to give birth at home, she knew that Vasili didn't have Teddy's cool head. He was already a nervous wreck at the prospect, and every time she moved in bed, he leaped up, his black eyes starting, a look of shock on his face. "Is it now? Is it now?"

"No, silly, go back to sleep." Serena would smile at him, and she lay in bed, thinking of their baby and the years ahead. Everything was peaceful between them and the episode of his heroin use seemed like a distant nightmare now, until one day in the first week of July Vasili didn't come home at night. At first she thought that something awful had happened, like a car accident perhaps, and then as the hours ticked by she began to wonder if it was all happening again. She was racked by terror and anger as she waited up for him until four thirty in the morning, and at five o'clock she heard him come up the front steps. The door slammed soundly behind him, and on bare feet she tiptoed down the front stairs, trembling, with the baby seeming to leap inside her. She was afraid of what she would see, but she had to see it and know if he was using drugs again. All the old terrors had started again, in only one night.

As she stood halfway down the stairs and he stood in the front hallway, his eyes met hers, and he attempted a false bravado, with an enormous movie-star smile.

She could see instantly from the way he looked that he was high on something, and he looked nervous and foolish as he raced toward her, trying to pretend that there was nothing extraordinary about coming in at 5 A.M.

"Hello, darling, how's the baby?" His voice sounded hoarse and she had noticed that during his drug use before Christmas too. He always sounded different when he used heroin, and she couldn't bear to think now that he had done it again. She didn't answer him, she just stared at him, and he ran up the stairs and tried to give her a kiss. But she shrank from him in horror, knowing full well what he had done.

350

"Where were you?" It was a stupid question and she knew it. The point wasn't where he had been, but what he had done. And without waiting for an answer, she turned on her heel and walked up the stairs as quickly as she could. She felt as though at any minute she might have the baby. She felt so tense and she was having so many contractions from her long night awake that she wasn't sure if she was in labor or just feeling ill.

"Don't be so goddamn square," he shouted at her as she reached their bedroom, and she turned to him with a look of fury.

"Be quiet or you'll wake Vanessa." But it wasn't anger she felt so much as terror and despair. Vasili's private demon had entered their life again.

"To hell with Vanessa, she's a little bitch anyway." But at the very sound of the words Serena lunged toward him. With a rapidly flailing hand she attempted to slap him, but he caught her wrist first and flung her backward against the wall. She stumbled as she fell, and she groaned as she reached the floor, but more than hurt, she was stunned. He stood over her, and when she looked up at him with tears in her eyes, she saw that his eyes had the mad nervous gleam they had had before when he used heroin. It was like reliving the same nightmare and she felt as though she couldn't bear it. She felt a rage rise up within her that was almost beyond control.

"You make me sick!" She rose to her feet, with every inch of her body trembling, and she reached back as though to slap him again, and this time he beat her to it. He caught her across the face with the back of his hand and sent her reeling. She came crashing to the bedroom floor, and it was at this moment that Vanessa came running in. "Go back to your room!" Serena said it quickly, not wanting the child involved, but before Vanessa could leave, Vasili pushed her, and she landed in a heap beside Serena.

"There, two whimpering women. You belong with each other." He turned away and then spat over his shoulder. "Fools!"

Serena whispered to the child to go back to her room, but

Vanessa refused, with a look of panic in her eyes. "He'll hurt you."

"No, he won't." She was afraid he would too, but she didn't want Vanessa to see it.

"Yes, he will." Vanessa began to sob and clutch at her mother.

"Darling, please." Carefully she stood up and led the child to her room, and it was half an hour before she returned to Vasili. He was sitting in a chair, his head on his chest, a cigarette burnt out in his fingers.

"What?" He picked his head up as though she had just spoken and squinted in her direction. "I heard you."

"I didn't say a damn thing." She closed the door softly behind her, hating him with every ounce of her soul. "But I'm about to. I just want to let you know now, you son of a bitch, that when you come to tomorrow morning, I'm going to my lawyer, and then I'm going back to the States."

"And what will that prove? Who will support your baby?"

"I will."

There was something evil and vicious about him when he used drugs, and as Serena saw him that way she began to hate him. It was as though it canceled out all the good she had seen in him, all the hopes, all the dreams. All she wanted to do was run away. She began to leave the room then, but even in his seemingly sleepy state he suddenly sprang from his chair and leaped toward her.

He grabbed her arm and pulled her toward the bed and then he pushed her onto it. "Go to bed."

"I don't want to sleep here." She was shaking but trying not to show it. And the contractions were so fierce that she could barely stand up straight. And then, in spite of herself, she began to try and pull away from him. "I don't want to be near you."

"Why not? Do I disgust you?" The evil eyes gleamed at her.

"Let me go. You're hurting my arm."

"That isn't all I'll hurt if you don't start behaving."

"What in hell does that mean?" She knew better than to argue with him when he'd been using and yet she couldn't

352

stop. She wanted to shake him. "Do you expect me to take this and stick by you? Well, I won't, damn you. You can go to hell. I'm getting out of here in the morning."

"Are you?" He took a step toward her again. "Are you?" She trembled uncontrollably as he stood over her, and then, as though the effort had been too much, she lay back on the bed and began sobbing. She cried for over an hour and he didn't come near her, and when her tears were spent, she fell asleep on the bed, and when she awoke, it was eleven o'clock and he was still snoring. She tiptoed out of the room to go and find Vanessa, but Marianne had taken her for a walk, and Serena walked around the house slowly. She knew that she had to leave, that she had to get Vanessa out before things got too far out of hand again, and she had to go for the sake of the baby, yet she felt a strange panic at the thought of going. Maybe he was right. Who would help her? Where would she go? She couldn't expect Teddy to help her with this baby. And there was no one else left. She felt trapped as she sat at the foot of the stairs, and didn't hear him approach her. She only felt the touch of his hand on her shoulder and she leaped off the step with a little scream. As she turned to face him she saw his ravaged face. This time the damage of the drug was apparent after only hours. The time before it had taken weeks to look as bad as he did now. He already looked haggard and ferret-faced and seedy.

"Are you all right?" The wan face wore an expression of terror. She nodded, looking at him with dismay, and was almost unable to keep from crying. He lowered his voice. "Did I hurt you?"

"No." She spoke very softly. "But you terrified Vanessa." It was as though she herself no longer existed, as though the only two people who mattered anymore were Vanessa and the unborn baby. For herself, suddenly she didn't care if he killed her. She just didn't want him to harm her children. And it all seemed so exhausting to defend them. She was at a time in her life when she needed someone to take care of her, and instead she was suddenly having to deal with this nightmare with him. "What are you going to do?" She stared at him with beaten eyes. He was no longer the man she knew. Already, in one night, he had vanished.

"I don't know. I can handle it myself this time. I've only used a few times."

"A few times?" She looked shocked. She hadn't noticed, and she was surprised that he was being so honest. In Athens, the previous spring, when she and Andreas had once discussed it, he said that Vasili was never honest about using drugs once he started. So if he said "a few times," how many did that mean? She looked at him in despair. "Why now?"

"How do I know?" He sounded irritable and nervous.

"Will you go into hospital again?" She looked at him imploringly and felt her swollen belly begin to contract again.

"I don't need to this time."

"How do you know?"

"Because I know, dammit." She was making him very nervous. "Why don't you go upstairs and rest?" She noticed then that he was wearing jeans and his shirt from the night before and shoes without socks.

"Are you going somewhere?"

"I have to pick up some film."

"Really. Where?"

"None of your goddamn business. Why don't you go lie down?"

"Because I just got up."

"So what? Aren't you supposed to rest? Don't you care about the baby?" As though, in attacking her, he could free himself. In spite of her haranguing and nagging he left the house five minutes later and he didn't come back until after midnight. She had spent the day pacing and wondering and hating him, and in spite of her threats the night before, she didn't call her lawyer. She ended up screaming at Vanessa, bursting into tears, and having contractions that almost made her call the doctor. And when Vasili came in at last, she saw that he had once again been using drugs.

"How long is this going to go on?" Her voice was near hysterical and he nodded out as he pretended to listen to her.

"As long as I want to, if it's any of your business."

"Last time I looked I was your wife, and we were having a baby. It's my business."

354

He smiled evilly at her. "Such a little square lady."

She felt her stomach churn with horror as she watched him. "Why don't you get yourself put on one of the state heroin programs then, list yourself as an addict and do it that way?" What a thought. As she listened to herself she almost shuddered, but maybe then it would regulate him to a dose he could live with and they wouldn't have to go through quite the same hell.

But he was sneering at her. "What? And lose all my work? That would be interesting."

"Can you work like this?" They both knew he could not. Whenever he went on a binge, his assistants covered for him.

"Mind your own fucking business, bitch." This time she didn't get up to slap him, she only turned her back to him and lay there in bed, wondering why she hadn't moved out that morning. It was as though she were unable to move, unable to function, as though she thought that if she stayed with him long enough he'd straighten out again. But he didn't. The nightmare only grew worse every day, as Serena helplessly sat by and watched it, feeling herself sink into a quagmire of despair. At the end of the first week every day he promised her that he would get help, and every day he went out and used again. He was always going to get help the next morning, she was always going to call her lawyer and leave for the States at a moment's notice. It was a merry-go-round of threats and promises and fear. But she realized in the first few days that, other than a hotel, she could go nowhere. She couldn't get on a plane to the States, she was much too pregnant. And at last her due date was only days away and she had sat in the same quicksand for almost four weeks, as Vanessa watched her. The child was almost as wide-eyed and pale as her mother.

"Are you all right?" Teddy called them from Long Island on her due date, and he was even more worried than he had been before. There had been more press of late about Vasili— shots of him at night spots, alone, with speculations that his marriage to "The Princess" was on the rocks. "How is he?"

"Worse and worse. Oh, Teddy . . ." She had started to cry.

"Do you want me to fly over?"

"No. He'd have a fit and it would just be worse."

Although that was hard to imagine. How could it be much worse?

"If you need me, I'll come."

"I'll call you." But as she hung up she realized how isolated she felt from him. She felt isolated from everyone, adrift in this nightmare of Vasili's creation, as she waited to give birth to their child. She was afraid all the time and worried and she felt ill. But she had said nothing to her doctor. She couldn't stand the shame of admitting to anyone, except Teddy, what she was going through.

Teddy called her back a few hours later. He couldn't stand it any longer. He was flying over in a few days.

Five minutes later Serena went to Vanessa's room and found her staring sadly out the window. "You okay, sweetheart?" Serena was horrified when she saw her. The whole tale of the last month's grim scene was written all over the child.

"I'm all right, Mom. How's the baby?"

"The baby's okay, but I'm more worried about you."

"You are?" Vanessa's little face brightened. "I worry about you all the time."

"You don't have to. Everything's going to be fine. I guess Vasili will eventually get himself straightened out, but meanwhile Uncle Teddy is coming day after tomorrow."

"He is?" The child looked as though Christmas had been announced four months early. "How come?"

"I told him what was happening here, and he wants to come over to keep you company while I have the baby."

Vanessa nodded slowly, and then looked into her mother's eyes with eight-year-old eyes filled with confusion and pain. She had seen her mother slapped, pushed, ignored, terrified, worried, deserted, neglected. It was something that no child should ever see and that Serena prayed she would never see again. She hoped most of all that it wouldn't mark her forever. "Mommy, why does he do it? Why does he get like that?" She knew he took drugs. "Why does he want to?"

"I don't know, sweetheart. I don't understand it either."

"Does he really hate us?"

"No," Serena sighed, "I think he probably hates himself.

I don't understand what makes him do it, but I don't think it has anything to do with us."

"I heard him say he was afraid of the baby."

Serena looked at her. She had heard so much, and absorbed even more than Serena thought. "Maybe the responsibility of it scares him."

"Does it scare you?"

"No. I love you with all my heart, and I'm sure that we're going to love the baby."

"I'm going to love the baby a lot." Vanessa looked at her mother proudly, and Serena marveled that all that she had seen hadn't also made her hate the baby. Instead all of her bad feelings were for Vasili. "It's going to be my baby, Mommy. And I'm going to be a terrific sister." She looked at her mother and kissed her cheek. "Do you think it'll come soon?"

"I don't know."

"Sometimes I get tired of waiting."

Serena smiled. "Sometimes so do I. But it'll be soon." She could tell from all the contractions she'd been having in the past few days that it could come at any moment. "Maybe it'll wait for Uncle Teddy." Vanessa nodded, and they hugged each other close for a minute, and then Serena went upstairs to call Andreas and tell him what was happening to Vasili. Andreas was horrified when she told him, and sympathetic to her.

"Poor girl, he's doing that at a time like this? He should be shot!" He sounded very Greek and Serena smiled.

"Do you want to come and try and talk him into the hospital, Andreas? I have no effect on him anymore."

"I'll try. But I can't come for a few days. Alecca is sick, and I can't leave her." His wife had been ill for several months, Serena knew, and everyone was beginning to suspect it was cancer.

"I understand. I just thought that maybe you could influence him."

"I'll do my best. I'll be there by the end of the week, Serena. And you take care of yourself, and little Vanessa. No baby yet?" He smiled gently and she felt sad. She hardly

357

had time to think about the baby. Vasili's addiction was the only thing on her mind.

"No, not yet, but soon. I'll let you know."

"I'll try to come before you have it."

That night she felt calmer than she had in weeks, knowing that Teddy and Andreas were both coming. She knew that Vanessa would be cared for, and with any luck at all Vasili would be put away for a while. Now all she had to do was try not to have the baby before they got to London. She lay thinking about it all night and Vasili did not come home, and as she began to doze off just before dawn she felt something damp and warm on her legs, as though she were swimming in very warm water. She tried to fall asleep in spite of the impression, not wanting to know what it was, and then suddenly she felt her whole belly seized as though in a giant vise, and she awoke with a start, knowing instantly what she was feeling.

"Damn . . ." she muttered softly. All the women she knew went into labor gently. They had mild pains for hours and wondered if what they were feeling was even labor, instead she leaped into it with both feet. But as she sat up in bed she remembered what both Teddy and her English doctor had told her. She knew she had to hurry if she didn't want to have another baby in her bed, and this time there was no one to help her. She got out of bed as quickly as she could, but she suddenly felt very awkward, the baby had dropped even lower in the past few hours, and she felt severely encumbered as she walked to the bathroom for some towels. As soon as she got there she had another pain, and she had to pant softly in order to bear it. She straightened up then, grabbed a dress off a hanger, pulled off her nightgown, slipped on the cotton dress, slipped her feet into sandals, and grabbed her handbag. She began to laugh softly to herself, feeling excited as she had almost nine years before. To hell with Vasili. She would leave him as soon as she had the baby. All she had to do now was wake Vanessa and get to the hospital. It was the maid's night out, and she couldn't leave Vanessa alone in the house with no one there with her. Particularly not with Vasili drifting in and out. She would never leave her alone with him.

She made her way gingerly down the stairs and walked into Vanessa's room. She shook her gently by the shoulder, bent to kiss her, smoothed her hair, and then gasped suddenly as she knelt beside the bed, but when Vanessa woke up, the pain was over.

"Come on, sweetheart, it's time to go."

"Time to go where?"

"To the hospital to have the baby."

"Now?" Vanessa looked startled and when she glanced out the window, she saw that it was still dark outside. Serena only wished that she could have waited until the arrival of the two uncles. Vanessa would just have to come to the hospital with her. They would set up a cot for her in another room if they had to. And she knew that Teddy would be there by Tuesday.

"Come on, love, get up. Just hop into some clothes and take a nightie. And a book," she added as an afterthought, and then she gasped as a horrifying pain ripped through her.

"Oh, Mommy!" Vanessa leaped out of bed, unprepared for the agony she saw on her mother's face. "Mommy, are you all right? Mommy!"

"Ssshhh . . . darling, I'm fine." Serena gritted her teeth and tried to smile. "Be a big girl and call a taxi . . . and hurry!"

Vanessa ran downstairs in her nightgown, carrying blue jeans and a T-shirt with her. She dressed while she waited for the cab company to answer, and when they did, she explained that it was an emergency, her mother was having a baby.

The taxi was at the front door less than five minutes later, and Vanessa helped Serena into it. She felt very grown-up as she helped her mother, and less frightened than she had been when she had seen the first pain, but she winced when her mother had another.

"Do they hurt that much?"

"They're just strong so they can push the baby out." Vanessa nodded, but she still looked worried. The pains seem to get harder as they approached the hospital, and when they arrived, Vanessa took the money out of her mother's bag and paid the driver. He smiled at them both and wished Serena luck, and two nurses came out to help Serena into a

359

wheelchair. She was smiling wanly at Vanessa and waving one hand as they wheeled her away, and Vanessa settled down in a corner of the waiting room, assuming that her little brother or sister would be born a few minutes later.

When nothing had happened an hour later, she asked a nurse, but they brushed her off, and by midafternoon she was panicked. Where was her mother? What had happened? Why hadn't the baby come? "These things take time," a nurse told her. When the shift changed at four o'clock, the nurses were kinder to Vanessa. No one understood why she was in the waiting room all alone, but finally someone realized that no one was coming for her and the poor child hadn't even eaten. She had complained to no one for fourteen long hours, and when finally one of the nurses brought her a sandwich, she burst into tears.

"Where's my mother? What happened? Why didn't she have the baby?" And then with huge eyes, "Is she going to die?" But when they smiled and told her that that was nonsense, she didn't believe them. When they left her alone again, she wandered off and began to drift down the halls, until she came to an ominous room with a smoky glass door marked LABOUR. As though she sensed what she would find within, she straightened her shoulders and slipped inside, and what she saw there made her gasp sharply. It was her mother, lying on a white table, her legs strapped onto what looked like boards high in the air, her face contorted with pain, her hands restrained, her blond hair matted, and her mouth open in a scream.

"Mommy!" Vanessa was instantly in tears as she came toward her, and there was no one in the room with Serena. "Mommy!" She instinctively began to free her hands and Serena looked at her blindly. It took her a moment to recognize her own child and then she began to cry as hard as Vanessa.

"Oh, my baby . . . my baby . . ." As her hands were freed she touched the long golden blond hair, and then suddenly she clutched Vanessa's shoulder. The child nearly screamed out with the pain, and sensing it, Serena freed her, but she was unable to restrain a horrible groan.

"What's wrong . . . oh, Mommy, what's wrong?"

360

Vanessa's eyes were huge with terror. Her mother was drenched with sweat and she was a ghostly color.

"The baby's . . . turned . . . around . . ." And then, as though she suddenly had a thought. "Vanessa . . . ask them for . . . my bag . . . I have money . . . call Teddy. Do you know . . . the number?" Vanessa nodded, still desperately afraid. "Tell him—" But she couldn't go on then, the pain was too ferocious. It was several minutes before she could start again. "Tell him the baby's breech . . . *breech*. Understand?" Vanessa nodded. "They tried to turn him and they couldn't. They're giving me a few more hours and they'll keep trying . . . go on . . ." Her eyes looked desperately at her daughter. "Tell him . . . tell him to come now, today. And hurry." Vanessa nodded again, and hesitated, but after the next pain her mother begged her to get her bag, find a phone, and call Teddy without waiting another minute.

Vanessa had a difficult time getting the nurses to let her have her mother's handbag, but when they realized that she didn't even have money to eat, they finally relented. She then stealthily went to a phone booth down the hall, closed the door, and put the money in to call the operator and make a collect call to Teddy. It was seven o'clock at night in London by then, but in New York it was only one in the afternoon and she knew that she would find him at his office.

"Dr. Fullerton?" The nurse sounded surprised. "Yes . . . his niece? I'll get him." Teddy was on the line a minute later, the call was accepted, and Vanessa almost got hysterical as she tried to tell him what she had seen and what her mother had told her.

"She's all tied up, Uncle Teddy, with her legs up in the air, and we've been here since five o'clock this morning, and she says . . . she says . . . the baby's beach, and they tried to turn him and can't, and—" She began to sob into the phone and he tried to calm her.

"It's all right, sweetheart, it's all right. Just tell me what she said."

"They're going to give her a few more hours and keep trying to turn the baby. She wants you to come right away, and she said hurry." At his end he almost burst into tears too. A breech birth three thousand miles away. Even if he caught the next plane, it would be anywhere from twelve to eighteen hours before he got to her. She needed a Caesarean section done immediately, and waiting useless hours to continue trying to turn the baby could kill her and lose the baby.

"It's going to be all right sweetheart," he told Vanessa, wishing he believed it. "Do you know her doctor's name?" At least he could call him, but Vanessa didn't. "The hospital?" She gave it to him quickly. "I'll call them and we'll see if we can't get things moving."

"Can't you come, Uncle Teddy?" It was obvious from her voice that Vanessa was beginning to panic.

"I'm going to catch the next plane, sweetheart, and with any luck at all I'll be there first thing tomorrow morning, your time, but maybe the baby will come before that." It would only be twenty-four hours by then, but he knew that for Serena, strapped to a delivery table, her legs in stirrups, with a breech birth, and a possibly unsympathetic staff continually trying to turn the baby, he could think of no worse torture for her to endure. "Can you get back to Mommy, sweetheart?"

"I'll try. I don't know if they'll let me."

"Tell her I'm coming. Do you know where Vasili is?"

"No, and I don't want him to come. He's crazy."

"I know, I know. I just wondered. Did you leave him a note at the house about where you are?"

"No."

"What about his brother?"

"Mommy said he can't come until the end of the week because his wife is sick."

"Okay, tiger, then you just hold the fort until I get there. Think you can do that? It may be a long night, but I'll be there, and pretty soon it'll be all over." He was already making notes for his secretary. He wouldn't even go back to his apartment. He could buy what he needed in London when he got there. All he would take with him was his medical bag and a briefcase. "I'm very proud of you, Vanessa darling. You're doing great."

"But Mommy—"

362

"She's going to be fine too. I promise. Sometimes it's a little hard having a baby, but it isn't always like that, and when it's all over and she has the baby, she won't even mind it. I promise."

"She looks like she's dying." Vanessa's voice broke on a sob, and Teddy prayed that Vanessa was wrong. But she might not be.

Five minutes after they hung up he called the hospital, spoke to the nurse in charge, and was unable to speak to a doctor. Mrs. Arbus, according to them, was doing fine. The baby was indeed breech, but they felt no need for a Caesarean as yet. They were going to wait until, at the very least, the following morning. And no, they had been unable to turn the baby, but they had every confidence that subsequent efforts would set matters aright. Subsequent efforts would mean that when Serena was in midpain, a nurse or an intern would shove both hands as far in as they could get them and try to turn the baby upside down. The very thought of it was almost more than he could bear when he thought of Serena. He went straight from his office to the airport and checked in at Idlewild at two thirty. The next flight to London left at four, and he called the hospital again. There was no change, but this time they sounded slightly more impressed. Not all of their patients had attending physicians flying in from New York.

The four-o'clock flight was due to reach London at two-o'clock the next morning, which was eight o'clock in the morning in London. He assumed that with any luck at all he could reach the hospital by nine or nine thirty. It was the best he could do, and once he was on the flight, he explained to the steward what he was doing. He was flying to London to deliver a baby by Caesarean with complications for a very important patient. What he needed was a police escort or an ambulance to take him as quickly as possible from the airport to the hospital. The steward spoke at once to the captain, the message was passed along once they established radio contact with London, and when they arrived, Teddy was whisked through customs, out a side door to a waiting ambulance, the sirens were put on, and they sailed through the streets on the way to London. Luck had also been on their side, the flight had arrived half an hour early. It was exactly five minutes after eight when Teddy stepped out of the ambulance into the streets of London. He thanked the ambulance driver, gave him an enormous tip, rushed inside, inquired for the maternity ward, and ran up the stairs, his bag in his hand, to emerge into a large unfriendly waiting room, where he saw Vanessa asleep in a chair. He hurried to the desk, spoke to a nurse, and she looked extremely startled.

"From America? For Mrs. Arbus?" She immediately went to get the head nurse, who in turn found the doctor on duty. Mrs. Arbus's physician had not actually been at the hospital for several hours, but of course if Dr. Fullerton had the proper credentials with him, perhaps if a Caesarean was indeed needed in due course, he would be able to assist the British surgeon. Teddy immediately presented the papers they would need, washed his hands, and asked to see Serena. And with a large entourage behind him he was led to the door where Vanessa had found her thirteen hours before. She lay almost breathless, semiconscious, drenched in sweat, and so stunned by the pain that she seemed to be barely breathing as Teddy got to her. He looked down at her, took her pulse, listened to the baby's heart. There seemed to be no sign of recognition from her. Her heartbeat was frantic and faint, the baby's was beginning to fade, and her blood pressure was so low that he wondered if they could even save her. Without thinking, he gave rapidfire orders to prepare her for surgery. He wanted to kill someone for not doing it twenty-four hours sooner. When he examined her to see how low the baby had come, he saw what they had done to her by continually trying to turn the baby, and it horrified him to see the condition she was in. He wanted to sweep her into his arms and carry her away from the nightmare she had suffered, but as he unstrapped her legs and laid her gently flat on the table and they began to wheel her away, she stirred and looked at him strangely.

"You look . . ." It was the barest of hoarse croaks. ". . . like . . . Teddy."

"I am Teddy, Serena. Everything's going to be okay. Vanessa called me, and we're going to take the baby by Caesarean." She nodded, and then a moment later she was screaming with the pain again. They rolled her directly into the operating theater, a young doctor appeared, a little flustered by the unusual procedures, and without further ado the anesthetic was given, and after scrubbing up and returning in operating-room garb, Teddy began to make the incision on Serena. The anesthetist and two of the nurses were keeping close tabs on her failing heart. Teddy felt himself working steadily against the clock as he could see her dying rapidly beneath his fingers. And a moment later he had the child, a perfectly formed, beautiful little baby girl, but as they brought her out of the womb there was no cry, she wasn't breathing, and he knew that he was about to lose both the baby and Serena. He gave terse instructions to the nurses who stood by as he continued the surgery on Serena. Every effort was made to keep her alive, and a pediatrician was summoned to help the nurses and the young doctor with their attempts to get the baby breathing. It seemed an eternity before they heard the first cry, but suddenly the room was filled with her lusty sounds, and at almost the same moment the anesthetist reported that Serena's blood pressure was rising slowly and her heartbeat was finally regular. He wanted to give a whoop of joy, but he still had work to do, and when it was all over, he looked down at the sleeping woman he had loved for so many years, and in a most unprofessional gesture he leaned down to her cheek and kissed her.

The operating-room staff congratulated him on his brilliant and speedy maneuvers, and he followed them slowly out of the operating theater. Both Serena and the baby were going to be all right, but he still had to see Vanessa. The poor child had been through an ordeal of her own, and when he reached her side at ten fifteen, she was still sleeping. He sat down beside her and as though she sensed him, she looked up with a puzzled frown, and he smiled at her. "Hi, kiddo. You have a big fat baby sister."

"I do?" Vanessa sat up, stunned. "How do you know? Did you see her?"

"I sure did. I delivered her myself."

"You did?" She threw her arms around his neck. "Oh, Uncle Teddy, you're terrific!" And then with an anxious look in her eyes, "How's my mom?"

"She's asleep." And then he explained about the Caesarean section.

"It sounds awful." She made a grim face. "I don't ever want to have a baby. They had her all tied up, and"—her voice drifted away as she remembered—"she was screaming . . . I thought she was going to die. . . ." He put an arm around her shoulders.

"But she didn't. She's fine. And the baby is so cute. Do you want to see her?"

"Will they let me?"

"If they won't, I'll tell them you're my nurse."

Vanessa giggled, and after a hushed conversation with the head nurse they led Teddy and Vanessa down the hall to a big picture window. There were at least two dozen babies there, but they held up "Arbus, baby girl" for Vanessa to see, and as she looked into her sister's face, she saw exactly what Teddy had seen when he delivered her. "She looks just like Mommy!" Vanessa looked stunned. "Except she has black hair." But she did look exactly like her mother. She was a tiny perfect mirror image of Serena. "She's too pretty, isn't she, Uncle Teddy?"

He put a hand on Vanessa's shoulder and looking at the baby with a small tired smile, he nodded. "Yes, she is."

CHAPTER FORTY-FOUR

Andreas arrived, as promised, at the end of that week and found Vasili in a stuporous state in his bedroom. He hadn't bathed in a week, his skin was broken out, his hair was matted to his head, his eyes were sunken and darkly ringed, and he was wearing a filthy bathrobe. Andreas tried to urge him to clean up before they left, but he was nodding out, and he saw with distaste and despair the hypodermic on the table. He also noticed a yellowish tinge about his brother's face, and feared that he had hepatitis. In the end he had to get his driver to help Vasili out of his chair, and they led him, just as he was, to the car and drove him directly to the hospital. He had not been to see his wife, recovering slowly from her ordeal and the emergency surgery. He had not seen his daughter, and he was barely aware that the baby had been born, when Andreas left him at the clinic.

"He's in bad shape this time," he told Serena bluntly when he came to see her. "But he should be all right soon." He didn't mention the serum hepatitis they had confirmed at the hospital and for a long moment she said nothing. And then she sighed. She was still in a great deal of pain, and the truth of what she had to do about Vasili had been nagging at her all morning.

"I think I'm going to divorce him, Andreas."

"And go back to the States?" Andreas looked crushed. He was fond of her and the child, and yet another part of him wanted them free of the nightmare.

"I think so. There's no reason for me to stay here." Having got pregnant so soon, she had never really established herself in London as a model. And now she had two children to support, instead of one. "I can go back to work in New York."

He spoke slowly and sadly. "You won't have to." Serena didn't answer. "Serena, if he cleans up again, will you give him one more chance?"

"Why, what would be different this time? According to him, he's been doing this for the last ten years."

"But it's different now. He has you and the baby." Andreas had been awed by the beautiful little baby girl. But Serena suspected that Vasili was going to be less impressed than Andreas.

"He's had us for the past year. Me anyway, and Vanessa. It hasn't changed a thing."

"But now he'll have the baby." He smiled then. "What will you call her?"

"Charlotte." And then she smiled at him. "Charlotte Andrea." He looked as though he would burst into tears, he was so pleased, and leaned down and kissed Serena.

"You're a beautiful girl." And then with a tone of sorrow, "I shouldn't let you waste yourself on my brother. But . . . I hate to see him lose you and the child." He stood up slowly then, and she saw that he was really a very attractive man. In his own way he was better-looking than Vasili. He had none of the dissipation, or the mischief, or the boyish good looks. What he had instead was an air of distinction, the same handsome face, and an aura about him that was all man. "Do what seems best for you. I know that you will, and if you go, let me know where I can find you, Serena. One day I will come to New York to visit my namesake." Serena inquired for his wife, and he avoided her gaze. He didn't want to face what was coming. Instead he kissed her gently on the cheek and left her to her own thoughts. She had as yet heard nothing from Vasili. But the day before she was to leave the hospital, she was walking slowly down the hall on the arm of a nurse, and she suddenly saw him. He looked clean, handsome, and very much like himself, but also desperately frightened, and for a moment when she saw him, she wondered if he would run away. She stopped walking and stood there, leaning heavily on the nurse's arm and wishing that she could run away quickly, but she couldn't, and he walked slowly toward her, and then he stood very still.

"Hello, Serena."

"Hello." She felt her knees turn to jelly beneath her. Part of her wanted to see him, and part of her wanted him to go away, perhaps forever this time.

"Are you all right?" She nodded, and the nurse began to squirm, sensing that this was an awkward meeting. "The baby?"

"She's fine. Have you seen her?"

"Not yet. I wanted to see you first. I just . . . I . . . uh . . ." He glanced at the nurse. "I just got back to town today." She noticed how pale he looked. The detox was always quick, but it took him a long time to look decent, and this time he had a slight cast of yellow to his skin. She knew what it was, but she also knew that the hepatitis one caught from needles was not contagious. But she was sorry as hell he had come. She didn't want to see him.

"Do you think we could talk?" She motioned toward her room, and the nurse led her back there slowly. When she got there, she lay down on her bed and she looked exhausted. Vasili was looking at her strangely, and then he hung his head and she saw that he was trying not to cry. "I don't know what to say to you, Serena."

"I don't think there's anything left to say, Vasili." For the first time in a long time, when she looked at him, she felt nothing. No disgust, no anger, no sorrow, no love. In her heart there was silence.

His head shot up and the black eyes met her green. "What do you mean, there's nothing left to say?"

"Just that. What can one say after all we've been through? I'm sorry? Good luck? Good-bye?"

"We could try again." His voice was sad and soft. But to her he still looked like a junkie. To her he always would. She would never forgive him.

"Could we? Why?"

"Because I love you."

"That's what you said before." She looked at him accusingly then. "If you'd been around and sober, I might not have almost died having this baby. Did you know that I almost died and we almost lost the baby? If Vanessa hadn't come to find me and called Teddy, we'd both be dead now."

"I know." The tears crept slowly out of his eyes. "Andreas told me."

"Could you have lived with that?" He shook his head, and then looked up at her again.

"I can't forgive myself for anything I've done, and I will understand if you can't forgive me either. But I'm different now, I came so close to losing everything, both you and the baby, and even myself. If we tried again, I know that this time everything will be different."

"I don't believe that anymore. How can you even say it?"

"I can't be sure. But I can tell you that I'll try with my whole soul. I can't give you more than that." He approached the bed slowly and reached for her hand and gently kissed it. "I love you. It sounds like very little, but it's the best I've got. I'll do anything to keep you. I'll beg you . . . I'll crawl . . . Serena, you don't know how much I love you." Her eyes filled with tears and spilled over as she listened. She bowed her head, and stricken, he reached out to hold her. "Oh, darling, please—"

"Go away . . . don't touch me." She didn't want to want him again. She couldn't let herself go through that.

He forced her face up to his then. "Do you still love me?" She shook her head, but her eyes said she did, and when he looked at her, he could see all that she had suffered at his hands and at the birth of their child, and he hated himself for it. "What have I done?" He began to cry, and then suddenly he took her into his arms, and the only sound in the room was that of Serena sobbing. He begged her for another chance, but she was too overcome to answer. And then at last she asked him if he wanted to see the baby.

"I'd love to." And then he remembered something. "Are you going home from the hospital tomorrow?"

"I'm leaving here." Serena blew her nose and avoided his eyes. "But I'm not sure yet if I'm going to the house or a hotel." She was thinking of staying at the same hotel as Teddy, the Connaught, before she made up her mind. He wasn't leaving for the States for a few more days.

"I see." Vasili offered her an arm, and laboriously she took it, making her way slowly out of her room again and down the hall to where they could see the baby through the window. The nurse smiled when she saw Serena, and looked with interest at the man at her side, and then she remembered him from his pictures in the paper, but he looked very different. Nonetheless she recognized him and she was impressed, as she picked up his baby girl and held her up for him to see for the first time. He stood mesmerized by the tiny child with Serena's face and his shining black hair, and tears filled his eyes again as he watched her and silently put an arm around Serena.

"She's so beautiful, and so small."

Serena smiled. "She looks big to me. Eight and a half pounds is big for a baby."

"Is it?" He grinned down at his wife with pride. "She's so perfect."

370

"Wait until you hold her."

"Does she cry a lot?"

Serena shook her head and for a few minutes she told him about the baby, and then he took her back to her room and they looked at each other. "Serena, can't we try it again? I don't want to lose you. Not now . . . not ever."

Trembling, she closed her eyes, and then she opened them again. She still loved him, and she owed the baby something, at least to try one more time, but she was afraid that if he used drugs again the horror of it would destroy her. But she felt so torn between what she owed herself and what she thought she owed the baby. "All right. We'll try it once more." It was barely a whisper. "But if you do it again, it's over. Do you understand?" She knew she should take her children and go now, but his magic still worked on her. He was still dug deep under her skin.

"I understand." He came to her then and kissed her, and in the kiss was all the ache that he felt over the pain he had caused her. He promised to pick her up to bring her home the next day, and as he left the room, with a sigh she reached for the phone to call Teddy, wondering how to explain this new madness to him. She knew it was wrong, and yet she wanted to think it was right. And she couldn't, and now she had to justify it to Teddy.

CHAPTER FORTY-FIVE

When Serena came home from the hospital with the baby, the house looked as thought it had been redone. There was still the striking white and chrome modern decor, with the enormous pastel paintings. But Vasili had been busy. There were flowers everywhere for her, mountains of gifts and equipment and goodies for the baby, a stack of dolls and new toys for Vanessa. He had bought them everything he could

think of, including an incredible diamond bracelet for
Serena. As before when they had tried again, he couldn't do
enough for them, and the first time he held the baby, his
face looked like a male Madonna. He was totally enthralled
by the tiny creature, and completely enamored with her
mother. He couldn't be with them enough, and he could
hardly wait until Serena could get out with him a little. After
two weeks at home she was allowed to go for walks nearby.
And after another week he took the baby and Vanessa out
with the pram for their first outing. By then it was early
September, the weather was balmy, and Vanessa had gone
back to school. She was in fourth grade now, and her ninth
birthday was approaching.

"Happy, darling?" He looked at her proudly as they
strolled along, his camera around his neck. He had already
taken hundreds of pictures of the baby.

"Very much so." But there was something subdued
about Serena now, as though she was never happy anymore
as she had once been. He sensed it and at times it made him
very nervous. He was always afraid now that one day she
would leave him. It was as though the days in the Garden of
Eden were truly over.

They went back to the house that afternoon and played
with the baby. He had still not gone back to work after his
own stint in the hospital to recover from his addiction. Now
he wanted time with Serena and the baby, and Serena began
to wonder if his constant absences weren't beginning to
affect his career. But Vasili didn't seem to care, and a few
days later he said he was going to attend to some business in
Paris. He left in great spirits and told her that he would call
her from over there, but he didn't. When she tried to reach
him at the apartment, she couldn't, and eventually she gave
up, and assumed that she would hear from him, but once
again the worries set in. She didn't know for sure until he
walked back into the house in London a week later, and she
felt her heart sink to her feet as she saw him. It was all over.
He had lost the battle again, and the signs of heroin were all
over him. She looked at him, feeling as though the end of the
world had finally come, but she said not a word to him. She
went upstairs, packed her bags, called Teddy, and made

reservations on the next plane. And then, trembling from head to foot, she set her bags on the floor just as Vasili walked into the room.

"What exactly do you think you are doing?"

"I'm leaving you, Vasili. I made it perfectly clear in the hospital. If you used again, I left. You're using. I'm leaving. I have nothing to say. It's all over." She felt tired more than anything else, exhausted to her very soul, and a little bit frightened of what he would do or say. He was always so erratic when he was on drugs. But she didn't care what he did now. It was over.

"I am not using, you're crazy." Just hearing him say it made her angry.

"No." She looked at him in white fury. "You're crazy, and I'm getting the hell out while I can. Nothing matters to you except that shit you put in your arm. I don't understand why you do it, you have every reason not to, but since none of that makes a damn bit of difference to you, I'm leaving." She spat the words at him. "Good-bye."

"And you think you can take my baby?"

"Yes, I can. Try to stop me and I'll have it in every newspaper in the world that you're a junkie." She looked at him with raw hatred, and even in his drugged state he knew she meant it.

"Blackmail, Serena?" He raised an eyebrow and she nodded.

"That's right, and don't think I won't do it. Your career will be over then and there."

"You think I give a damn about that? You're crazy. What do I care about some lousy pictures for an ad or a magazine?"

"I guess not much or you wouldn't be using. Not to mention me and the baby. I don't suppose we weighed much with you either."

He looked at her strangely for a moment. "I don't suppose you did."

He disappeared again that night, and when she left the house with the children the next morning, he hadn't returned yet. She got to the airport with Vanessa and the baby and the suitcases she had brought and the things she needed for the baby, and they got on the plane with no problem. Ten hours later they landed in New York, exactly thirteen months after they had left it. Serena looked around her at the airport after they landed, and wondered if she was in a dream. For the first time in her life leaving had not been painful. She was totally numb. She moved as though in a daze, with the baby in her arms and Vanessa clinging to her hand. For an odd moment she had the same feeling she had had arriving with the nuns and other children during the war, and as the thought crossed her mind the tears began to slide down her face, and she began to sob when she saw Teddy, as if seeing him unleashed the feelings in her.

He led them all gently out to his car and then drove them to the furnished apartment he had rented for a month. Serena looked around at the stark little room, clutching the baby to her. There was only one bedroom, but she didn't care. All she wanted was to be three thousand miles away from Vasili. She had almost no money with her, but she had brought the diamond bracelet he'd given her last month and she was going to sell it. With luck it would give her enough funds to subsist until her modeling picked up again. She had already asked Teddy to call Dorothea.

"Well, how does it feel to be back?" Teddy smiled at her, but there was concern in his eyes. Serena looked worn out and Vanessa looked scarcely better.

"I think I'm still numb" was Serena's only answer as she looked around her. The walls were bare and white, and the furniture was Danish modern.

"The Ritz it ain't," he apologized with a smile, and for the first time she laughed.

"Teddy, my love, I couldn't care less. It's a roof over our heads, and we're not in London." Vanessa smiled too, and Teddy reached out for the baby.

"How's my little friend?"

"Hungry all the time." Serena smiled.

"Unlike her mother who looks like she never eats." She had lost all the weight she'd gained while she was pregnant, along with an additional fifteen pounds. And all in the six weeks, since the birth of the baby.

"If I'm going to model again, it's just as well. What did

Dorothea say, by the way?''

"That she awaits you with bated breath, as does every photographer in New York." Serena looked pleased.

"Well, that's good news." But the best news of all, to her, was that she had escaped Vasili. There had been a time when she thought she never would, that she would be trapped with him forever. It had been like escaping from a jungle. But it was all over now, and Vasili knew it. She had told Andreas too. And she hoped that she never saw Vasili again. She had listened to enough lies and suffered enough trauma to last her for a lifetime.

"Do you think he'll follow you over here?" Teddy asked when Vanessa had gone to bed.

"It won't do him any good. I won't see him."

"And the baby?"

"I don't think he'll really care. He's too involved in himself and his drugs."

"Don't be so sure. From what you said he was crazy about her."

"Not enough to stop using heroin though."

"I still can't believe it."

"Neither can I. Sometimes I wonder if I'll ever be the same again."

"You will. Give it time." She had survived so much in her life that he felt sure she would survive this too. And he thanked God she had left Vasili.

She sighed and closed her eyes before facing him again. "I don't know, Teddy. I guess you're right, but it's been such a nightmare, it's hard to understand what happened. You know . . . I think that stuff makes him crazy."

"It's pathetic." She changed the subject then and they discussed a school for Vanessa. The poor child had been through a great deal in the past six weeks. Serena was almost inclined to give her some time off from school while she readjusted, and all Vanessa wanted to do anyway was take care of the baby. She was totally enamored of her baby sister, whom she called Charlie, instead of Charlotte. Serena could hardly get the baby away from Vanessa when it was time to go to bed, and Vanessa was marvelous with her.

"She's a great kid." Teddy spoke of his niece with obvious pride and Serena laughed.

"Yes, she is."

He left them alone then to settle into the apartment, and Serena fell into bed after feeding the baby. She slept a deep dreamless sleep and woke up feeling slightly less exhausted.

She went to the Kerr Agency a few days later, and Dorothea looked at her pointedly with a hand on one hip.

"I told you, didn't I?" She grinned at Serena. "But I sure am happy to have you back."

"Not as happy as I am to be here." They had a cup of coffee, and Dorothea gave her the latest gossip around New York. There was a new girl in town who had been the rage since the summer. She was German and looked a little like Serena, but Dorothea felt certain that there was still room for "The Princess" too. "They've missed you, there's no doubt about it." She could also see that there was something new and interesting in her face since she'd had the baby. She was even thinner than she had been, and there was something wiser and more serious about her eyes. It was that that told Dorothea she had been through an ordeal with Vasili.

"And what about Vasili? It's all over?"

"Finished."

"Forever?" Serena nodded and said nothing. "Want to tell me why?"

But she only shook her head and patted her old friend's hand. "No, love, I don't. And you don't want to know. It was like going to a place I thought I would never come back from. And now that I'm here, I don't want to remember or reminisce, or even think about going back. My only pleasant memory of the past year is Charlie, and she's here with me."

"Thank God." Dorothea looked impressed. Serena's year with Vasili had apparently been worse than she had suspected.

By the end of the week Vasili had started calling the agency, and Dorothea thought she was going to go nuts. He wanted to know where Serena was, where he could find her, how he could call her. Serena had given out strict instructions not to tell him. It was only when one of the models happened to answer the phone for someone, as a favor, that Vasili struck pay dirt. She looked up Serena's number and address among the file cards, and gave it to him without a second thought, having no idea of what she had just done.

The next day he flew to New York to find her, and when he reached her apartment, he found her about to go out. "Serena . . ." She opened the door and heard her name and almost jumped out of her skin when she saw him. She could tell by his eyes that he was still using and obviously half out of his mind and she backed slowly into the apartment. The children were in the living room with the baby-sitter and she wanted to slam the door but he shoved his way past her, muttering darkly that he had to see his baby and that she couldn't do this to him, and she slammed down her portfolio and watched him look down at Charlie, as she felt the old fear and anger well up inside her. All the ugliness of the past year seemed to dance before her eyes as he turned to face her, his eyes cloudy and wild.

"How the hell did you find me?" Her voice was sharp and her eyes were blazing. She had come three thousand miles to escape him and now here he was again.

"I had to." He stared at her blankly. "You're my wife." The baby-sitter sat there staring at him, looking frightened, and Vanessa instinctively reached over and took the baby protectively into her arms. She was watching her mother grow angrier by the moment and Vasili looked as though he were totally crazed. "Why didn't you come back?"

"I'm not ever coming back. And I don't want to discuss this here." She glanced worriedly at the children. Vanessa had seen enough of this in the past, and she didn't want her seeing more now.

"Then, let's go in there." He pointed to the bedroom, and Serena followed him into it with long angry strides, "I want you to come home!" He turned to face her, and she shook her head from side to side.

"No. Do you understand? No! I am never coming back to you, Vasili. Now get out of my house and get out of my life."

"I won't!" He was shrieking. "You took my baby, and you're my wife, you have to come home to me if I tell you."

"I don't have to do a damn thing. You're a bloody junkie and you almost destroyed me and my children—"

"But I didn't, I didn't . . ." he interrupted her. "I love you . . . I love you . . . I love you . . ." And as he said the words he advanced on her, his maddened black eyes flashing into hers, his hands instinctively closing on her throat and squeezing harder and harder and harder, and she suddenly began to choke and then turned purple as he shouted, "I love you! . . . I love you! . . . I love you!" In the room beyond, Vanessa heard him, but after a few minutes she didn't hear her mother, and suddenly terrified, sensing that something was amiss, she burst through the door, with the baby still in her arms. What she saw in the bedroom was Vasili, kneeling, sobbing, on the floor, his hands still around Serena's neck, as she lay with her head twisted at an odd angle, her eyes open, her portfolio spilled out on the floor.

"What have you done to my mother?" She shrieked at him, clutching Charlie.

"I've killed her," he said softly. "Because I love her." And then sobbing hysterically, he collapsed on the floor beside Serena.

CHAPTER FORTY-SIX

The publicity for the next two weeks was of international proportions. The death of Serena Fullerton Arbus caused no small stir. Her background, her parents' death, her marriage to Brad and then to Vasili, were all exposed again and again in the press. His history of heroin use became public knowledge, his marriages were rehashed, his stays in mental hospitals to dry up, were discussed at length. And the hint of a custody battle over the children was superficially mentioned. It was a scandal second to no other, but the main issue at hand was the children's fate. Just as Brad, when he died five years earlier, Serena had left no will. And whereas her remaining funds could be evenly divided between her daughters, the biggest question was where and with whom they would live. Would both stay together or would it become a war of *Fullerton* v. *Arbus?* A custody hearing was set for late in October, in which all of the parties would be heard and, hopefully, the matter decided. Teddy wanted to adopt both of Serena's children, and his mother was appalled. In fact she promised to stop him. "I won't allow it. God knows what those children will turn out to be with a mother like that, and in the baby's case a history of murder and drugs."

"And Vanessa? Can you think of something unkind to say about her too?" He was furious with his mother. He had been grief-stricken and numb ever since Serena's death, and even in the midst of the horror she had no kindness to spare for her only grandchild, and it soured the last of his feelings for her. Only Pattie seemed unusually sympathetic. Most of the time now Greg was too drunk to give a damn. But Pattie spoke constantly about what she read in the papers, and said that it was tragic that all of this should have happened to Brad's only child. For a time Teddy was touched at her concern for Vanessa, but as the days went by, it seemed to become an obsession with her and it made him nervous. She called him at the office to discuss it, and a few days before the matter was to be heard, she asked for the name of the judge.

"Why?"

"I'm wondering if Daddy knew him."

"What difference would it make?"

"It might make things a little more pleasant."

"For whom?"

"Why, Vanessa, of course. Maybe he'd be kinder and make the arrangements more quickly." It didn't make a lot of sense to Teddy but it made some, so he told her. He assumed that she could have found out anyway, if she wanted to badly enough. He had enough on his hands with worrying about Vanessa. But the children had been living with him since their mother's death, and Vasili had been locked up at Bellevue, pending an immigration hearing. His brother had been doing everything possible to get extradition. He had promised that if they would allow Andreas to take him to Athens they would put him in a hospital there. What he was terrified of was a murder trial for his brother. He was deathly afraid that Vasili would never get out of jail.

But Teddy's worries were even greater. Vanessa had been in a kind of stupor ever since she had seen her mother killed. She had begun screaming that morning, and the baby-sitter said she had screamed until the police came, and then they had gently led her away. She had clutched Charlie to her until Teddy arrived and took the baby from her. He had taken both children home with him, called a doctor for Vanessa, got a nurse for the baby, and since then he had taken Vanessa to the doctor several times. She seemed to have totally blanked out everything that happened, and she seemed to remember absolutely nothing from day to day. She moved through each day like a little robot, and when Teddy tried to hold her, she just shoved him away. The only one she wanted and whose love she would accept was little Charlotte, whom she would hold in her arms and croon to for hours. But she never mentioned her mother, and the doctor had told Teddy not to say a word. At some point it would all come back to her, it was only a question of when. It could take twenty years, the doctor warned him, but in the meantime it was important that she not be pushed.

As a result Teddy saw to it that she didn't go to the funeral. It was almost more than he could bear himself. The only woman he had truly loved had been murdered, and he went alone and stood in the second pew, his eyes riveted to the casket, tears pouring silently down his cheeks, as he longed just to touch her once more . . . to see her walk across the room, beautiful and proud, her green eyes dancing. He couldn't believe that she was gone and he felt empty to the depths of his soul without her.

He too was still in shock, in a way, as he filed into the courtroom and the judge began the custody hearing. He tried to force himself to think rationally as the judge droned on. A petition was filed by Teddy's attorney, offering to take custody of both girls, and he had hoped to convince the judge that it was a sensible decision. The only obstacle was Andreas Arbus, who explained quietly to the judge that arrangements had been made in Athens to quietly put Vasili away. The immigration officials and the district attorney's office had approved it that morning. They would be leaving for Athens, with two guards, later that day. But, he went on to explain to the judge, since the child so recently born to Serena had no other blood relations, he felt it imperative that he take her back to Athens too, to grow up among her cousins and aunts and uncles who would love her. It was only right that she should be among her own. The judge seemed to give this some serious attention, and as Teddy tried to catch his breath and prepare the argument that the girls shouldn't be separated, he looked up in astonishment at a petition being made to the judge by an attorney he knew well. It was a petition made on behalf of a Mrs. Gregory Fullerton, who wished to offer to take custody of her niece. Teddy's jaw almost fell open as he listened while she claimed that she and her husband had been fond of the child for years, and while her brother-in-law was of course a suitable father, there was no mother for Vanessa in his home since he was single.

Again the judge seemed impressed with what was argued, and Teddy thought frantically of how to stop them, before the worst could come. Why in God's name did Pattie want Vanessa? he wondered—except that she was Brad's child and she could have no children of her own. Could she still love him after all these years? But that was crazy. Or was it simply a final act of vengeance against Serena? To steal her child from her now that she was dead, as Serena had stolen Brad from Pattie in Rome. Greg was a drunk. Pattie was vicious. There was nothing maternal about her. He made whispered remarks to his attorney, an objection was made, which was discussed with the judge, but half an hour later it was all over. Charlotte Andrea Arbus was awarded to her paternal uncle, since Teddy was no blood relation to the baby, and Vanessa Theodora Fullerton was awarded to her paternal aunt and uncle, Gregory and Patricia Fullerton, because Theodore Fullerton, as a single man, had a less suitable home in which she would live.

Pattie stood in the courtroom, smiling victoriously as they watched Vanessa being led in, with the baby in her arms, and the judge explained to her what had happened.

"You're giving him Charlie?" Vanessa looked at Andreas with such shock and hatred that it frightened Teddy to watch her eyes. "You can't do that, she's mine. She was my mommy's." But the judge insisted and when she resisted them, a bailiff simply took the baby away, handed it to Andreas, and with tears in his eyes, he attempted to talk to the older child. But almost as though she had become catatonic, Vanessa didn't hear him. She just sat on the floor of the courtroom, rocking back and forth. Teddy rushed forward and signaled to Andreas that it was best for him to go quickly, and Teddy reached out and touched the child he loved. He didn't even have time to give a last glance at Charlie. She was gone forever before he could turn his head.

"Vanessa . . ." His voice was firm but it didn't reach her. "Baby, it's all right. I'm here. Everything's going to be all right."

"Can we go home now?" She turned her eyes to his at last, and it was as though she had retreated yet another step. And this time he was obliged to shake his head.

"You're going to go home with your aunt Pattie, sweetheart. She wants you to come and stay with her."

"Not with you?" Her eyes filled with tears. "Why."

"That's what the judge wanted, so you'd have an aunt and an uncle like a mommy and daddy."

"But I need you, Uncle Teddy." She was pathetic as she sat there, and held up her arms to him.

"I need you too, sweetheart." It was almost more than he could bear. "But I'll come to see you. And you'll be happy with Uncle Greg and Aunt Pattie." He felt like a liar and a beast for what he was saying. He couldn't imagine her anything but miserable with Greg and Pattie, who were total strangers to her, but for the moment they had to comply with what had been ruled in the courts. The matter of Charlotte he knew was over. What the judge had said was true. He had no blood claim on the child, only his love for her mother, and that would never hold up in court. But with Vanessa it was a different matter, he and the child had a relationship that had been built up over nine years.

And as he watched his sister-in-law lead Vanessa from the courtroom, he decided to appeal.

"Do I have a chance?" he asked his lawyer as they watched Vanessa glance back over her shoulder helplessly as she left with Pattie.

"We can try," his lawyer answered. "We can always try."

Teddy nodded then and followed him from the courtroom, his face grim.

CHAPTER FORTY-SEVEN

When Teddy went to see Vanessa at Pattie and Greg's apartment, it tore at his heart in a way that nothing ever had before. She sat in her room, staring out the window, and when he spoke to her, she seemed to hear nothing he said. She didn't stir until he touched her shoulder and shook it gently, calling her name. Then she turned to him with wide, empty eyes that told him almost more of her grief than he could bear.

He tried to talk to Greg about the insanity of Pattie's taking custody of Vanessa, but it was virtually impossible to talk to Greg. He was no longer ever sober past noon. He sat in his office purely to maintain the fiction that he still ran the law firm, but there were other people to do that for him. He only had to sit in his office and drink quietly, and manage not to fall out of his chair. To speak to him coherently about anything, Teddy had to get to him first thing in the morning, which after a week of fruitless efforts he finally did, collaring him in his office only moments after he got there and before he had had time to pour himself a drink.

"For chrissake, man, how can you let her do this? You and Pattie are strangers to that child. She doesn't know you. She needs people she's comfortable with right now. She's lost her mother, her home, her baby sister. The child is in shock, for chrissake. When you look at her, her eyes are glazed." He had been unable to speak to her about anything important, but even discussing trivia, she seemed to shy away. "Pattie doesn't even know her, what's more she hated her mother. What in hell do you want with a nine-year-old girl?"

"I don't." Greg stared at him blankly. "But she does. She always wanted a child." And then he pulled a bottle of bourbon out of his desk, as Teddy stared at him in horror. "She told me once that she always wanted Brad's baby. I can't have any, you know. Got the goddamn clap when I was in school." He shrugged and took his first sip. "I told her before we got married, she said it didn't matter to her." Then he looked up at Teddy with a sad little look in his eyes. "But it did matter. I always knew it. I guess I should have told her before we got engaged but I didn't." He looked up at Teddy sadly and then stared into his drink for a minute. "You know, I don't think she ever really loved me. She married me to get even with Brad. But I don't think he gave a damn what she did. He was crazy about Serena. Pretty girl too, I think Mother has been wrong to carry on the vendetta. Too late now though."

"No, it isn't. You can still do something decent. Let me have Vanessa—she needs me."

Gregg shrugged. "I can't. Pattie's decided that she wants the kid, Teddy, and there isn't a damn thing you or I can do about it. You know how she is. In some ways she's worse than Mother, stubborn and mean and vengeful." He said it helplessly as he finished his first bourbon, but Teddy's eyes narrowed as he looked at him.

"Yes, there is something you can do, dammit. You can refuse to keep the child. Pattie doesn't love Vanessa. I do."

"Do you?" Greg looked at his brother in amazement. "Why? I don't much like kids myself." It was hardly surprising to Teddy. Greg didn't like anyone, least of all himself. Besides, he had been stewed for the past ten years, it was a wonder he even knew he was alive. "I don't know why the hell you'd want her, except"—he looked Teddy over as he poured himself another drink—"you always loved her mother, didn't you?" Teddy didn't answer. "What's wrong with that? I've had a few babes myself in my day." Teddy felt his stomach turn over slowly. His brother was thirty-nine years old, and he talked like a broken-down old man. But the worst of it was that he looked like one too. No one would have guessed his age if they'd seen him. He looked easily to be in his late fifties. The long years of boozing hadn't been kind. "Did you ever sleep with Serena, Teddy?" Greg sat back in his chair with an ugly grin.

"No, if it's any of your damn business. And I'm not here to discuss Serena. I'm here to talk about Vanessa, and why the hell your wife got temporary custody of that child."

"She wants to adopt her." Greg sounded totally without interest in the matter, and inwardly Teddy raged.

"That's totally crazy. She doesn't love her."

"So what, for chrissake? What the hell difference does love make? Do you think our mother loved us? Shit, who knows and who cares."

"Greg." Teddy leaned forward and grabbed his arm before he had time to pour another drink. "Tell the courts you don't want her. Please. The child is miserable with you and Pattie. I'm sorry to be so blunt about it, but all you have to do is look at her. She's dying inside. She doesn't ever see you, she's ill at ease with Pattie. You can't keep her in that household like a prisoner, for chrissake . . ." Teddy's eyes welled up with tears and his brother freed his arm and poured himself another drink.

"So we'll buy her some toys."

"Toys!" Teddy jumped to his feet. "Toys! The child has no father, her mother was just murdered, she has seen her baby sister probably for the last time, and you want to buy her toys. Don't you know what that child needs?"

Greg stared at him in annoyance. "She'll have everything she needs, Teddy. Now, for chrissake, forget about it. You can come to see her when you want to. If you want kids so damn much, get married and have some yourself. Pattie and I can't."

"But you don't want children. And it isn't a question of that, dammit. It's a question of what's right for the child."

"If you don't like it"—Greg got up and strolled the room, and Teddy saw that he was already unsteady on his feet as he glanced over his shoulder—"then take it back to court. They knew what they were doing. They gave the other kid to the Greeks, they gave Brad's kid to us. You don't have a wife, Ted. The kids needs a home with a man and a woman. You can't bring up a child as a bachelor.''

"Why not? If your wife dies, what do you do, put your children up for adoption?''

"She was never your wife?''

"That's not the point.''

"Yes, it is.'' Greg returned to face him. "I think that is the point. You were always in love with that sexy Italian broad Brad married. You hated Pattie, and now you want to rock the boat for me again.''

Teddy looked stunned. "When did I ever rock your boat?''

"Shit?'' Greg snorted and tossed off the last of his drink. "When didn't you? Everything you ever did Dad thought was terrific. You were Mom's baby, and Brad was the star. Every time I started to get their attention, you'd come along and play baby face and fuck up the whole thing.'' He looked petulantly at his younger brother. "I had it up to here with you years ago''—he indicated a line near his eyebrows— "and now you want to make trouble for me with my wife. That woman hasn't got off my back for one thing or another since the day we got married, and if this is what she wants, this is what she gets. I'm sure as hell not going to side with you and make her give the kid back. She'd drive me nuts, so forget it. Just forget it.'' He glared at his brother and poured his third drink in half an hour. "Get the message, buddy? Fuck off!''

Teddy stood there watching him for half a minute, almost detachedly wondering how soon he would die of cirrhosis, and then without another word he turned on his heel and left. His next stop that morning was to his mother, but his results with her were no better than they had been with Greg.

"It's ridiculous.'' Her face had begun to wrinkle badly, but she was still beautiful, and her hair was still the same thick snowy white. "That child doesn't belong in this family. She never did. And now she doesn't belong with you, or Greg and Pattie. They should send her back to those Greeks where she belongs. Let them have her.''

"Christ, you never change do you?" He felt heartsick that no one would help him. He desperately wanted to have Vanessa, because he loved her, and because in a way she was an extension of Serena. But it was precisely that that made his mother hate her. And the fact that she was Brad's that made Pattie want her. "They'll destroy that child. You know that, don't you?"

"That's not my problem, or yours?"

"The hell it's not. She's your grandchild and my niece."

"She's the daughter of a whore." Her voice was vicious and quiet.

"God damn you!" Teddy's eyes filled with tears and he made a gesture as though he might slap his mother, but the violence of his own emotions shocked him, and he turned away, trembling.

"Are you quite finished now?" He didn't answer. "I suggest you leave and don't come back here until you've regained your senses. Your unreasoning passion for that woman has clearly affected your mind. Good afternoon, Teddy."

He left without saying another word and the door closed quietly behind him.

CHAPTER FORTY-EIGHT

The first hearing of the appeal seemed to take forever. It began the week after Christmas and droned on for almost two weeks. Teddy and his attorney presented every kind of evidence they could think of, Pattie and Greg brought out all of Pattie's friends to testify as to how fond they had been of Brad and how much they wanted his daughter. They claimed that Serena had been jealous and that was why they had never been "allowed" to see the child. Their testimony was heavily laced with pure fabrication, and doggedly Teddy attempted to convince the court that his home was the right place for the child. He promised to buy a larger place, to only tend to his practice four days a week, to hire a female housekeeper and a nurse for the child. He brought out people who had seen him over the years with Vanessa. All to no avail, it seemed. And on the last day of testimony the judge requested that they bring forth the child. She was too young to have any say in the matter, but the court wanted to hear her answer some questions. In a little pleated gray skirt and white blouse, shiny Mary Janes and white socks, her shining blond hair in braids, she was led forward by a matron and seated on the stand. Teddy's mother was watching the proceedings as well, but she had taken the stand for no one. She was merely watching, and most of all she had kept an eye on Greg. Miraculously he had stayed sober for all of the court proceedings, and she had pointed out frequently to Teddy that if he were truly an alcoholic he wouldn't have been able to do that. And Teddy said that wasn't true. As it was, they all knew that within ten minutes of leaving the courtroom he was usually too drunk to get out of the car. But that was just tension, his mother insisted. Teddy didn't choose to argue the point, although he had had his lawyer suggest to the court that Mr. Gregory Fullerton had a problem with alcohol. His wife denied it, under oath, on the stand, and the family doctor was so evasive and protective of privileged information, that Teddy ended up looking like a fool for the accusation.

When Vanessa was called, she sat as she always did now, her feet planted on the floor, her arms hanging down beside her, her eyes staring straight ahead. Teddy was never allowed to be alone with her anymore, but he had the impression for months that she was slipping more and more into herself. Her eyes seemed glazed and the child who had been so full of life and her mother's magic was listless, but he could never talk with her long enough to pull her back.

The judge looked at her for a moment before beginning. He didn't want either of the attorneys asking her questions. They had already agreed to let the judge handle the questions, and both sides would attempt to be satisfied with that. But she seemed not to hear the judge at first when he spoke to her, and then finally she turned her face up toward where he sat when she heard her name.

"Vanessa?" His voice was gruff but his eyes were kind. He was a big man and he had grandchildren, and he felt for this child with the bleak gray eyes. They looked liked dead fields in winter, and he suddenly wanted to take her into his arms. "Do you understand why you're here?" She nodded in silence, her eyes wide. "Can you tell us why?"

"Because Uncle Teddy wants me to come and live with him." She glanced at him, but she looked more frightened than pleased. She was frightened by the entire proceedings. It reminded her of something else, but she wasn't sure what. She just knew it hadn't been pleasant, and neither was this.

"Are you fond of your uncle Teddy, dear?" She nodded, and this time she smiled.

"He always comes to help me. And we play good games." The judged nodded.

"When you say that he comes to help you, what do you mean?"

"Like if something bad happens." She began to look more animated than she had. "Like once, when . . ." She began to look troubled and very faraway. ". . . when my mommy was sick . . . he came to get us . . . I don't remember . . ." She looked up vaguely, as though she had forgotten the story, and Teddy narrowed his eyes as he watched her. She had been referring to when Serena was giving birth to Charlotte. But had Vanessa really forgotten, or was she afraid to tell the story? He didn't understand. "I don't remember." She began to look glazed again and sat in the chair staring at her hands.

"It's all right, dear. Do you think you might like living with your uncle Teddy?" She nodded and her eyes searched him out, but there was so little emotion in her face that it was frightening. She looked as though when Serena had died she had died too. "Are you happy in the home of your aunt and uncle now?" She nodded again. "Do they treat you well?"

She nodded and looked at him sadly. "They buy me a lot of dolls."

"That's nice. Are you close to your aunt, Mrs. Fullerton?"

For a long time Vanessa didn't answer and then she shrugged. "Yes."

He felt so sorry for the child, she looked so broken and so lonely. It was obvious that she needed a mother to comfort her. A man just wouldn't be enough. "Do you miss your mother and sister very much?" He said it very gently, as though he really cared, but Vanessa looked up at him in surprise.

"I don't have a sister." She looked blank.

"But you did of course . . . I meant . . ." He looked a little confused and Vanessa stared at him.

"I never had a sister. My daddy died in the war when I was three and a half." She said it as though she were reciting, and where Teddy sat a light dawned in his eyes. He was the first to understand, as Vanessa went on. "And I didn't have any brothers and sisters when he died."

"But when your mother remarried—" The judge persisted with a puzzled frown, and Vanessa shook her little head.

"My mother never remarried."

With this, the judge began to look annoyed, and Teddy whispered something to his attorney who signaled the judge, but he was silenced. "Vanessa, your mother remarried a man named—" But before he could continue, Teddy's lawyer hastened toward the bench. The judge was about to reprimand him, when he whispered urgently to the judge, who raised his eyebrows, looked thoughtful for a moment, and then signaled Teddy to the bench. There was a moment's whispered conference, during which the judge looked both chagrined and worried. He nodded then, and Teddy and the attorney went back to their seats. "Vanessa," the judge went on more slowly, watching the child carefully as he spoke, "I'd like to ask you some questions about your mommy. What do you remember about her?"

"That she was very beautiful." Vanessa said it softly and looked as though she were in a dream. "And she made me very happy."

"Where did you live with her?"

"In New York."

390

"Did you ever live anywhere else with her?"

Vanessa thought for a moment, began to shake her head, and then seemed to remember. "San Francisco. Before my daddy died."

"I see." Now the other attorney was beginning to glance strangely both at Vanessa and the judge, but he signaled him to remain silent. "You never lived anywhere else?" She shook her head. "Have you ever been to London, Vanessa?" She thought about it for a minute and shook her head.

"No."

"Did your mommy ever remarry?"

Vanessa began to squirm and look uncomfortable in her seat, and everyone in the courtroom felt for her. She began to play with her braids and her voice cracked. "No."

"She had no other children?"

The eyes glazed over again. "No."

And then the shocker. "How did your mommy die, Vanessa?" They whole courtroom was stunned into silence and Vanessa only sat there, staring straight ahead. At last, in a wisp of a voice, she spoke. "I don't remember. I think she got sick. In a hospital . . . I don't remember . . . Uncle Teddy came . . . and she died. She got sick. . . ." She began sobbing. "That's what they had told me. . . ."

The judge looked appalled, and he reached down and stroked her hair. "I only have one more question, Vanessa." She went on crying, but she looked up at him at last. "Are you telling me the truth?" She nodded and sniffed. "Do you promise?"

She spoke in a brave little voice with those two shattered eyes. "Yes." And it was obvious that she thought she was.

"Thank you." He signaled for the matron then to take her away and Teddy longed to go to her, but he knew that he couldn't. The door closed behind her, and the courtroom exploded into a hubbub of chatter as the judge pounded his gavel and literally roared at both lawyers. "Why didn't anyone tell me the child was disturbed?" Pattie was put on the stand and insisted that she didn't know it, that she hadn't dared to discuss the murder with Vanessa before. But there was something about the way she testified that told

391

Teddy she was lying. She knew how disturbed Vanessa was, but she didn't give a damn about her, Vanessa was an object—or worse, a prisoner of war. Teddy insisted that he was never allowed enough time with the child to determine anything, although he had begun to suspect it from little things that she said. The hearing was postponed pending further investigation. A psychiatrist was assigned to get a full evaluation of Vanessa before any further decisions were made. Meanwhile the story had leaked to the press and it was all over the headlines that the granddaughter of the Fullertons, and the daughter of the internationally known model, was allegedly "catatonic" after witnessing the murder of her mother, at the hands of Greek-English play-boy Vasili Arbus. It went on to discuss Vasili's other wives, the fact that he had been spirited out of the country and was currently in a sanatorium in the Swiss Alps. And the article further explained that Vanessa was now the object of a custody fight between both of her father's surviving brothers: Greg Fullerton, head of the family law firm, and "socialite Surgeon," Dr. Theodore Fullerton. The articles every day were awful, and eventually Vanessa had to be taken out of school. Before that, some effort had been made to maintain normalcy for her, but she had followed almost nothing in her classes, and much of the time she hadn't gone at all.

The psychiatrist took a full week to come to his conclusions. Vanessa waited in the judge's chamber as the doctor's testimony was given. The child was in a state of severe shock, suffering from depression, and had partial amnesia. She knew who she was, and remembered her life clearly up until the point at which her mother had married Vasili Arbus. In effect she had totally blocked out the last year and a half, and she had repressed it so severely that the doctor had no idea when she would be aware of the truth, if ever. She had some recollection of her mother being extremely ill, and it was, as Teddy had suspected, her memory of her mother in the hospital in London that had conveniently surfaced, but she did not recall that it had happened in London or that the reason for the "sickness" was that her mother was in labor. Along with all memory of Vasili, the

392

memory of the baby she had loved so much, tiny Charlie, had vanished. She had repressed it all to avoid the agony it had brought her.

She was not crazy, the doctor insisted. In fact in some ways what she had done was healthy, for a time. She had cut out the part of her life that was so painful to her, and buried it. It had happened unconsciously, possibly moments after her mother's death or, as the psychiatrist and Teddy both suspected, at the moment when the baby had been taken from her and given to Andreas Arbus in court. It had been at that moment in time that it had all become too much for her. And she hadn't been the same since. She would recover, the psychiatrist felt certain, but whether she would ever remember the truth was a question he could not answer. If she did, it could come upon her at any time, in a month, in a year, in a lifetime. If she didn't, in some way the unresolved pain would always haunt her. He advocated psychiatric treatment for a time, to see if the memories would surface. He insisted though that she should not be pushed or prodded, that the way her mother had died should not be told to her. She should be left alone with her forgotten memories, and if they came of their own, it was all to the good. If they wouldn't come, she should be allowed to keep them buried. It was a bit like living with a time bomb, because one day they would probably surface, and it was impossible to say when. He hoped, he explained to the court and all of the parties involved, that when the child felt more secure again, her presently traumatized psyche would relax enough to allow her to deal with the truth. It would have to be dealt with, he said sadly. One day. If not, it would severely damage the child.

The judge inquired whether the doctor felt that she was in particular need of a mother figure, or if he thought that she would fare as well without.

"Absolutely not," the doctor exploded. "Without a woman to relate to, that child will never come out of her shell. She needs a mother's love." The judge pursed his lips then, and Teddy waited, and half an hour later the decision was announced. Permanent custody was to be granted to Greg and Pattie. Greg looked relieved as he left the court, and Pattie was elated. She didn't even look at Teddy, as she forced Vanessa to walk ahead of her. The child walked like a machine, without looking, seeing, feeling. Teddy didn't even dare reach out to touch her. He couldn't bear it. And as he walked slowly down the steps in the chill air, his mother came up beside him.

"I'm sorry, Teddy." Her voice was husky and he turned to her with angry eyes.

"No, you're not. You could have helped me, and you didn't. Instead you've left her to those two." He indicated the limousine pulling away from the curb, carrying Vanessa back to their apartment.

"They won't do her any harm her mother didn't already do. And you'll see enough of her." He said nothing, but walked away from her as quickly as he could.

He sat home alone that night, in his darkened rooms, staring out into the night. It had begun snowing. And tonight he planned to be just like his brother. He had taken out a full bottle of Scotch when he got home, and he planned to drink it all before morning. He was halfway into it when the doorbell rang, and he ignored it. There was no one he wanted to see now and his lights weren't on, so no one could know he was home, but after the bell rang for almost fifteen minutes, someone began banging on the door. They pounded repeatedly and finally he heard muffled shouts of "Uncle Teddy." Startled, he put his glass down, jumped to his feet, ran to the door, and pulled it open, and there she was. Vanessa, carrying a paper bag in one hand and an old doll he had given her years before in the other.

"What are you doing here?"

She said absolutely nothing for a minute, and suddenly she looked afraid. "I ran away."

He wasn't sure whether to laugh or cry as he looked at her. They were both standing in the light from the hallway. And self-consciously, he flicked on the lights in his apartment. "Come on in and we'll talk about it." He knew, however, that there was nothing to talk about. He would have to take her back as soon as they had discussed it.

As though reading his thoughts, she braced herself stubbornly in the hall. "I won't go back."

"Why not?"

"He's drunk again, and she hates me."

"Vanessa," he sighed tiredly, and wished he hadn't drunk the half bottle of Scotch before she'd got there. He wasn't thinking as clearly as he should, and he was so damn glad to see her. "She doesn't hate you. She wouldn't have fought so hard to get you if she hated you."

"She just wants me like a thing." Vanessa sounded angry. "Like all those clothes she buys, and the crystal stuff on the coffee table and the dolls she buys me. It's just stuff. That's all I am to her. More stuff." Teddy knew that she was absolutely right but he couldn't say so. "And I hate them."

"Don't." He knew she was going to have to live with them for a long, long time. The court had ruled.

"I won't go back there." She glared at him and he sighed as he flicked on the lights.

"Vanessa, you have to."

"I won't."

"Come on, let's talk this over." He was feeling a little unsteady on his feet and it was a welcome relief to sit down with her.

But Vanessa looked as stubborn as the proverbial mule. "I won't go back to them, no matter what."

He ran a hand through his hair. "Will you please be reasonable for chrissake? There's nothing we can do. You can't live with me if the court gave them custody."

"Then I'll just keep running away, and they'll send me away to school."

He smiled sadly. "They wouldn't do that."

"Yes, they would." Vanessa looked matter-of-fact. "She said so."

"Jesus Christ." For this they took her away from him? To threaten her with boarding school. "Look, nobody is going to send you anywhere, Vanessa. But you can't stay here."

"Just for tonight?" The eyes were so big and sad that he melted and reached out his arms to her with a smile.

"Oh, princess, how did all of this happen to us?"

There were tears in her eyes when she turned her little

face up to his, and once again he saw the face of his brother in this small child. "Why did Mommy have to die, Uncle Teddy? It's so unfair."

"Yes." He could barely speak as he thought of her. "It is."

"Oh, please," she said, clinging to him, her little hands warm against his shirt, "don't make me leave you. Just for tonight?"

He sighed, feeling suddenly very, very sober, and then he nodded. "All right. Just for tonight." But he never got a chance to call Greg and Pattie. Pattie called him before he could get up to call. He reached for the phone, and she shrieked at him instantly.

"Is she there?"

"Vanessa?" His voice was strangely calm. "Yes."

"God damn it, Teddy, bring her back here! The court gave her to us, now she's ours!" Like a vegetable, or a suitcase. The very thought chilled him.

"I'll bring her back to you in the morning."

"I want her now!" Pattie was strident, and Teddy's eyes began to blaze.

"She wants to spend the night."

"Never mind what she wants. She's ours now, she's to do as I say. I'm coming over to get her."

"I wouldn't do that if I were you." His voice was smooth as velvet, but it had an edge of steel. "I told you, I'll bring her back to you in the morning. She can sleep here."

"No, she can't. You heard what the judge said. It's unsuitable, you're a bachelor. She is not allowed to spend the night at your house," Pattie said archly. "I want her home right away."

"Well, she's not coming. I'll see you in the morning."

But what he saw in the morning was not Pattie, but the police. They arrived just as he was making breakfast for Vanessa. The doorbell rang, an officer asked if he was Theodore Fullerton, he said that he was, he was told that he was under arrest, handcuffs were clapped on him, and in front of Vanessa's horrified eyes he was led away. Another officer turned off the fire under the breakfast and gently told Vanessa to get her things. For a minute she started to get hysterical and looked around her frantically. . . . There was something about the uniforms . . . the police . . . she couldn't place it but they terrified her. . . . She grabbed her doll and ran for the door, looking for Teddy. But when she got downstairs, accompanied by the other officer, the car carrying Teddy to the station had already pulled away. Vanessa was driven back to Greg and Pattie's apartment, where she was returned to Pattie with a kind word and a smile.

At the exact same moment Teddy was downtown at the station, being booked for kidnapping. Pattie had brought charges against him during the night. Bail was set at fifteen thousand dollars, an extortionate amount, and a hearing was set in front of the very same judge the next day.

The next morning, looking unshaved and exhausted, Teddy was led into court, the handcuffs were removed, and the judge glared at him for several minutes before clearing the court. He ordered everyone out of his courtroom, especially the reporters—the headlines that morning had been bad enough: SOCIALITE SURGEON KIDNAPS NIECE. There was even some subtle intimation in the piece that, given his passionate interest in her, perhaps Vanessa was his child and not Brad's.

"Well, Doctor Fullerton, I can't say that I'm pleased to see you here again. What exactly do you have to say about all this? Off the record, just for the information of the court."

"I didn't kidnap her, your honor. She arrived at my door."

The judge looked troubled. "Had you told her to do that?"

"Of course not."

"Did she give you a reason?"

"Yes." He decided to be honest. He had nothing to lose now. "She hates my brother and his wife."

"That's not possible, she said nothing about that in my courtroom."

"Ask her again."

The judge looked angry. "Have you primed her?"

"I have not." Teddy's eyes flashed. "My sister-in-law is

397

already threatening to send her to boarding school, that's how much they love her, your honor. If I do say so myself''—he looked chagrined as he smiled ruefully at the judge—''you made a very poor choice.''

The judge looked anything but pleased with Teddy's comment. ''She's a very disturbed child, Doctor. You know that. She needs a normal household with a mother *and* a father. As much as you may love her, you are only a man.''

Teddy sighed. ''My sister-in-law doesn't have a maternal bone in her body, your honor, she hated Vanessa's mother with a passion. Vanessa's father jilted her for the child's mother. In a way I think Pattie—Mrs. Fullerton—wants to get even. She wants to finally 'take possession' of his child at all costs, to prove something. She doesn't love Vanessa, your honor. She doesn't even know the child.''

''Is it true that the child's mother hated Mrs. Fullerton?''

''I don't think so. I think the hatred was all on Mrs. Pattie Fullerton's end. She was wildly jealous of Serena.''

''Poor woman. . . .'' He thought of Serena and shook his head. ''And your brother Gregory?'' The judge looked mournful, it was the worst case he'd had in years, there seemed to be no right solution for Vanessa. ''Is he fond of the child?''

''Your honor,'' Teddy sighed, ''my brother is an alcoholic. In my opinion he's in the very last stages of it. Not a very pretty scene for Vanessa to see, or anyone else for that matter.''

The judge shook his head and sat back heavily in his chair with a sigh. ''Well, I've got kidnapping charges on you to deal with, and it looks like I should reopen the case on your niece. . . .'' He looked as miserable as Teddy. ''I'm going to do something very unusual, Doctor. I'm going to give you thirty days in jail for the alleged kidnapping of your niece after my verdict. You may request a trial on the matter if you wish, but I'm not going to charge you with kidnapping. I'm going to charge you with contempt of court. There is no bail for contempt, and you will serve the full thirty days. In that way I can be quite sure that you won't truly kidnap her.'' He glared at Teddy, who listened with dismay. ''And during the thirty days I'm going to have an extensive investigation done on this matter, and I will restate my verdict in the custody matter exactly thirty days from today. That will be"—he looked briefly at his calendar—"March fourth." With that, he signaled to the bailiff, and without further ado Teddy was removed.

CHAPTER FORTY-NINE

On March fourth, at 9 A.M., Teddy was led back into the courtroom, clean-shaven and well groomed but almost twelve pounds thinner after his month in jail, and he found himself looking at his brother, his sister-in-law, and Vanessa. For him it had been an endless month and he hadn't been able to see Vanessa for the whole time, and now as he saw her his heart leaped, and he began to smile. Her eyes lit up too, and he saw that she looked a little better. Maybe she would be all right with them, after all.

The bailiff called the court to order, everyone was told to rise, the judge came in, and he frowned at them all. He informed them that the investigation conducted regarding Vanessa's custody had been the most extensive of any of his career on the bench. He told everyone present that he truly felt that they were all worthy people and that it was not a case of finding one person suitable and the others not. It had become an issue of the greatest good to Vanessa. There were certain peculiar problems to this case—the judge looked in the grown-up's eyes, knowing that they would understand him—that made it especially difficult to select the right home for the little girl. Whatever happened, he hoped that they would all remain friendly, because he felt certain that Vanessa needed all of them around her, no matter whom she lived with. It was quite a long speech for a normally taciturn judge. He cleared his throat then, shuffled through some papers, and looked from Margaret Fullerton to her youngest son.

"Doctor Fullerton, I think you have a right to know that I had a lengthy talk with your mother." Teddy glanced at her with instant suspicion, but he could read nothing in her eyes. "And it would seem that your devotion to the child has been not only admirable but of long and steady duration. Apparently you remained close to her mother after your brother died, from what I understand, and both Vanessa and her mother came to rely on you greatly. It is also my understanding that Mr. and Mrs. Gregory Fullerton had no contact whatever with Vanessa and her parents." Teddy glanced at his mother in sudden amazement. Had she told the judge all that? But why? Why would she suddenly help him? "Therefore, it would seem to me that residing with you, despite the fact that you're not married, would give Vanessa a sense of continuity, which, according to the psychiatrist, is much needed. So, Doctor Fullerton, I am granting you final custody of this child." There was a gasp from Vanessa, and she ran toward him. He threw his arms out and held her to him, and he was crying as he held her. The judge looked at them both and felt his own eyes grow damp. And when Teddy glanced at his mother, he saw that she was wiping her eyes, and he felt gratitude overwhelm him. She had finally done something decent. Only Pattie looked as though she wanted to kill them all as she stalked out of the courtroom, but Greg stopped to shake Teddy's hand and wished them both luck. He knew that it was the right thing for Vanessa.

Margaret Fullerton watched her youngest son, thinking of what had led her finally to soften toward Vanessa. The past was over with, the child was so lost without Teddy. It seemed time to let history become memory. "Perhaps I'm getting old," she said to herself and smiled.

In the courtroom Teddy was still holding Vanessa and the two of them were laughing, and when they walked triumphantly out of the courtroom hand in hand, the photographers had a field day and they didn't give a damn.

She ran down the courtroom steps, holding Teddy's hand, like a little movie star, smiling at him from ear to ear and holding so tightly to his hand that his fingers almost went numb. He hailed a cab outside the court, and they went directly to his apartment. He hadn't seen it or Vanessa in a month, and as he turned the key in the door it felt as though he had been gone for a year. He stood at the threshold, looking down at his beloved smiling niece, not sure whether to carry her over the threshold or not, after all, they were starting a new life. Instead they stepped over it together, holding hands, and when they reached the other side, they shook hands ceremoniously, and then she stood on tiptoe and kissed him on the cheek.

"Welcome home, princess."

"I love you, Uncle Teddy."

"Oh, sweetheart." He folded her in a great big hug. "I love you too. I hope you'll be happy here." He wanted to make up to her for the past, but he knew that he couldn't do that, all he could give her was the present and what he was.

"I'll be happy, Uncle Teddy." She looked at him with a big smile, and for the first time in months she looked like a nine-year-old child. There was no trace of the tragedy or the trauma or the anguish of all that she had been through. She threw herself on the couch, giggled loudly, threw her hat in the air, and looked like a mischievous little elf as she lay there and kicked off her shoes.

The headline that night read SOCIALITE SURGEON BECOMES BACHELOR FATHER, and it went on to reiterate for the thousandth time about his month in jail, the kidnapping charges Pattie had tried to make stick that had become contempt of court, and again all the details about the custody case. The papers had been strictly kept from Vanessa all along, and Teddy hoped that they would all get lost somewhere over the years. He didn't want any of that coming back to haunt Vanessa. She still remembered nothing of Vasili, or the baby, or her mother's murder, but she seemed much more herself now. It was just a matter of time.

Book Three

VANESSA
AND
CHARLIE

CHAPTER FIFTY

"Vanessa? Vanessa? Are you home?" Teddy walked sedately through the front door, put his hat on the hall table, took off his coat, and peeked into the study. She wasn't there, but as he wandered through the house he suspected that she was in the darkroom. For the past four years she had spent most of her time there. He had had to give up the guest bedroom on her behalf when she discovered photography in her freshman year at Vassar, but she was so good at what she did that it was actually a pleasure.

During the thirteen years she had lived with him almost everything had been a pleasure. They had grown up together, hand in hand, learning and growing, and occasionally fighting like cats and dogs, but there was an enormous respect between them. His mother had died when Vanessa had been twelve, but that was no particular loss to Vanessa. Her grandmother had never accepted the child, and that never changed right up until her death. She left Vanessa none of her vast fortune. She left it all, equally divided, between her two sons. Two years later Greg had died, predictably of cirrhosis, and Pattie had eventually moved to London and married "someone terribly important." From the rumors he occasionally heard, Teddy assumed she was happy, but he didn't really care if he never saw her again. Once she lost custody of Vanessa, she had entirely lost interest in the girl, and they never saw her. So over the years Teddy and Vanessa had been alone. He had never married, and he had devoted himself wholeheartedly to the task of being a bachelor father. It had its moments of absolute despair, there were moments that were hysterical beyond words, and moments that were worth an entire lifetime. When she had graduated from Vassar the previous spring, it had been a moment that he knew he would always cherish. In some ways she was as lovely as her mother had been, but it was more a similarity of spirit. She had grown up to look exactly like Brad, and sometimes it amused Teddy to see how much she was like him. She had his same long lanky blond good looks, her sense of humor was much the same, her eyes were the same gray-blue, and when she laughed, it was as though he had come back for another life, as a woman. It was extraordinary to watch her, and be with her, she was so dynamic and so alive. It was her energy and her drive that she got from her mother. And she wanted to be not a model but a photographer. She had studied fine arts at Vassar and done very nicely, but all she cared about was what she saw in her camera lens, and after that what she did with it.

Teddy knocked softly on the door, and Vanessa answered.

"Yeah? Who is it?"

"The big bad wolf."

"Don't come in, I'm developing."

"Will you be through soon?"

"In a few minutes. Why?" It seemed to him that most of their conversations were through that door.

"Want to go to dinner?"

"Wouldn't you rather play with kids your own age?" She was always teasing him that he should get married.

"Mind your own business, smartass."

"You'd better be nice to me, I could sell that picture I took of you last week to the papers. Famous surgeon seen dressed as a bunch of grapes." He roared with laughter at the memory. She and half a dozen friends had gone as the Fruit of the Loom insignia to a Halloween party, and at the last minute the guy who was supposed to be the grapes couldn't come, and she had pressed Teddy into service. He had been a good sport, but they had also won the prize, so Vanessa had had someone take pictures of them. "How would that look in the medical journals?"

"That's blackmail."

"You'd better be nice to me. I just sold another picture to *Esquire*." She had been free-lancing for five months now, and she was doing very nicely.

"You're moving up in the world." He was still standing in the hallway, talking to the door. "Are you ever coming out of there?"

"No, never," she shouted back.

"What about dinner?"

"Sounds good. Where are we going?"

"How does P.J. Clarke sound to you?"

"Terrific. I'm wearing jeans and I don't want to change."

"So what's new?" He was teasing. She was always in jeans, with her incredible blond hair swinging, and assorted army surplus jackets and vests, which made up the rest of her wardrobe. She wanted to be comfortable enough to take pictures at all times. She was in no way preoccupied with her wardrobe.

"I'll get dressed."

He disappeared into his own bedroom and loosened his tie. He had led two lives for years, that of a sedate, successful surgeon at Columbia Presbyterian, in dark pin-striped suits, white shirts, and dark ties, and then a whole other life with Vanessa. A life of ice skating and pony rides and the zoo and father's days at camp, and hockey games and ice cream parlors. A life of blue jeans and sweat shirts and pink cheeks and windblown hair. She had kept him even younger than his forty-five years and he hardly looked more than thirty. His own blond good looks had held up well, and he actually looked a great deal like her. They had the same lanky frames, the same shoulders, the same smile, it was perfectly conceivable that she could have been his daughter. Once in a while when she was little, she had introduced him as her "Daddy," but she still called him Teddy, and most of the time she told friends that he was her uncle. She remembered in every glorious detail the day she had been finally awarded to him in court, but of the ugliness of the past, she still remembered nothing.

He had consulted several psychiatrists over the years and they had eventually convinced him not to worry. It was disturbing that none of that had ever surfaced, but it was possible now, they all felt, that she would never remember. She was happy, well adjusted, there was no reason for any of the past to come leaping out. And they also suggested that if he wanted to, once she was an adult, he might want to tell her. He had decided not to do that, she was happy as she was, and the burden of knowing her mother had been murdered by her husband might have been too great for Vanessa. The only possibility that could be of concern was if she suffered some major trauma. In that case, perhaps, some of the memories could be dislodged. When she had been little, she had had frequent nightmares, but she hadn't even had those in years, and eventually Teddy had stopped worrying about it completely. She was just like any other child, happy, easygoing, better natured than most, they had never had any teen-age problems. She was just a terrific kid and he loved her as though she were his own child. And now that she was almost twenty-three, he couldn't believe how quickly the years had flown past them.

He returned to the darkroom twenty minutes later, in blue jeans and a dark brown cashmere jacket with a beige turtleneck sweater. She shopped for him sometimes at Bloomingdale's, and came back with things he would never have bought for himself, but he had to admit that once he had them he liked them.

"Are you ever coming out of there, Mrs. Cartier-Bresson?"

The door opened just as he said it, and she stood before him in all of her towering beauty, her hair flowing around her shoulders like a wheat field, and a huge smile on her face. "I just developed some truly great pictures."

"Of what?" He looked into her eyes with pleasure. It seemed for all her twenty-three years she had been the hub of his existence.

"I took pictures of some kids in the park the other day, and they're just stupendous. Want to see?" She looked at Teddy with pleasure and he followed her back to the dark-room. She switched the light on, and he looked at the prints. She was right. They were fantastic.

"You going to sell these?" They were really lovely.

"I don't know." She cocked her head to one side, and the blond mane fell over her shoulder. "There's a gallery down-town that wants my work. I was thinking I might let them show them."

"They're beautiful, darling. You've done some lovely work in the last few weeks."

She pinched his cheek and kissed him. "That's just because I have an uncle who buys me great cameras." He had bought her a Leica for Christmas, and another Nikon for her graduation. She had got her first one for her eighteenth birthday, which was what had got her started.

They walked out of the apartment arm in arm, and they got in a cab that took them to P.J.'s. They went out often in the evening together now that she was back from college. He liked taking her out and going to fun places with her, and she liked being with him, even though sometimes Teddy felt guilty about that. She hadn't had a lot of friends when she was in school. She was kind of a solitary child, and she had always clung to him. At Vassar she had made some friends, but she seemed happier alone with her camera. And with her twenty-third birthday looking at her in a matter of weeks, she was still a virgin. There had been no important men in her life and she seemed to shy away from them. A touch on the hand, a hand on her arm, almost always made her shudder. It was something that worried Teddy a great deal. As the first psychiatrist had said in the courtroom many years before, all of the buried horror she had seen would leave a mark on her life, if it never surfaced. It hadn't, and Teddy wondered if unconsciously she remembered seeing Vasili kill her mother and was afraid because of it. Or was it buried so deep that it didn't affect her? Like shrapnel left over from a long-forgotten war?

"You're awfully serious tonight, Uncle Doctor. Why so quiet? Something wrong?" She was always very straightforward with him.

"I was just thinking."

"What about?" She was munching on an enormous hamburger and looked about fourteen. He smiled at her.

"About you. How come you're such a good kid? It's not normal."

"I'm retarded." She grinned at him and set down the hamburger. "Would you rather I got into drugs?" She grinned, knowing how he felt about the drug epidemic. Though she didn't know what a deep-seated horror Teddy felt or why.

"Please. I'm eating."

"Okay, so just be grateful I'm boring." She knew what he was working toward. She should be going out with some nice young man and not her old uncle. She had already heard the speech ten thousand times, and she always told him in answer that he should be married.

"Who said you were boring?"

"You were about to start picking on me again for being a virgin."

"Was I?" He looked amused. "You know me awfully well, Vanessa."

"Hell, I ought to," she chuckled, "we've been living together for thirteen years." She said it too loud and several people turned around to stare at them, in particular two women who glared at them in obvious disapproval.

Teddy leaned toward them with his most charming smile. "My niece," he said sweetly.

"I've heard that one before," snapped the woman and she turned around at her table as Vanessa burst into laughter.

"You're more outrageous than I am, do you know that?"

The trouble was that they liked each other so much and were so comfortable with each other that neither of them was highly motivated to go looking for anyone else, which wasn't good for either one of them. He had never really got over Serena, and his years of single parenthood had kept him busy enough that he could use it as an excuse not to look seriously for another woman. There had been women now and then, but they never meant very much to him. And in Vanessa's case, she just seemed to shy away from any kind of serious involvement with a man. She grew oddly shy and uncomfortable around them. Teddy had seen her do it. So instead she hid behind her camera, saw all, and felt as though no one saw her.

"It's a damn waste, kid." He looked at her with a grin as he paid the check.

"What is?"

"You hanging out with me all the time. Besides, I'll never get you off my hands like this. Don't you want to get married?" But whenever he mentioned marriage, there was always terror in her eyes.

"No, never. That's not for me." It was then that he could see the bits of shrapnel surface. It was always there. She just didn't know it.

The next morning they sat peacefully over scrambled eggs and bacon. They alternated making breakfast every morning. On her days they had scrambled eggs, on his they had French toast. They had it down to a science. They read the paper in sections, with perfectly harmonized rotations. Watching them in the morning was like watching two people perform a ballet. It was all perfectly synchronized, and no one spoke a single word until after the second cup of coffee.

But this morning, when he held out his cup, nothing happened. Instead she sat staring at the paper, with a blank look on her face, and sensing something, Teddy watched her.

"Something wrong?" She shook her head, but she didn't answer. He got up and came around behind her then; and what he saw gave him a jolt. It was a photograph of Vasili Arbus. She was reading the article, but her eyes kept straying back to the picture. The article was brief and said only that he was dead of a drug overdose at fifty-four. It said also that he had spent five years of his life in a mental hospital for having committed murder, and he had been married six times. But for once none of his wives were listed. Not even Serena. Teddy wanted to say something as he watched her look at the picture, but he knew he shouldn't do it. He had to let happen what would happen. It wasn't fair to help her repress it all again. He said absolutely nothing, and she went on looking at the picture for another ten minutes, and then suddenly she looked up at Teddy with a troubled smile.

"I'm sorry. That's crazy. It's just . . . I can't explain it . . . I feel as though I've seen that man somewhere before, and it's bothering me." Teddy said nothing and she shrugged. "Hell, he's been married six times, maybe he has some kind of hypnotic power over women. Looking at that picture was like going into a trance." Teddy almost shuddered. After all those years here it finally was. But she seemed to have cast the mood off. She poured his second cup of coffee and went on reading the paper, but he saw a few minutes later that she had turned back to Vasili's picture again. It was interesting also that they didn't say whom he had murdered. He was grateful for that. That would have been a terrible shock for her. This way her own memory had to do the work, but it was like trying to stir Rip Van Winkle.

Teddy watched her closely that morning, but when he left for work, she seemed herself. He took the paper with him, just as a precaution, so she wouldn't fixate on it while she was alone. He was nervous about all of that coming to the surface when she was by herself somewhere. And after twenty minutes of trying to concentrate on his patients at his office, he gave up and called Vanessa's last psychiatrist, but it had been eight years since she'd seen him. It turned out that he had retired, and a woman had taken over his practice. Teddy explained the case, and she went to get the file. She was back on the line a moment later, pensive as she glanced through it.

"What do you think? Do you think I should tell her now?" He sounded very nervous, and the woman was annoyingly calm when she answered.

"Why not let her work through it? She'll only remember as much as she can handle. That's the whole point of that kind of repression. It's the mind's way of protecting itself. As long as she couldn't handle it, she didn't remember. When she can, if she can, it'll come back to her. Probably in little pieces, and as she digests each one the next one will come to her."

"It sounds like a long process." Also depressing, he thought.

"Not necessarily. The whole thing could be over in a day, or it may take weeks, or months, or even years."

"Terrific. And I just sit there watching her ruminate, is that it?"

"That's right, Doctor. You asked me. So I told you."

"Thanks." Her name was Linda Evans and he wasn't sure he liked her.

"You know, there's another thing you might want to be aware of, Doctor. She may have nightmares. That would be fairly normal, while things push their way up to the surface."

"What do I do?"

"Be there for her. Talk to her if she wants to talk. It may

412

come out very quickly that way." And then she thought about it for a minute. "If you need me, Doctor, call me. I'll leave word with my service. This is kind of a special case. I'd be happy to come over, no matter what time."

"Thank you." It was the first really nice thing she had said. "I appreciate that." And then he chuckled. "And if you ever need your spleen removed, I'd be happy to take care of that for you too." She laughed, amused at the bad joke. Doctors seemed to be famous for them, but he had a nice voice, and she felt genuinely sorry for his niece. Besides, it was a case that had always intrigued her. She remembered studying the file when she'd taken over the practice.

They hung up and Teddy went back to work, not feeling greatly encouraged, but when he went home that night, Vanessa was busy in the darkroom again and seemed in good spirits. The maid had left them a pot roast and they ate dinner at home, they both talked about work, she went back to the darkroom for a while, and he went to bed early. And when he awoke with a start, he saw from the clock on his night table that it was two thirty in the morning. He knew instantly that it was Vanessa who had woken him. In the distance he could hear her screaming. He jumped out of his bed and ran to her bedroom. And he found her sitting there, staring into space, muttering darkly. She was still asleep, and it was obvious that she had been crying. He sat beside her for the next hour, and she muttered and whimpered and cried softly for a while, but she never woke up, and she didn't scream again. He called Dr. Evans back in the morning and reported to her. She urged him to relax and just see what happened, and the same thing happened again the next night, and the night after that. It went on for weeks, but nothing really surfaced. In the daytime Vanessa was cheerful and busy and entirely herself, and at night she lay in bed and moaned and cried softly. It was as though deep down some part of her knew, but the rest of her didn't want her to know it. It was agonizing watching her that way every night, and at the end of three weeks he went to see Dr. Evans.

He waited in the waiting room for fifteen minutes, and then the nurse told him that she was ready to see him. He was expecting, he had decided, a short, heavyset, serious-looking

413

woman with thick legs and glasses. What greeted him instead was a statuesque brunette, with a radiant smile, big green eyes, and her hair pulled back in a chignon like a ballet dancer. She was wearing a silk shirt and a pair of slacks, and she looked at the same time both relaxed and intelligent. As he walked into her office Teddy felt surprised as well as unnerved.

"Something wrong, Doctor?" He saw from a quick glance at the degree on her wall that she had gone to Harvard, and he calculated quickly that she had to be about thirty-nine, but she didn't look it.

"No . . . I . . . I'm sorry." He smiled at her then and looked more himself. "You're not at all what I expected."

"And what was that?" She was very much in control of the situation and he felt silly.

"Someone . . . well . . . different . . ." He burst out laughing. "Hell, I thought you'd be ugly as sin and about two feet tall."

"With a beard? Just like Freud? Right?" She laughed at him, and then blushed faintly. "You're not what I expected either."

"Oh?" He looked amused.

"I thought you'd be very stuffy, Doctor. Pin-striped suit, horn-rimmed glasses"—she looked at the attractive blond mane—"no hair."

"Why, thank you. As a matter of fact, I do usually wear pin-striped suits. But I took the afternoon off to come and see you. So I came in my civvies." He smiled at her. He was wearing gray gabardine slacks and a blazer. And he looked very handsome. "May I make a suggestion? Could we possibly stop calling each other Doctor? It's an awful lot of 'Doctor'-ing." He grinned and she smiled and nodded agreement.

"Call me Linda."

"I'm Teddy."

"All right." She sat back in her comfortable black leather chair and looked at him directly. "Tell me about your niece. In detail." He told her everything that had been happening, and she nodded. And when he had finished his recital, she told him gently, "Do you remember? I told you it could take months, or even years. There was a possibility, with the initial shock, that she might have been jolted into remembering the whole story. What seems to be happening instead is that it's leaking slowly into her subconscious. It could take a very long time, or it may all subside again. It's unlikely that anything would happen to shock her again the way that photograph did. That was kind of a fluke."

He agreed. "But it was amazing how it struck her. She stared at it for about half an hour."

Linda Evans nodded slowly. "She must have some awful memories of that man. It's not surprising that the photograph haunted her."

"You don't think we should just tell her and get it over with?"

"No, I don't."

"Do you think she ought to come to you?"

Linda thought about it for a moment and then shook her head. "On what grounds? Why would you be suggesting such a thing? You see, she has no idea what's happening yet. If she wakes up one day and wants to see a therapist, that's one thing, but if you suggest it, it may put her on edge. I think we just have to let her be for the moment." Teddy nodded, chatted with Linda for a moment, and then shook her hand and departed. But a week later he was back to talk to her again, and eventually he became a regular visitor to her office. He no longer took the afternoon off to come to see her, he arranged it during his lunchtime instead.

"See, I told you. Pin-striped suits." She laughed with him. There really wasn't that much to say about Vanessa, and after a month or two she began having fewer and fewer nightmares, but Teddy had come to enjoy talking to Linda Evans. They seemed to share a myriad common views and opinions, common interests and likings for many of the same things. Eventually he suggested that they spend the lunch hour in a restaurant instead of her office, and from there it was only a step to dinner. Normally she had stringent views about not going out with patients, but Teddy wasn't really a patient. He was the uncle of a patient she had never even met, but whose file she had inherited with the practice, and he was a fellow doctor. Besides, she was amazed at how much she enjoyed him. And Teddy was equally amazed at his feelings—he wondered once or twice if, in speaking of Vanessa's past to Linda, he was somehow healing the ghosts of his own. For the first time in a long time he could speak of Serena without a stab of pain and it dawned on him slowly that he was falling in love with Linda. They went to dinner two or three times a week, occasionally went to the opera or the theater. He even took her to a hockey game with Vanessa, and was pleased at how well the two women got along. It also gave Linda her first look at Vanessa. She found her a delightful girl and saw no sign of inner torment.

By spring Teddy and Linda saw each other almost every night, and Vanessa had begun to tease them. Linda was becoming a regular visitor at the apartment, and Vanessa teased that if she was going to hang around as much as she was, she was going to have to start taking a shift for breakfast. It was also beginning to occur to Vanessa that she needed her own apartment. She didn't want to hurt Teddy's feelings, but she was twenty-three years old, she wanted to combine a studio with living quarters of her own, and it was obvious that he was crazy about Linda Evans.

"Why the hell don't you ask her to marry you, Teddy?"

"Don't be crazy!" he growled at her over one of her breakfasts. "Besides, your eggs were lousy today." But the thought of marriage had already crossed his mind and he didn't want to tell her.

"That's it!" She pounded a hand on the table and he jumped. "I'm moving out!"

"Will you stop that!" She was making him very nervous, but suddenly he saw something gentle and sad in her eyes. She had been teasing at first but now she meant what she was saying and he knew it.

"I kind of mean it, Uncle Teddy." She looked just like a little girl as she said it, and he felt his insides turn over.

"Why?" He looked very upset. "Because of Linda? I thought you liked her." He looked so disappointed that she hugged him.

"I do, silly. I'm just turning into a big kid now, and I

416

want to get a studio to work in, and . . . well . . . a place of my own." It felt like such a betrayal, she felt like a monster.

"Have you started looking yet?"

"No, I thought I'd start in the next few weeks."

"Already?" He looked pale, and then retreated behind his paper, and when he left for his office, he looked shaken. He called Linda half an hour later. "Vanessa wants to move out." He sounded as though his wife had said she was divorcing him, and at her end of the phone Linda grinned, but when she spoke to him, her voice was gentle.

"What did you tell her?"

"I didn't really, I was too upset. She's too young, and . . . what if she starts having nightmares again, if it all comes back to her?"

"Then, she'll call you. Besides it may never happen. You said that she had settled down again."

"But she might see something." He sounded frantic and Linda was smiling.

"Sweetheart, she's a big girl now. Your baby is leaving the nest. You're going to have to face it."

He groaned softly. "You know, I feel like a complete jerk, but it just about turned my insides upside down." He was smiling now too, and he felt comforted by the sound of Linda's voice. Suddenly he needed her more than ever. For years Vanessa had filled an enormous void in his life, a void that had been left by Serena. But now little by little Linda was moving into that space and he was letting her do it.

"You're not alone. This happens to all parents. It's especially hard on fathers to see their daughters grow up, and very hard on mothers to have their children leave the nest. You're a mother and father rolled into one, so it's hitting you doubly hard. Guess what, Doctor? It's normal."

"You know, I almost cried."

"Sure. Who wouldn't?" She had such a nice way of making him feel that everything was all right and he wasn't crazy.

"You know something? You're terrific. How about lunch today?"

She glanced at her calendar. "Sounds delightful." And then she had an idea. "Want to meet me at my place?"

He chuckled in his office. "Now, that is a splendid idea, Doctor Evans. A consultation?"

"Of course." They both laughed and hung up, and at noon they met in her apartment and made love until two thirty. With Linda, Teddy was feeling a passion that he hadn't felt in years. And for the first time in years, after they made love, he didn't feel empty or guilty. The ghost of Serena was finally fading.

"You know," he said, looking at her pensively as he drew a lazy finger around her breasts, "I used to think it was all over."

"What?"

"Oh, I don't know . . ." he sighed. "I haven't been in love in so long, Linda." He looked at her sadly for a moment. "I was so much in love with Vanessa's mother that I never really wanted anyone else."

"It must have been very traumatic for you when she was killed."

His eyes were bright with tears as he looked at Linda. "I wanted to kill the son of a bitch myself. I'll never understand how he could do it . . . and they let him out of the country."

"He must have had an awful lot of pull."

"He did. His family was very influential. Anyway, I don't know. After that I poured out everything I had on Vanessa. There was never much left for anyone else. I think maybe I was numb." He smiled at the beautiful woman lying at his side, and she touched him gently.

"You certainly aren't numb anymore."

"Thank you, Doctor." He kissed her and a moment later he felt desire surge within him again. They made love one last time, and parted regretfully afterward to go back to work, even though they were meeting again for dinner that night.

As Vanessa's preparations to move gained momentum they seemed to spend more and more time together. It was as though, in letting her go, Teddy was better able to reach out to Linda. Vanessa finally moved into a studio apartment of her own on May 1, and on the following weekend Linda stayed for four days. After that Teddy wound up spending most of the following week at her apartment. She returned

418

to his place for the weekend and spent the week. They never seemed to leave each other anymore, except to go to their offices, and when the three of them went away for a weekend in Cape Cod in August, Teddy looked at Vanessa sheepishly and cleared his throat.

"I have something to tell you, sweetheart." Linda watched him, feeling tenderness mingle with amusement. In some ways he was still very shy. But it was part of what she loved about him, and there was a great deal about him that she loved.

Vanessa looked at him with a question in her eyes, and for just an instant the two women's eyes met and held, and then Linda looked away. She didn't want to spoil the surprise. "What is it?" Vanessa tried to seem nonchalant but she wasn't. She suddenly felt an electric thrill of excitement and anticipation course through her.

"I . . . uh . . . Linda and I . . ." He almost choked on the words and then took a breath. "We're getting married."

"Well, it's about time." Vanessa beamed. "When's the wedding?"

"We haven't quite figured that out yet. We thought maybe September."

"Do I get to take pictures?"

"Of course." He looked at her searchingly, wanting her approval, and she was beaming, and suddenly she threw her arms around his neck. They had had something so special for so many years, and now it had altered slightly, but in a healthy way for them both, and she was so pleased that he was marrying Linda. They were perfect for each other, in every way. And neither one of them had ever been married, he at forty-six and she at thirty-nine.

"I'm so happy for you, Uncle Teddy." She held him close and Linda felt warm just watching them. And then Vanessa reached out to hug her, and as the two women embraced there were tears in their eyes.

"Do I get to be an aunt, or . . ." She looked puzzled. "What would I be? A cousin? Gee, seems like I could have a better title than that." And then her eyes clouded strangely. She had been about to say sister, but something had stopped her. Teddy and Linda both saw it and no one said a word.

"Can I be an aunt?"

"Sure." Linda grinned. "But you're a little ahead of yourself, Vanessa. I'm happy to announce that this is not a shotgun marriage."

"But I could arrange that." Teddy grinned and put an arm around each of his women, as they strolled down the beach, talking about the wedding, and he felt as though he were the happiest man alive.

CHAPTER FIFTY-ONE

The wedding was lovely. They had it at the Hotel Carlyle in mid-September. They invited about a hundred friends, and Vanessa took all the pictures, and by Christmas her wish had come true. As they sat around the fireplace after the turkey dinner, Linda reached out to touch her husband's hand, and then looked at Vanessa.

"I have something to share with you, Vanessa." She wore a mysterious little smile, and Vanessa looked at her in the firelight, thinking that she had never seen her look more lovely. She wore a peacock-blue silk dress, with her hair loose around her shoulders. Her eyes looked greenish blue and her skin had an almost rosy blush that made her look much less than her thirty-nine years.

"If it's more food, Linda, I can't." Vanessa lay down on the floor with a groan and smiled up at her aunt and uncle.

"No, it's not more food." Linda giggled and Teddy grinned. He was wearing an expression of beatific contentment that Vanessa had never seen before, as Linda went on. "We're having a baby."

"You are?" Vanessa looked stunned. It took her a moment before she actually looked pleased. Again one could almost see her hearing an echo, and Teddy watched her nervously, afraid that the news would cause her pain. But an instant later her eyes danced and her face was radiant. "Oh, Linda!" She threw her arms around her friend, and then around Teddy, and clapped her hands with glee.

The next day Vanessa went out and bought the baby an enormous teddy bear, and for the next five months she bought things for the baby in a never-ending stream, pandas, giraffes, silver rattles, hand-made quilts, tiny nightgowns made of old lace, little caps, and she even knit a pair of bootees. Linda and Teddy were touched by the gifts, but occasionally, when Linda looked at her, she was worried. There was an odd kind of tenseness about her lately, a sense of something about to happen. Linda tried to talk to her about it once or twice, but Vanessa herself didn't seem to know what was the matter and insisted that she wasn't aware of it. It was an almost indefinable impression one got when one looked at her closely. It was as though, deep within, she was desperately unhappy. And it grew more marked as the time for the baby's birth came closer.

Linda on the other hand seemed to grow happier and calmer as she got larger. There was a serenity about her that struck everyone who knew her. Even her patients were touched by what one of them called "the rosy glow of the Madonna" about her. There was a luster in her eyes, a warmth to her smile, that told everyone how happy she was about the baby. At forty she was finally having the baby she had wanted all her life but had decided would never come.

"And suddenly there you were one day in my office"— she smiled at Teddy one night as she told him—"and I knew that you were it. Prince Charming." She beamed at her husband and he grinned.

"Oh, you did, did you? Is that why you had me come back for all those consultations?"

"I did not!" she tried to look incensed. "You wanted to come back to talk about Vanessa."

"Well, I did at first." He looked suddenly thoughtful. "Speaking of which, have you seen her lately?" He looked worried and Linda nodded. "I'm worried about her. She's lost weight and she looks very nervous."

"I think she is. I tried to talk to her about it the other day."

"Anything important?" He looked worried. After all, in a sense Vanessa was still his first child, and Linda understood that. But she looked pensive as she answered.

"Honestly I don't know. I think that maybe the baby has set off some old impressions for her. I'm sure she doesn't know it, but whether or not she's aware of it, there's a definite deja vu in it for her. It's bound to rattle up something." She sighed unhappily for a moment. "And I think the latest man she's met has her upset too."

"Why?" Teddy looked surprised. "Who is he?"

"She didn't say anything to you?"

Teddy sighed. "She almost never does. By the time she gets around to telling me, they're usually already off the lists." It always made him sad to see how she closed herself off from men and any kind of close relationship. The only people she was close to were Teddy and Linda, with them she was wide open to her feelings and to theirs, but with anyone else she ran like a frightened deer if they came near her. She was twenty-four now and Teddy knew that she had never been physically involved with anyone. "Who is he?"

"I think he's a photographer's agent, she met him at a party. She said that he was very nice, and apparently he was interested in representing her work. She was thinking about it too, but then he asked her for a date and she got nervous."

"Did she go?" Linda nodded.

"Yes. I think they went out three or four times. She really liked him. They had a lot in common, he was crazy about her work. She says he made some very good suggestions about how she should market herself. Everything was fine."

Teddy looked bleak. "And then he kissed her."

Linda reached out and touched his hand. "Don't take it so personally, Teddy."

"I can't help it." He looked at his wife. "I keep thinking that if I'd handled it right, if I'd been the perfect role model, she wouldn't be afraid of men."

"Teddy, she saw a man kill her mother. Be reasonable. How can anything you did or didn't do alter that?"

He sighed. "I know, I know . . . but in my heart I keep thinking—" He looked sadly at Linda then. "Do you think I should have told her?"

Linda shook her head. "No, I don't. And I don't think telling her would have changed a damn thing. She'd still have to live with the same nightmare, consciously or not. If she's going to trust men, or even just one man, it will come to her on her own, if the right man comes along. It's still possible, you know, Teddy. She's a young girl. She isn't totally averse to the idea. She's just frightened."

"So what's happening with this guy?" Teddy looked a little more hopeful after Linda's speech.

"For the moment, nothing. She called a halt on dating him until she decides if she wants him as her agent. She says that if she does, then she doesn't want to go out with him, she'd want to maintain a businesslike relationship with him."

"Sounds like you." He leaned over and kissed her, and then gently patted the enormous belly. "You sure that's not twins, by the way?"

She laughed and shook her head. "Not according to my doctor. The kid's probably got big feet like me." She smiled at her husband. "Or he's carrying a football."

"Or a purse." They both laughed, and Teddy sighed as he thought of Vanessa. "Think she'll start seeing this guy again?"

"She might."

"What's his name?"

"John Henry."

"John Henry what?"

"That's it. John Henry."

"He sounds like a phony." Teddy frowned.

"And you," Linda laughed at him, "sound just like a father. One minute you're all upset that she'll never go out with him again, the next minute you think he's a creep."

"Have you seen him?"

"No. But Vanessa's a bright girl. If she says he's a terrific guy, I'm sure he is. She certainly isn't easy about men, so if she likes this one that much, I'd say he's probably a winner."

"Well, we'll see what happens."

"Yes, we will." Linda was looking at her husband. "Don't worry about it so much. She's all right, Teddy."

"I hope so." He lay back on the bed. "I've been so worried about her lately." But much of the time his worries about Vanessa were eclipsed. He was so excited about the baby that he could hardly wait until the due date. He was more than a little concerned about Linda having her first baby at forty. Medically speaking, they both knew the dangers of giving birth to a first baby at her age, but her doctor seemed to feel confident that there would be no problems.

But more and more Teddy found himself remembering Serena's pregnancies. He remembered the golden glow she had seemed to have before the birth of Vanessa, and how he had delivered her himself that afternoon, alone in the house in the Presidio. He told Linda about it one night, and she watched him. Something so gentle and so sad always happened to his face when he spoke of Serena. It gave her just a hint of what the woman must have been like, and always made her wish that she had met her. She had seen photographs of her among some of Teddy's old things, and she was really incredibly beautiful. It was funny, only Vanessa's shape was actually reminiscent of her mother. Her face and everything else about her was exactly like her father. It was only in looking at the old photographs or remembering cherished moments that Serena still came alive to Teddy.

"Weren't you terrified?" Linda was referring to when he had found Serena on the floor, already in hard labor.

"Scared shitless." He grinned. "I had been in med school for exactly four months, and the only thing I knew about delivering babies was what I had seen in the movies. Boil water and smoke a lot until the doctor comes out of the room, wiping his hands. And suddenly the whole damn movie was upside down and I was the doctor."

"Did she have a hard time?" There was a tiny edge of fear in Linda's voice as she spoke. In the last few weeks she had started to get a little nervous. But Teddy knew instantly what was happening and he kissed her and shook his head.

"No, she really didn't. I think most of all we were both scared because we didn't know what was happening. But once she started pushing, it went great after that."

424

"You know"—she smiled sheepishly at Teddy—"I hate to admit it, at my age, and with my training . . ." He smiled, already knowing what was coming. ". . . but lately I've been getting nervous about it."

"I hate to tell you this, Doctor, but that's perfectly normal. All women get nervous before childbirth. Who wouldn't? It's a major happening in anyone's life, and physically it's always a little scary."

"I feel so silly though. I'm a psychiatrist, I'm supposed to be able to handle things like that." She looked at him in sudden panic. "What if I can't stand the pain? . . . if I freak out . . .?" He took her in his arms and stroked her dark hair.

"You're not going to, and it's going to be wonderful."

"How do you know?" She sounded like any of a million patients and he loved her better for it.

"Because you're in good health, you've had no problems at all, and because I'm going to be right there with you the whole time."

Linda has been so excited about this first baby that she had bought everything in sight since the day she found out she was pregnant. The nursery was a sea of white eyelet with blue and pink ribbons, there was an antique bassinet draped in white organdy, a cradle a patient had sent her, shelves filled with dolls, handmade quilts, and lots of little goodies knitted by Linda's mother. A dozen times a day now she walked into the room, looked around, and she always felt that something was missing. It was five days before her due date when she finally realized what it was that was missing, as she laughingly told Vanessa over lunch.

"It's the baby!" They both laughed at the revelation. Linda had retired from her practice the week before, and she was enjoying the last days of waiting. "I must admit, I'm a little antsy. But part of that is just not working for the first time in fifteen years. I feel guilty as hell about that." But she was going back for half days when the baby was a month old, so the five weeks she'd taken off were really no more than a healthy vacations.

"Your patients will wait."

"I suppose so," Linda sighed, "but I worry about them."

"You're as bad as Teddy. Before he met you, he'd have a nervous breakdown if he took two weeks off. There's something about doctors. They're compulsive."

Linda grinned. "I think we like to call it conscientious."

"Well, I must say, I admire it. But I don't have that problem. I spent all of last week sitting on my ass and I loved it."

"Oh?" Linda looked intrigued. "With anyone special, or is that an indiscreet question?"

There was a twinkle in Vanessa's eyes when she answered. "I saw John Henry again. I decided not to use him as my agent." For Vanessa that was a major step, Linda knew. She had been almost certain that that was going to be the way out Vanessa would have selected. She would hire him as her agent and then claim that she couldn't get involved with him after that.

"That's an interesting decision." She sounded non-committal, and Vanessa grinned.

"You sound like a shrink."

"Do I?" Linda laughed. "I apologize. I meant to sound like an aunt."

A warm look passed between them. "You're not bad at that either. No, I don't know. I thought about it a lot. And in a funny way I think we were already too involved with each other for me to do business with him coherently. The funny thing"—she looked at Linda in a puzzled way—"is that I'm attracted to him."

"Is that such a shock?"

"For me, yes. Most of the time, Linda"—she shrugged—"even if I like them, I don't want to go to bed with them. I just . . . I just can't . . ."

"When the right one comes along, it'll be different."

"How do you know?" Vanessa looked very young as she asked her. "Sometimes I think maybe I'm just strange. It's not that I don't like men, it's just that . . ." She groped for the words. "It's as though there were this wall up between them and me, and I just can't get past it." That was exactly what was happening, as Linda knew only too well. She only hoped that one day Vanessa would find the door, or have the courage to climb over the wall.

"There are no walls too high for us to climb, love. Some walls just take more work than others. I think that it may just depend on how badly you want to."

"I don't know." Vanessa didn't look convinced. "It's not really that . . . it's like I just don't know how to begin, or what to do. . . . But," she sighed softly, "it's crazy, John seems to understand that."

"How old is he?"

"Twenty-seven." Linda found herself wishing that he were older, and perhaps more mature.

"But he seems a lot older than his age. He was married for four years. They got married when he was in college. Childhood sweethearts and all that. She got pregnant, so they got married when he was eighteen. But—" She hesitated, realizing that she had just made a ghastly faux pas, and she looked up at Linda. "Never mind. It's a long story."

"I'd like to hear it." And the worst of it was that Vanessa wanted to tell her. She wanted to share what she was thinking about John. She needed to get it off her chest, and she could always talk straight to Linda.

"I'm sorry, love. It's a lousy story. But maybe since you're a doctor . . . Their baby was born defective. It had some terrible birth defect, and I guess he and his wife hung together because of the child. It sounded really awfully when he told me. They took turns sitting at the hospital for the first year, and after that they had him at home until he"—she almost gulped—"until he died. I gather that it took a terrible toll on the marriage. When the baby died, they split up, and that was it. That was five years ago, and I think it shook him up for a long time."

Linda looked shaken too, but birth defects were certainly no news to her, and to Vanessa's relief she didn't look overwhelmed by the story. "That's understandable, and so is the divorce. A lot of times couples don't survive tragedies like that one."

Vanessa nodded. "I'm sorry to tell you that now. I didn't think when I started—"

"It's all right." Linda touched Vanessa's hand. "I'm a big girl, you know. I'm even a doctor." They smiled at each other.

"You know, the odd thing is that I like him so much. I feel comfortable with him, it's as if he really understands me."

"Does that surprise you so much?"

"Yes." She sighed softly. "Everybody else has always pushed me. They're on the make and they want to get you to bed in one night. I tried explaining to John how I felt, and he understood it. He said that after his little boy died and he broke up with his wife, he didn't sleep with anyone for two years. He just didn't want to. He thought that there was something wrong with him too, but there wasn't, it was just as though he were numb or something."

Linda nodded. "He's right. It is very common."

"You know, he asked if anything ever happened to me to make me feel the way I do." She shrugged and smiled. "But I just told him I was crazy from birth, I guess." She laughed, but it was a hollow sound, it was almost as if her eyes asked Linda a question.

Linda spoke very quietly. "I think it must have been a tremendous trauma for you when your mother died, and the custody case. You never know how those things will come out later."

"Yeah." She looked wistful. "Some people wind up with a stutter. Me, I'm frigid." Her eyes were sad when she looked at Linda again but Linda shook her head.

"That's not necessarily true. In fact I seriously doubt it. You've never made love with anyone, Vanessa. You don't know what you are yet."

"That's the truth. I'm nothing." She looked disappointed in herself and Linda felt for her.

"Give yourself time. John sounds like a nice man. Maybe he'll come to mean something to you."

"Maybe." She sighed again. "If I let him." It was not as if she were unaware of her problems. She was even beginning to think of seeing a shrink again, which pleased Linda. Maybe she would finally get it all out, after all. Maybe it was time for her. The blockage that had sat there for so long was finally making her uncomfortable.

For two nights Linda had trouble sleeping, the baby had

428

dropped, and it felt so heavy that she could barely walk. A heat wave came along, and she was miserable and restless. At five o'clock one morning she got up, her back ached, she had heartburn, she couldn't sleep, and she finally gave up and made herself a cup of coffee. The coffee gave her cramps, and she felt like a lion in a cage by the time Teddy got up at seven.

"What time did you get up, love?" He looked surprised to see her so wide awake and so busy. She had been in the baby's room since six o'clock, folding clothes again and checking the suitcase she had packed for the baby. He hadn't seen her this busy in months, and then suddenly, as she made a funny face, he began to watch her. "Something wrong?" He said it as casually as possible, as she checked the supplies in the dressing table.

"That damned cup of coffee gave me cramps." And then just as she said it her face pinched and she gently felt her stomach, and suddenly she understood what was happening. She looked up at Teddy in surprise, with a broad grin. "My God, I think I'm in labor."

"What time did you get up?"

"About five o'clock. I was restless and I couldn't sleep, so I came in here and got busy."

He grinned at her. "For a doctor you're not very smart. When did the cramps start?"

"About five thirty." But they were so gentle, she hadn't even realized she was in labor.

"Why don't you give your doctor a call?"

"Already?"

He nodded. "Already." She was forty years old. He was not going to play games and wait until the last minute. In fact he insisted on taking her to the hospital right away, even though she was barely in labor. But the whole thing seemed like an adventure, as she showered, put on a clean dress, and kissed him in the doorway.

"When we come back here, we'll be a mommy and a daddy."

The thought of it made him smile, and he kissed her longingly. They hadn't been able to make love in weeks, and he was hungry for her body. "You'd better get your ass out of here, Doctor Evans, or I'm going to rape you right here in the hallway." But as soon as he said it she had her first good pain, and she made a little surprised sound, as he supported her with an arm around her shoulders. "I think, my love, that we'd better go. The last baby I delivered at home was twenty-five years ago, and I'm not exactly dying to try that again."

"Chicken." She grinned at him.

By the time they got to the hospital, Linda was getting excited and the pains had begun to come at regular intervals, five minutes apart. She was smiling at everybody and exploding with energy and excitement. He helped her unpack her Lamaze bag at the hospital and then they prepared her, and when he came back, she was lying on her bed in a pink hospital gown, with a lollipop between her teeth, her hair tied back with a pink ribbon.

"Good Lord, woman, you look like you're starring in a movie, not having a baby."

She looked proud of herself as she rode out another pain. "Isn't this how women look when they're having babies?"

"I don't know. Ask an expert." The doctor had just come in, he examined Linda and declared that all was going splendidly. She was going to try to have the baby by natural childbirth, though he offered her medication if she wanted it. But both she and Teddy had agreed that it would be better for the baby if she tried not to.

A few minutes later the pains picked up in speed, and an hour later Teddy was telling her to pant softly. Her eyes had begun to look a little glazed and there was a faint veil of sweat on her brow, her hair had begun to stick to her face, and she was beginning to clutch at his hand when the pains came. "This isn't as easy as I thought." She looked at him anxiously, and when the next pain came, she clenched her teeth and he had to shout to make her do her breathing. When it was over, he ran a damp cloth over her forehead, gave her ice, held her hand, and told her how wonderfully she was doing. Nurses came and went, and offered her encouragement, they told Linda she was doing great, and outside in the hall they all gossiped about Linda and Teddy both being doctors. They had seen Lamaze practiced before, and in 1971 it was already fairly common, but they had rarely seen it practiced with such devotion. Linda and Teddy were both working hard, and he was marvelous with Linda.

The next stage lasted until late afternoon, and by six o'clock Linda looked exhausted. Her face looked ravaged by the pain, her hair was glued to her face and her neck, and she was trying desperately not to whimper, and then suddenly with the next pain she gave a scream and lunged toward Teddy. "I can't do it, I can't . . . I can't . . . tell them to give me something . . . please . . . oh, God . . ." But he talked her through it. He could tell how well it was going. It was a whole other world than he had seen with Serena. When he had arrived in London that morning, he had known that she was literally dying. Had they left her there long enough, her heart would have eventually stopped from the strain, and the baby would have died too if they hadn't moved quickly. But in Linda's case everything was different. She was obviously in enormous pain, but things were moving at a reasonable pace, and she wasn't being beaten by what was happening. The labor was moving along nicely, and what had happened was that she was finally in transition. After thirteen hours of labor she was nearly eight centimeters dilated, and in a little while she could begin pushing. But they both knew from the Lamaze class that she had just entered the hardest part of her labor. The next two hours were absolutely grueling, and Teddy stayed with her every moment, holding her hand, urging her on, breathing with her, holding a paper bag for her to breathe in, and cooing softly to her almost as if she were the baby, and then suddenly with a final scream a look of victory came to her face, and with no urging at all she began pushing. He tried to make her hold back, but the doctor came quickly, gave the sign to the nurses, and without further ado they wheeled her bed from the labor room right into delivery. She was shifted onto the table, her legs put in the stirrups, and five minutes later she had begun pushing in earnest. The entire delivery-room team urged her on while Teddy held her shoulders, and sweat ran down his face and his back and his arms as profusely as it did down hers. Linda had never worked as hard in her entire life, and Teddy felt as though he were pushing with her.

"Come on, push!" they all shouted at once as Linda's face grew red and she groaned with the effort. It seemed to take forever, but finally the doctor grinned and held up a hand to announce, "The baby's crowning . . . come on, Linda . . . come on . . . I can see hair! . . . Come on, *push*!" Linda tried again and the baby moved another inch, the top of his head was almost out now, and Teddy could feel tears sting his eyes when he looked in the mirror. At forty-seven years of age he was having his first baby and he had never loved a woman as much in his life as he loved Linda at that moment.

"Come on, sweetheart . . . come on, you can do it . . . oh . . . that's it . . . come on . . . *more*!" She was pushing as though she would burst and suddenly with a gasp and a groan the head came free all at once and the room was filled with a hearty wail. The doctor grinned, the nurses laughed, and Linda and Teddy began to cry at once, smiling and laughing along with them.

"Oh, what is it?" Linda struggled to see, and when Teddy held her up, she could see the baby's face, angry and red and scrunched up as it cried.

"We can't tell yet." The doctor smiled broadly. "Give us a few more pushes and I'll tell you what it is."

"That's not fair," Linda gasped, smiling at her husband. "God ought to put their sex organs on their heads, so you can tell . . . right away. . . ." But she was already working again. Two more pushes and the doctor freed his shoulders, and then, with one enormous final push, the baby was born and he lay in the doctor's hands.

"It's a boy!" he cried triumphantly. "A great big beautiful boy!" Linda's and Teddy's eyes filled with tears as they looked at him. Linda laughed and reached up to kiss her husband, and he smoothed back her hair and looked down at her with unlimited adoration.

"You're the most beautiful woman I've ever seen."

"Oh, Teddy . . ." She smiled through her tears. "I love you."

"I love you too. Oh, look at him. . . ." He couldn't get over it, the baby was perfect.

"Eight pounds, twelve ounces. Good work, Mrs.

Fullerton." The doctor looked pleased as he handed the baby to his father.

"And you thought it was going to be twins." Teddy grinned and looked into his son's face, held him for a moment, and then gave him to his mother. "Here's your boy, Mom." Their eyes filled with tears again as she held him.

It was a night filled with jubilation and excitement. When they got back to Linda's room, she was so high she could almost fly. She got out of bed and walked down the hall to see her son in the nursery window, and she stood holding on to her husband's arm, and they both looked like the proudest parents alive.

"Isn't he beautiful, Teddy?"

"He sure is." Teddy couldn't take his eyes off his son. "What'll we call him?"

She looked at Teddy with a smile. "I kind of thought we could call him Bradford, for your brother." As she said it Teddy felt a lump in his throat, and he reached out and held her and said nothing.

That night a bond had formed between them that he knew that nothing would sever. They had waited half their lives to find each other, and he had thought he would never get over Serena. But Serena had been a dream for him, an unattainable woman he had always loved, and who had never really been his. She had belonged to Brad and then to Vasili, and never really to him. She had loved him, but she had never belonged to him. This woman who had just borne him a son was now his, and he knew it, just as he was hers and would never belong to anyone else again. And as they walked slowly down the hall, back to Linda's room, it was as though the ghost of Serena di San Tibaldo quietly tiptoed away for the last time.

CHAPTER FIFTY-TWO

"A boy? Hurray! Oh, Teddy, that's super!" Teddy called Vanessa at eleven thirty that night, and she was ecstatic. "Oh, that's beautiful!" and then with a worried voice, "How was it for Linda? Was it hard?" Vanessa had always had nervous feelings about giving birth, and she always said that she never wanted to have children. When the time came, she would adopt. It was something that she and John Henry agreed on. Next time he wanted to know what he was getting. He couldn't imagine going through the agony of a birth-deformed baby again, and the horror of waiting for nine months to know that it was normal terrified him. Yet, like Vanessa, he wanted children.

But Teddy sounded jubilant as he reported. "No, she was just terrific. You've never seen anyone go through it better. And she looked just beautiful." He almost cried again. "Wait until you see the baby!"

"I can't wait to see him. What's his name?"

"Bradford, for your father. It was Linda's idea. We'll call him Brad, I guess."

At her end Vanessa smiled. "You've got yourself one terrific lady, Teddy."

"I know." He sounded as though he could barely believe his good fortune. "She was so great, Vanessa. You should have seen her!"

"I'll see her tomorrow, first thing."

"Good. Why don't you bring your friend John Henry? Maybe he'd like to see the baby too." Teddy was curious about him, and he was dying to show off the baby. Vanessa understood and chuckled at him.

"I'll see if he's free." But she knew that he wouldn't be able to go. There were some things that still upset him, and going to a hospital to see a newborn was one of them. He had already told her that he wouldn't do it. He had told her that he'd see the baby later, at home. And she had understood. "I'll probably come alone, Teddy. I don't want to share the baby with anybody anyway, not even with you!" He had laughed, but when she arrived the next morning at the hospital to see them, she looked very pale as she got off the elevator on the maternity floor.

As Teddy watched her get off the elevator, she seemed disoriented. He started to walk toward her with a smile, but then he stopped. She looked almost gray. He wanted to say something to Linda, but there wasn't time. Vanessa stood next to him in a moment, her eyes very big and gray, and she looked frightened.

"You okay, sweetheart?"

She nodded. "Yeah, but I think I have a headache or something. I worked in the darkroom late last night, and I think that did it." She smiled but it didn't look real, and then she forced herself to look more cheerful still. "Where's my nephew? I'm dying to see him."

"In his mother's room." Teddy looked at her with a smile, but he was still worried as he followed her inside. Linda was sitting on the bed, nursing the baby. Vanessa stopped for a moment, she had snuck in her camera, and clicked several frames, before she put the camera down again and came toward them. There was something terribly serious in her face as she looked at Linda, and then without saying a word, her eyes went to the baby. She couldn't take her eyes off of him. She just stood there staring, her eyes big, her face pale, and her hands trembling.

"Do you want to hold him?" She heard Linda's voice as though from very far away, and without saying a word she nodded and reached out and Linda give him to her. She sat down in a chair with a look of awe, holding the tiny bundle. The baby had gone back to sleep at his mother's breast, and now he lay round and content in Vanessa's arms as she looked down at him. She said nothing for long moments, as Teddy and Linda exchanged a smile, and then suddenly Linda looked at Vanessa. There were tears running down Vanessa's face in steady streams, and a look of pain on her face that tore at Teddy. But before he could say anything at all, Vanessa had begun to speak softly.

"She's so beautiful . . . she looks just like you, Mommy . . ." She didn't look up at Linda as she spoke, and Linda sat very still, worried about both Vanessa and the baby. "What'll we call her?" And then softly, she began to croon her name. "Charlotte . . . Charlie. I want to call her Charlie." She looked up at Linda then, but her eyes were blind to the people around her. She cradled the baby gently and began to sing softly, as Teddy and Linda watched her. Some deep-seated maternal instinct told Linda to take back the baby, but another sense knew that it was important that she leave him with Vanessa.

"Isn't she pretty, Vanessa?" Linda's voice was like a whisper in the quiet room, and Teddy watched with awe what was happening. "Do you like her?"

"I love her." Vanessa looked straight at Linda, and saw her mother. "She's mine, isn't she, Mommy? She doesn't have to be his. She's ours. He doesn't deserve her."

"Why not?"

"Because he's so mean to you, and . . . and those things he does . . . the drugs . . . and when he didn't come back . . . and . . . Uncle Teddy said you could have died. But you didn't." She looked at once agonized and relieved, as they watched her relive it. "You didn't because Uncle Teddy came and got the baby out." She winced then, remembering how she had seen her mother, near death, her legs in stirrups, strapped helplessly to the table. "Why did they do that to you? Why?" Instinctively Linda knew.

"So I could have the baby. That was all. They didn't mean to hurt me."

"But they did, and they almost let you die . . . and he wasn't there . . ."

"Where was he?"

"I don't know. I hope he's gone for good. I hate him."

"Does he hate you?"

"I don't know . . ." Vanessa started to cry. "I don't care . . ." She continued to cradle the baby, and then, as though she'd had enough, she held him out to Linda. "Here, I think she wants you." Linda nodded, took the sleeping infant from her, and handed him to Teddy, nodding toward the door. Teddy left with him immediately, and returned a

436

moment later, alone, to watch the drama unfurl. He was terrified at what was happening to Vanessa, but he had always known that it would have to come one day, and it was best if it came now, all at once, with Linda there to guide her.

"Does he hate you, Vanessa?"

"I don't know . . . I don't know . . ." She jumped out of the chair and went to the window, staring out of it blindly. And then she wheeled around and looked at Linda. "He hates you . . . he hates you . . . he hit you . . . oh, Mommy . . . we have to go away . . . back to New York, to Uncle Teddy." And then suddenly her face clouded again and she seemed to stare into space with a look of horror. "Back to Uncle Teddy . . ." It became almost a chant. "Back to New York . . . oh, no . . . oh, no . . ." She looked around frantically, from Linda to Teddy, and he wondered for an instant if she would ever be the same again, if she would ever be sane. "Oh, no! Oh *no*! . . ." And then a wail. "He killed her! That man . . . he killed my mommy!" She began to sob and reached out to Linda. "He killed you . . . he killed you . . . he killed you . . ." She looked up then as though for the first time she really saw Linda, and it was not the face of a child that Teddy and Linda saw as they looked at her, but the face of a ravaged young woman. "That man"—it was a hoarse whisper, she had come back—"the one I saw in the newspaper that day . . . he killed my mother." She stared at Teddy, seeing him too, and then she went on, as though waking from a dream and trying to remember. "And then . . . the police came and they took him away, and I was"—she looked at them, puzzled—"I was holding a baby." She closed her eyes then and trembled. "Charlie. Her name was Charlie . . . the baby Mama had in London . . . and they took her away from me in a courtroom." She began to cry great gulping sobs then. "And they made me live with Greg and Pattie . . ." She looked at Teddy and held her arms out to him. "And then I came to live with you . . . but I never knew . . . I never remembered, until"—she looked at Linda in shock and despair—"until I saw that baby . . . and I thought . . ." She looked up at her uncle and his wife. "I don't know what I thought . . ."

Linda helped her at last. "You thought it was Charlie."

She looked at Linda then. "Is all of this true? I feel like I dreamed it."

Linda looked at Teddy. "It's true. You repressed it all after it happened, and it's been waiting to come out for years."

She looked frightened then. "Is there more? Did something else happen?"

Linda was quick to answer. "Nothing else. You remembered it all. It's all over now, Vanessa. It's out." Now all she had to do was learn to live with it, which Linda knew wouldn't be easy either. She watched the girl closely. She had had a tremendous shock. "How do you feel?"

She looked blank for a minute. "Scared . . . empty . . . sad." And then two huge tears rolled down her face. "I miss my mother." She hung her head down and began to sob again. "He killed my mother . . ." She was shaking all over. "When I came into the room, she was . . . she was lying there . . . her eyes open, his hands were on her neck and I knew she was dead . . . I knew . . ." She couldn't go on, and with tears streaming down his face, Teddy took her in his arms.

"Oh, baby . . . I'm so sorry."

"Why? Why did he do it?" The questions were sixteen years later.

"Because he was crazy. And maybe because he was into drugs, I don't know. I think he loved her, but he was terribly disturbed. She left him, and he thought he couldn't live without her."

"So he killed her." For the first time she sounded bitter, and then she looked up at her uncle with a look of shock. "What happened to Charlie? Did they give her to him?"

"No, they put him away in an institution. For a while at least. Your sister was given to Vasili's brother. He was a decent man, I think. He was as distraught as I was at the time, and he wanted Charlotte." Teddy smiled sadly. "He was very fond of you too. Do you remember him at all?" She shook her head.

"Have you stayed in touch with him over the years?"

Teddy sighed. "No, I haven't. The judge discouraged us

from having contact with each other. He said that you and Charlie had gone to separate lives. I don't know how Arbus felt about it, but I was nervous about you, because you had repressed it all. I didn't want anyone coming along to surprise you over the years." She nodded slowly in understanding and spoke softly after a little while.

"She would be almost sixteen now. I wonder what she looks like." Her lip trembled again. "When she was a baby, she used to look just like Mommy."

Teddy began to think of something but he thought it was too soon to suggest it. Perhaps in time, when Vanessa had absorbed it all, they could all go to Greece and look up Andreas Arbus. Vasili, he knew from the article, two years before, was dead now. It was, of course, that article and Vanessa's subsequent nightmares that had led him to Linda. He smiled at his wife. She had handled it all so beautifully.

"I'm sorry I spoiled everything, Linda. I came to see the baby and to be happy for you, and instead I went crazy." She looked rueful and blew her nose. She felt very strange, as though she had just run ten miles or climbed a mountain, it wasn't so much a feeling of exhilaration but of being drained.

Linda reached out to her and put an arm around her in maternal fashion. "You didn't go crazy. You did something very healthy. You finally reached back into the past and opened a door that's been locked for years. And the reason your psyche let you do it is because you were ready. You can handle it now, and your mind knows that. What you did took sixteen years to do, and it wasn't easy. We all know that."

Vanessa nodded, unable to speak for the tears, and Linda looked cryptically at Teddy and he understood.

"I'm going to take you home now, sweetheart, so you can get some rest." He took her gently from Linda. "Want to come home with me?"

She looked at him sadly and tried to smile. "I'd like that. But don't you want to be here with Linda?"

"I'll come back later."

"I need some rest anyway." Linda smiled at them both, and there was a special smile in her eyes for her husband.

She had loved him even more than before since they had shared the birth of their baby. The baby created a bond between them that they could already feel. "You two take it easy today. Brad and I will be home in a few days. That'll be plenty of time for all of us to be together." She kissed Vanessa again and told her that everything she was feeling was normal and healthy and she should go with it and just let it flow, let the memories come, cry with the sadness, feel the grief and the pain and the loss, and then it would finally be done with once and for all. And then she said gently, "I think your friend John could tell you something about that."

But Vanessa looked shocked. "How can I tell him? He'll think I'm crazy."

"No, he won't. Try him. From what you've told me, I don't think you'll be disappointed."

"What? And just tell him that sixteen years later I remembered that my mother was murdered. It sounds nuts to me." She sounded bitter again but Linda was firm with her.

"Well, it isn't nuts, so you'd better understand that. What has just happened to you is the most normal thing that's happened to you in twenty-five years. And the fact that your mother was murdered isn't your fault, Vanessa. You couldn't help that. It's not a reflection on you, or even on her. It happened. Her husband was obviously crazy when he did it. And you couldn't have stopped him."

"He was crazy long before that." Vanessa remembered him clearly now, and hated him all over again, and then she turned to Teddy.

"Did my mother love you?" It was a blunt and painful question for him. Serena had loved him, he knew, but never as he had loved her.

He nodded slowly. "Yes. I was someone she could depend on. I was like a brother to her, or a very special friend." He looked at his wife now. It was the first time he had told her that, and he wanted her to know it too. And there was something gentle and loving in her face as she looked at him.

"Why didn't they let you keep Charlie?" That had been

bothering her for the past half hour.

"Because she was no blood relation to me, and you were. Her uncle wanted her, and he had a claim to her."

"Would you have taken her?" Vanessa needed to know that. Suddenly she wanted to know everything about what had severed her from her sister. It was as though she had to know all the whys.

"I would have taken her. I wanted to very much." Vanessa nodded, and a moment later they left. Teddy took her back to his apartment, and she lay down on the couch and they talked for over an hour, about her mother, about the first time he'd seen her, about when he delivered Charlie in London, about Vasili and how Serena had fallen in love with him, and then, as though she had had all she could take for the moment, Vanessa closed her eyes and fell asleep on the couch. Teddy stayed near her all day and called Linda several times. He was worried about Vanessa, but she assured him that she felt things had gone very well. He suggested that he stay with her, and when she woke up four hours later, he could see that she felt better than she had. There was a terrible aura of sadness about her, as though she mourned now in a way she hadn't dared when her mother had died. He remembered now that frozen little face, those blank eyes, and in the woman she had become he could see the grief that she had carried hidden for so many years.

At five o'clock she decided to go back to her own apartment. She had a date with John Henry, and she suddenly felt a longing to see him.

"I'm going to be lousy company tonight, but I don't really want to call it off." She looked at her uncle. "Thank you, Uncle Teddy." Her eyes filled with tears. "For everything . . ." She choked on a sob. "For so many years." They held tightly to each other, and Teddy cried softly too. It was as though, that day, they had finally buried Serena together, and the pain of it, even remembered, was almost more than he could bear too.

CHAPTER FIFTY-THREE

Linda and the baby came home from the hospital three days later, and when Vanessa came to see them, she looked a great deal better than she had a few days before. Her eyes looked bright and she wasn't so pale, but she still looked worn and tired as she held Brad for the first time. But this time there was no trauma, no ugly memories to haunt her. The ugly memories were out in the open now, along with the good ones, and she felt sharply the loss of Charlie as though it had happened to her only the week before. But this was a different baby, and she knew it. She held him and crooned to him, and laughed when she thought he was smiling. She adored him, and Teddy and Linda were thrilled. On the whole she seemed to have recovered very well from her trauma, but it was clear to Linda as the summer wore on that the pain of it hadn't really left her.

"What's happening with John?" She finally dared to ask her in August. She hadn't wanted to press her before.

"Nothing much." She sounded vague. "We still see each other."

"Oh, has it cooled?" He had come to see the baby once or twice with Vanessa, and Linda and Teddy both liked him. Vanessa's appraisal of him had been correct, he was handsome and intelligent, gentle and kind, and mature well beyond his years. He had declined to hold the baby, but had stood playing with him over his crib. It was obvious that there were still too many memories for him, wrapped up with the infant. He was more comfortable talking to Teddy, or Linda, in the other room. In truth it was a malaise that he and Vanessa shared. There were times when the baby still reminded her of Charlie, but nonetheless she came to see him almost all the time. She had come to visit the baby again on the day when Linda was asking her about John Henry.

442

"I don't know. Maybe we're just destined to be friends."

"Any special reason?" But Linda already knew what it was, as Vanessa turned to her almost with defiance.

"Yeah, despite what you said, I seem to be frigid. I just don't want to go to bed with a man."

Linda sighed as she watched her. "I think you're being premature again, Vanessa. You had an enormous shock two months ago. You have to give yourself time."

"How much time? I'm almost twenty-five years old." She sounded angry at Linda, but they both knew that she was angry at herself.

"You told me that when John's baby died it took him two years before he wanted to make love again."

"How long's it been for me? Sixteen?" She was sick to death of her own problems, of trying to live with them, overcome them, forget them. It was all she had thought of for two months.

"How long have you known? Only two months. You're being very unfair with yourself."

"Maybe I am." But she stopped seeing him entirely a month later. She said that she couldn't handle a relationship until she sorted things out in her head, and he was very understanding. He told her simply that he loved her, that he wanted to stand by her, to help her work it out, but if she needed to be alone, he would respect that. He asked only that she try to stay in touch and let him know from time to time how she felt. The day he left her apartment for the last time he stood in the doorway with a look of sorrow in his eyes as he looked at her.

"I want you to know two things, Vanessa. One, that I love you, and two, that you're not crazy. You've been through a horrendous experience and it may take you time to sort it out. But I'll be here if you want me. In a year, in a day. I've never met anyone like you. So when you work it out, just call."

Her eyes filled with tears and she nodded, but then she turned away as he closed the door. And after he had left, she had never been as lonely in her life. She wanted him desperately, emotionally, physically, mentally, in every way she could think of. But every time she thought of making love to him, she thought of Vasili standing over the body of her mother, and she couldn't bear it. It was as though, if she let anyone that close to her, he would do the same thing to her.

"Is that normal?" she finally asked Linda one day in her office. Linda had gone back to work full-time in the fall, and it was now late September.

"Yes."

"How the hell do I get over it?"

"Time. And your good mind. You have to remind yourself over and over again that John is not Vasili, and just because Vasili did something doesn't mean that John will do it to you. Vasili is not all men. He is one man. And you are not your mother. I never knew her, but I suspect that you are very different. You're a whole other person, with a totally different life. You just have to say that to yourself over and over, and eventually it will start to take." She smiled gently at Vanessa. It had been a difficult few months for the girl and it showed. But she was growing from her efforts to wrestle with the problems.

"You know, I've been thinking of going away for a while."

"I think that's a great idea. Any place special?"

Vanessa looked at her for a long moment, and then said it. "Greece."

Linda nodded slowly. "Want to tell me why, or do I have to guess?"

Vanessa took a deep breath, almost afraid to say it, but she had to. "Ever since the baby's birth I have this overwhelming urge to find Charlie."

"I understand." Linda's voice was soft.

"It's a little crazy really, I know she's not a baby anymore, but she's my sister. My mother and father are gone, and other than Uncle Teddy, she's all I have left of the past. I have to find her. And at the same time I'm so damn scared. Maybe I won't have the guts to see her, after all. Maybe I'll just go to Europe and float around."

"It might do you good." And then, hesitantly, "Any news from John?"

Vanessa shook her head. "I told him not to call me, and he won't."

"You could call him."

444

"I'm not ready." And then with a sad shrug, "Maybe I never will be."

"I doubt that. Maybe he's just not the right one."

But Vanessa shook her head again. "That's not true. If there were someone," she said very softly, "I would want it to be him. He's the kind of man I'd like to spend the rest of my life with. We have a lot in common. I've never . . . I've never been able to talk to anyone the way I talk to him."

"That's how I feel about Teddy. It's a very important thing. Maybe after you get back from Europe . . ."

Vanessa shrugged again, looking noncommittal. "Maybe."

She thought about the trip for another week after that and then she made the reservations. She was leaving on the first of October, and the night before she left she called John and told him where she was going. He asked her the same questions Linda had, and she told him the same things.

"I want to go to Greece but I don't know what I'll do. I've decided to start out by making kind of a pilgrimage in honor of my mother. Maybe then I'll be able to let go."

"That sounds like a good idea." He had been so happy to hear from her, and he wished he could see her before she left, but he knew that she would not agree. It was almost as though she were afraid to see him, afraid of what he represented, and of how much he cared for her. She had told him once at the end that she had nothing to give him, that she thought that she had given herself to people who no longer existed, and she had no way of finding her way back. "Where are you starting out?" He brought the conversation back to the trip after a moment.

"Venice. I know she lived there with her grandmother for a while. I don't know where. But I'd like to see it. Everyone says it's a beautiful town, especially in October."

He nodded at his end. "It is."

"After that, Rome. I want to see the palazzo, wander around a little to some of the places Teddy says my father talked about. And then—" She hesitated. "I'll see. Maybe Greece."

"Vanessa." He said it almost urgently. "Go."

"To Greece?" She sounded surprised.

"Yes."

"Why?"

"Because that's where you'll find the missing piece. You gave yourself to Charlie and they took her away, you have to go back there to find her or to find you. I have the feeling that you won't be happy until you do."

"You may be right. I'll see."

"Will you let me know how you are?" For a moment he sounded worried.

"I'll be okay. What about you?"

"I'm all right. I miss you though. A lot." The damn thing was that she missed him too.

"John . . ." She wanted to tell him that she loved him, because she did. But there seemed to be so little she could offer him. He was a man who deserved so much more than she had to give. And then she decided to say it anyway. "I love you."

"I love you too. Promise me that you'll go to Athens." She laughed nervously into the phone. "I mean it."

"All right, I promise."

"Good."

She hung up then, and the next morning she took the plane to Paris, where she changed flights at Orly Airport, and then flew on to Venice, where the pilgrimage began.

CHAPTER FIFTY-FOUR

Vanessa spent two days in Venice and loved it. It was the most beautiful city she had ever seen, and she walked for hours, getting lost in the maze of crooked little streets, wandering over narrow bridges, sitting in gondolas, looking at the Lido or the assorted palaces. She wished that she had known which one her mother had lived in as a child but they were all so lovely that it didn't matter. She was enchanted with her stay and wished that she had seen it with John.

After that she went to Rome, and was a little over-whelmed when she saw the Palazzo Tibaldo. The few times she'd seen the Fullerton house in New York she had been struck by how grand it was, but it was nothing like this. To her the palazzo looked immense.

It had been taken over in recent years by the ambassador of Japan, and there were Japanese soldiers standing outside it when Vanessa went to have a look. She wished that she could walk in the gardens, but she knew that she couldn't. She remembered her mother talking of Marcella, who had died many years before. For the rest of her stay in Rome she wandered around the many piazzas, the Piazza Navona, Piazza di Spagna, sat on the Spanish Steps with the other tourists, went to the Trevi Fountain, sat in a café on the Via Veneto and drank wine. All in all she was having a wonderful vacation, but after four days in Rome she began to get anxious about why she had come. The first two laps of her pilgrimage were almost over. There had been plenty to see and she had taken lots of photographs, but she knew only too well that that wasn't why she was there. On the fifth morning of her stay in Rome she lay in bed and remembered her conversations with Linda, and suddenly her promise to John rang in her ears. She knew as she lay in her bed at the hotel that morning that she had no choice. She had embarked on a journey on which her life rested, and now she had to take the next step. She picked up the phone, asked for the concierge, and booked a seat on the next flight to Athens. The flight was scheduled to leave at two o'clock that afternoon.

She reached the airport in good time, checked her bag, and boarded the aircraft, and an hour later she arrived at Hellinikon Airport in Athens, looking wide eyed and feeling desperately afraid. She could no longer remember why she had thought this part of the trip so important. She was terrified of what she would find there, of how she would feel, and she didn't really understand why she had come. When she reached the hotel in Athens, she felt weak from her anxieties, and she went to her room with trembling knees and set down her bags. And then, as though she couldn't wait a moment longer, she went to the telephone book, and holding it close to her, she sat on the bed. But she couldn't

447

read the Greek letters in it, so, as though she were trapped in a dream, she went downstairs to the front desk and asked them to look it up for her. She wasn't going to call them. She just wanted the phone number and the address—"in case." The man at the desk looked it up for her quickly. Andreas Arbus lived on a street in a quiet residential section, the man at the desk explained. He gave her the address and the phone number and told her it wasn't very far away. Somehow that made it all worse when Vanessa went back to her room, and ten minutes later she had to escape. It was almost unbearable knowing that perhaps now she was very close. She hailed a cab and explained to him in English that she wanted to see a little bit of Athens. She paid him handsomely in drachma, and after an hour's tour they stopped at a café and shared a carafe of wine.

The weather was absolutely gorgeous, the skies were blue, and the buildings looked brilliantly white, and Vanessa sat staring into her glass of wine, wishing that she hadn't come. It was as though she were trying to delay the inevitable every moment, and as she walked back into her hotel room, she knew with a feeling of panic that it was time. Like a woman condemned to a death sentence she walked to the phone with dragging feet, picked up the receiver, and dialed the number she'd been given by the man at the desk.

A woman answered and Vanessa felt her heart go into trip-hammer action. The woman on the other end spoke no English at all, and all Vanessa could do was ask for Andreas. A moment later there was a man's voice on the phone.

"Andreas Arbus?" Vanessa sounded desperately nervous and he answered her in Greek. "No . . . I'm sorry, I don't understand . . . Do you speak English?"

"Yes." Even with the one word, he had a charming accent, but she still couldn't imagine what he looked like. "Who is this?"

"I—" She was terrified now and she didn't want to tell him. What if he hung up on her? What if her sister was dead? She forced the crazy thoughts from her mind. "I've come from the States and I'd like to see you."

He sounded intrigued. "Who are you?" There was laughter in his voice, perhaps he thought it was a joke, and

448

she realized then how absurd it was to expect him to meet her if she wouldn't tell him her name. She took a deep breath and almost choked on a sob.

"My name is . . . Vanessa Fullerton." It came out in a rush. "You may not know who I am, but my mother was married to your brother and—" She couldn't go on, as tears clogged her throat.

"Vanessa?" The voice was gentle. "Are you here? In Athens?" He sounded stunned, and she wondered if he would be angry. Perhaps he didn't want her around. God only knew what they had told Charlotte. "Where are you?"

She gave him the name of the hotel. "The man at the desk says it's pretty close to where you live."

"It certainly is. But I am astonished to hear from you. Why have you come?" He sounded gentle and as though he genuinely cared.

"I—I don't really know, Mr. Arbus. I—I think I just had to. It's a long story. I . . . perhaps . . . we . . ."

"Would you like to get together?"

She nodded. "Yes, I would. Would that be all right?"

"Of course, my dear. Are you busy now?"

"No. No, I'm not."

"I'll be there in half an hour. Is that all right with you?"

"Thank you. That would be fine." Well, she had done it, she told herself after she hung up. She had called him. And she had no idea at all what to expect now. Surely he would come alone. He would not bring Charlotte with him. But at least she would see him, and maybe she would get some answers from him. The only trouble was that she was not yet sure of the questions, but perhaps when she would see him, she would know.

She waited nervously in her room, tapping her foot and waiting. She had combed her hair, washed her face, she was wearing gray slacks and a cashmere sweater, brown Gucci shoes and, as always, there was a camera over her arm, and she nervously took it with her when at last she went downstairs. She stood rooted to one spot in the lobby, watching people come in, and then realized that she hadn't told him what she looked like, and she had no idea what to expect of him.

449

She stood there for another ten minutes, wondering if perhaps he were already there, and then, as she watched the door, she saw him. She had no recollection of him at all, yet when she saw him, she knew it was he. He was well built, and very elegant, he was wearing a dark blue suit that looked as though it had been made in London or Paris, and he had an interestingly chiseled face and salt-and-pepper hair. His eyes as he looked around were quick and intelligent, and his face was heavily lined, she noticed. He looked like an interesting man, and as he inquired at the desk and then came toward her, she felt a magnetism in his eyes that surprised her. He was an odd combination, she could see. In some ways he looked very young, and at the same time in a certain way he looked quite old. He was in fact fifty-eight years old, but he didn't look it. He had kept his body youthful, and he looked no more than forty-eight or so. He came toward her slowly, as though afraid to approach, and the dark eyes were smiling gently.

"Vanessa?" The voice rang a distant bell. "I'm Andreas." He held out a hand and she walked toward him. There was something in his eyes that made her trust him.

"Hello." She smiled and he watched her. Her face was not very different than it had been sixteen years before.

"Do you remember me at all?" He stood before her, looking down at her gently and she shook her head, but then she smiled.

"But I've had a bit of a problem with that."

"Oh?" He looked at her with concern and then indicated the bar. "Shall we go in there? Perhaps we can find a quiet corner." Vanessa nodded and fell into step beside him. It was odd, there was something so virile about him that one felt more of a woman at his side. Vanessa felt it as she walked along beside him, and he glanced at her, smiling at the beautiful hair. "You've grown up to be a beautiful woman, Vanessa." He found a table and they settled down. "But I always knew you would." He looked at her quietly then. "Do you want to tell me why you're here?"

She sighed again. "I really don't know why I'm here. I just knew that I had to come here." He said not a word about Charlotte. He only nodded. And then suddenly she felt compelled to tell him the story of how she had repressed it all and remembered it only recently at the birth of Teddy's baby. She had to fight not to cry as she told him, and it seemed absurd to be telling this totally strange man. After all, he was the brother of the man who had killed her mother, and yet she couldn't bring herself to hate him, and she realized when she finished her story that he was holding her hand. He patted it then and released it, looking deeply into her eyes.

"You had forgotten completely about Charlotte?" It was hard to believe.

"Completely." Vanessa nodded. "It all came back to me at once." He shook his head as though feeling her pain.

"How terrible for you."

And then Vanessa couldn't help asking the question. "Does she know about me?"

He smiled. "Yes. She knows all about you." He sighed then. "All that I knew to tell her. Your uncle didn't wish any contact, and the American court had discouraged it. Of course." He looked troubled. "I can understand . . . it was a terrible time." This time there were tears in his eyes. "Vanessa, my brother was a very strange, very sick man." Vanessa said nothing. Part of her didn't want to hear about him, and another part of her did. It was all part of why she had come. "He was not really evil, but so wrong in his pursuits, his ideas. It was as though he had taken a bad turn in his youth." He sighed again. "We never really got along. And he was always in trouble . . . women . . . drugs . . . terrible things. His wife before your mother committed suicide." He stopped abruptly, looking at Vanessa, afraid to go on. "And then of course there was the tragedy that happened in the States."

"Does Charlotte know?" It was odd asking this stranger questions, and yet she knew that she could, that she had to.

He looked at her quietly. "That her father killed her mother?" He said it so bluntly that Vanessa was shocked. "Yes, she knows. She knows the good about him, and she knows the bad. And she knows everything I knew to tell her about your mother. I wanted her to know it all. She has the right. She has the right to try to understand in her own way.

I think she accepts it. It is horrible, and it hurts her, but she never knew either one of them. To her they are only people in a story.'' He said it sadly. ''It is not as if someone told her that I had killed someone. That would be different, that would tear her apart, but Vasili . . . your mother . . . they are only names to her.'' He spoke very softly.

Vanessa looked at him and nodded. ''Did she have a woman to bring her up?''

He shook his head. ''My wife passed away when Charlotte was two. She doesn't remember her. She had my daughters, who are like big sisters to her, and she has had me.'' Something sad crossed his face then, but Vanessa couldn't read it. ''And you? Did your uncle marry when you were young?'' He was looking at her so intently, as though to drink in her face, as though to see something that Vanessa herself didn't know was there. It seemed strange to her at first but she got used to it after a few minutes. There was something extraordinarily compelling about the man.

''No, my uncle only married last year. We were alone while I was growing up.''

''Did you mind?'' He seemed curious and she shrugged, thinking over her answers.

''I don't think so. Teddy was like a mother and father rolled into one. I missed my mother, but that was different.''

He spoke very gently. ''I think that Charlotte has always been very curious about you. She talked often as a child of her American sister, she used to play games with you, using her imagination, once she wrote you a letter. I still have it somewhere. I used to wonder if you would come back.''

''Have I been here before?'' She looked momentarily startled and he nodded.

''A few times with Vasili and your mother. We used to play checkers, you and I. . . .'' His voice drifted off and it was as though she could see something in the distance. She closed her eyes and she began to remember. She could see him, and his wife and his children. . . . When she opened her eyes, they were filled with tears.

''I remember.''

''You were a wonderful little girl.'' And then his face clouded. ''I remember when Charlotte was born, I came to

London. . . ." He shook his head and looked at Vanessa squarely. "You went through a great deal. Your mother should never have married Vasili."

Vanessa nodded agreement, thinking of how strange their lives had been, interwoven, and then broken apart, and then back again.

"And you?" He looked at her with a warm light in his eyes. "You're not married yet?"

"No." For a moment she looked distant and then she smiled.

"A beautiful girl like you? That's a waste." He wagged a finger and she laughed, and then she asked him another question.

"Does she look anything like me?"

He looked at her closely, and then shook his head. "Not really. There is a kind of impression. It's more in the way you move, the shape of your body. Not the face, or the eyes, or the hair." He looked at Vanessa very hard then and she felt his eyes bore through her. "Do want to see her, Vanessa?"

She was honest with him as her eyes met his. "I don't know. I'm not sure. I want to, but . . . what then? What will it do, to both of us?"

"Perhaps nothing. Perhaps you will meet as two strangers, and part the same way. Perhaps you will meet as sisters. Or you will grow to be friends. It is difficult to say." And then, hesitantly, "Vanessa, you should know, she looks a great deal like your mother. If you remember your mother at all, it may upset you to see her." It was odd to think of it, why should this girl she had never seen look anything like her mother? The whole idea of having a sister was suddenly almost more than Vanessa could understand. She felt suddenly exhausted again as she sat there with Andreas, and he saw all the emotions crossing her face and reached out a hand for hers. "You have time to think it over. She is away for two weeks. On a cruise with some friends." He looked sheepish. "She is supposed to be in school, but . . . it's a long story, but she talked me into it. My children say I spoil her rotten, but she's a good girl."

Vanessa thought about what he had said. "When will she be back?"

"Two weeks from today. She left last night." Vanessa thought it over with exasperation. If she hadn't lingered in Rome, she could have come to Athens the day before, and it would be over. She would be on her way back to the States by now, with whatever impressions she had gathered and the deed done. Now she would have to wait for fourteen days.

"I suppose I could go somewhere else, and come back. . . ." She mulled it over and he watched her. When he thought there was no one looking, there was something unbearably sad in his face.

"Wouldn't you like to stay here, in Athens?" He smiled the smile of a host. "You could move into the house, if the hotel is a problem." But Vanessa smiled and shook her head.

"You're very kind, but it isn't that. I'm just not sure what I'd do sitting here for two weeks. I could go to Paris, I guess." But she really didn't want to. She wanted to take a look at Charlotte and go home. She had decided that much now, but wait another two weeks?

"Why don't you try waiting here?" He inclined his head in a gentlemanly fashion. "I will do my very best to entertain you."

"No, really, I couldn't impose on you—"

He interrupted her. "Why not? You have waited sixteen years for this moment. May I not share it with you? May I not help you to live through the fears, to deal with the anticipation, to have someone to talk to?" As he said it she wanted to let him take care of her forever, he had that kind of way about him, a way of giving in every way he could, so that one felt as though one had been given a part of his very soul.

"You must have better things to do."

"No." He looked at her very strangely. "I don't. What you are doing is much more important than anything I was attending to when you arrived. Besides," he said, shrugging easily, "October is a slow month in Athens." He laughed in his husky way. "Athens is slow all year." And then he smiled as he asked a question. "And what do you do in New York, Vanessa? Your uncle is a doctor, I believe."

"He is, and so is his wife. I'm much less respectable than they are." She smiled at Andreas. "I'm a photographer."

"Are you?" He looked pleased. "Are you good at it?"

"Sometimes."

"Then we'll have to take pictures together. I enjoy photography too." They began to talk then of a recent exhibition that had come to New York and also to Athens, and the time began to drift by as if they were old friends. And at ten o'clock they both remembered that they hadn't eaten. Andreas insisted on taking her to a restaurant nearby, which turned out to be a beautiful little place with marvelous food. When he brought her back to the hotel at one o'clock in the morning, she was exhausted and happy, and felt like a different woman than when she'd arrived. She tried to share the feelings with him, but he only hugged her and kissed her on both cheeks. "Never mind, Vanessa. It is I who thank you. I shall see you tomorrow. Does that suit you? We'll go and take pictures on the Acropolis, if you'd like that." She could think of nothing better. They said good night again, and she went back to her room.

She found herself musing over things he had said, as she undressed slowly, and she found her mind full of him as she fell asleep. The prospect of waiting two weeks to meet Charlotte still didn't thrill her, but at least for a few days she could spend some time with Andreas, and after that she'd have to see.

When she awoke the next morning, the maid was bringing in an enormous bouquet of flowers. They were fragrant and brilliantly hued in a big handsome white vase, and Vanessa looked stunned. The card said only WELCOME. ENJOY YOUR STAY. ANDREAS, but she was very touched and told him so when he picked her up. He was driving a large silver Mercedes, and in the back seat he had a whole basket of Greek goodies for her to eat. In addition he had brought along for her a picnic basket, in case they didn't want to go back to eat. She looked at him strangely for a moment, as though she didn't understand him, and he met her eyes.

"Yes?"

"Why are you so good to me, Andreas?" Perhaps he felt sorry for her, or he felt an obligation, but there was something very different in his eyes.

"For one thing, you are a very lovely young woman, possibly the loveliest I've ever seen. For another thing, I care about you, Vanessa. I did a long time ago when you were a child." How blessed she had been then to have two men who had cared so much about her. Teddy, and perhaps even this man. "You were special to me even then."

"But you don't know me now." She was still puzzled, and she wanted to know what he saw.

But he looked at her very deeply. "I do know you, little one. I knew what was happening to you then, and I can see what has happened to you now." It was almost like having a father, and yet it was not like that at all. He was unusual and special and terribly attractive, she felt herself being swept away on a current she didn't understand at all.

"How can you see what has happened?" She tried to look amused, but she was not.

"I can see it in your eyes."

"What do you see, Andreas?" She spoke softly and he stopped the car and pulled off the road.

"I see how much you have been hurt, Vanessa. I see what Vasili must have done to you as a child. It is as though something in you has been beaten." And then, in a matter-of-fact voice, "I can also see that you're afraid of men." She started to deny it, and then, feeling defeated, she shook her head.

"Does it show so easily, then?"

"No." He smiled at her and looked more handsome than ever. "I'm just a very wise man."

"Be serious." She began to laugh at him and he laughed too.

"I am serious." And then he turned toward her and asked a question that shocked her. "Are you still a virgin, Vanessa?"

"I . . . no . . ." She blushed beet-red and looked away.

"Don't lie to me."

"I'm not." And then after a moment's pause, softly, "I am."

"Is there someone you love?" It was odd to be answering all these questions he asked her, and yet she wanted to. It was as though she wanted to give herself to him.

"Maybe. I don't know. I haven't made up my mind."

"But you haven't gone to bed with him?"

She sighed softly. "I can't." And then as they drove into the hills around Athens she told him how it was with her and men—how she'd feel afraid when they got too close to her and she held them at bay, even more so since she remembered the murder, she would picture his face and feel all over again how panicky she was then.

"One day, Vanessa, you will forget that." And then he shook his head. "No, that is wrong. You won't forget it. But it will not haunt you. Most of all, you must stop being afraid."

"But how?" She turned to him as though he had all the answers, and in some ways he did.

"Time. Everything heals in time. It hurt me a great deal when my wife died."

"That's not the same thing."

He glanced at Vanessa. "No, it's not."

"What about Charlie? . . . Charlotte . . . is she like me at all? . . ."

Andreas chuckled softly. "No, little one." But his eyes sobered then as he patted Vanessa's hand. "But she has nothing to remember. She was only a baby. And she is young and beautiful, and all the boys love her and she loves them. She is a tease and a flirt and a little beast. That one"—he rolled his eyes and laughed again—"will lead some poor man a merry chase." Vanessa envied her as she listened. It seemed part of another life. But Andreas understood her and looked at her seriously again. "It is a great deal harder to be who you are. All that Charlotte has ever known is that she is greatly loved. She is the fruit of an unfortunate union between two people who flew across the sky at each other and crashed like falling stars. They met and exploded in a hailstorm of beautiful comets. She is one of those comets, and the falling stars simply vanished from the heavens as they died."

"You make it sound so lovely."

"It was lovely, for a time, Vanessa. They loved each other very much."

"But look what happened then." She sounded mournful, and he looked at her severely.

"No, you must stop looking at that, Vanessa. You must look at the beginning, at when it meant something. If you look always at the trail of dust behind the car, you will never see the beauty of the machine." The allegory amused her and she smiled. "Everything is beautiful for a time. Some things have great meaning in a lifetime, what they become later doesn't always matter so much. In your mother's case it was tragic, but it still meant a great deal. They had a child who is a joy to everyone who knows her, and especially to me. Just as you were the fruit of your mother's love for your father. When he died, none of the beauty could ever be forgotten, because there was you. You must learn to hold the moment, Vanessa, only the moment . . . not to try to seize an entire life." She was silent for a long time after he said it, and in time they reached the Acropolis, took all of their photographs, and then ate their picnic on the hills. For the rest of the afternoon they stayed away from difficult subjects, and made each other laugh with funny tales and memories. They compared their cameras, took pictures of each other, cavorted and laughed and had a wonderful time. It was as though he were her own age and not old enough to be her father, and when he took her back to the hotel, she was sorry to see him go.

"Dinner tonight, or are you tired?" She wanted to say no to him, but she couldn't. It didn't seem right to monopolize all his time, but she enjoyed being with him and she had nothing else to do.

They met again for dinner that night, and the next night, and the night after. And on the fifth night they went dancing, and when he brought her home, he seemed unusually quiet.

"Is something wrong, Andreas?" She looked at him and saw that the lines around his eyes seemed deeper.

He smiled. "I think you've worn me out. I'm an old man, you know."

"That's not true." It was certainly hard to believe looking at him.

"Well, it feels true, and when I look in the mirror . . ."
He made a terrible face.

She invited him into the hotel for a drink, and although he looked tired, he accepted, and as they sat over ouzo and coffee she felt oddly nostalgic. Her days in Greece were the happiest of her life.

"What were you thinking just then?"

She looked at him for a long moment, and without her thinking, the words slipped out. "That I love you."

He looked as though she had reached deep inside him and touched his heart. He looked startled and gentle and deeply touched. "The nicest part of all that is that I love you too."

"It's funny." She looked at him and he took her hand. "I came to see my sister, and in the last few days I've forgotten about her most of the time." For a moment Vanessa looked embarrassed. "All I think about is you."

"I've been falling in love with you since you got here, my love, but I didn't think it was right . . . a beautiful young girl and such an old man."

"Stop saying that." She looked hurt. "You're not old."

He looked at her in an odd way. "I will be very soon."

"Does that matter?" Her voice was very soft, and she could feel his breath, soft on her face as he sat very close to her. "It doesn't matter to me, Andreas, not at all."

"Perhaps it should." His voice was as soft as hers.

"What about the falling stars? Don't we have a right to be falling stars too, for one moment before we fall out of the heavens, never to be seen again?"

"Is that what you want, only a moment instead of a lifetime? My darling, you deserve much more."

"You told me that I was wrong, that I should search for the moment, and not the lifetime."

"Ah." He smiled gently at her. "You see . . . the foolish things that I say . . ." But he was looking at her so profoundly and with such love that she moved gently toward him, and a moment later she was in his arms and he was kissing her as he hadn't kissed a woman in half his lifetime, and all he wanted in what remained of his life was this splendid young girl. "I love you, Vanessa . . . oh, darling. . . ." He held her close. He wanted to take her upstairs to her hotel room, but more than that, he wanted to take her home with him. He laid some money on the table, stood up with a gentle smile, and held out his hand to her. She asked no questions. She followed him out of the hotel, got in his car, he drove her home, and ten minutes later they were standing in his palatial home with the fountains and the atrium and the courtyard, the exotic plants and the priceless objects he had collected from around the world. Quietly, holding her hand, he led Vanessa to his room, closed the door and locked it, so none of the servants would surprise them in the morning, and then led her to the small study where he often sat, staring into the fire. He threw a match into it now, and in a moment there was a cozy blaze before them, and he sat beside her and kissed her, and then knelt before her, with her face in his hands. He touched the lines of her face and ran his fingers through her hair, touched her throat and her neck and her breasts and circled her waist with his hands. He touched her and held her and caressed her, until the fire began to grow dim, and then he looked at her gently and asked her permission to take her to his bedroom.

"Will you come with me, Vanessa?" He said it so gently that she would have gone to the ends of the earth with him. She followed him quietly, let him undress her, and a moment later they lay side by side in his bed. Here again he lingered over the graceful curves of her long, supple body, and marveled at how beautifully she was made, and at last, gently at first, and then with ever greater urgency, he took her. She cried out at first and he knew that it hurt her, but he held her close to him, sharing her pain, and when it was over, he held her and caressed her and loved her, and in a little while they made love again.

When she woke up beside him in the morning, there was a smile on her face and a look of peace in her eyes that had never been there before, not so much because she had made love with Andreas but because she had given her heart to him, she had come to trust him, and with that, she had at long last unlocked the long-hidden door she had never, until that moment, been able to find.

CHAPTER FIFTY-FIVE

The next days sped by much too quickly, as Andreas and Vanessa spent all of their time together, going for long walks in Athens, discovering markets, going for drives and once a sail on his yacht. She moved out of the hotel the morning after they had become lovers, and he ensconced her in a handsome guest room just down the hall from his suite. She spent each night in his bedroom, and in the morning, like two children, they ran into her room and tousled the bed so it looked as though she had spent the night there, and then they laughed, and one morning he had insisted on making love to her there, so that the disorder would appear real. She had never been so happy in her life, and it was as though the rest of her life had been forgotten. Teddy and Linda and the baby all seemed part of a distant dream, and whenever she thought of John Henry, she gently pushed the thought away. She didn't want to think of him now. She only wanted to be with Andreas, for as long as they had, however long that was, a moment or a lifetime, to share their hours and their dreams.

She noticed once or twice that he seemed a little vague in the morning, and noticed also that there were vast quantities of pills in his dressing room. But she felt that it was indiscreet to ask him questions about it. Now and then he was still sensitive about the difference in their ages. He wanted to introduce her to his family though and it was Vanessa who suggested that they wait until she met Charlie, and now the day was approaching when her sister would come home.

The last night they spent alone together they went to a quiet restaurant, came home early, and made love, and afterward Andreas fell into a deep sleep. Vanessa wandered slowly around his bedroom, looking out at the view and wondering what the next day would bring. What would she think of this girl who though a total stranger was her closest kin?

From some of what Andreas had said, she suspected that Charlie had been spoiled rotten, and since she was living in the midst of the Greek shipping magnates, it was certainly likely that that was the case. Andreas had already tried to buy two diamond bracelets for Vanessa, and she insisted that that wasn't what she wanted. Instead he bought her some marvelous lenses for her camera and gave her a beautifully cut simple emerald ring.

"But I can't keep that, Andreas, it's so expensive!"

He was amused at her concern. "I promise you, my darling, I can afford it." He had kissed her passionately and quelled her objections, but after they had made love, she mentioned it again.

"I shouldn't, it's too big a present."

"Ah, how refreshing, a woman who wants *smaller* emeralds!" He looked amused. "Believe me, darling, my wife had none of those reservations." Vanessa had to laugh at him and shook her head. In the end she had agreed to keep it, and now she saw it sparkling darkly on her left hand. It looked, in a way, like an engagement ring, and it meant a great deal to her. It symbolized the love that she had for this man, and all that he had done for her. He had freed her from her lonely tower and brought her down into his arms. Had he asked her to marry him at that moment, she would have, but there was never any talk of the future between them. He seemed to live entirely in the here and now.

The next morning Vanessa rose early and was already dressed by the time Andreas came out of his room. He was going to pick Charlotte up at the dock and bring her back to meet Vanessa. Vanessa had insisted that she didn't want to shock her, but he insisted again that Charlotte was a sturdy, happy child and it would not upset her to be surprised. In the end Vanessa let him talk her into going, and they drove down to the port after they got the phone call that his friend's yacht had returned. Vanessa sat playing with the emerald ring and looking out the window, feeling a cascade of emotions rush over her and trying to fight back a lump in her throat.

He leaned over and kissed her as he stopped the car and smiled at her. "Are you all right, my love?" She nodded, looking at the handsome, lined face and touching the silvery hair.

"Yes, thanks to you, I've never been better." And then she sighed. "I'm just scared."

"Of what?" And then suddenly he understood. "That she will reject you?"

"Maybe. I don't know. I loved her so much when she was a baby, and now I'm meeting a total stranger. What if she doesn't care about me at all?"

"She always has, in the stories she told me about you, in her fantasies. You were always the big sister whom she loved."

"But she doesn't know me. What if she hates the real thing?"

"How could she"—his eyes glinted with affection mingled with passion—"when I love you so much?"

"Oh, Andreas, what was my life before you came along?" She could barely remember it now. After two weeks with him it was as though she had belonged to him for her entire lifetime.

He pointed the yacht out to her then, it was a magnificent piece of work, painted black with three enormous masts and full sails. It slept eighteen in the cabins, with a crew of twelve. Charlotte must certainly have had a very pleasant trip.

"What shall I do? Shall I wait here?" She wanted to run away and Andreas smiled at her.

"Why don't you? I'll go on board and talk to her alone for a few minutes, and then we'll come up to get you. Maybe you'd like to see the boat?" But he could see in her eyes that all she cared about was seeing Charlotte. The boat could have sunk once her sister got off it, the rest just didn't matter at all. He had to smile at her.

"What are you going to tell her?"

"That you're here, that you came all the way from New York to see her, that you didn't know where she was until now."

"Will you tell her about us?" Vanessa looked worried, and suddenly wondered if Linda had at one time felt that way about her.

463

But he shook his head. "No, darling, not now. One thing at a time. She's only sixteen."

Vanessa agreed with him. It was a relief. It was hard enough to meet a sister, without having to tell her that you were madly in love with her uncle, and highly desirous of becoming her aunt. She turned the emerald ring around on her finger, and Andreas walked quietly toward the gangway, and a moment later disappeared.

It seemed hours before he emerged again, but it was actually more like twenty minutes. He had taken Charlotte quietly aside after greeting his friends and had had a talk with her. He had explained that Vanessa was in Athens and all of the things he had told Vanessa he would say.

"She is?" Charlotte's eyes flew open wide. "She's *here*?"

"Very much so." He smiled at the enthusiastic response. "Where is she?"

"Charlotte . . . darling . . ." Suddenly he was worried too. Maybe Vanessa was right. Maybe it wouldn't be easy. "She's outside."

"On the dock?" Charlotte stood to her full height, her sheaf of black hair flung straight as onyx threads over her shoulder. Her hair was Vasili's, but the rest of her, every inch, was Serena. "She's right out there?" Charlotte pointed with all of her sixteen-year-old disbelief and excitement, and with a slow smile Andreas nodded, and as he did she took off, ran out of the room, up to the deck, across the gangway onto the dock, and stood looking around with excitement, and then she saw her, standing so tall and quiet and blond beside her uncle's car. She looked exactly as Charlie had dreamed her. So exactly that it stunned her now to see the real thing. It was as though she had always known her, always carried an image of her in her heart, and as she stood staring from the distance, Vanessa suddenly stiffened. She had seen her coming off the boat, the black hair, the long legs, all of it. It was exactly like seeing her mother. Vanessa gave a small anguished sound and stood there, rooted to the spot, it was as though her mother had come back to life, in the body of this girl coming toward her. Without thinking, Vanessa began to run toward her, and she didn't stop until they stood in front of each other, the tears pouring down Charlotte's face as well as Vanessa's, and without saying a·word, Vanessa held out her arms. Charlotte flew into them, and they held to each other, as from the deck Andreas watched them, with tears flowing from his eyes too. The two girls clung to each other for an endless moment, and it seemed as though Vanessa was never going to let go.

"Oh, baby . . ." she kept saying over and over. "Oh, Charlie."

"You came back." Charlotte looked up at her rapturously, with the face of her mother and the eyes of a child. "You came back."

"Yes, love." Vanessa looked down at her, a woman at last. A smile lit her eyes behind the tears. "I did."

CHAPTER FIFTY-SIX

For the next two weeks the threesome was inseparable. Vanessa went everywhere with Charlie, except when she was in school, and then Vanessa spent her time with Andreas. They were alone again at night, after Charlie went to bed, and then their life continued as it had before Charlie had got back to Athens. It was an idyllic time for them all, and Vanessa had never been happier. She had everything she wanted, a man she loved, a sister she adored, and now all the good memories returned as she put away the others. She remembered times she had had with her mother, and seeing Charlie brought it all back to her. She dared now to touch the past, like a magic blanket she had brought with her over the years and always hidden.

It was during the second week that Charlie had come back that Vanessa got up one morning and Andreas didn't come to breakfast. She was worried when he didn't come down as he always did, trim in his English suits, and his perfectly starched white shirts, his hair impeccably in place, and smelling of lavender and spices.

"Is he all right, do you suppose?" Vanessa looked at her sister with a worried frown. He had seemed all right the night before, but she didn't mention that to Charlie. They were keeping their love affair a secret.

Charlie looked troubled too as she buttered a piece of toast. "I think it may be one of his bad days. If it is, we can call the doctor after breakfast." The ravishing child swung her hair over her shoulder and began to munch on her toast.

"One of his bad days?" Vanessa looked confused.

"Sometimes he has them." She looked at Vanessa strangely, a question in her eyes, but Vanessa seemed not to understand her. "Was he all right while I was gone?"

"He was fine." Vanessa felt worry begin to tighten her chest. "Is he ill?"

For a long moment Charlotte said nothing. She sat in all her silky black splendor, her enormous green eyes piercing into Vanessa's. They were bright with tears when she spoke again, but her voice was calm. "He hasn't told you?" Vanessa shook her head.

"He has cancer." For an instant Vanessa felt as though she could feel the room twirl, and then clutching the breakfast table, she stared at her sister.

"Are you serious?"

Charlotte nodded quietly, with all the dignity of her mother. "He's had it for two years. He told me almost right away. He said I had to know, because there was no one else to take care of me afterward. He said I would have to grow up quickly because of that." The tears began to slide down her face and it was difficult to continue. "I could live with any of his children, but"—she gulped—"it wouldn't be the same. And he's right." She was crying openly now, looking at Vanessa. "It wouldn't."

"Oh, my God." Vanessa went around the table to where she sat, and sat down with her arm around her. "Oh, poor baby." But her thoughts were in a jumble as she cradled her sister on her shoulder. "Can't they do anything for him?"

Charlie sniffed loudly. "They have. They've done wonders. We almost lost him last year." Her English was precise and Vanessa loved her accent. She loved everything about her. "But then he got better again. He wasn't too well just before I left, but then he seemed to be all right, and he promised me that if he got sick he'd call me on the boat and I'd come back. It's in his liver and his stomach." Vanessa thought over the meals they had shared, and remembered noticing that he ate very little. She thought at the time that it was vanity and that was why he ate so little, to keep his figure. Now she felt heartsick at what she had heard. The man that she loved was dying. For an instant she felt sorry for herself, remembering that she was about to endure another loss in her life, but almost at the same moment she could hear Andreas's voice telling her that they had to grab the moment . . . and now Vanessa had Charlotte to think of. The loss of Andreas would be a tremendous blow to her. The two girls sat that way for a long time, and then Vanessa looked at her watch as she saw the chauffeur in the hallway.

"You'll be late for school."

"Will you go in and see him? And don't believe a word he tells you. If he looks sick, call the doctor."

"I promise." She walked Charlotte to the door, waved at the retreating limousine, and hurried back to the door to Andreas's bedroom. She knocked softly and went inside when he answered her knock. She found him lying in bed, looking deathly pale, but trying to look cheerful as she entered. "Andreas . . ." She didn't know what to say. He wanted to play a game, and she didn't know how to play it with him.

"Sorry, I overslept." He sat up with a wan smile, and overnight he seemed to have radically altered. Charlotte had warned her that that was how it was on his "bad days," and then suddenly he would seem better again and look like himself for a while. But the doctor had told her the month before that the good days would be coming to an end soon. "You must have worn me out last night."

"Darling . . ." Her voice trembled as she sat down, and he smiled at her. She had become a woman in one short month. There was nothing left of the frightened girl she had been when she arrived in Athens. "I . . ." She didn't know how to say it, but she knew that she had to. The pretense would be impossible to keep up. And as long as Charlie knew, there was no reason why she shouldn't too. With enormous gray eyes she looked at him and held his hand. "Why didn't you tell me?" There were tears in her eyes and he looked startled for a moment, as though she had caught him unprepared.

"Tell you what?"

"I spoke to Charlie this morning—" She faltered and he immediately understood and nodded.

"I see . . . so you know." He looked sad for a moment. "I didn't want anyone to tell you."

"Why?" The sorrow that she felt showed in her eyes and it tore at his heart to watch her.

"You have had enough loss in your life, my love. I was going to send you home while I was feeling well, with nothing but happy memories to take with you."

"But that isn't real if the reality is this."

"The reality is both. All that we have shared, all the love, the excitement, the happy moments. Vanessa." He looked at her gently. "I have never loved any woman as I love you. And if I were younger, and"—he skipped over the words—"things were different for me now, I would ask you to marry me, but I can't do that."

"I would, you know."

"I'm happy to know that." He looked pleased. "But what I want you to take away from here is better than marriage. I want you to take a better knowledge of yourself, an understanding of how much you have been loved. I want you to take not the past but the future with you."

"But how can I leave you here? And if you're ill, I want to be with you."

He shook his head with a gentle smile. "No, my darling, that I cannot allow. What we lived was that brief moment I talked to you about before. Perhaps it will come again, perhaps I will be better again tomorrow. But when I am, this time you must go. And when you go—" He hesitated for a moment, obviously in pain. "I want you to take Charlotte."

Vanessa looked stunned. "Don't you want her here with you?"

"No." He spoke very clearly. "I want the two people I

love to go to their new lives. In your hearts you will take me with you. You have been dear to me, little one, for all of these years that I remembered you as a child. Now you will remember me for a lifetime.'' She knew that it was true, but she didn't want to leave him. He shook his head though, vetoing her objections. ''My children will be here with me, Vanessa. I will not be alone. And soon,'' he said very softly, ''it will be time to go.''

She bowed her head then and began to cry, and at last she raised her eyes to his face. ''Andreas, I can't leave you. I can't give up what we had.''

''You won't. You will take it with you. Won't you?'' He looked at her so gently that it made her cry more. ''Won't you always remember?''

''You've changed my whole life.''

''As you've changed mine. Isn't that enough? Do you really want more? Are you so greedy?'' His eyes were teasing and she smiled through her tears and blew her nose in the handkerchief he gave her.

''Yes, I am greedy.''

''Well, you can't be. And you must fulfill an important task for me. For two years I have agonized about what will happen to Charlotte. I had thought that she will be with my children. But she needs something more. She is a special child. She needs someone who will love her as I have.'' Now his eyes were damp too. ''I like watching the two of you together. You are so good to her.'' And then, as a single tear slid down his face and tore at Vanessa's heart, ''Will you keep her with you?'' It was like receiving a sacred gift, the Holy Grail, and Vanessa was dumbfounded that he would ask her.

''Yes, but don't you want her here with you?''

''No, I want her away from all this. I know what it is. It will get very ugly. And''—his face grew stern—''she is not to come back afterward for my funeral. That's barbaric and unnecessary.'' He glowered and Vanessa made a face.

''Stop running everyone's life.''

''No, my darling.'' He smiled at her more gently again. ''Only yours, and that's because I love you.''

''Are you serious? Do you really want me to take Charlie

back to the States?'' He smiled. Vanessa was the only one who called her Charlie, but Charlotte loved it. "Won't she be terribly lonely?"

"Not with you. Put her in a good school." He cleared his throat slightly. "She will have an enormous income, run by her trustees. With her father's death she inherited a considerable fortune." Vanessa nodded.

"I lead a very simple life. Do you think that would be enough? She is used to such grandeur."

"I think that she would like it. I will see to it that you both have all the necessary comforts." But Vanessa shook her head.

"I can't let you do that. I have enough as things are. One day I know that Teddy has provided for me. I make enough money from my photography. It's just that—" She looked embarrassed. "It's not fancy."

"She doesn't need fancy. She needs you. Vanessa, please." His eyes pleaded with her. "Take her."

Vanessa looked at him then. "I want to ask her first. That seems only fair." He looked doubtful, but finally he agreed.

And that afternoon when she came home from school, Vanessa quietly put the question to her. She seemed shocked for a moment. "He wants me to leave?"

"I think so." Vanessa looked at her sadly. "But I won't take you if you don't want to go. You can stay in Athens with him if you want to." He couldn't force her to take the girl away, after all. And she could always come back for Charlie later.

"No." She shook her head. She knew Andreas better than Vanessa. "He'll send me to Paris or somewhere. He doesn't want me here in the end." They had talked about it for two years. And then slowly she nodded at Vanessa. "I want to come with you." Vanessa said nothing more, she only took the girl in her arms and held her. All the mothering that she had thought she would never have had come out and was pouring forth for this child, who looked so much like her mother. It was like returning something she had been given a long time before. They had come full circle.

They told Andreas that night that Charlotte had agreed, and he said that he would have his lawyers arrange for

470

transfers of funds and whatever else would be needed. His secretary would see about schools in New York. He thought that a Catholic school run by nuns would be a good choice, and Charlie was not overly delighted about it. She wanted to go to something "free thinking and American," not more nuns, which was where she went to school in Athens. But she was so delighted at the prospect of going back to the States that it eclipsed all her complaints about the school. But on the whole the atmosphere in the house for the next two weeks was bittersweet, all of the excitement was tempered with sorrow.

Three days before they were to leave, Vanessa called Teddy and Linda and told them that she was bringing Charlotte. She had written them long letters about how it had been and how happy she was in Athens. And she told them how marvelous Andreas had been, but she didn't tell them that she had had an affair with him. She felt private about that, and Linda had sensed that there was something she wasn't telling.

"Will you meet our plane?" Vanessa sounded tired but not totally unhappy. She had explained about Andreas's illness and they understood only too well how hard it was on her. But they couldn't know fully how hard it had hit her. They didn't know how much she loved him.

"Of course we'll meet the plane." Teddy sounded ecstatic. "We'll even bring the baby." And then he had a thought. "Do you want me to call John Henry?"

"No." Her answer was instant.

"Sorry."

"That's all right. Don't worry about it. I'll call him when I get back." But she sounded vague.

"He's called here a couple of times, wondering if we had news. I think he was worried."

"I know." She had only sent him two postcards in the beginning of her trip, and nothing at all since she had reached Athens. But she couldn't write to him. She couldn't concentrate on them both. She had become totally involved with Andreas. "I'll take care of it." But Teddy suspected that it was over and told Linda so when he hung up the phone.

471

"I think she's still not ready."

"Maybe not." Linda looked worried but had to go look after the baby.

And in Athens the preparations went on, until at last the valises were packed. Several boxes had been filled with things to ship, like Charlotte's stereo. Andreas had told her once that she could come home in five months for Easter, but very little was said about that. In the past few days it had become apparent that his cancer was moving very quickly.

The night before they left, Vanessa sat next to Charlie's bed and told her about her life in New York, Teddy and Linda, the baby. "Don't you have a boyfriend?" Vanessa shook her head, and she looked disappointed. "Why not?"

"I just don't. I have friends." She thought of John Henry and felt a little shiver of guilt. She owed it to him, in a way, that she had come to Athens. He had made her promise to do it. "And there is one nice man I see."

"What's his name?"

"John Henry."

"Will I like him? Is he handsome?" She looked suddenly very much sixteen as she snuggled in her bed and Vanessa smiled at her.

"He's sort of handsome, I guess. And I think you'll like him."

"I'm going to find a boyfriend." She said it with determination, and Vanessa grinned and stood up.

"Well, first get some sleep." They had said very little about Andreas. It seemed odd to Vanessa, but Charlie seemed as though she had made her peace with the situation. There was something fatalistic about her, as though she were wise well beyond her years. Andreas had prepared her well. "Sleep tight. I'll see you in the morning."

"Good night." And then as Vanessa stood in the doorway, "Are you going to Andreas?" Did she know? Vanessa looked stunned.

"Why?" She stood very still.

"I just wondered. He loves you, you know."

And then Vanessa had to say it. "I love him too. Very much."

"Good." Charlie didn't seem disturbed. "Then we will

love him together." It was as though, as he had said, they would be taking him with them on the morrow.

Vanessa gently closed the door and went down the hall to Andreas, where they spent the night in his bed, holding each other tight, and at last he slept soundly in her arms. She knew at that moment that for the rest of her life she would take him with her.

CHAPTER FIFTY-SEVEN

Their parting was brief, heroic, and brutally painful. Charlotte clenched her teeth, held him close, and stood back for a moment, looking at him.

"I love you, Andreas."

"I love you too." And then, "Good-bye."

With Vanessa it took a moment longer. He reached out and held her to him, felt her warmth against him for a moment, and then set her free. "Take what you learned and use it well, my darling. I give you two gifts, that of my heart and that of courage." He said it so softly that no one could hear him, and when he stepped back, he pressed a small box in her hand. His eyes insisted that she take it. And then suddenly they were being rushed onto the plane and he was gone and she and Charlie were both crying. They boarded the plane with their arms around each other, and it wasn't until after they took off that they felt like talking. Charlie was subdued, and Vanessa looked at her, thinking that she looked absolutely splendid. She was the prettiest girl Vanessa had ever seen, and she had noticed a number of heads turn as they had taken their seats. It was the combination of the ivory skin, the emerald eyes, and the sheet of black satin hair. It was a dazzling combination.

It wasn't until later that Vanessa opened the small package Andreas had given her. A thin gold chain fell into her hand, and at the end of it a starkly beautiful single diamond in a setting that made it look like a star, and as she hung it around her neck she understood its meaning. It was their falling star. As she touched it with her fingers she felt her eyes fill with tears again. She had only known him for six weeks, but it seemed like a lifetime.

The plane landed in London an hour and a half later, and they had to change planes, and discovered that they had to wait for two hours until they could board the plane to New York.

"Do you want something to eat?" Vanessa looked at her sister after they had checked in, and Charlotte looked excited. She had bounced back after leaving Athens, and now there was a fresh spark in her eyes. She had met two English boys and a girl her own age on the plane and had talked to them at length. They were on their way to London, she explained to them that she was on her way to New York. Vanessa marveled at how lively and open she was, at how easily she talked to people. She had none of Vanessa's restraint, no fears at all about being hurt or rejected. She was used to being loved, to spreading joy wherever she went.

They walked into the coffee shop arm in arm and took a table, and Charlie ordered a hamburger and Vanessa ordered tea.

"Don't you want to eat?" Charlie looked surprised, but Vanessa seemed suddenly nervous. "Is something wrong?"

"I don't know." Vanessa looked strained. "I think it's this airport." And then as she said it the memories began to flood back, the times she had been there with her mother . . . with her mother and Vasili on their way to Athens . . . when they had left London the last time for New York. Vanessa looked into Charlie's eyes and trembling a little, she recalled it all, even the appalling scene in the hospital in London, when she had called for Teddy to come and save her mother's life. "What were you thinking just then?" Charlie looked worried, but Vanessa slowly smiled.

"About when you were born. . . ."

"Andreas said that Mommy almost died."

"She did." Vanessa answered gravely. "My uncle Teddy

came and delivered you by Caesarean." Charlie nodded.

"Where was my father?"

Vanessa looked distant as she answered. "I don't know. He had disappeared." She sighed deeply then. "He was awful to my mother in those days . . . to our mother," she corrected, and Charlie nodded.

"He used to scare me. After a while Andreas wouldn't let me see him." She had been five when he had got out of the institution, and fourteen when he died. But she had only seen him four or five times over the years. They said nothing more about him, and Vanessa sat lost in her own thoughts.

"What was it like when you were little?" Charlie looked at her with her big green eyes and Vanessa smiled.

"It depends when. Some of it was wonderful . . . and some of it wasn't." But she seemed to look at it differently now. She looked at everything differently since she had met Andreas. None of it seemed quite as overwhelming as it had before.

"Do you remember your father?" Charlie was curious about all of it now. She was crazy about her sister in every way.

Vanessa shook her head. "Not really. Just from pictures. The only man I really remember from my childhood is my uncle Teddy." But now she remembered Vasili too. It was odd now that she remembered him so clearly, he seemed ugly to her, in the things he had done to her mother, but he didn't frighten her as he had before. When she thought of him, it was with anger and sadness at what he had done, but she thought also of Andreas and the love she had just shared with him. Vasili was only one man now. He no longer represented all men. And as she thought of it she looked at Charlie, and then glanced at her watch with a sudden thought.

"Are we late?" Charlie still wanted a milk shake.

"Go ahead. I want to make a phone call."

"To who?" The sixteen-year-old eyes were always curious and Vanessa laughed.

"A friend in New York."

"From here? It will be so expensive!" Andreas had made her a speech about not being too extravagant in New

York. "Why don't you call from there?"

"Because I want him to meet us at the airport, Miss Nosy, that's why." She grinned at her sister and went to the phone booth just outside the restaurant, as Charlie ordered a chocolate milk shake and a piece of pie, none of which showed on her figure.

The phone rang twice and he answered it, and her voice sounded strained at first. She told him that she was fine and that she was arriving with Charlie. And then after an awkward pause, "I'd like to see you, John. . . ." She didn't know what else to say, how to tell him. . . .

"At the airport?"

"Yes."

"I'll be there."

And when they landed in New York, he was. Vanessa and Charlie came off the plane, looking rumpled and tired and expectant. They came through customs, and as they did Vanessa looked up high at the glass-enclosed deck, and she pointed them all out to Charlie.

"There they are, love, waiting for us." There was Teddy and Linda and the baby, and John Henry standing beside them, looking terribly serious, as his eyes never left Vanessa's face. She looked different to him as he watched her, more sophisticated, he thought, and somehow more womanly than she had before. And as she stopped to speak to a customs officer, he looked down at her neck and saw something sparkle. It was the diamond Andreas had given her when she left.

"Are you ready?" She looked at Charlie with a smile as they prepared to leave the customs area.

"Yes." Charlie said it almost breathlessly.

Hand in hand they were going into their new life. The doors opened automatically and they stepped into the terminal, and for an instant Vanessa could see Teddy catch his breath. Seeing Charlotte for the first time was like seeing Serena return to life. Only the black hair was different but even that seemed not to matter as one looked into the familiar green eyes. Teddy stood very still, looking at her, his eyes filled with tears, and then with a sudden gesture he brushed them aside and hurried toward her, he took her into

476

his arms and he held her, remembering the last time he had seen her, when she was only an infant in court. And now she was back with them, sixteen years later. And he held her, knowing that Serena's baby had come home at last.

Linda watched him and held their baby, as Vanessa walked slowly toward John Henry. He only looked at her and he said nothing. There were no words that had to be spoken between them. She had gone to Athens as he had told her, she had touched her past, found her sister, and she had come back. She felt his arms tremble for a moment as he held her, and when he looked into her face and saw her smiling, he knew that all was well. John held tightly to Vanessa's hand, and Teddy slipped an arm around Linda, and Charlie walked between the two couples, with a broad smile.

"Welcome home." John Henry said it over his shoulder. And Teddy whispered softly, "Welcome back."

WANDERLUST

Danielle Steel

At 21 Annabelle Driscoll was the acknowledged beauty, but it was her sister Audrey – four years older – who had the spine and spirit. She had talent as a photographer; she had the restless urge of a born wanderer.

Inevitably it was Annabelle who was the first to marry, leaving Audrey to wonder if life were passing her by. The men she met in California were dull, worldly. Even in New York, they failed to spark her. Only when she boarded the *Orient Express* did she realise she was beginning a journey that would take her farther than she had ever dreamed possible . . .

FINE THINGS

Danielle Steel

Living on the crest of a highly successful career, he was moving too fast to realise that he had everything – except what he wanted most . . .

Sent to San Francisco to open the smartest department store in California, Bernie Fine becomes aware of the hollowness of his personal life. Despite his success he grows increasingly disenchanted with his existence – until five-year-old Jane O'Reilly gets lost in the store.

Through Jane, Bernie meets her mother Liz, who finally offers him the possibility of love. But the rare happiness they find together is disrupted by tragedy and Bernie must face the terrible price we sometimes have to pay for loving . . .

Other bestselling Warner titles available by mail: